THE RED DEATH MURDERS

JIM NOY

The Red Death Murders copyright © Jim Noy 2022

'The Masque of the Red Death' by Edgar Allan Poe is out of copyright; annotations © Jim Noy 2022

Cover design by Felix Tindall
www.felixtindall.com

ISBN: 9798411493580

To Lani,
20 years later.

CONTENTS

...and thus it happened, perhaps, that more of thought crept, with more of time, into the meditations of the thoughtful among those who revelled.

'The Masque of the Red Death'
Edgar Allan Poe

PART ONE

A Thousand Hale and Light-Hearted Friends

ONE

At first, Thomas failed to recognise the blood; it was the rising hair on his arms and the shiver passing through his chest that made him look a second time.

In the confusion following that baffling attack on the Prince, when they had realised Sir Oswin's absence from among them, Sir William had dispatched everyone to a different level of the castle to search. Thomas, perhaps on account of his familiarity with the servants' quarters, had been sent to the top floor. And now, standing in front of the closed door of the privy, he was willing to bet that he had found the man they sought.

Even though it was only for this last of his thirteen years that people had come to fear the redness and the horror of blood, the possibilities of that crimson stain against the worn wooden planks of the floor roared in his ears with the fury of white water crashing over rocks. That trail of blood, stretching the length of a hand from beneath the wooden screen, could represent a death as certain as being pulled into the depths of any river – more so, in fact: water could be forced from the stomachs of men rescued from rivers and lakes, and life restored to them; no-one had ever come back from the Red Death.

After a moment of hesitation, Thomas turned and headed for the nearest staircase, only too happy to put distance between himself and the blood as he spiralled down. Sir William would need to be told, of course, but in this moment of sudden fear Thomas sought the convenience of nearer company. On the floor below, he called Sir Marcus' name in a voice that he hoped failed to give away the fear rising within him; the scrape of boots on wood brought that huge shambling figure out of the dimness, and safety came with it.

"Found him?"

"I-I think so."

"Show me."

Back up the spiralling stairs they headed, Thomas leading the way. At the wooden screen, Sir Marcus crouched and lowered his own candle to the floor, examining the red stain closely. He then raised a fist and banged the door harshly:

"Oswin? Oswin are you in there?"

There was no reply. Sir Marcus stood.

"I'll get Will." He turned and walked away down the corridor, disappearing around the corner.

Thomas waited in silence, shamed at the panic in his own chest when Sir Marcus could react so calmly, realising now that he had even failed to check whether Sir Oswin was alive before turning and running for help. The roar of white water deafened his ears anyway, and he turned and pressed his forehead to the rough stone of the inner wall, soothed by the coolness. His pulse slowed, his breath deepened. Only at the sound of the slamming door to the roof, the shuffle of feet on stone steps, did he stand straight again, in no way desiring to appear the boy he was to the men who surrounded him.

Sir William – slim where Sir Marcus was broad, clean shaven where his brother was bearded, his cropped hair in contrast to his brother's unruly mane – preceded Sir Marcus around the corner. At his glance, Thomas pointed to the red line on the floor, and Sir William turned, stepped forward, and looked down at the blood.

"This is the privy," he said, placing a hand against the screen, his back to them.

"Aye," Sir Marcus replied.

"Did Oswin use the privy?"

"Unlikely."

Sir William turned to face Thomas. "Did you open the door?"

Thomas tried to swallow the dryness in his throat, shook his head.

"Very wise." His master reached out for the candle in Thomas' hand. "May I?"

Thomas passed the light to him and watched as Sir William turned to face the door in the middle of the screen, keeping the blood to his right-hand side. He pressed his right hand against the door and pushed it gently.

The door remained closed.

Sir William pushed again, more firmly, but still it refused to move. He turned and looked at Thomas, and then to Sir Marcus.

"Two nails, I think," Sir Marcus said, making a circle in the air with a finger.

"I'm sorry?"

"There are no bolts on the doors up here—" it was unacceptable that servants might be able to lock their doors against their masters, "—but I think Fenwick was worried about people queuing up to watch him defecate, so they used nails here: one in the back of the door at the edge, the other at the same height in the frame. Hung a length of twine from one, and just," again he made a circle in the air, "wrapped that around both nails to hold the door shut."

Sir William turned to the door again, and banged it several times with the underside of his fist. "Oswin, are you in there? Are you hurt, Oswin?"

No reply.

He stepped back, turning his head to take in the whole of the wooden screen. "This is from one of the bedrooms?" he asked Thomas.

"Yes."

The privy had existed for maybe fifty days; it was difficult to keep track with so little happening. As more and more servants had fled the castle, several of the important men and women who remained had proved reluctant to empty out the toilet stands in their rooms. At a meeting called in the main hall to discuss the matter, some had suggested that the task should fall to the remaining servants, regardless of the house they served, but Prince Prospero himself had intervened and so the suggestion was put aside.

A few days later, a plan had been devised to create a toilet for those who objected to cleaning out their own. Since the western wall of the castle abutted the moat, and since the bay window on the top floor overhung the moat on that side, could that window seat be turned into a means for the waste to dispose of itself?

Objections had been obvious – any opening might allow access to animals carrying the Red Death – but, over the water and on the fourth floor of the castle, arguments for its safety were simple. And so the place where Thomas had told Isobel of his love for her, and had asked her to spend the rest of her days with him, became a privy to save rich people from unpleasantness.

Quick measurement had showed that the wooden screens fronting the servants' bedrooms would fit between the wooden walls either side of the bay window. Such a screen, with a door at its centre, could be pushed at least halfway back before its top met the rising stone arches supporting the battlements above them. And so the wooden panels had been removed from the front wall of an empty bedroom and the frame there cut loose, moved into place in front of the bay window, and nailed to the floor and walls on either side. The panels from the front of the frame had then been reaffixed to afford some privacy.

The door was solid wood, but Sir William turned his attention on the upper row of panels to the right-hand side – those reaching from waist height to the top of the doorframe. If the panel nearest the door was removed, they would be able to see inside, to confirm the source of the bleeding.

The heads of the nails holding the panel in place glimmered dully in the light of the candle as Sir William examined them.

"Shall I get a hammer?" Sir Marcus asked.

"No," Sir William handed the candle to his brother. "This wood is thin, we can break in more quickly."

Unsheathing the knife from his belt, Sir William slipped his fingers through the looped handle designed to protect the hand when punching, the flat blade protruding from the underside of his curled fingers. He raised his fist to the panel, indicating to Sir Marcus where he intended to strike, then spread his feet, drew back his arm, and looked over his shoulder at Thomas.

"Take a step back. Just in case."

Thomas did.

"Oswin, if you're in there, keep away from the screen," Sir William called loudly, and then swung a punch at the panel that set it rattling. He drew his arm back again and hit the panel a second time, then a third, gouges making themselves clear on the surface of the wood. At the fourth strike the panel creaked, and at the fifth it splintered under the handle of the knife, a flash of daylight showing through. A sixth, seventh punch followed, and the centre of the panel split fully open and Sir William was able to sheathe his knife and pull with his bare hands at the splintered edges of the gap he had made. Before long, a ragged hole had been opened in the wood, from just above Sir William's waist to just below the top of his head and wide enough for most men to fit their shoulders through.

Thomas watched Sir William's back, and saw his shoulders stiffen as he leant in through the hole. After a few moments, he stepped back from the panel and looked first at his brother and then at Thomas, a weight in his eyes.

"It's Oswin. He's dead."

Neither reacted. They had become so used to death. Corpses could be found at the foot of castle walls, or floating in rivers, or hanging from trees in woodland – usually victims of the Red Death, though often dead by their own hand having taken a quicker and more appealing escape from the horror that surrounded them.

Sir William stepped away from the screen, and the soft morning light coming through the window on the other side was blocked again as Sir Marcus, placing his own candle on the floor, stepped up and looked in. He ducked his head to lean through the ragged hole, his hands flat against the wood either side to support his weight. After a few moments he ducked his head again and stepped back, "The Man Who Would Never Die…"

Since coming to the Prince's castle, Thomas had heard people occasionally use this title when they spoke of Sir Oswin Bassingham, apparently a reference to the Thousand Days War.

"…dead by his own hand."

Sir William had sunk to his haunches, his back against the privy door. At Sir Marcus' words, he dropped his hands from his face as if coming to a decision.

"By his own hand? No, Marcus, this is murder."

Thomas jerked his head up to look at his master, and saw Sir Marcus stand straighter with the same surprise.

"Mur—? Will, he killed himself. You can see the cuts on his wrists from here."

A picture of wounded flesh, of that terrifying blood pouring out of the body, flashed in Thomas' mind, and he tried to deny the quickening of his own heart in response.

Sir William shook his head without looking up. "No, Marcus."

"Will," Sir Marcus crouched down to his brother's level, his voice becoming soft. "He is in there alone with slit wrists, the door is fastened shut with twine wrapped around the nails as I said—"

"I know."

"—the screen reaches the ceiling, so unless he was killed by a rat no-one got out that way. There are no hinges on the window and no glass missing, the only hole in there is the one they crap through, which is smaller than a clenched fist—"

"I know, Marcus."

"—no-one could have killed him and sealed the door that way and escaped, and there's nowhere to hide, so no-one is still in there with him." He reached out and placed a hand on his brother's knee. "It is unpleasant to face, I know, but...be sensible. He killed himself."

Sir William patted his brother's hand and rose calmly to his feet.

"I am unable to tell you how it was done," he said as the other man also stood, "but he was murdered and left there so we would think him a suicide."

Sir Marcus looked away.

"If you are unwilling to believe me," Sir William continued, and Thomas felt a shiver of both anticipation and fear at what he knew was coming, "I'll have Thomas explain it to you."

Sir Marcus glanced from his brother to Thomas and back again. There was no hostility in the look, no resentment. They would often pose problems in this way, getting Thomas to suggest answers and explain his thinking, often challenging him to take sides against one or the other of them, all without any bad feeling. A death, possibly a murder, was something new, however.

"Do you feel up to it, Thomas?" Sir William asked. "Would you care to tell us which of us is wrong this time?"

Thomas took a breath, and approached the screen.

TWO

The sight of the blood on the floor reminded Thomas the risk they ran being here, and stopped him in his tracks.

"He is untouched by the Red Death," Sir William said, seeing his hesitation. "His eyes are open, and there is no blood in them. I promise you, you are perfectly safe."

The screen hiding Sir Oswin's body seemed both terrifyingly close yet far enough away to exhaust even Terrington Fenwick's horses. Thomas approached it on legs he begged would show no tremor or hesitation and, ensuring his feet were well-spaced either side of that trickle of blood, he leaned in through the gap Sir William had made.

The seat in the window was perhaps two long paces away on the other side of the screen, and Sir Oswin Bassingham sat in the centre of this, as if using the privy. The shape of the corpse's torso was cast largely in silhouette, but Thomas was relieved to see trousers still clad Sir Oswin's legs; he had liked Sir Oswin and, given how little dignity was found in these days, he was pleased that some remained with this man in death. The corpse's upper body leaned back from the waist, the shoulders and head resting against the diamonds of glass in the window behind him, the neck held at an angle surely too uncomfortable to maintain if any flicker of life remained. A candle holder containing the merest stub of wax stood on the seat.

Then Thomas' eyes adjusted to the light, and he saw the blood.

The sleeves of Sir Oswin's shirt had been rolled up to expose his forearms, his hands resting palm upwards either side of his hips. The single cut along the inside of each wrist, halfway to the elbow, was clearly visible. Thomas' eyes were drawn to the left arm, where blood had drenched the skin in overlapping patterns, and even at this distance he was sure he could smell its smoky richness. Jagged lines of crimson extended away from the body and over the floor, some having seeped out from beneath the screen at his feet.

His toes began to itch.

He glanced nervously at Sir Oswin's face and saw, below his ragged fringe only lightly touched with grey, that the open, staring eyes showed none of the red speckling that was the first indication of the Red Death.

Blood was hardly new. Sir Marcus had been teaching Thomas to slaughter animals in the home of Sir William and Lady Suzann since the age of five, but to see it running so freely from another person in the time of the Red Death gave him pause. He swallowed the sourness in his throat and glanced across at the right arm of the corpse, the cut here equally long and straight and deep, the staining of blood on the forearm far less pronounced. Red spots speckled the corpse's rough brown trousers and thrice-buckled leather boots.

Thomas took in more details: Sir Oswin's military belt clinching the fabric of his long shirt at his waist, the scabbard empty against his right hip. Leaning in slightly, Thomas saw Sir Oswin's military knife on the ground behind the door, having supposedly come to rest there after falling from the dying man's hand. Another mistake.

Thomas stepped back from the panel and turned to face his expectant watchers.

"He was probably killed, yes," he said quietly. He felt dizzy.

"Why?" Sir Marcus asked evenly.

"The knife is too far away."

Two long paces from the body to the screen, too far away to have fallen from dying fingers; doubtless dropped there by the killer as they left.

"Is…that it?"

Thomas shook his head. "The cuts."

"The cuts?"

"And the blood is wrong."

"You will need to explain," Sir William said after a pause.

It had always been like this; for as long as Thomas could remember they had pushed him to think, to reason, to be clear why he came to the conclusions he did. Sometimes they would disagree with him just to provoke further explanation, and any questions he asked of them were generally met with more questions in return.

"The cuts are the same length, and straight. If Sir Oswin cut his own wrists the second cut would be less…steady."

Because he would have been bleeding to death.

"And," he continued, before either of the brothers could interrupt, "there's too much blood on his left wrist."

"Too much…?" Sir Marcus looked at Sir William, who gestured with his fingers that the point was Thomas' to explain.

"Sir Oswin was left-handed," he patted his right hip, where a left-handed man's knife would rest in its scabbard for easy access, "so he would have cut his right wrist first, and more blood would have come out there. But there is more blood to the left side of him, so that was cut first. And the right wrist has hardly bled at all, so he was probably dying or already dead when his right wrist was cut open."

Sir Marcus cursed, and turned to look upon the body. Sir William waited in silence, his eyes cast downward and a faint smile pulling at his mouth.

Sir Marcus turned back to them. "But that's impossible."

"Yes," Sir William replied. "Yes, it is."

"That door is secured shut on the inside by two nails here, like I said," the big man touched the door halfway up, "one in the door frame, one in the back of the door itself. There is a piece of twine wrapped around both of them," again he made the circle in the air with his finger, "several times. Someone could hardly do that and then walk out through the door they had just sealed, so it would have to have been done from out *here*," he stamped a foot on the floorboards. "And that's also impossible."

Sir William was unconcerned. "I know, Marcus."

Sir Marcus spread his hands and looked from Thomas to Sir William, "Then he killed himself.".

Sir William shook his head. "I agree with Thomas. Someone, in a hurry, cut open Oswin's wrists in the wrong order and then left him there to be judged a suicide."

"But *how*?" his brother demanded.

Thomas thought of the insanity that had already opened the day, "Could it be whatever attacked the Prince? Th-that vanished into thin air, too."

The brothers exchanged an uneasy glance.

"I think," Sir William said slowly, "that we should guard against jumping to any conclusions yet. How might it be possible for someone to secure this door and then make their escape?"

"Down through the seat?" Sir Marcus asked, frustration in his voice.

"The hole is too small," Sir William replied.

"And the planks are nailed down," Thomas said. In the too few moments he and Isobel had shared there when both freed from the requirements of servants in the castle, he had always been acutely aware of the nail heads scratching the backs of his legs through the thin fabric of his trousers

"I know *that*. I mean," Sir Marcus mimed lifting something, "removing the slats and climbing out through the hole that would make."

"And go *where*?" Sir William asked. "They'd be four storeys above a sheer drop into the moat. Once they're on the bracings below the window, they could possibly climb up to the roof, but how do they get back in?"

Sir Marcus raised an arm, indicating the roof on the other

side of the tower. "They could have unlocked the door ahead of time."

This was true: everyone except Thomas had a key to the hatch that opened onto the roof, though since there was no access to the lock from the outside it would need to be unlocked first if someone wished to enter the castle that way.

"Or," Thomas suggested quietly, "they could walk around the castle walls to one of the watchtowers, then down the steps into the courtyard and back in through the wicket gate in the castle's door if they had unlocked it in advance."

A moment of silence followed.

"That's a good idea," Sir Marcus said, looking to his brother, "I'm glad we decided against feeding him to the pigs as a baby like you suggested."

In spite of the seriousness of the situation, Thomas smiled.

"Either way," Sir William said, "the boards of the seat would be loose. Whoever climbed out would be unable to nail them back down once outside."

Sir Marcus turned to the broken panel and reached through to unwind the string around the nails.

"Wait," Sir William said, and his brother turned. "Thomas, did you see the nails?"

Thomas shook his head. The knife on the floor had commanded his attention.

"Marcus, I'd like Thomas to see them, too, in case we're wrong and they become important later."

Sir Marcus stepped back and Thomas approached. Leaning through the gap again, he looked down and to the left where the door met its frame and saw, as Sir Marcus had described, two nails halfway up the door's height – one in the back of the door close to its edge and a second, roughly a thumb length away at the same height, in the frame. The nails protruded from the wood to about half the length of a finger, the rough twine used throughout the castle wound tightly around them several times.

"Seen enough?" Sir William asked from behind him

"Yes."

"Then you can unwrap it."

Thomas reached in with his right hand, and took hold of the loose end of the twine hanging down from the nail in the back of the door. Lifting this up and over the other nail, the one in the door frame, he then guided it under both nails and continued slowly unwrapping the coils, counting as he did. Eventually, the string came loose in his hand and he stepped back from the screen.

"How many times was it wrapped around?" Sir William asked.

"Six."

"You're sure?"

Thomas was. Lady Suzann had taught him to count to over a thousand and, while he sometimes got confused in the hundreds, the words all becoming very similar, six presented no difficulty at all.

Sir Marcus stepped passed him, placed his right hand against the door, and pushed. The door opened inwards, scraping against the wooden floorboards, revealing a pattern of parallel curved scratches there. Thomas coiled the string around his hand, the rough ends prickling his fingers, and placed it in the hip pocket of the long shirt he wore, then turned to watch through the broken panel.

Sir Marcus stepped up to the left-hand side of the seat and plucked with thick fingers at the wooden struts that formed the horizontal surface. Nothing came loose, so he stepped past the body and tried at the other end, with the same result. The seat was firmly nailed in place; no-one had exited that way.

The big man turned to face them, the growing light through the blurred glass of the window casting him slightly in shadow. Thomas watched him crouch down out of view and then straighten up with the knife from the floor in his hands. He turned, wiped the blade clean on Sir Oswin's trousers, and placed it on the seat beside the stump of candle in its holder.

"I can think of only one other method," Sir William said, and looked at Thomas. "How about you?"

Thomas had one: "Could the string be wrapped around the nails with the door open? Whoever was in there could then squeeze out underneath it and pull the end as the door closed so that the twine appeared wrapped around the nails."

As the smallest among them, it fell to Thomas to test this, and it soon became clear that the length of string they possessed would only loop around the nails once in order for the door to remain open wide enough for him to leave. Two nails had also been hammered in at the very top of the door – directly above those the that twine had been wrapped around, one at the edge of the door and the other in the frame. These may also have been used in securing the door at one time, but whichever pair they tried the result was the same: no more than one loop of twine could be made, and six was out of the question. Since everyone else in the castle was a grown man, and would therefore need a bigger gap to squeeze through, this method also provided no solution.

Sir William's idea was that panels which made up the screen may have been removed and then nailed back in place on the frame holding them. Plenty of tools had been left behind by the men who had modified the castle to the Prince's tastes, with hammers, hand-powered augers for drilling holes, several different types of saw, and more besides easy to come by. However, a careful examination of the panels – those from the floor to halfway up the door, those from the middle of the door to the top, and the shorter, wider panels that ran along the very top of the screen above the door – found no nails loose or missing, and none that could have been removed without leaving some mark upon the wood. The heads of the nails, too, were dull, and had therefore been in place for a long time, rather than recently hammered back in once the killer had exited the privy.

On the inside of the screen, no wooden panels had been fastened, leaving instead a skeleton of horizontal beams and vertical braces holding them in place. This made it possible to see that the nails in the floor and walls holding the screen in place were deep in the wood and clearly old. Much as opening the door had scratched pale marks in the floor, the prising out of a nail or hammering it in a second time would leave some small traces which this close scrutiny would have discovered.

The floorboards were examined, too, and no marks found that would indicate their having been removed and replaced. And anyway, how could they have been nailed back in place once the killer had left the privy?

Sir Marcus examined the glass of the window – diamond-shaped panes no longer than a man's thumb, held in place by bands of lead – and found none loose, nor any sign that the window itself, fixed into the stonework surrounding it, could have been removed and replaced. If any glass were broken in such an operation, as seemed likely, it would be practically impossible to hide the damage. And in this age of the Red Death, who would risk breaking a window and providing a potential point of entry for any small animal that might find it?

Since the door opened inwards, towards the seat, the hinges were also protected from external tampering, but Sir William checked these closely anyway for signs or scratches upon the metal bands at the door's top and base. No indication of how the room could have been left sealed was found.

Eventually, defeated, the three of them sat on the floor outside the privy, their backs to the wooden walls on either side; Thomas and Sir Marcus faced Sir William across the gap, the dried trickle of Sir Oswin's blood on the floor between their extended feet.

"So," Sir Marcus said, "there was no way out."

Sir William was holding Sir Oswin's knife by the point, tapping the handle against the wooden floorboards between his legs.

"He was in there alone," Sir Marcus pressed.

Sir William nodded.

"But you two insist he was murdered."

Sir William nodded again.

"You're sure," this to Thomas, with a note of wryness in it, "that the twine was there the whole time? Will might have wrapped it around the nails when he broke the panel in, just to give us something to puzzle over."

Thomas smiled faintly, and a thin, humourless smirk flashed on his master's face. The door had been sealed when Thomas had first reached it, and Sir William's hands had remained outside the privy the entire time he was breaking in, and Sir Marcus knew this. The answer to the puzzle would be cleverer than that.

The big man threw his own hands up in exasperation. "Well, then."

Thomas felt again the desire to voice his suspicion that whoever, or whatever, had attacked the Prince earlier that morning might be responsible. If a man could vanish from one room with locked doors and solid stone walls then surely he could vanish from another. It seemed to be the only answer, even if it was no sort of answer at all.

"What shall we do?" Sir Marcus asked.

"We summon the others," his brother replied after a pause.

Sir Marcus slapped his knees and clambered to his feet with a groan. "I'll ring the bell."

He was almost out of view when Sir William called his name to summon him back.

"For the time being, say nothing about murder."

Thomas tried to hide his surprise.

"Someone thinks they have gotten away with this. I want

them to keep thinking that."

Sir Marcus nodded and turned away a second time.

It was only when the older man had disappeared from view again that Thomas realised the meaning in Sir William's words: one of the men in the castle had killed Sir Oswin and tried to make it appear a suicide. There were, he counted carefully, only nine of them in the castle now – no, eight, with Sir Oswin's death. Thomas knew that he was innocent, and he knew that Sir William and Sir Marcus were similarly innocent, and it seemed impossible that the Prince would kill Sir Oswin. That left four men. Four men who had been living here for close to two hundred days.

Why murder someone in the middle of a plague? And why now?

They sat in silence for a little while, Thomas certain that his master was turning the same questions over in his mind.

Eventually Sir William rose to his feet, slipping Sir Oswin's knife into his belt, and Thomas also rose, waiting while his master stood looking through the open door at the corpse. The two men had, in recent weeks, been spending more and more time talking together, and Thomas wondered if they had become friends.

The bell began to toll then, almost immediately above them, the sound clear and loud and deep and exceedingly musical, summoning everyone back from their searching, back to the main hall.

And one of the men responding to its call was a murderer.

THREE

Perhaps two hundred days ago – Thomas had lost count, they all blurred together after a while – when everyone had first gathered at the castle, the main hall had looked beautiful. The space had been filled with circular tables around which the invited men and women had crowded, their excited, chattering voices rising and swelling into the open tower above them.

Even the kitchens, to which Thomas was dispatched with the rest of the servants, had thrummed with a lively energy he had never before encountered. To have so many people gathered together after so many days of uncertainty and fear had felt like a new beginning. No more would they remain terrified of their neighbours. No more would faceless death stalk them, their livestock, their livelihoods. The King may have hidden himself away, offering nothing to his subjects in their time of greatest need, but now Prince Prospero had summoned them, and many were convinced that he had a plan to push back the tide of the Red Death.

Now, the hall stood empty but for the single circular table at its centre, around which could be seated every inhabitant of the castle. The departure of Terrington Fenwick some thirty days prior had seen most of the ever-decreasing group who had remained for that long also take their leave. People had been drifting away from the castle since that first day – many seeming to come to themselves soon after being sealed inside, a few hurrying away later in the embarrassment of their servants having fled in the night – but the departure of Fenwick and the power he represented seemed to Thomas to be the final gasp of hope out of the drowning sea of the Red Death that surrounded them.

The circular tables that had seated the heads of the richest and most important families in the kingdom stood on their edges around the six walls of the hall, the chairs they had

20

occupied long since placed in storage rooms. Now, even Thomas had been invited by Prince Prospero himself to come out of the kitchen at mealtimes and sit with the men at the table. At the same time, the Prince had also declared that, in reward for his dedication, Thomas should come down from his room in the servants' quarters on the top floor and sleep in one of the rooms on the first floor where everyone resided, giving him a room one door away from the Prince's own.

Four of them sat at the table now, awaiting the others.

In the seat to Thomas' right sat Sir Marcus, beyond whom stood the empty chair Sir Oswin would never again need. In the next chair around sat Sir Baldon Gregory, the only other person to have returned from searching, his eyes fixed on the middle distance as he slouched in his seat. Thomas had watched an uneven grey-patched beard sprout from Sir Baldon's face over the last few months and, like the close-cropped hair of the rich men who surrounded him, it had taken some getting used to. Sir Marcus had pointed out to Thomas that Sir Baldon had likely grown the beard because, his servants having abandoned the castle some months before, his own hands shook too much these days for him to be able to shave himself.

The chair to Thomas' left was usually occupied by Prince Prospero, and the chair to the left of that was reserved for the Prince's bodyguard, Zachariah – both stood empty. In the next seat was Sir William, and between him and Sir Baldon there stood two more empty chairs: those of Laurence Tolworth and Fergus Highstone.

"Must we wait, Sir William?" Sir Baldon asked, the irritation in his voice clear on his face.

"Well, some of us are missing, Baldon," Sir William replied with a smile, gesturing to the table, "and I do so hate repeating myself."

"Could we perhaps hurry them along?"

"You're welcome to try, Percy," Sir Marcus replied. "I told Zachariah why we were meeting on the way down and he refused to move from outside the Prince's door."

Sir Baldon sniffed, ignoring the use of his birth name, and Sir William stepped in – perhaps to retain some sense of unity in the lunacy of the morning:

"Perhaps try again. He should know of this."

Sir Marcus rose from his chair, and made for the stairs.

"And the others?" Sir Baldon asked, pressing his point.

The main hall was open all the way to the very top of the castle, where the bell hung far above their heads in the tented roof that topped this six-sided tower. The rope by which the bell was rung hung down from on high and was fixed to the wall behind Sir Baldon's chair, next to the door that led to the kitchens.

Sir William gestured to the rope and said, with what would have sounded to anyone unfamiliar with his ways like kindness, "You are welcome to ring for them again, Baldon. But I'm sure they heard it and are making haste."

"Even in the dungeons?" Sir Baldon asked, ignoring the invitation.

Sir William paused and turned to Thomas. "Baldon has a point. Thomas, would you collect Laurence? He may have been unable to hear the bell from down there."

Thomas stood from the table. A set of stairs, all reaching from the dungeons to the servants' quarters on the top floor, opened on each of the six corners of the main hall. Thomas paused, unsure where best to look for Laurence in the vastness of the revel rooms below.

"I'd try," his master pointed at the staircase to the right-hand side of the main hall's fireplace, itself opposite the door to the kitchens, "that one."

"Should I take a key?" Thomas asked.

Guests had keys, servants only went where the guests

allowed, and so he would need to borrow one from either of these men.

"Just knock," Sir William said. "He'll hear you."

What little light reached the main hall spilled only onto the top few steps, but fetching a candle to aid his descent would waste time. As Thomas descended, the spiralling stairs grew darker and darker, until he was advancing by memory and feel alone, his right hand brushing the roughness of the curving outer wall. After four full rotations, the ground flattened and he reached out with both hands and felt the rough wood of the door in front of him.

He knocked as loudly as he could: "Laurence! Laurence!"

Silence greeted him when he stopped. He wondered if he would even be heard in the vastness of the dungeons.

"Laurence!" He hammered the door with the underside of his fist, stopping only to rub the sore flesh there. He was about to start again when he heard a scrape and the click of the lock, and the sound of the door sliding open.

The darkness lifted slightly, subdued daylight filtering through the green and white windows at the back of the room beyond.

"Alright, Tom, keep it down, some of us are trying to sleep. Who are you looking for?"

He could hear the smile in Laurence's voice, and smiled in return.

"We're meeting in the hall, Laurence. Did you hear the bell?"

"No," the dim shape of Laurence replied, and Thomas felt a hand ruffle the stubble atop his head, "thank-you. Run along, I'll be up in a moment."

Thomas turned and headed back up the stairs towards the light, advancing carefully in the gloom. When halfway up, he heard the door below close and a key turn in the lock. Footsteps followed him slowly and, when he emerged into the hall and took his seat, Sir William tilted his head in a silent thanks. A few moments later, Laurence emerged from the same doorway.

The closely-cropped hairstyle most of the men in the castle had adopted – a guard against lice and mites now that their usual treatments were unavailable – suited Laurence Tolworth. His dark blonde hair looked darker cut short, and for some time now he had sported a trim goatee that made him appear younger than his thirty-some years. He walked up behind Sir William and clapped him on the shoulder, then pulled his chair out, and sat down with a tilt of the head to Sir Baldon.

"Terrible news about Sir Oswin," he said, shaking his head.

Sir William nodded in agreement just as Sir Marcus emerged from the next stairway round. The Prince's bodyguard Zachariah followed him into the hall, stopping short as he entered, apprehension on his face.

"Where is Highstone?" he said in his accented voice.

"He'll be here," Sir Marcus assured him, and gestured to the table. "Take a seat."

Zachariah stood, the expression of displeasure on his tanned face made somehow more threatening by the dark hair falling past his shoulders.

Sir Marcus rounded the table to his seat, raising his fingers in greeting to Laurence. "Zachariah," he said, seeing the bodyguard's hesitation, "the Prince is safe – we are all here, or will be soon. Besides," he added with the ghost of a smile, "this way if anything happens to him you'll know it had to be Fergus who did it."

The bodyguard was about to object when Fergus Highstone emerged from the stairway behind him.

"Bugger, sorry," the big man said as he saw everyone else waiting, "I wanted to check on the Prince since we were meeting. Took longer than I thought."

Sir Baldon addressed Highstone as he and Zachariah

approached the table and took their seats. "And how is he?"

Highstone dragged out his chair and sat down heavily, his face red. Like everyone else in the castle he wore long trousers and a long-sleeved shirt that reached to mid-thigh and was clinched at the waist by a belt. However, in keeping with his status, the fabric of Fergus Highstone's clothes was noticeably finer than those of the military men who surrounded him, and the sleeves of his shirt were, from wrist to shoulder, a close-fitting crimson silk of a type and quality that Thomas had only seen in the revel rooms of the dungeons below. His belt, too, was without the dagger that the others wore, being instead a twist of fabric the same colour as his sleeves.

"He has had...quite a shock," Highstone said after a moment's deliberation, rubbing at his horseshoe of greying hair.

"Will he live?" Sir Baldon pressed.

"Oh, yes," Highstone said easily. "Most certainly."

Sir Baldon sat up straight, his hands flat on the table. "Thank-you, Fergus." He looked around at the seven other men – six men and one boy – and then stood. "Shall we call this meeting to order?"

Having lived all his life in Sir William's household, there was much about the conduct of the Prince's castle that had been new to Thomas. As the most senior person at the table, it was Sir Baldon's role to start this meeting, even though he was unaware of what Sir William and Sir Marcus had found and why they had summoned everyone here. This made no sense to Thomas, but then neither did why Sir Baldon was more senior than Sir William and Sir Marcus – Prince Prospero had given them their titles for their service in the Thousand Days War; Sir Baldon, Thomas knew, had adopted his name and title from his own father, the previous Sir Baldon Gregory. All he'd had to do was wait for an old man to die. Surely fighting for the King was a more noble way to earn a title.

"I believe, Sir William, that you have news?"

Sir William waited for Sir Baldon to sit before he stood. "We found Oswin, I'm afraid. He appears to have secured himself in the privy on the top floor and ended his own life." He ran a finger down the inside of his arm.

"He slit his wrists?" Laurence asked without standing, looking up at Sir William, and Thomas saw Sir Baldon's eyes squint in irritation.

"He did."

One of these men would be extremely pleased to hear this. Sir Baldon, Fergus Highstone, and Zachariah – one of them must have killed Sir Oswin. It was wrong to suspect Laurence, Thomas realised now. Laurence was his friend. And surely Zachariah could be freed from suspicion. The valuable rings on the bodyguard's fingers spoke of the gratitude shown by the various rulers in whose armies he had served. The stories whispered about Zachariah were the stuff of legend: that he had once killed seven men with a single swipe of his sword, had killed one man simply by touching him. Someone that fearsome – fearsome enough to guard Prince Prospero – would have cut Sir Oswin's head off for all to see rather than disguise his act as a suicide.

Sir Baldon stood again: "Do we take this as an admission?"

"An admission?" It was Laurence again, his elbows resting on the arms of his chair and his fingers steepled in front of him. "Of what?"

"Of his…" Sir Baldon looked around the table, seeking some agreement, "of the attack on the Prince."

Laurence's voice snapped out, cold:

"A man is dead. Our–" he pointed at Sir William and himself, never taking his eyes from Sir Baldon, his frustration clearly growing, "commanding officer, who served the King faithfully for his entire career, is dead, and your first thought is to accuse him of treason against the Prince?"

Sir William placed a hand on Laurence's arm, then rose to his feet. "No, Laurence; we must acknowledge that Baldon has a point, even if it is something we find unpleasant to face."

To Thomas' eye, Sir Baldon stood a little straighter.

"Will," Laurence said, a begging note in his voice, but Sir William spoke over him.

"The Prince is attacked. Within an hour, Oswin turns up dead by his own hand. They might be related."

"When did he die?" Zachariah half-growled without standing. Thomas waited to see who of Sir William and Sir Baldon would sit down first, but neither did.

"I, hurrum," Fergus Highstone leaned forward to answer the question and then, realising his mistake, rose to his feet as the two standing men sat. "I would be happy to inspect the body. Was it stiff?" he asked Sir William, who looked at his brother for guidance.

"We failed to check."

Highstone rubbed at the island of bare skin in the middle of his head. "Bodies grow stiff for some time after death. That may give us an idea."

Having said his piece, the medical man sat down.

"Even if – if it *was* Sir Oswin who attacked the Prince," Laurence said, still agitated, still seated, "in fact, whoever it was – how did he...?"

Everyone fell silent, and Laurence slouched in his chair with a frustrated gesture.

Thomas was sure that there were eyes upon him. After all, it was he who insisted on the vanishing of the robed figure. He felt heat rise to his face.

"How do we know the man vanished?" Zachariah asked from his seat.

Laurence pointed across the table. "Thomas."

Zachariah turned to Thomas. "You chased him."

Thomas nodded.

"You were very brave."

The kindness in the bodyguard's voice took Thomas by surprise. All of the discussions here took place around him, in the full knowledge that his own involvement was unasked, and he felt suddenly awkward at being addressed directly.

Sir Baldon coughed into the silence and rose to his feet. "I think perhaps that when we find out who was responsible, maybe they will be able to tell us what *really* happened."

Sir Baldon's tone brought Thomas up short.

He's calling me a liar.

"And where do you suggest we look, Sir Baldon?" Laurence asked from his chair, throwing his hands wide. "Because if *somebody* did it, it would have to be one of us."

"Unless it *was* Sir Oswin," Highstone muttered, half under his breath.

"Now hold on…," Laurence snapped at his neighbour.

Highstone, unmoved, straightened in his chair and ran his eyes over Laurence. "Where else would you suggest we look, Laurence?"

"Now *hold on*…" Laurence said again, rising to his feet, his finger hovering close to the end of Highstone's nose. Thomas glanced at Zachariah and saw something like amusement in the bodyguard's eyes as he watched the men argue.

"Gentlemen, please. We have important things to do," Sir William rose to his feet and took his friend by the shoulders, turning him away from Fergus Highstone. Behind Laurence, Thomas saw Highstone sit back and relief flood his face.

They're terrified, he realised. *They're just as scared as I am.* These men hid it better, but the attack on the Prince had shaken them because they could make no sense of it, any more than he, a thirteen year-old boy, could. For the first time, he felt as if he actually belonged at this table.

Sir Baldon stood and, raising his faintly-trembling hands for silence, waited until Sir William had coaxed Laurence back into his chair.

"It seems to me, gentlemen," he said, his eyes roving over the men at the table and avoiding Thomas, "that, if we are to accept Sir Oswin's innocence as Laurence insists, then the first people under consideration–" and suddenly his eyes fixed on Thomas, and Thomas found himself unable to blink or to look away, "would be the King's enemies."

Sir Baldon's eyes moved on, and he glanced around the table with his eyebrows raised.

Oh no.

Thomas had found Sir Oswin's body.

Thomas had been present when the Prince was attacked.

Thomas was the one who claimed that the robed figure had vanished.

He risked a glance around the table. Sir Marcus and Sir William held each others' gaze, Fergus Highstone was examining his fingers, Laurence sat staring straight ahead, and Zachariah had confusion written all over his features as he glanced from face to face.

They're going to say it was me.

His head throbbed. He realised he was standing, having pushed himself away from the table. Every face turned to him, and all Thomas could see was seven men with more influence and power than he would ever know; seven men who could blame him, whose collective word would never be questioned. They were going to accuse him of treason, because it was better to have an easy answer that was wrong than to accuse someone close to them.

His vision distorted and blurred, and he realised he was crying.

"I would never..." he gasped out, and suddenly it overwhelmed him – the terror of being thrown from the castle, cast out in disgrace, to face the Red Death alone.

"Thomas," he heard Sir Marcus' voice as if from a great

distance, and looked over to see Sir William's eyes struck wide as if realising what Thomas now knew.

"I WOULD NEVER...!" he yelled through his tears, and suddenly felt a great crush of hands on his back and a press of rough fabric covering his face. The familiar smell of Sir Marcus engulfed him. Thomas tried to lean back, to explain, but every time he drew breath it simply fuelled the furnace of his fear and set him crying more intensely.

"I think we're done," he heard Sir Marcus say to the room at large, his voice close. And then, quieter, "Come on, let's go and boil those frogs."

Thomas, tears still streaming, allowed the gentle pressure of Sir Marcus' hand at his back to steer him towards the doorway that led to the kitchens. Lacking the courage to look up as he left, he kept his eyes fixed on the ground, the air of suspicion and fear thick around him.

FOUR

They crossed the corridor that ran around the main hall, and entered the kitchens by the doorway immediately opposite. Sir Marcus eased the door shut behind them and ushered Thomas into one of the stools at the central table where they would ordinarily have eaten their breakfast that morning.

Taking up this entire side of the castle, the kitchens were divided into three sections by the two huge fireplaces – the length of room between them twice that between each hearth and the end wall. Thomas blindly groped his way towards the seat and sat bent forward, his feet twitching, his knees bouncing.

Sir Marcus pulled up a stool nearby, and let him cry.

"Do you want to talk about it?" the big man asked gently after a few moments.

Thomas shrugged, and wiped at his nose with his sleeve. It would sound stupid said out loud. And how could this titled man ever understand? He would always be free from the suspicion that Thomas knew was gathering against himself.

The squeak of hinges made Thomas open his eyes and look round to the door. Behind Sir Marcus' seated form, Thomas saw Sir William enter the kitchens, with Laurence immediately following. Laurence closed the door and stood back as Sir William approached, crouching down to Thomas' level.

"Thomas, what happened?"

He had known these men his entire life. He had served in their house, slept under their roof, eaten at their table. William and Marcus Collingwood, and Sir William's wife Lady Suzann, were the only family he had ever known. And Laurence was their friend, the only regular visitor at the manor, and perhaps the only other adult who had ever shown any interest in Thomas. Without these people, who else did he have?

He took a breath.

"They're going to blame me." His voice scraped his throat, the words thick and heavy.

Sir William glanced at his brother as if seeking explanation and, with none forthcoming, looked back at Thomas. "I'm sorry?"

"I was there when the Prince was attacked, and no-one believes what I saw. And I found Sir Oswin's body."

The growing heat in his head threatened to overwhelm him, and his throat closed up again in terror.

Sir William's voice was soft. "Thomas, believe me, no-one is going to accuse you of attacking the Prince. Marcus was there, too; he saw what you saw."

"Still got the bruises to prove it," the older man said, half a smile in his voice.

"But Sir Baldon—"

"Baldon?" Sir William seemed surprised.

"He looked at *me* when he said it: 'the King's enemies'."

Sir William dropped his head. "I see."

Laurence stepped forward. "He would never accuse you, Thomas, believe me. Baldon just wants to be sure he's safe. He wants to remind us all that, if we're looking for enemies of the King, he will never come under suspicion."

Thomas wanted to believe him, but the question seemed unavoidable: "Who *are* the King's enemies, then? Here in the castle, I mean."

His master smiled like a man in pain. "That is what needs to be found out."

Laurence stepped further forward, past Sir William, and rubbed his hand over the stubble on Thomas' head, as if ruffling his hair. He knew Thomas hated it, that was the joke between them now: he had no hair, so there was nothing to stop Laurence disarranging it. "There's nothing to fear, Tom. I promise."

Thomas tried to ignore the heaviness that his friend had set growing inside of him. Surely Sir William or Sir Marcus had spotted it, too…

Laurence squeezed Thomas' arm in a manner that would have been reassuring at any other time, and turned to Sir William. "I would like to see Sir Oswin before Baldon and Fergus pull him around too much; there may be a detail they overlook that will tell us what happened."

Sir William stood up and touched his friend's elbow in thanks. Laurence, with a final look back, opened the door and stepped through.

And still the heaviness in Thomas grew.

"It's been a strange day for all of us," Sir William said, and Sir Marcus snorted in agreement. "I think we forget sometimes how difficult this whole situation must be for you."

Thomas closed his eyes, hating this.

"There's something else." He had to say it now or he never would.

The brothers waited.

"Laurence," he lowered his voice, in case his friend – the thought of betraying that friendship was bitter – was still outside the door. "I said nothing to him about…about Sir Oswin being dead. I just told him we were meeting in the hall."

Understanding dawned in Sir William's eyes.

"But," Thomas continued, "when he came into the hall the first thing he said was…"

"'Terrible news about Sir Oswin'," Sir Marcus finished, softly.

Thomas' back and shoulders twitched involuntarily. He wanted to throw up.

Sir William, his face controlled, pulled a stool from beneath the table, and sat on it.

"I'm sorry, I…" Thomas felt the prickling in his eyeballs again, and the rising uncertainty about whether he had just done the wrong thing. He was a servant, after all. Raising doubts about those more senior than him – which, really, meant anyone – was doubtless a flogging offence in any other household. And Laurence was more than just *his* friend, he was the closest friend of these two men.

Sir William twitched a hand in the air to brush aside the apology, looking between Thomas and Sir Marcus. "We owe Laurence the opportunity to give an explanation for that. I'll speak to him."

"Wh-what if he denies it?"

Sir William looked at Thomas then, really *looked* at him, and understood the real question being asked.

"Thomas, if you tell us that you said nothing to Laurence about Sir Oswin's death, we believe you. I am so sorry if you feel untrusted. I'm sorry you're caught up in this, all of it, but whatever happens know that Marcus and I believe you."

Again Thomas' eyeballs prickled, but this time with an entirely different kind of heat. He tried blinking it away, and Sir William stood.

"You did the right thing in telling us. I will speak to Laurence, it is easily resolved. Is there anything else you want to say?"

Thomas shook his head.

Sir Marcus also rose to his feet, with an air of wishing to move things along. "We should do the checks, then."

Sir William and his brother exchanged a look, and the squeak of hinges told Thomas when the younger man left the room. Sir Marcus got to his feet and walked around the table to the bench along the back wall, collecting the leather bag he had placed there after dinner last night.

"Ready?"

Thomas rubbed his eyes and stood.

In the right rear wall of the kitchen were two doors. The first led to the covered walkway out to the well from which they drew their water, and the second led to the spiral staircase down to the dungeons. It was to the second they now headed, walking past the fireplace at that end of the kitchens.

The kitchen fireplaces were open at both sides, their mantles far taller than those in the bedrooms above, easily the height of a man's chest. Sir Marcus took a wooden torch from its bracket on the chimney and pressed the crown into the low-glowing embers always burning there until a flicker of flame could be lifted away.

Handing the torch to Thomas as the flame grew, Sir Marcus unlocked the door to the stairway and preceded Thomas down. Four full rotations of the spiral stair brought them to the bottom, and in the flickering light of the flame Sir Marcus inserted his key into the lock and opened the door to the dungeon, to the revel rooms.

They emerged into the blue room and, even after all this time, the sight of it still made Thomas catch his breath.

The room was, as the name suggested, entirely blue: under their feet, the rug which ran from the back wall to the narrower front wall was of a rich shade rarely seen in nature, and the furniture filling the space – couches, lounging chairs, tables – had been upholstered in equally pristine material of the same hue. Massive sails of this material hung from the ceiling and covered the front and rear walls, and even the mantle of the fireplace in the front wall had been stained blue to match.

Far from the disease-ridden prisons about which Laurence had an apparently endless supply of stories that thrilled even as they appalled, the dungeons of this castle had been turned into a paradise where the Prince entertained only his most honoured guests. Thomas still remembered the thrill of stepping into this room for the first time, the buzz of the crowd as they were admitted, the overwhelming feeling of release, the joy of sharing an experience that only the most privileged would ever know. The rumours that had circulated the kingdom regarding the Prince's dungeon were almost legendary, and the rooms themselves more than lived up to their reputation.

More amazing than the existence of this striking room in blue was that, from within this sea of colour, you could see the exact same room replicated again – to the left as they stood now in deepest crimson and, to the right, in pure black. From where he stood, Thomas could turn to his left and walk in a ring through six rooms that differed only in the colour they had been rendered: from blue to red, then stark white, onto lush green, to purple, through black, and back to blue where he had begun. Even the wood that went into the fireplaces was treated in such a way that the flames burned with hints of the appropriate colour. He squirmed to remember the eagerness with which he had run to see the black fire Isobel had solemnly promised him burned in that room, and the way she grinned at him when, fooled, he had returned to her, his face hot with embarrassment.

In the rear wall of each room, where they now stood having emerged from the kitchen stairs, was a window the height of two men, filled with coloured glass that matched room it overlooked. Illumination from behind these windows sent shadows of the appropriate hue dancing around the shapes and people present. When filled with the laughing, excitable guests here at the Prince's invitation, in their costumes of every manner and taste, there had been much of the beautiful, much of the wanton, much of the bizarre, something of the terrible, and more than a little of that which might have excited disgust for the eye to fall upon.

After a lifetime of stone walls, mud, trees, and animals, such vibrant colours in such concentration stirred the embers of excitement and unease within Thomas still. Daily exposure to it had in no way lessened the fascination.

"Come on, lad," Sir Marcus said gruffly, entirely unmoved, the spectacle around them only vaguely implied by the dim morning light filtering through the great windows, "there's still work to do."

Locking the stairway door behind them, they stepped over the invisible boundary into the red room and, lifting a fold of fabric away from the wall, Sir Marcus unlocked the door hidden there and ushered Thomas ahead of him.

They stepped out of luxury, and back into the real world.

The stone passageway here was as stark as the rooms they had just quit were luxurious. A bare stone wall faced them, stretching up to where a grate wide enough for four men to lie side-by-side opened at ground level into the castle's courtyard. Beneath each grate stood the brazier which lighted the windows into the revel rooms.

This passage ran in six continuous sections around the six coloured rooms, a brazier atop a tripod in front of each window except the room garbed in black. This room had a window, and the glass in it was indeed stained black, but – as the corridor there ran beneath the castle's moat – no grate could be installed and so no brazier had ever burned there.

Sir Marcus, after locking the door behind them, turned to the left. Taking the torch from Thomas, he climbed one-handed up onto the tripod by the blue window and raised the torch above his head, placing the flame to the brazier's oiled wick. Once the flame had taken, he climbed down and ground the head of the torch into the stone floor to extinguish it.

The Red Death had first emerged over a year ago, the early signs of its presence in anyone easy to spot – blood in the eyes came first, then that blood running freely from the nose and mouth as the afflicted became aggressive and unpredictable, attacking any living thing within reach in the short life the disease allowed them.

When the blood of the attacker touched the wounds of their victim, the Red Death found itself a new host and so, if shut off from the aid and from the sympathy of their fellow men, the unlucky souls touched by the plague could have been identified quickly before they died, before they had a chance to spread the insanity to anyone else.

It was impossible to imagine now, but the Red Death should have been easily tamed.

But then animals had also started showing signs of the affliction, and so the tide of misery and death had spread.

The lurching walk, the bleeding from the face – these signs were present in everything the Red Death touched. But where all other living things were granted at most an hour in which to suffer before expiring, it was soon noticed that rats were living for up to ten days with the Red Death upon them. And one such rat – aggressive, unmindful of its own survival – could spread the disease to a lot of men and animals in that time.

Every day, Sir William examined the roof, chimneys, and castle walls for any birds that may have died in flight and fallen into the grounds. Every day, Sir Marcus and Thomas came down here to check for any vermin that might have swum the moat and entered the courtyard through the drainage holes at the base of the castle's walls. Such vermin could enter the castle itself through the grates above their head now, since those were at ground level outside the castle, and would nest in the wood store that opened off this passage. All the doors that could be – those to the stairs leading to and from the revel rooms, the hatch onto the roof, that other to which none but the most honoured had ever possessed a key – were kept locked, and any animal found in the castle was killed. Sir William kept a bow and arrows on the roof for such purposes, and long-handled clubs were here in the dungeon for the same reason.

So far, none of the rats they had encountered down here had shown any sign of being touched by the Red Death. But it would only take one. Thomas was charged with finding and killing any animals discovered in this corridor. Wearing the gauntlets from the castle's lone suit of armour, he would carry the carcasses to the brazier and place them into the flame. If thrown into the land surrounding the castle, they might attract other scavengers, who would return over time and potentially draw others, raising the risk of the Red Death finding them here. Fire was the only thing the Red Death feared. Burning the corpses was the only way to banish that scourge. Sir Marcus carried, in the leather bag, the poison they used against those rats that evaded capture: stale bread soaked in a mixture of water and ground apple seeds salvaged from the dried fruit that made up so much of their diet.

This morning, Sir Marcus headed for the wood store to check for nests and Thomas worked his way through the black corridor and into the purple, emerging with several carcases for burning, only to see ahead of him that Sir Marcus had, perhaps to save time so that they could return to the mystery of Sir Oswin's death, also lit the brazier by the green window ahead. He was about to climb one-handed up the tripod to the platform that housed the flame when he heard Sir William's voice calling: "Marcus? Thomas? Are you there?"

Thomas quickly threw the dead rats up onto the platform, trusting the heat of the flame to burn them, and continued on the way he had been heading, drawing off the gauntlets as he went. Sir Marcus, who had come from the other direction, met him at the door and unlocked it. Hanging up the gauntlets, Thomas stepped out into the red room.

The light of the brazier through the blue window threw dancing shadows around the furniture scattered in the adjacent room. Sir William could be made out standing halfway across the room, between Thomas and the door on the inner wall which provided access to spiralling stairs back to the main hall.

"Is it Laurence?" Thomas asked, seeing the concern on Sir William's face. "What did he say?"

The muted brightness of the room, the dancing shadows, vanished as Sir Marcus snuffed out the brazier, leaving only the gentle morning light creeping down through the grates in the brazier corridor to illuminate the windows and the rooms they overlooked.

"No," Sir William replied, cast suddenly in silhouette, and Thomas heard the door behind him open and close, the key turn in the lock, as Sir Marcus joined them.

Sir William's shadow turned minutely towards his brother.

"There's a problem."

"Is it Laurence?" Sir Marcus asked.

"No, it's… Fergus and Baldon went to examine Oswin's body, to see if they could work out when he died."

Thomas remembered this from the discussion earlier.

"And," Sir William said, "it's gone."

"What?" Sir Marcus asked quietly, somewhere between a cough and a laugh.

Thomas was unable to see the expression on Sir William's face, but his voice carried the confusion they all felt:

"It's gone. Oswin's body. They say it's disappeared."

FIVE

"There was...was so much blood...we should really think about...about burning everything in the...the privy...though in this heat...we should...probably..." Fergus Highstone's words burst out hurriedly between shaking breaths as he led the way up the winding staircase. "I'm sure there's a...a simple explanation for all this...anyway," he continued, and Sir Marcus suddenly came to a stop in front of Thomas, indicating that Highstone, at the front of the procession, had himself stopped.

Thomas listened to the older man's breath rasping in the confines of the stone walls, and wondered why they had allowed the oldest person in the castle – Highstone must be at least sixty – to lead them to where they knew they were going anyway.

"I'm sorry, Sir William," Highstone's voiced echoed back. "All this excitement...and now...up and down these stairs..."

Sir Marcus muttered something Thomas failed to hear but was certain had been impolite.

"Take your time, Fergus," Sir William said. "If Sir Oswin's body has already gone, there is no rush for us to get there."

They were between the second and third floors at this point, heading up the stairway that continued all the way to the roof, having met Highstone in the main hall. And while Sir William was correct in there being no rush to see something that was no longer there, Thomas was desperate to get to the privy and confirm with his own eyes that the dead body of Sir Oswin Bassingham had indeed vanished.

"Perhaps," Highstone swallowed loudly, "perhaps you should go ahead."

"Yes," Sir Marcus said, his voice flat. "Perhaps we should."

Sir William may have been about to answer – they had

been in too great a rush to stop and collect candles from the stores, so it was difficult to see much in the gloom between floors – when the sound of what might have been a footstep on the stairs above reached them. How likely was it, Thomas wondered, that with only eight people in the castle, five of them should end up in the same stairway at the same time?

"Who's there?" Sir William called. "Is that you, Baldon? Laurence?"

Again a scrape of a boot on stone, with something unsteady in it.

"Hello?" Sir William called again, as the uneven scraping sounded nearer.

"...Will?" came the voice, quiet and carrying a note of distress that froze Thomas' insides.

It was Laurence. He sounded...ill.

Suddenly they were all trying to move at once; Thomas heard Fergus Highstone at the head of them struggle to his feet and lead the charge up the staircase. Thomas, fighting down panic, hurried close at the rear. Sir William shouted Laurence's name, as did Sir Marcus, and over the din Thomas thought he may have heard Laurence's reply, weaker than before.

Then suddenly he heard Highstone, with horror in his voice, say "Oh, Laurence!" and panicked confusion surged in his mind. Thomas saw, in the light drifting down from the third floor, a brief glimpse of his friend's face contorted in fear. He heard Sir William shout Laurence's name again, this time with an edge to it Thomas had no desire to contemplate.

Thomas allowed the panic to take hold.

He tried to fight his way past Sir Marcus, heedless of what he was doing, and the bearded man turned around and simply engulfed Thomas in a bear-hug to hold him still.

"It's well enough, lad," Thomas felt the deep voice rumble in his chest, "they've got him. Let's just wait."

Thomas tried to wriggle free, concern for Laurence flooding

his might as he fought past the point of exhaustion and yet still had energy to fight some more. Sir Marcus held him close, and eventually Thomas sagged, spent. He felt Sir Marcus' body twist as if looking around, and then found himself released.

"Now," Sir Marcus said, his voice heavy, "we'll go up. But slowly."

Desperate to find out what was happening, Thomas pressed impatiently behind Sir Marcus' bulk as they ascended into the light.

The first thing he saw as the big man moved out into the corridor was Fergus Highstone standing against the wooden screens that fronted the bedrooms on the opposite side of the corridor, his eyes wide and mouth open, blood on his chest and his hands. Thomas wondered if Highstone was hurt, but, though the tall man was breathing heavily, he looked far more confused than alarmed. The blood must have come from somewhere else, from some*one* else.

Then Thomas saw the feet, lying on the ground.

The thrice-buckled boots were worn by all military men, and Thomas blanched at either possibility of who this pair might belong to. Sir Marcus' shoulders were slack as he stood looking down at whoever was lying there, his bulk obscuring everything from the knees up, and Thomas pushed past him to see the dark head of Sir William who had sunk to his haunches to examine the prostrate form.

Oh, no.

His master was crouching over the body of Laurence Tolworth.

The cold, drenching shock that struck Thomas was overpowering. Tears sprang to his eyes for the second time that day and, wordlessly, he stumbled away from the body as if distance alone might make its existence less true. It was a few moments before he noticed the handle of a knife – that looped handle of a military knife, through which the fingers may be passed – protruding from Laurence's chest, the blade driven between his ribs.

Sir Marcus rubbed roughly at his beard as if steeling himself, and started to crouch down by his brother's side.

Sir William raised a hand to stop him.

"No, Marcus. Look."

And then Thomas, his senses scrambled by the shock of discovery, saw – and among all the madness the day had already offered, this was surely the deepest yet.

The lifeless eyes of Laurence Tolworth, staring blindly skywards, were stained red.

It was unthinkable. This was all happening too quickly. The Prince had been attacked, Sir Oswin had been murdered, his body found in impossible circumstances before apparently vanishing, and now Laurence had been murdered, too.

And, somehow, the Red Death was inside the castle.

Thomas' head spun, thoughts crowded in and then, when he tried to grasp at one, fled and left him staring, struck dumb. He was aware that he should feel sad, but was too confused to feel *any*thing.

They all stood staring down at Laurence's body; eventually, Sir William spoke.

"Marcus," he said without looking up, "get Baldon, get Zachariah, get Prospero out of bed if you can, get everybody downstairs. Now."

Sir Marcus nodded, his face slack.

"Fergus," Sir William said, and then, when the medical man failed to respond, louder: "Fergus!"

"Yes?" the tall man looked up, dazed.

"Are you injured Fergus?"

"I…" he looked down at his hands as if in disbelief, then back to Laurence lying on the floor.

"Have you injured yourself, Fergus?" Sir William's voice was slow but hard.

Highstone collected himself with a visible effort. "I think it is all Laurence's blood."

"Well," Sir William ran his hand through his short hair, his fingers pressing hard into his scalp, "I suppose we'll find out soon enough." He looked at his brother and then to Thomas. "Get Thomas downstairs, collect the others."

Sir Marcus glanced around himself as if in a dream.

"Fergus," Sir William said sharply as Highstone turned to walk away. "I would like you to remain; I need you."

"But," Highstone, too, seemed in shock, rubbing his bloodied palm down the side of his tunic like a naughty child, "I must burn these clothes at once. The blood, Sir William, the blood…"

Sir William approached him, and placed a hand on his shoulder.

"Fergus. *Fergus*."

Finally, the medical man looked at him.

"I need you, Fergus, I need you here. Go and change, but come back quickly, yes? I need you to tell me what happened."

Sir Marcus, clearly working hard to master his self-control, turned away, and indicated to Thomas that they should leave.

"Yes," Thomas heard Highstone say sadly as he started down the stairs, "I had a feeling you might."

~

Four of them sat around the table in silence: Thomas staring at Laurence's empty chair, Sir Marcus to his right, then, after Sir Oswin's empty chair, Sir Baldon, a cup in front of him. To Thomas' left, on the other side of Prince Prospero's empty chair, sat Zachariah, unhappily dragged away from outside the Prince's room. It seemed to Thomas that only the grimness with which Sir Marcus had broken the news of Laurence's death had convinced the bodyguard to accompany them to the main hall without objection.

"Must we wait?" the bodyguard said at last. Thomas had no way of knowing how long they had been here. Half an hour? Laurence was dead. The Red Death was in the castle. Everything seemed to be happening at a distance.

"We must," Sir Marcus said.

"I should be with His Highness."

"Yes," Sir Marcus replied, his voice clipped, "because you were so helpful to him last time."

Zachariah surged to his feet. "Nobody speaks to me that way—"

"Well I will!" Sir Marcus bellowed, also rising. "My friend has just been murdered, bodyguard, and you will sit down in that chair until my brother says otherwise or I will nail you into it."

Thomas swallowed nervously at this unfamiliar rage.

Something dark and unpleasant danced in the bodyguard's eyes. "You know, the Prince, he told me about you."

"Oh, *did* he?" Sir Marcus asked, disinterested, as he dropped back into his chair.

"And I told him—"

"No-one cares, bodyguard. Sit down. Now. Or I *will* make you."

Sir Baldon lifted his cup and drank.

The bodyguard stood, breathing heavily, looking at Sir Marcus for a few moments. The other man deliberately avoided his eye, glancing down at his own hands and then into the distance.

Slowly, without taking his eyes from Sir Marcus, Zachariah sat.

"I must ask," he said, his faintly-accented voice lilting with false politeness, "where *were* you when Prince Prospero was attacked?"

Sir Marcus looked at the bodyguard with red-rimmed eyes

and, with the same heavy disinterest as before, cocked a thumb in Thomas' direction. "Outside the door, with this one."

"And so—"

But whatever he said was cut off with an irritated gesture from Sir Marcus as Sir William and Fergus Highstone, the latter in clean clothes, appeared from the stairs to the roof, their faces unreadable.

"Thank-you for waiting," Sir William said as he approached the table, ignoring, Thomas noticed, Sir Baldon who had half-risen as if to start the meeting. "Fergus and I have examined the body." Both men took their seats, "Fergus, you can probably explain better."

Sir Baldon sat back in his chair, and took another drink.

"There are," Highstone said without standing, "some old scratches upon Laurence's hands, and what looks like a fresh cut on his thigh, but beyond that we see no evidence of him having been...of anything having bitten or attacked him. Of any way for the Red Death to have entered his blood."

"There was also a knife in his chest," Sir Marcus muttered darkly.

"Yes," Highstone apparently took this suggestion seriously, "but that only raises more problems. For if the Red Death entered Laurence's blood when he was stabbed, how did it get onto the knife in the first place?"

Nobody could answer that.

Thomas had, of course, heard of Fergus Highstone's exploits in studying the Red Death. You could hardly stay in the castle for as long as they had, surrounded by company as starved of gossip as the Prince's guests had been, without hearing the same tale trotted out: how, watching cows drink from a stream in which floated a corpse with the Red Death clearly upon it, Fergus Highstone had come to realise that the plague would spread only when blood met blood. So brilliant an observation could have been made by no less a mind than the Prince's personal physician.

"It would be good to know," Sir William said, as if forcing the words out, "what happened when you both went upstairs."

Sir Baldon and Highstone exchanged a glance and, since the former showed no eagerness to talk, the latter started:

"Sir Baldon and I, after we had met here, went to examine Sir Oswin's body in the hope of establishing how long he had been dead. When we climbed the stairs, however, it was – well, Sir Oswin *was* in the privy, am I correct?"

Sir William and Sir Marcus nodded.

"Well, by the time we got there, he was elsewhere," Highstone said simply.

This made no sense to Thomas. Sir Oswin was clearly dead, so could hardly have moved by himself. And there had been no time for anyone to move him. And *why* move the corpse? The death of Sir Oswin would have known to everyone in the castle soon after the discovery of his body, and the condition in which the privy had been left – the panel to the right of the door broken open by Sir William, the door itself unsealed – left no possible doubt that the body *had* been discovered.

"We thought," Highstone continued, "that it may have been hidden in one of the bedrooms, and so I elected to search the rooms one side of the privy and Sir Baldon took the other side. After a short time I heard noises from the corridor and went to look – and found Laurence exiting the privy. Doubtless Sir Baldon heard us talking?"

His face blank, Sir Baldon took a draught from his cup.

"Did you *hear* them, Percy?!" Sir Marcus demanded.

Sir Baldon swallowed. "I think so."

"Laurence told me he was going to examine the roof. I wanted to come down here to inform you all of Sir Oswin's inexplicable vanishing, so we walked to the stairway and parted ways – he headed up, and I down."

A moment passed before they realised that Highstone had stopped talking.

"And that's it?" Sir William asked.

"That is. Unless Sir Baldon has anything to add."

They looked to Sir Baldon, who, his eyes glassy, said nothing.

A loud *crack!* as Sir Marcus slapped his hand on the table made them jump. "Do you have anything to *add*, Percy?"

"No," Sir Baldon finally said, as if the sound of his own voice caused him pain. He seemed more affected by the shock than anyone. Or maybe it was simply that the contents of his cup had once again proved too alluring this morning. "I was in the f-front rooms then. I h-heard Fergus and Laurence talk and then a bang which I assumed was Laurence opening the hatch to the roof."

"And what did you do after you finished searching?" Sir William asked.

Sir Baldon looked at him, wide-eyed, as if wondering himself. "I went back to the privy and waited." He gestured to Sir Marcus "Y-your brother came and f-found me, and told me what h-had happened."

Sir William watched him silently for a moment before he spoke: "Laurence was stabbed with his own knife – it was driven between his ribs and into his lungs and...and heart." He took a deep breath and blinked rapidly. "We know he was injured before he came down the stairs looking for help, because we heard his voice and his...his step was..." his voice faded, and he sat, head bowed, looking at the backs of his hands.

Everyone waited in silence.

Sir William clenched and extended his fingers as if trying to dig gouges in the surface of the table. His face completely blank, he raised his right hand into the air, curled it into a fist, and brought it crashing down into the wood. Before anyone knew what was happening he did it again, and then a third time, the circular table rocking beneath the fury of the blows he rained upon it.

His expression remained blank; he made no sound.

Thomas watched, horrified.

The fist was raised a fourth time and, as it came plunging down, Sir Marcus was suddenly at his brother's side, grabbing the arm to stop its descent, lessening the force of the blow. Sir William tried to shake his hand free, swinging his other fist to knock Sir Marcus away, and the bigger man simply wrapped his arms around his brother's chest and lifted him bodily out of his seat, the chair crashing to the ground.

Sir William, now furious, screamed and thrashed in his brother's grip, snapping his head back to try and strike at the man holding him. Hit on the bridge of the nose, Sir Marcus dropped Sir William in surprise and, when the smaller man turned on him, took a punch to the stomach and one to the face without flinching, absorbing his younger brother's rage. The bigger man shoved his brother in the chest and, when Sir William raised his fist to swing in a wild punch, stepped under the descending arm and enveloped his would-be attacker in a bear-hug that trapped the arm in midair, flailing wildly, light blows tapping the top of his head.

Sir William screamed and writhed, trying to swing a punch, trying to stamp his feet or swing his legs, his body contorting, his loud breathing and grunts of discomfort filling the otherwise-silent hall.

Sir Marcus held him until he was still, until he went limp in his brother's arms and started to weep.

Highstone had half-risen from his chair, but the rest of them simply sat and watched, spellbound. Thomas became aware of the cold sweat in which he was covered.

Fergus Highstone stood and lifted up the fallen chair, turning the seat to face the standing men. Sir Marcus' red-rimmed eyes looked at Highstone over his brother's shoulder and he shook his head. Gently releasing Sir William from his embrace, the bigger man turned him unresistingly towards the nearest stairway. Sir William stood, his back to the table and his face in his hands, and Sir Marcus wrapped an arm around his shoulders and gently steered him from the room.

Thomas, on the verge of tears himself, remained still.

The room was silent for several moments.

Highstone swallowed. "If I may, Sir Baldon – w-we should consider b-burning the body as quickly as we can. If the Red Death is here among us, fire is the only way to banish it."

No-one objected. If they kept the body in the castle, it was only a matter of time before it would begin to smell; left outside, it would attract the very scavengers they worked so hard to guard against, especially in the current unceasing warm weather. Thomas hated the idea of his friend burning, and was aware that no-one would listen to the objections of a servant boy in any case, but fire was the only way.

Highstone stood. "I will prepare the body. If I may?" He looked to Sir Baldon who, glassy-eyed, tilted his head indifferently and lifted his cup.

The meeting broke up, and everyone drifted away.

~

Thomas saw nothing of Sir William until that evening, when, grey-faced, he emerged with Sir Marcus through the hatch at the front of the roof to join everyone else overlooking the courtyard.

Like the dungeons and the main hall, the castle and the courtyard in which it sat had six sides, the western wall of both standing hard against the moat. From this rear wall, one could walk out along the courtyard's containing wall, atop which was a pathway wide enough for two men to stand abreast. At each of the six corners of the surrounding wall, watchtowers had been built to allow sentries to oversee the forests and land beyond; the raised drawbridge stood between the two towers in the eastern wall.

Fergus Highstone had stitched Laurence's body into a sheet from an empty bedroom. Shortly before this ceremony, Thomas had watched from the roof as Sir Marcus had carried his friend out into the middle of the courtyard, the death shroud now a white smear on the grey stone five storeys below.

At the appearance of the Collingwoods on the roof, Fergus Highstone touched the tip of the arrow he was holding to the flame of the oil lamp Sir William had hung on the front of one of the chimneys there – as a sign of occupation, he'd said, to anyone passing who may need their aid – and strung it to his bow. Stepping to one of the crenels at the front of the roof, he fired the flaming arrow into the shape in the courtyard.

The faint crackle of flesh was soon audible even at this height, and the smell of the lamp oil with which the body had been treated rose to them before being carried away on the slight breeze. They stood in silence for maybe half an hour, the shadows around them lengthening as the sun lowered and grew dimmer at their backs.

Zachariah was the first to make his way inside through the hatch in the tented roof behind them, with Sir Baldon soon following, and Highstone leaving shortly thereafter.

Sir William, Sir Marcus, and Thomas stood at the front of the roof, their backs to the chimneys, and watched Laurence burn.

The evening was far from cold, but Thomas shivered – with grief, with fear, he was unable to tell. The baffling attack on the Prince and the murder of a man they had shared lodgings with was horrible enough, but the death of someone close to them all, and seeing that shake the foundations of the men who had raised him, was a sadness Thomas had been able to delay examining too closely until now.

He wanted time to himself, and for these men to have their own private grief. He shivered again and looked at Sir Marcus, who was watching Sir William closely. Feeling eyes upon him, the big man turned his tear-streaked face to Thomas. After a moment, he nodded.

Thomas pursed his lips in thanks, turned to the roof, and climbed down through the hatch, leaving the brothers alone.

PART TWO

Folly to Grieve

SIX

When Thomas awoke the following morning, his sadness at the loss of Laurence sat as a weight in his lungs. In the curtained darkness of his too-large bed, he worked to master the sense of emptiness that his friend's murder had left, and tried to spot any pattern in the previous day's unfathomable events.

Thomas thought of the men in the castle – remaining after the others had left because, he supposed, they were either bound to the Prince by position or sought the safety he offered – and asked himself again which of them could have upon their minds the obvious touch of insanity to justify the chaos that had erupted after so much fear had been dulled by so much time to so much boredom.

No answers were forthcoming.

With tiredness clinging to him, Thomas roused himself from bed and dressed. After sleeping four or five to a room this size on the top floor, having space to himself again was a relief. Perhaps touched by the manic energy of the revels in which their masters and mistresses were engaged, the other servants had tended to play tricks on him, probably because he was the youngest and therefore the easiest target. They would hide his clothes, steal his food, throw water or worse on him while he slept, all the while laughing at him and with each other, their faces looking to Thomas more twisted in anger than in the merriment they claimed.

Sometimes Isobel would intervene on his behalf, and that would only make things worse.

It was the departure of Terrington Fenwick from the castle – the sign which many of the others who had clung on past the dying days of the revels seemed to have been awaiting – that had spurred the last exodus of guests, and with them their servants, Isobel included. When Prince Prospero had said at dinner that evening that Thomas should be given a room with the remaining men here on the first floor, a room one door away from the Prince's own, Thomas had assumed it was just another jest in which he failed to see the wit.

Time had long since ceased to matter, but a glance out of the two windows in the outer wall told Thomas the youth of the day. He could feel a slight chill, bringing to mind an image of fine mist clinging to the ground, waiting to be banished by the approaching sun. He sat on the edge of his bed and ran his eyes over the furniture of the room – the vanity screen in the corner, hidden from view when the door opened, behind which stood his toilet stand; the small table by the head of his bed on which he placed his candle holder; the hearth in the wall opposite the foot of his bed – and was running his eyes along the floorboards, practising counting in larger and larger jumps, when Sir Marcus' knock came at his door.

The lands the Prince had bestowed upon the Collingwoods following the Thousand Days War took four full days to ride around. After years spent checking their borders, protecting livestock from poachers, and ensuring all within the lands was running well – absent from the manor several days at a time, camping out in the fields – an early start to the day had found its way into the marrow of Sir Marcus' bones. In the first days at the castle, when the revels would continue early into the mornings, Sir Marcus was the only one who had risen early and come to the kitchens for food, and Thomas had wondered why the older Collingwood brother had bothered to join the guests at the castle if he had so little interest in enjoying the Prince's hospitality.

By the time the revels had eventually ceased, with too few people remaining for them to feel like the joyful escapes the Prince had intended, Thomas had stopped wondering. Time and repetition dulled even the sharpest curiosity.

He drew back the simple bolt and, pulling the door towards him, smiled as he always did to see Sir Marcus bent low in a mock courtly bow. The big man straightened, his face showing, perhaps, just a trace of his private sadness, and indicated with a sweep of the arm that Thomas should lead the way. Stepping into the corridor and leaving his door open – the light through the windows helped illuminate the inner corridor, so any unoccupied room typically stood with its door open – Thomas turned to his right to walk past Prince Prospero's room. Then the memory of the previous day asserted itself, and he turned to the left instead, and they took the first staircase in that direction down to the main hall.

In the faint morning light, the round table tops stacked against the walls appeared as a phalanx of shields, the spindles at their centres protruding into the room like the spears of soldiers taking shelter. Thomas crossed the space to the door out to the kitchens and, crossing the corridor, stepped into that room.

No-one else was ever about this early, so Thomas and Sir Marcus fell into their habit of long practice and prepared their food without speaking. The circular bread plates from which the previous day's meal was eaten had been stacked to one side; finding their own, they selected the dried meat and fruit from the rations Sir Marcus had laid out the previous evening.

Thomas had seen the stores – in the rooms at the back of the castle, where it was coolest – and knew how carefully Sir Marcus had tried to ration out what they possessed to last for as long as possible. There was plenty of flour, an apparently endless supply of the bitter wine that Thomas always left untouched at mealtimes, and they could draw all the water they needed from the well even in this heat, but the barrels of cured meats and dried fruit were significantly less plentiful than anyone would have liked – always assuming that anyone besides Sir Marcus paid any attention. These men were so used to having everything, it may have never occurred to them that what they wanted might one day be unavailable.

The thought flashed into Thomas' mind that, with two men dead, the supplies would now last slightly longer. Might that be why the killer had struck? In a race between starvation and the Red Death, the first could be denied for a little longer if there were fewer mouths to feed.

They ate in silence, consuming the dry, tasteless food on their plates and then the thin bread plates themselves. Thomas baked a new batch of these every few days, with fresh plates laid out each evening and consumed the following morning. When the meal was complete, Sir Marcus took from around his neck the twine on which he wore his key and asked, as he always did, "Shall we boil these frogs?".

Collecting the leather bag and lighting the torch on the low-burning embers of the fireplace, they descended to the dungeons. Emerging into the blue room – dimly visible this early in the day with the torch providing the only illumination, but still magnificent in Thomas' mind – Sir Marcus locked the door behind them, and they stepped into the red room and unlocked the door to the outer corridor there.

"Just one flame today," Sir Marcus said, walking to the tripod by the red window and hauling himself up one-handed to light the wick there, "save the fuel."

This morning there were, thankfully, no interruptions. Thomas donned the gauntlets, took up a club, and hunted out any vermin living or dead. Collecting their carcasses and carrying them back to the red brazier, he climbed up to the flame and rubbed the fur of the rats against the oiled wick to ensure they would burn. He remembered then to check the brazier at the green window, where he had simply thrown the vermin yesterday, and found two unburned bodies that he carried back around for destruction. At various points he could hear Sir Marcus piling up wood in the stores and swearing at the rats he found nesting there, and this familiarity was a much-needed comfort after yesterday. With the Red Death having somehow found its way into the castle, it was sensible to wonder if this vigilance came too late, but the routine was reassuring. There was so little to do, anything that distracted the mind was to be seized upon.

The outer corridor checked, they carried armfuls of the thick, heavy wood which was burned in the kitchen fires upstairs, a time-consuming job on account of the need to unlock and relock the doors as they passed through. This done, they returned to the red brazier. Seeing that the vermin there had burned, Thomas picked up the snuffer – a rod with a hinge at one end holding a metal hood that could be lifted and placed over the brazier's wick – and killed the flame to preserve the oil. In preparation for tomorrow, he carried the snuffer round to the next brazier, that by the white window, and laid it on the floor there.

Locking the doors behind them as they went, they ascended to the kitchen for the final time. Emerging in the corner of that big room, they could hear someone moving around in the wide central section, the view cut off by the chimney and fireplace.

"That you, Will?" Sir Marcus asked, and his brother, jaws working, stepped into view.

"How are the frogs?" Sir William asked after he had swallowed his food. Thomas had never understood why they called the rats 'frogs', and it seemed too late to ask now.

"Little bastards keep getting in."

"Probably drawn by the smell of cooking last night," Sir William said flatly.

Because, yes, Thomas realised, before the burning oil had caused the flesh of Laurence's body to blacken past recognition on its way to becoming simply ash, Laurence would have cooked for at least a little while. And Thomas could well understand how the smell of cooked meat would draw hungry animals.

"He always did enjoy making life difficult for us," Sir

Marcus said, his voice somewhere between tenderness and dismissal, and Sir William pinched out a painful, fleeting grin in response before turning away.

Laurence had been one of the few visitors Thomas could remember ever spending time at the Collingwoods' manor, and it was clear that everyone – Sir William, Lady Suzann, Sir Marcus, Cook, Elena who helped in the kitchen – was always pleased to see him. Thomas would hope that, as they sat around the table telling jokes and silly stories, Sir William and Laurence might also tell him about the heroics of the King's soldiers in the Thousand Days War when they had served together to defeat the King's enemies. Cook, however, had always warned him sternly that the topic should never be raised, that the war had done damage that neither man wished to remember. Instead Laurence would teach them magic tricks or quiz Thomas on a range of subjects, or profess amazement at the improvements in his counting and calculating, pouring praise on Lady Suzann for teaching him so much. Thomas always hated being ushered away to bed, leaving the men sitting up late into the night.

Now, the three of them took seats at the central kitchen table and Thomas tried to ignore how tired his master looked, his face so pale that the dark lines of his eyebrows and the stubble on his chin stood out even more starkly against the skin. Thomas wondered whether Sir William had slept at all – if his grief had kept his mind stirring all night, or if the shock and fear was so great that, like Thomas, exhaustion had simply swept over him the moment he lay back in bed.

It was Sir Marcus who broke the silence.

"Do you remember," he said with a smile in his voice as he plucked the apple seeds from his brother's plate, "when he showed up that time sick as a dog – eyes streaming, sneezing, barely able to stand?"

Sir William's eyes were far away as he smiled. "The

bloody idiot brought us all down with it."

"Except this one," Sir Marcus cocked a thumb at Thomas, and Thomas smiled. The entire household had been too ill even to rouse themselves out of bed, and he had needed to run from room to room with food and water as people required, the sickness somehow overlooking him. "Favouritism, I call it."

"I liked his dancing," Thomas said, remembering how Laurence would spring into action at the first sound of music. In the revels below, he had been easily one of the most sought-after dance partners while the musicians still remained.

"You should have seen him at our wedding."

"No," Sir Marcus said to Thomas with mock seriousness, "nobody needed to see that."

"I think he spent more time dancing with Suzann than I did."

"He was a better dancer than you."

"He was a more *enthusiastic* dancer than me."

They would do their friend no justice by being sad, Thomas realised. The only person besides Thomas who ever accompanied Sir Marcus when he would patrol their land, the only person outside their household who Lady Suzann seemed truly pleased to see, the only comrade of Sir William and Sir Marcus' war service who was spoken about, scant crumbs of information about the war though Thomas could get from them – Laurence had meant too much, brought too much joy. When they gathered to discuss him, sadness would be no memorial to such a man.

Nevertheless, Thomas was unable to deny his sadness.

"We will find who killed him," Sir William said softly. "The three of us."

Sir Marcus held his brother's eye in agreement.

"And Sir Oswin?" Thomas asked. "And who attacked the Prince?"

Sir William watched him for a moment in silence. "Do you

think they're linked?"

Thomas recognised this as the test it was. "Maybe someone saw Sir Oswin attacking the Prince and killed him in ret-reali...relati..."

"An attack on the Prince is treason," Sir Marcus said. "The punishment for treason is death. Why seek retaliation, if the guilty man would die anyway?"

"Besides," Sir William said, "if Oswin attacked the Prince, how did he get from the dungeons up to the privy?"

"By the usual route, surely," Sir Marcus said. "The stairs."

"But how did he get to them? Remember, I followed Baldon into the dungeons – if someone got past him, I would have seen them. And so would you."

Sir Marcus nodded, almost reluctantly.

"And however Oswin got away – if it *was* Oswin – no-one else could have also been upstairs killing him. Everyone was clustering around Prospero, and then they were down in the dungeons with us."

"Except Zachariah."

Sir William met his brother's eye. "Except Zachariah."

The bodyguard, Thomas remembered now, had refused to join the others in the dungeons following the attack, claiming that his place was with Prince Prospero.

"So, could Sir Oswin have been killed sooner?" Thomas asked. "*Before* the attack on the Prince?"

"I am certain of it," Sir William replied.

They fell silent.

"How do you feel about Percy?" Sir Marcus asked darkly.

"For Laurence's murder?" his brother returned, and Sir Marcus nodded. "Yes," Sir William said with a sigh, "I did wonder about Baldon."

"What?" They were moving too fast for Thomas to keep up.

Sir William turned to him. "If what Fergus says is true and he left Laurence going to the roof before coming downstairs himself, that means Baldon alone was on the top floor with Laurence, and so Baldon alone had the chance to stab him."

The shock of it hit Thomas harder for how obvious it should have been. "That's it, surely. That's who killed him…"

"But why?" Sir Marcus asked.

"Why?" Thomas again felt left behind.

"Mm. Let us say that Laurence was killed because he saw something that told him Percy killed Oswin. Why would Percy have killed Oswin? And why now?"

"Maybe he hated him."

Sir Marcus snorted. "Plenty of people have *plenty* of reasons to hate Oswin Bassingham, believe me, but I think only Will, Laurence, and I had ever met him before."

"Really?"

"Yes," Sir William said. "After his successes in the war, Oswin became one of the King's most trusted advisors, and spent most of his time in the King's court. He was only here now because the King wanted someone he had faith in to keep an eye on his son."

"H-how do you know that?" Thomas asked. The King had been hidden away since news of the Red Death had begun to spread. Despite many rumours circulating during the revels here, no-one could claim actual *knowledge* of what was happening at the palace.

"Oswin told me," Sir William replied, simply.

"So why would Percy kill a man he barely knew?" Sir Marcus asked. "And," he raised a hand which tremored elaborately, "can you really see *Percy* beating Laurence – who must be at least twenty-five years younger – to his own knife?"

That mention of Laurence as if he were still alive was agonising.

Sir William exhaled through his nose, as if resenting the problems mounting before them. "And remember the candle."

"The candle?" Thomas was pleased to see Sir Marcus

looking equally confused.

"Oswin had a candle with him in the privy, so we can assume he met someone there during the night – taking the light to ensure he met with the *right* person. You've both seen Baldon at the end of the evening meal; he is unlikely to remain awake long enough to arrange to meet and kill someone later that night."

"Maybe someone else killed Sir Oswin, then," Thomas said, unwilling to let go of Sir Baldon's guilt, "and Sir Baldon killed Laurence to protect *them*."

Again Sir Marcus snorted. "Percy only cares for tradition – you've seen him at the table, always trying to shore up the old ways; anything to bring him closer to Prospero and his circle. I am unable to name a man in this castle he would kill to protect."

But there was, Thomas realised.

"Unless—" Suddenly it struck him that the thought should remain unfinished.

The two brothers watched him, waiting.

"I have things I need to do today, Thomas," Sir Marcus said. "Out with it."

"Unless," Thomas swallowed and lowered his voice, "unless Prince Prospero killed Sir Oswin."

He was relieved when Sir William inclined his head.

"Unless Prince Prospero killed Sir Oswin," his master repeated quietly, as if voicing a thought he had been entertaining for some time.

They fell silent, Thomas wondering if he had just committed treason.

"Where do you want to start, Will?"

Sir William looked at his brother without seeming to see him. "It's all so confused. Where did it even begin?"

"The attack on the Prince," Thomas said. Sir Oswin's death had probably happened first, but what Thomas had seen following the attack on Prince Prospero haunted him, and he was desperate to have it explained.

The brothers exchanged a look.

"The attack on the Prince?" Sir Marcus asked.

Sir William bobbed his head, looking unhappy. "The attack on the Prince. We shall start there and see where it gets us."

SEVEN

The three of them climbed the stairs to the guest bedrooms on the third floor, reasoning that this re-enactment was best done without the knowledge of anyone else in the castle and away from the resting Prince. Sir Marcus continued up the stairs, presumably to perform the checks on the roof that Sir William would be unable to complete now that this was occupying his attention, and Thomas and his master picked a room at the left-hand end of a corridor so its fireplace would be in the right-hand wall as it was in the Prince's room.

"Before we start," Sir William said, extending his arm, "you should have this."

Thomas reached out, and a key tied to a loop of twine was placed into his hand.

"It was Laurence's."

Unable to meet his master's eye, Thomas lifted the loop over his head, tucking the key inside his shirt where it rested, cold and heavy, against his chest.

"And so," Sir William said, perhaps keen to move on, "how do we start?"

Firstly, they rearranged the furniture so that it was placed as in Prince Prospero's chamber: the double bed moved from the left-hand wall to stand instead between the two windows in the outer wall of the castle; the clothes trunk at the base of the bed, so that one lifted the lid with their back to the door; the small table at the head of the bed on the right-hand side; a chair either side of the fireplace. They would simply have to imagine the doorway that stood in the rear left corner – a unique feature of the Prince's room.

"Now," Sir William said, "tell me what you saw."

Thomas stepped into the corridor. Through the open door, behind Sir William, the curtains at the base of the bed hung closed.

He pointed. "The curtains were tied back."

Sir William arranged them and stood aside.

"I came out of my room," Thomas pointed to his right, to the third door of four on this side of the castle. "Sir Marcus was following me. We usually go down the stairs near the kitchens."

Sir William waited.

"As we passed the Prince's room, Sir Marcus stopped and asked me if I'd heard a noise, like something being knocked over. We listened and heard—" he struggled to describe it, "a muffled shout. Sir Marcus called the Prince's name and knocked on the door – and, as he did, the door eased open under his hand."

The door should have been bolted, especially that early in the morning – only unoccupied rooms were left unlocked. Even so, it was probably treason to burst into a prince's bedroom, no matter how noble your intentions.

"We waited for a moment, and then heard a sort of...whimpering noise, so Sir Marcus looked at me and opened the door fully and—" Thomas stepped into the room and pointed to the bed. "The curtains were open, we could see the head of the bed. At first it looked like the Prince was kneeling on the bed, facing away from us, holding his face to the wall. And then—"

And then, partially blocked by the corner post, he had seen the figure standing beside the bed, its back partially towards them: a red hood covering the head, a floor-length red robe, red sleeves reaching forward, red gloves on its hands wrapped around the Prince's neck from behind, pressing him against the wall.

"And what happened?"

Thomas swallowed. "Sir Marcus shouted, and...*it* straightened and turned to look at us."

He blinked, the image more powerful now. Of course he

should have recognised it, but it had made no sense in that first moment. Now, though, it seemed to fit perfectly within the madness that was to descend upon them that morning.

The head of the robe had turned to the side, and the blunt white nose, grinning teeth, and black eyes of a horse's skull had come into view.

Whoever it was strangling the Prince, they were wearing Terrington Fenwick's costume of the Red Death.

~

Maybe two hundred days ago, sitting in the main hall when it was still beautiful, the source of excitement was two-fold: first, simply the invitation – summons, really – to the Prince's castle, where he threw his exclusive and lavish parties, and second the hope it gave to those present; perhaps, in his father's absence, the Prince had devised a plan for how the Red Death could be faced, halted, driven back.

When the Prince had emerged and his true purpose made clear, the rising excitement of many had been matched only by the swirling anger of a relative few. Prince Prospero, smilingly, apparently unsurprised, had wished a safe return journey to all who chose to leave and extended to the rest a warm welcome to his castle – bidding them ascend to pick out rooms and be ready for the tolling of the bell that would indicate the start of the revel below.

Thomas remembered the disappointment and fear of those who now faced confronting the Red Death a second time by leaving. Several servants had broken down in tears as their masters indicated no desire to remain and be part of such folly. As the Prince had said, they might bid defiance to contagion by remaining here, leaving the external world to take care of itself, but several of the great and powerful thus gathered had hoped for so much more.

A frenzy of excitement and competition grew among those who elected to stay. As the carriages of the disappointed began to exit the courtyard outside, inside a clamouring for the best costume, for only the finest raiment to display for the Prince's pleasure, had begun. As servants were pressed into the urgent work of getting from the carriages those clothes that the foresighted had brought with them, and the back-breaking work of hauling belongings up the outside of the castle using the winch on the roof began, it became clear to Thomas just how many of those in attendance had guessed the Prince's true intent. When the gaily-coloured crowds spiralled into the dungeons several hours later, their manic energy a spark in the dried leaves of their exhaustion, costumes far too gaudy, too fantastic – delirious fancies such as the madman fashions – showed that many had known this was no ordinary visit to a royal residence.

For all their efforts, none could outdo Terrington Fenwick.

In such an assembly of phantasms, it may well be supposed that no ordinary appearance could have excited such sensation. Fenwick's costume – a long-sleeved robe that reached the floor, of a scarlet colour matched only by the decorations of the red revel room – would have seemed dowdy but for the hood that covered his thinning hair and the mask the hood held over his face: the bleached skull of one of the snub-nosed battle horses with which he had made his fortune, its teeth locked in a permanent grin, its shortened nose and blackened eye sockets hiding the wearer's face from view.

As Thomas had moved through the crowds of that first revel, refilling cups with wine, carrying food down from the kitchen and returning there with empty plates, he had been aware of Fenwick above all others, even in that sea of masqueraders. Fenwick had been seemingly everywhere: an arm around a shoulder one moment, a lady sitting on his knee the next; he would chase others playfully through the coloured rooms, or creep up with exaggerated care behind women to lunge out and molest them and be greeted with squeals of delight. The attention he drew, and the favour it brought upon him, was all he desired.

And he had called himself the Red Death.

At subsequent revels, the costume had been borrowed by others – Fenwick happy to surrender it, the effect no longer the same – and for a while within these walls when people spoke of 'the Red Death' it was the costume and its wearer to which they referred, rather than the tide of fear and ruination which had washed them here. As the revels had extended beyond the castle's dungeons, the drunken guests spilling upwards and parading through the corridors, many a night had seen the red-robed figure shrieking and gibbering as it ran amok, probably never the same wearer twice within. Many a morning Thomas would wake to find that one of those pressed into service, sleeping five or six to a draughty top floor room while their masters indulged themselves below, had lost patience with this exhibition, stolen a key from a drunken guest, and left in the night: the open door to the roof and a rope descending from a watchtower showing their means of escape.

Over time, the mood in the castle began to shift.

Those gathered on the Prince's hospitality became more sombre, the feverish heart of life beating less within them as the days began to stretch, to take on a repetitive aspect, and still no end to the plague in sight. Guests could be found wandering the corridors in the daytime, as if uncertain where they were or why they remained. Perhaps being closed off from the outside world reminded people how much they valued it – whatever the reason, the guests began to leave, sometimes simply abandoning their possessions and fleeing as if in disgrace, perhaps in shame.

To those who expressed the desire to leave, the Prince was sympathetic, and yet, perhaps for want of some activity to fill their days, out of these departures came a new entertainment. For each person who left on any given day, the remainder would gather in the main hall and, cheeringly, burn a chair in the huge fireplace there. Those possessions left behind were also burned for a while, though – given that many took to abandoning entire wardrobes in hasty departure – before long this was abandoned and the best raiment simply divided among those who were quick enough to claim them.

Before too long, even these amusements were forgotten.

When reports reached them that the Red Death had found its way into the stables outside the castle's walls and killed many of the horses kept there, panic settled in. Calm, or a version of it, was restored only by Terrington Fenwick: sending with the one carriage able to leave a request for his own horses to be brought by men in his employ, that those remaining in the castle who wished to leave may do so.

While they waited, and with no revels to cater and fewer of the wealthy and powerful to please, Thomas had more time to spend with Isobel, and she had told him of life in Terrington Fenwick's service. Appalled at the treatment they received, Thomas begged her to stay when Fenwick left – he had already told her he loved her, and she, being four years older, had gently diverted his outpourings – but knew she had to leave when Fenwick decided. It would be dangerous to turn your back on the richest and most influential man in the kingdom, even in these days.

The horses came, the carriages were loaded up, the drawbridge lowered, and Thomas bid Isobel a tearful goodbye. The drawbridge was raised for a final time, securing the eight men who had endured – those most desperate, Thomas suspected, to huddle close to the flame of the Prince's power. The revels were forgotten, the coloured rooms visited only by Sir Marcus and Thomas, and the laughing in the face of fear replaced by a quiet resistance of creeping and inevitable death, the Red Death once more banished to the outside world.

And now it had returned.

~

Sir William cleared his throat, bringing Thomas' attention back to the present.

"Marcus said it was Terrington's Red Death costume. I suppose whoever used it last simply left it behind."

Thomas considered this, part of his mind still on the past.

"What did you see?"

"When he straightened up—" it had to be a man, there were only men remaining in the castle, "it took us a moment to see that he was strangling the Prince. His thumbs were—" Thomas tapped the back of his neck, "and the fingers around the Prince's throat."

"And what did you do?"

Sir Marcus had expressed amazement at Thomas' bravery, but the truth was that Thomas' legs had seized, his body refusing to respond in the indecision of fear.

It was Sir Marcus who had dashed forward, lunging at the figure over the base of the bed, the clothes trunk preventing him from getting close enough to reach it. The robed figure had thrown the Prince down onto the bed and jumped over him as Sir Marcus hurried to where it had been standing.

Sir Marcus had lunged out again, grabbing at nothing, and Thomas remembered clearly the figure rolling off the far side of the bed, the thrice-buckled boots on its feet showing as it landed on the floor and sprang quickly to its feet.

"Fergus is feed from suspicion, then," Sir William observed. The medical man wore the soft-soled shoes of the wealthy.

"He is too tall."

"Sorry?"

"Whoever was wearing the robe was shorter than Sir Marcus. Master Highstone is taller."

Sir William dipped his head. "And then your heroics."

"All I did was stand still."

"It's more than many would have done," his master replied. "And, no modesty, Thomas, you did much more than stand still."

The figure had truly *sprung* to its feet – Fergus Highstone was also too old to be so nimble – and then advanced on Thomas in the doorway, clearly hoping to leave before Sir Marcus could get to it.

Thomas, terrified, had simply watched.

And then...

"Why did it hiss at me?"

Sir William pursed his lips. "You were in the way, I imagine. You delayed him and, if he ran past you, you might shout and summon the others. Having been caught throttling the Prince, he knew he'd be hanged – I imagine it was a sound of frustration."

It had sounded like a hiss to Thomas.

Sir Marcus, advancing around the bed, had kicked the clothes trunk and stumbled, falling to the floor, and this seemed to make up the figure's mind: it turned and bolted for the back of the room.

"Had you forgotten about the other door?" Sir William asked, pointing to the rear left corner, which in this room contained only the vanity screen and toilet stand.

Thomas was unable to explain his thoughts at the time. Everyone knew about the Prince's staircase. It was his personal access to the revel rooms, and a way of bringing up with him – or, as usually happened, sending up ahead of him – whomsoever he favoured to share his bed. Only two keys to that door existed: one kept by the Prince, the other handed to the lady of his choice for the evening. At the revels, everyone's eyes would stray occasionally to the door at the bottom of the staircase in the hope of being the first to spread the news of who the Prince had selected – desperate for *something* to gossip about, in the little while before it became common knowledge.

The figure had turned and headed straight for the doorway, kicking the door open and vanishing from view as Thomas watched.   Sir Marcus had struggled up from the floor and scrambled for the doorway, shouting back at Thomas as he went 'Get help! Call for help!' and, as the big man gave chase, Thomas had turned to the doorway and shouted—

He had no memory of what he had shouted. He simply remembered turning back to the room and, after only a brief pause…

"Why did you follow Marcus down the stairs?"

"He might have needed me."

Something twitched in Sir William's mouth.   "And you wonder why he sees what you did as brave?"

Thomas was puzzled. "Why? If I could help?"

"Never mind. Carry on."

The echoing of Thomas' breath in the spiralling stairway, and the scrape of his boots on the stone steps, were all he could hear as he had descended in darkness. Going carefully to guard against tripping and falling, it seemed to take forever. He had eventually emerged into the dungeons where the green and white rooms met, and in the faint early morning light on those bright surroundings, he could see Sir Marcus on all fours on the floor in front of him. The robed figure, its back to Thomas and the doorway, stood over the fallen man and kicked him twice, savagely, in the side.

Sir Marcus had curled up in a heap and, looking past his attacker, had half-coughed out Thomas' name, the weak waving of his hand indicating that he, Thomas, should keep back.

The Red Death had then turned to face him.

Heart pounding, terrified, barely aware of what he was doing, Thomas had stepped out of the doorway, intent only on the safety of the man who had helped raise him. The robed figure hissed again and, after a moment's thought, turned to its right and ran.

Without thinking, Thomas had followed.

"You might have been killed."

"But he might have made it to one of the staircases and gotten away, escaped into the castle and taken off the robe so no-one would suspect him. If he fought me, I could rip off the robe and see who it was."

"And he might have killed you to keep that secret."

Thomas swallowed. He had failed to consider that. Knowing what had happened next, he almost wished he had let the man get away.

The Red Death had perhaps half a room's head start, well across the purple room by the time Thomas entered it. In the half-light, he tried to keep the figure in sight as it dodged furniture and made for the black room, its path always curving to the right-hand side, getting closer to the central walls and the staircases that Thomas was sure meant its security.

As the figure pulled further away entering the black room, Thomas pushed himself to run faster and, with his eyes fixed ahead as he entered that unlighted space, he collided at full speed with a chair rendered invisible in the darkness. He dropped to the floor painfully and grabbed at furniture as he fell, hauling himself up as the figure vanished from view into the blue room. Slowed, winded, Thomas ran after it, reaching the far boundary of the black room before a sudden spark of fear touched him as he saw that the figure had turned and was running back towards him. Knowing the man to be a solider by his boots, and knowing him to be in fear of his life, Thomas knew also that he stood no chance in a fight, and struggled to a stop, the need to flee uppermost in his mind.

Thomas had taken a backward step before he saw that the figure coming towards him moved more slowly now, had the wrong shape. The light around it danced, rather than on red silk, on the dull colours of the everyday clothes now worn in the castle. And then he recognised that, instead of the Red Death, it was Sir Baldon Gregory who approached, and following half a room behind him had been Sir William himself.

Pulled back to the present, Thomas looked to his master.

Sir William nodded. "I had followed Baldon down from the Prince's room. We saw Marcus on the floor and he sent us round in the other direction to you in the hope that we might capture between us the man you were chasing."

Except...

Except there was no-one to catch.

Whoever Thomas had been chasing should have run full into view of Sir Baldon and Sir William, there was barely any time between Thomas losing sight of the robed figure and seeing the two men heading towards him. When the Red Death was out of Thomas' view, Sir Baldon and Sir William would have already been in the dungeons and heading towards him, and the robed figure must, even in the half-light down there, have been visible to them as they approached from the other direction.

But as Thomas was to discover, Sir Baldon had seen only Thomas himself, and Sir William half a room behind Sir Baldon would also insist that no-one had passed either of them as they ran towards him.

The Prince's attacker had simply vanished into thin air.

EIGHT

"I know it makes no sense."

Sir William raised a hand. "As of this moment, no."

At the time, they had checked all the doors nearby – those to the kitchen stairs, to the outer corridor, and the inner doors between the black room where Thomas had seen the figure last and the white room where Sir Marcus would have seen anyone coming – and found them locked. All the furniture, upholstered in colours matching the room in which it was located, was searched, the skirts that hid legs from view raised and no sign of a person found beneath. Sir William had investigated the fabric falling down the rear walls in case the gathering of the sails at floor level provided shelter for a standing or hiding body. The chimneys above the fireplaces, Thomas knew from experience, were barred and admitted no escape, but he checked them anyway and found no sign of disturbance.

Sir William had then ascended to the Prince's room to gather everyone down in the dungeons, and things had only gotten worse.

Laurence, Fergus Highstone, and Zachariah were all in the Prince's room when Sir William had arrived, and all three of them avowed that none had left since reaching it. Sir William had then gone to Sir Oswin's room to rouse him, and had found the door unlocked and the room standing empty. He had returned to the dungeons and broken this news to the others – Zachariah having refused to leave the Prince's side – and it was decided, before anything else was done, that they would search for the missing man.

Sir William had dispatched them all to different floors of the castle to search: Laurence was to stay in the dungeons, Sir Baldon to go to the ground floor, Zachariah had refused to leave the Prince and so the first floor was excluded for now, Highstone was sent to the second, Sir Marcus the third, and

Thomas the top floor servants' quarters. Sir William himself took the roof. Whoever found anything – they might have suspected then that Sir Oswin was dead, but Thomas had been too distracted, too disturbed, to consider it – was to ring the bell and summon everyone back to the main hall. If anyone finished searching their floor before the bell sounded, they were to search the first floor.

Sir William and Laurence had stood discussing the search, and Thomas remembered the two keys tied on the length of twine in Laurence's hands – one to the private stairway which Sir William must have brought down from Prince Prospero's room himself, and the other which opened all remaining locks in the castle – as he had turned away from the group. The memory of his friend, and the warm weight of Laurence's key against Thomas' skin, were all that remained of him now.

"Well," Sir William said, "at least we know that there is *some*one we can talk to."

Was there? The only person they could trust was Sir Marcus, and he had seen even less than Thomas. Surely everyone else was under suspicion. And then Thomas remembered the thrice-buckled boots that had shown beneath the robe, and the figure standing shorter than Sir Marcus in the Prince's chamber.

"Master Highstone."

"Yes, let us see what Fergus can tell us."

~

It was no longer early, but that was no guarantee that anyone would be out of bed. Waiting for Fergus Highstone to rouse himself and go to the kitchens – always assuming he ate in the mornings – might mean further delay. Instead, they descended to Highstone's room on the first floor, two storeys immediately below the one in which they had just been speaking.

Sir William listened at the door before knocking.

"Yes?" came Highstone's muffled voice after a short delay.

"Fergus, it's William. I wondered if we might talk."

A creak and a shuffle of feet, and the bolt sliding back. The door eased open to about the width of a hand to reveal Highstone in a floor-length nightshirt of a startlingly purple hue. Around the older man's ankles Thomas could see the legs of the close-fitting undergarments in which they all slept to keep warm in the chill of the castle's nights. However stiflingly warm the weather got at the height of the day, even in the unrelenting warmth of these last two weeks, the castle remained cool.

"Sir William," Highstone said, smiling, "Thomas. To what do I owe the pleasure?"

"May we come in? It is perhaps better discussed in private."

The other man paused. "Of...of course."

He opened the door, stepped back, and bade them enter.

In the wooden-panelled walls of Highstone's bedroom – curtained bed standing with its head against the left-hand wall, fireplace in the right-hand wall, vanity screen in the back right corner beneath one of the windows – there was more than enough room between the door and the bed for the three of them to stand comfortably. Thomas pushed the door closed, the bottom brushing over the length of rug, running from one side of the doorway to the other, placed in all guest bedrooms to prevent draughts from intruding into the room.

Such comforts failed to extend to the top floor.

"This is a little irregular, Sir William."

"I understand, and I appreciate your forbearance, Fergus. But we have important business."

Highstone waited. The formless, flat smell of unfamiliar lodgings rose to Thomas' nose.

"We wish to identify the man who carried out the

81

treasonous attack on the Prince," Sir William said, and even in the half-light of morning Thomas saw the look of surprise that jumped into the taller man's eyes. "Thomas has made me realise that you were in no way involved, Fergus, and we're hoping that you will be able to help us by answering a few questions."

A smile played out on Highstone's lips. "This is hardly what I had been expecting, Sir William, but I would, of course, be only too happy to help."

"Thank-you," Sir William dipped his head in gratitude.

"May I ask how you have decided that am free from suspicion? Aside from my excellent character, of course."

Sir William flashed his tight-lipped grin. "You are too tall, Fergus."

"Too tall?"

"Indeed. Thomas," Sir William gestured to him, "witnessed the attack and saw that the figure in the robe stood shorter than my brother. As that description excludes only yourself, we are certain of your innocence. And," he smiled properly this time, "because of your excellent character, of course."

Highstone returned the smile with somewhat less warmth in it. "Of course."

"We would," Sir William glanced round at Thomas, including him in the request as if the presence of a 13 year-old servant boy made it any more acceptable to demand favours of a man appointed to his position by the King himself, "like very much to hear in your own words what you saw yesterday morning upon reaching the Prince's chamber."

Highstone sat on the edge of his bed.

"I heard a shout and then raised voices, someone shouting about the Prince, or so I believed, so I instantly got out of bed and ran into the corridor, hearing what sounded like a commotion from the other side of this floor. I assumed, naturally, that it was coming from the Prince's room and so immediately headed there—"

"A moment, please," Sir William interrupted, "which way did you go?"

"Which...? Oh, I see – to the left, as you leave the room. It is the quicker route."

This would, Thomas knew, take Highstone past the rooms of Laurence – who had slept on the other side of the empty room next to this one – Sir Baldon, Sir Oswin, and Zachariah.

"Thank-you, please continue."

"Well," the sitting man thought for a moment, "it was Zachariah whom I found there – he was in the Prince's room, over by the open door to His Highness' private stairway, and shouting down the stairs. In fact—" he turned to Thomas, "he was shouting your name, Thomas. I understand he had just seen you run down the Prince's private stairs."

Highstone's raised eyebrows left Thomas feeling as if he were being corrected on another point of expected behaviour in this castle. Of course the stairway was intended only for the Prince and his chosen companions, but would it *really* have been better to remain in the room and allow the Prince's attacker to escape?

"Laurence arrived almost immediately with me – he practically pushed me out of the way as he entered the room, obviously in a great rush – and His Highness was still awake at the point, rasping something about having been attacked and the man having run down the stairs." Amusement showed in Highstone's face. "I believe that Zachariah, having just seen you leave, Thomas, took this to mean that *you* had been the one to attack Prince Prospero, but Laurence was able to convince him otherwise, and the Prince himself confirmed this."

This explained why Zachariah had been so hostile to Sir Marcus: once it became known that Thomas had followed the older Collingwood down the stairs, Zachariah would have assumed, at least at first, that it was Sir Marcus whom Thomas had been chasing.

"I tried to examine the Prince to see how bad his injuries were, but Laurence and Zachariah's concern for his safety were obviously great and it took some effort to convince them to stand aside. When Sir Baldon appeared in the doorway I'm afraid I was rather terse with him and directed him immediately down the stairs to see what was happening below. Another person in that room would have been quite intolerable."

"That would make sense," Sir William replied. "I arrived about then and followed Baldon because I wondered where he was going – I'm sorry to say that it occurred to me he might be creeping off to hide something, and so I kept behind him in case he had a role in whatever was happening."

Highstone dipped his head. "A wise precaution, Sir William."

"When I got to the dungeons after Baldon, Marcus was curled up at the feet of the Prince's stairway and he sent me after Baldon – in the opposite direction to that which Thomas had chased the attacker. And, of course," Sir William raised his hands, the fingers spread, "we have no idea of where the man went after that."

"It seems to me," Highstone said after a moment's thought, "that your problem is a deep one, gentlemen. I will swear to the presence of Zachariah and Laurence the entire time, as I'm sure Zachariah will for me, until you, Sir William, came up from the dungeons to collect us. Since Thomas and your brother chased the attacker away, and since Sir Baldon, Zachariah, Laurence, and I could be in no way involved – well, that only leaves Sir Oswin, surely?"

And yet, Thomas reflected, the figure dressed as the Red Death had been too nimble for a man of Sir Oswin's age, who was surely of Sir Baldon and Fergus Highstone's vintage.

Sir William sighed, unhappily. "It does. And it is therefore a shame, Fergus, that his body disappeared before you were able to tell us how long he had been dead."

"Might that be," Highstone said, "why his body has been hidden from us? So that we remain in ignorance of Sir Oswin's involvement, I mean. I claim no understanding of these events, but if a reason is to be suggested, that seems to me a strong one."

Sir William ran his fingers through his hair.

"So either Oswin was alive when the Prince was attacked and someone wants us to think he was dead – which makes no sense, unless they wish the attack to appear the work of darker forces – or he was dead at the time of the attack and they want us to think him alive to deflect suspicion his way. But surely we would suspect him anyway, since everyone else is accounted for."

Try as he might, Thomas could find no way to explain it.

They all waited in silence, thinking.

"I feel no envy for your task, gentlemen," Highstone said eventually. "It seems a dark and a deep one. Perhaps you will, after all, need to examine more than just the attack on the Prince – the murder of Sir Oswin seems inseparable from that problem, and to a man with the stain of treason in his soul mere murder is no quandary at all."

"We can only hope," Sir William replied, "that the picture becomes clearer with more examination, and that we have good news for the Prince when he awakens. If they are linked, as you suggest, and if we can find the man responsible, that would indeed be a cause for celebration."

"The man responsible may feel differently."

Sir William gave no reply, caught up in his own thoughts, and eventually raised his head to look directly at Highstone.

"Thank-you, Fergus. I do appreciate your help."

Fergus Highstone spread his hands and bowed his head. "Anything for the service of the Prince, Sir William. I wish you both good hunting."

Sir William turned away, but then stopped and pivoted back to face Highstone. "We would, of course, appreciate you keeping this to yourself. Whoever is responsible walks among us somehow, and is perhaps best kept ignorant of our attempts to unmask him."

"Of course, Sir William. As you request."

They turned to leave.

"Oh, Sir William," Highstone said, rising to this feet as they turned back to him. "I believe that you might have the key to the Prince's private staircase. I remember you giving it to Laurence before he searched the dungeons, and when I prepared Laurence's body for...his funeral he was without it. Did you take it from him?"

"I did."

"This is," Highstone twitched his fingers, "a little awkward, but it would appear the Prince has locked himself in his room and, unless we break in the door, we have no means of assessing his safety. It may become necessary to – well, much as I hate to say it, to use that staircase to assure ourselves of his condition."

Sir William hesitated, giving Thomas the impression that he was unwilling to surrender the key. "Of course, Fergus."

Turning around to face Thomas, Sir William drew from his pocket a length of twine on which three keys were tied. Unpicking the knot in the cord, he slid one key off and, turning back around, handed this to the other man.

Highstone smiled in thanks. "We must hope, of course, that such action is unnecessary, but it is good to be prepared."

A confusing series of bows and nodding occurred, and then Thomas and Sir William were in the corridor again, Highstone's door closing on them. Without a word, Sir William turned to his right. Thomas followed him as far as Laurence's room, where his master pushed open the door and entered, sinking into a chair.

"Close the door," he said as Thomas entered, and, that done, "take a seat."

Thomas leaned against the clothes trunk at the base of the bed – as in the Prince's room, Laurence had placed his bed with the head against the outer wall of the castle, the foot facing the door; the clothes trunk, however, stood against the left-hand wall as you entered, facing the fireplace across the room.

"So," Sir William asked, "which do you want?"

"Which…?"

"Either Sir Oswin Bassingham – war hero, general, and right-hand man to the King – attacked Prince Prospero, ran downstairs when discovered, and vanished in a puff of smoke only to reappear elsewhere and then seal himself in the privy and commit suicide in, we presume, regret – forgetting in his distress that he has been left-handed his entire life – or the plague which has trapped us here took on physical form to enact a vendetta against the Prince for reasons unknown, and is able to stalk us through stone walls while strangling some of us, stabbing others, and slitting the wrists of yet others behind sealed doors for reasons we are yet to discover."

As he spoke, Sir William's voice quickened in anger – against himself or the unknown killer Thomas was unable to tell.

"And anyone clever enough to kill Sir Oswin behind a locked door is going to be clever enough to notice us trying to catch them. Time, I fear, is against us in this."

Thomas had only the one suggestion to offer at this stage: "Could Prince Prospero have seen someone killing Sir Oswin, and that person then attacked *him* to keep him from telling anyone?"

Sir William thought it over in silence, and then did what Thomas knew he would: "Why does that seem unlikely?"

Thomas barely had to think, he had been trying to ignore the flaw in this idea even as he had voiced it: "He would have said something."

"Most likely, yes. Prince Prospero was unlikely to quietly return to his bed having seen Sir Oswin being attacked. He would have shouted the place down, knowing his word would be accepted without question."

"Would we have heard him?" Sir Oswin had been killed on the top floor after all.

Sir William looked down, his brow creased as if considering this for the first time. "That is an excellent point."

"Or Prince Prospero might have failed to realise anything was wrong," Thomas continued. "Maybe he failed to realise it until later. Unless it *was* Prince Prospero who killed Sir Oswin, and the attack on him was in rela...retaliation for that."

He was going round in circles.

"The Prince was still awake when Master Highstone and other others found him. That might explain why he said nothing to them about his attacker: because he was afraid that one of them may have consip...copsin—."

"Conspired."

"...conspired to harm him."

"But, if Prospero was attacked *because* he killed Sir Oswin, that makes things even worse: with Oswin dead, it would have to be one of us who attacked him, and none of us could have because everyone knows where everyone else was when you were chasing the attacker round the dungeons." Sir William sighed. "Nothing fits."

There was only one possible explanation that Thomas could see: "Someone else is in the castle."

With nine of them in the castle for the last thirty days, it would surely be possible for someone to hide amongst all the empty rooms – perhaps someone they assumed had left the castle before was in fact hiding all this time, waiting for their opportunity. Or on one of the occasions when the drawbridge had been lowered, the carriages making their exit all those days ago, someone may have crept in and hidden. It would have to have been then, since the lowering and raising of that great door made enough noise to be heard in every corner of the castle and so could hardly have been done secretly, even under the cover of darkness. And if someone had crept in, and brought with them a dead animal touched by the Red Death, that might explain the signs of the plague upon Laurence when he died...

Sir William was watching him closely.

"It's possible," he said, but Thomas knew the idea was fanciful at best.

If someone had gained access to the castle, never mind how, they must have then waited, hidden, for thirty days before acting...for which delay there seemed no explanation. The more he thought it through, the more he wished he had kept the idea to himself.

Sir William stood up, and Thomas matched him.

"Come on," his master said, "this gets us nowhere, and there's still more to do. Let's go and find Marcus."

They left the room, and headed to the stairs that led to the roof.

NINE

Of the six spiral staircases around the inner wall of the castle started in the dungeons and wound their way up to the servants' quarters on the top floor, only one then continued upwards to the roof, opening among the thick rafters strung around the chimneys that rose from the revel rooms below. It was here that the bell hung under the peaked roof of the tower, and from here that the rope by which the bell was rung plunged straight down through empty space until it reached the main hall with its single table below.

The roof sloped inwards above their heads at the top of the stairs, a triangular hatch set in the base of one side providing access to the battlements. Sir William pushed this open without pausing to unlock it and hauled himself through into the sunlight that temporarily blinded them both. When the space above him was clear, Thomas followed.

Emerging into the outside world always brought with it an almost dizzying sense of freedom. To feel the air moving around you, even in these warm, sluggish days, and to fix your eye on a point more than ten paces away – to be able to see distances so great that any detail in them was lost – these simple delights meant so much more when each day was marked by so much confinement. Thomas blinked as he stepped into the sunlight and inhaled deeply, gratefully, as the dizziness that always greeted this emergence struck and then swiftly departed.

Sir Marcus was waiting for them, sitting on the ramparts at the front of the roof where they emerged, a garment Thomas was unable to make out gripped in his hand.

"All ready?" Sir William asked, and the big man nodded.

Two chimneys rose from the bedrooms to emerge through the walkways on each of the six sides of the roof, leaving enough space for a man to walk either side of them. In each of the peaked roof's six sections, another chimney also rose from the revel rooms below. Thomas turned to his right and followed Sir Marcus and Sir William past the chimneys, until they stood at the rear wall, where the castle abutted the moat.

"W-what are we doing?"

The two chimneys on the walkway here had rope wound around them and tied in place, a long coil resting at their feet.

Silently, Sir William beckoned Thomas to him and pointed to a spot on the ramparts along the back wall. In the shadow of the chimneys it took Thomas' eyes a few moments to adjust, but once he knew where he was looking it was easy to see: a rusty smear marking the top of the stone in the crenel there.

"Blood?"

"Probably."

Thomas could think of only one explanation: "Sir Oswin?"

"Probably," Sir William said again, taking the garment his brother proffered.

"There's nowhere to bury a body. Burning it or chopping it up would attract notice," Sir Marcus said, his voice low. "We searched the castle from top to bottom last night and found no sign of it—" Thomas felt a pang at being excluded from this, "so it seems likely that…" he whistled a rising note and made a diving motion with his hand.

"Laurence wanted to see the roof for a reason," Sir William had put on the garment now, a long-sleeved leather coat, and was collecting coils of rope in his hands. "We think this was why."

He stepped to the ramparts and hoisted the rope he had collected over the stone barrier there. They watched the tangle spool up from the ground and disappear over the stones, and Thomas realised what was afoot.

"You think Sir Oswin's body is in the moat?"

"We do," Sir Marcus said.

"And y-you're going to climb down there to find it?"

That much rope could only have come from the winch at the front of the roof.

"He is," Sir Marcus jerked a thumb in his brother's direction. "His brains are less valuable than my looks."

"But...why do you think it's there?"

Sir Marcus looked confused. "The blood, lad. Keep up."

"No, I mean it will have floated away, surely. It's connected to the stream," Thomas pointed out into the lands beyond, roughly in the direction of the stream that ran from the coast.

"The channel is closed off when the moat is filled," Sir William said, before hooking a toe into the ramparts and pulling himself up onto the upper edge of the stone. "The moat is standing water." He looked down over the edge of the castle, straight down, Thomas imagined, to the water below, and made a face. "I forgot about the privy," he said, with an edge of irritation in his voice. "I'll have to climb to the side of it."

And suddenly Thomas saw.

"That's it!"

The brothers turned to look at him.

"I know how it was done," he turned from one to the other in his excitement, "Sir Oswin – I know how he was left in the privy and the door was sealed."

Sir William, standing at the edge of an unimaginable drop and as calm as Thomas had ever seen him, simply waited.

"The killer loosened the roof of the privy first, from inside." Why had they left the roof unexamined yesterday? It was so obvious now. "Sir Oswin was then killed up here," pictures raced through his mind, "and the body lowered over the side through the roof."

He realised now that checking the privy roof from inside would have made no difference: it would have been nailed on again from *outside*, so the tell-tale marks would be found there – out of sight unless you were willing to climb over the side of the castle to look for them.

"They climbed down after the body, cut his wrists, sealed the door, and then climbed up the rope again and nailed the roof back in place from out here."

"Hanging one-handed from a rope over a drop like that?" Sir Marcus asked, and Thomas deflated a little at the doubt in his voice. "Did they hammer the nails back in while holding them between their toes?"

Sir William, however, seemed to give the idea some consideration.

"It's unlikely, but worth a look since we're here." He glanced down at the bay window below him, beyond Thomas' view. "Either the roof will be loose because it was secured badly, or there will be marks where the nails were struck."

At this he bent and lifted the rope at his feet, tugging it once, twice to test its safety. He crouched and took from his brother's outstretched hand a pair of leather gauntlets, pulled them on and, holding the rope again, backed to the edge of the ramparts.

One slip, and the five storey drop into the water below would kill him.

There was a tension now in his master's face as, standing at the very edge, keeping his legs straight, Sir William began to let out the rope, lowering himself almost into a sitting position, his feet out in front of him on the lip of the stone. Sir Marcus turned and climbed onto the sloped roof to keep his brother in sight; Thomas felt too sick to want to watch.

Five storeys.

Straight down.

Sir Marcus smiled and waved his hand happily, "Shout if you need anything," and the laugh that bubbled up from inside Thomas only made the tension worse. They stood listening to the rope creak as Sir William eased his way down it, the scrape and shuffle of his feet against the stone wall occasionally rising to them.

"I'm at the roof of the privy," the voice rose to them thinned only faintly by distance. Some thumping followed "The roof seems secure. Hold on."

The knots on the ropes looped round the chimneys creaked and shifted, and Thomas could picture Sir William easing his way over the top of the privy roof to examine the other side. More noises followed.

"Nothing feels" —*thump*— "loose" —*thump*— "It seems secure. I just…"

Again the rope creaked.

"No," the voice rose to them again, "there's definitely nothing loose at all. And…and the nails look—" —*creeeeak*— "old and untouched and…and deep in the wood. I'll check…"

They waited in silence, Thomas' chest fluttering. He was unable to tear his eyes from the rope disappearing over the stone ramparts. Having used the winch at the front of the roof and having rung the bell in the tower on occasion, Thomas knew how thick the rope in the castle was – he could only just close the fingers of one hand around it – and how strong. But it looked now like the finest thread imaginable, ready to snap at any moment.

"The sides are secure, too," Sir William said, and the rope creaked and shifted, slipping across the top of the stone as they watched from safety. "Both sides. Looks like we're in need of a new idea."

Thomas had been convinced he was right; surely there was no other way. Ashamed, he glanced at Sir Marcus and saw the big man looking at him.

"Still a better idea than any I've had."

Thomas stayed silent, feeling foolish now he knew it to be wrong. Would someone really kill a man on the roof and climb over the edge like this to hide the body inside the castle *at night*? Maybe Sir Oswin *had* killed himself, after all.

That would be easier to believe, but for Laurence having been—

"I'm going down now," Sir William called up and what sounded to Thomas like a series of high-pitched buzzing noises rose to them – each following quickly upon the last. The noises became less frequent, quieter, and Thomas was kept silent in his unease only by the watchful stillness of the big man beside him.

Eventually the waiting became too much and Thomas was about to speak when the rope suddenly lost all its tension and sagged in front of him. He looked, panicked, to Sir Marcus again, but saw only calmness on the big man's face.

"Yes," he said, unworried, "he's something of a show-off at times."

"H-he's down *already*?"

"That he is."

"How?!"

Sir Marcus stepped to the chimneys and, laying his arm along the rope, wrapped his forearm around it and brought his hand back on top, gripping the rope that was now wrapped around the arm. He looked at Thomas and gestured to his entwined arm with his free hand, his eyebrows raised.

The leather jacket made sense now: Sir William had simply, one-handed, slid down the rope by degrees, the tough leather protecting his clothes and skin as the rope rubbed past him.

"A show-off, as I say," Sir Marcus said casually.

"But the rope's slack – his weight should be…"

"There's a narrow walkway down there, between the moat and the castle," Sir Marcus replied, then smiled. "What, you thought that he'd be hanging one-handed over the moat? Bloody hell, lad, you go from very clever to very…otherwise very quickly."

Thomas felt himself redden as the big man grinned.

He turned his attention to the lands that extended away from

95

the castle in all directions. Scrub grass and clusters of trees –
dried past green and into browns now by the endless warm
weather – dotted the landscape all the way to the hills that rose
on the western horizon half a day's ride away. Against the
morning sky, two birds wheeled crazily, swooping around each
other in a way that, a year ago, would have looked playful.
Thomas brought his eyes back down to the trees and the plain
below, and wondered how many animals out there were, at this
very moment, attacking their kin under the insanity of the Red
Death.

He glanced up at Sir Marcus and saw that he, too was
watching the birds.

"Should we…?"

"I already did," Sir Marcus replied, never taking his eyes
from the sky, and Thomas followed the twitch of his hand and
saw for the first time the bow and quiver of arrows resting at
the foot of the pitched roof.

As they watched, the birds darted to and fro, wheeling,
spinning, lunging with claws extended, and eventually turning
away and vanishing into the distance. Maybe they had been
playing after all.

The rope shifted and creaked.

"Should we pull him up?"

Sir Marcus snorted, amused. "Let him get the exercise."

The ease with which the rope could be climbed down – a
twist around the arm and leg to slow your descent – balanced
out the difficulty of climbing up. It would be hand-over-hand
work, up five storeys on the outside wall of the castle. Thomas
tried to banish the thought of any slip, any error, and the
plunging death that would result.

The rope creaked and then rested, creaked and rested.
Thomas could picture Sir William with his toes dug into the
edges of a protruding stone in those moments of quiet,
releasing the rope with each gloved hand in turn to shake out

any tiredness, then drawing in a breath to ascend once more.

Hand-over-hand.

Five storeys up.

Sir Marcus stood alert and silent the entire time.

Eventually, the sound of Sir William's breathing reached them and, soon after, Sir Marcus leaned over the stone rampart and seized his brother's arm, pulling him to safety. Sir William lay atop the stone, heaving in breaths, and Thomas fought the urge to jump up there and hug him with relief.

After his brother had caught his breath, Sir Marcus helped Sir William down to the walkway, the water and mud on the younger man's clothes leaving damp patches of both on those of the elder. Sir William sat on the pitched roof, his elbows resting on his raised knees and, as his breathing slowed, shook his head.

"One of you two can do it next time," he said. The shoulder of the leather overcoat was torn, and mud caked his legs to the groin and arms to the shoulder.

"Did you find Oswin?" his brother asked.

"I did. He's tied to the rope below. We shall pull him up shortly."

The lightness in Thomas' head was almost overwhelming, the relief a far stronger sensation than the dizziness he had experienced earlier. They had finally answered one of the questions hounding them. It no longer felt as if they were just making work to keep themselves busy. They were at last on a scent, following the traces their quarry had left behind.

When Sir William had rested, he and Sir Marcus hauled the body of Sir Oswin up to the roof, wrapping the rope around the chimneys as they pulled to reduce the difficulty. The dead, waterlogged weight finally made it to the roof again, and the scramble to get it over the ramparts and onto the walkway left them both exhausted. The brothers sank into sitting positions on the pitched roof once again, and Thomas eyed the result of their labours cautiously.

The soaking, mud-caked body was a grim spectacle – the limbs hung absurdly loose and at disturbingly unnatural angles, the result of so long a drop from the ramparts, and the face was caved in where it had likely struck the water first – but Thomas had seen many worse in his life. He was looking over the shattered arms and twisted legs when a question struck him:

"Why did you want to bring him up?"

Sir William and Sir Marcus, still breathing heavily, simply looked at him.

"I mean – finding him down there tells you he was thrown from the roof; so why bring the body up for us to see?"

Unless…

Shame swept through him: what if they wanted to honour their friend, to say goodbye as they had with Laurence? Sir Oswin had been Sir William's commanding officer, after all, and the two had spent many hours together in recent weeks. Being dropped into the moat, with no gifts upon the body to assure him when he woke on the other side that he had been known and loved in his lifetime, was no send-off for a man who had protected the King.

Thomas' face burned and his eyes prickled with embarrassment.

"Sorry, I…"

Sir William stood wordlessly and walked to where the body lay staring skywards. It was still clad as they had last seen it: rough trousers, the smear of blood where Sir Marcus had wiped the knife the only mark upon them, the long-sleeved shirt reaching to mid-thigh, now caked in mud, and thrice-buckled boots. An image of Laurence, similarly dead in the same position, flashed in Thomas' mind.

Sir William unbuckled the belt around the corpse's waist and pulled at the long shirt covering the torso, raising it so the skin beneath was visible.

Thomas stared.

At the bottom of the ribcage, the flesh of the torso was livid with several wounds, puckered red puncture marks Thomas could have poked a finger into, now ragged after the body's drenching, distended and weeping water.

Sir William looked at Thomas and Sir Marcus, and the brothers seemed again to communicate in the silent way that had grown between them.

"I see," the older man said.

"I wanted to be sure," Sir William said, straightening and letting the corpse's shirt fall back over its torso, "and I wanted you both to see it."

"W-what is it?"

"It's an old army trick," Sir William replied, "a way of hiding bodies during an attack. Left lying around they may be discovered too soon, digging a grave takes too long, and thrown into water they float. So you puncture the lungs before dropping them in a river, and the water floods in more easily and they sink, staying hidden."

Thomas understood. Thrown into the moat, with no current to move the body on, this had been the surest way to hide the corpse. Now that he knew there were there, he could make out the holes in the thigh-length shirt where Sir Oswin had been stabbed after death.

"Still fail to see why they bothered," Sir Marcus said. "We knew he was dead, so what was the point in hiding him? Whoever killed Oswin wanted it to look like suicide, hence that sealed door we are unable to explain. Maybe they realised the mistake they had made and knew we suspected it was murder, but if they'd left him alone we'd never be *sure*."

"I agree," Sir William replied. "But there may be more to this than we realised."

Something in his master's tone caught in Thomas' chest. He swallowed drily.

"The moat was full when we first arrived here, and in this heat—" Sir William waved his hand at the growing warmth of the morning, "the level of water has dropped and so it was easier to see now." He brought his eyes back from the horizon and turned to them both, "I'm sorry. There are more bodies down there."

"What?!" Sir Marcus surged to his feet at his brother's words, and Thomas' stomach dropped.

Sir William met his brother's eye calmly.

"There are other bodies down there and it…it looks like they have been hidden in the same way."

Thomas' head reeled. The Dukes and Duchesses, Lords and Ladies had all departed in horse-drawn carriages, the drawbridge lowered by two men, the Prince smiling and wishing them good luck on their journey. None of the guests could have left the castle any other way without it being noticed, without something being said. It was those who roomed on the top floor who had vanished in the night, unseen and unsuspected, a rope left tied to a watchtower so no questions would be asked.

"Someone has been killing people at this castle," Sir William said. "And they've been doing it for a long time."

TEN

"How many?" Thomas wanted to know. "How many bodies?"

"Beside Oswin, at least three."

Thomas tried to think. More than three servants had vanished; close to twenty, he estimated, had crept away during the days of the revels. Surely some, most, of them would have lived. He wanted to remember the faces of the men and women who were assumed deserters, but found none forthcoming.

"The towers, though," Sir Marcus said stonily, and Sir William nodded.

For a moment Thomas failed to understand, and then, as he caught the meaning in the words, another wave of dizziness hit him: bodies could have been dropped into the moat from other places – they would have to be spread out, lest they pile up – and all six watchtowers stood against the edge of the water. Someone clever enough to ensure the bodies sank would have thought of that, would have dropped them from more than one location.

How many more might be down there?

Sickness and fear warred inside him. And, under it all, something new.

Anger.

"So this could have nothing to do with Oswin," Sir Marcus said.

"Why do you say that?" his brother asked.

The older man rolled his shoulders. "If Laurence thought of searching the moat – the obvious place for a rapidly-hidden body – someone may have killed him simply to stop him discovering the other bodies down there."

They looked at each other, the conclusion clear:

"So whoever has done this," Thomas said slowly, "could still be here. In the castle."

Sir Marcus tilted his head. "Or it's someone who wishes to

help keep their secret."

One of the men remaining in the castle – Sir Baldon, Fergus Highstone, Zachariah – may have committed these murders, or knew who did, and may have therefore killed Laurence to protect that knowledge. Sir Baldon stood out in Thomas' mind because he alone had been on the top floor when Laurence was attacked, but surely he was too intelligent, even when in his cups, to risk so obvious a suspicion being directed against him.

Or maybe he had panicked. Fear could make a man stupid.

Then a thought struck him: surely stabbing Laurence would get some blood on his attacker. But only Highstone had blood on him, from Laurence stumbling down the stairs, dying, into him. Thomas saw now how this might be achieved. Sir Baldon was searching rooms in which large numbers of clothes had been abandoned, so it would be easy, having stabbed Laurence and with blood upon his shirt, to change into a similar one and to hide his original, blood-stained garment somewhere out of the way. Sir William and Sir Marcus had searched the castle last night and found nothing, but they had been seeking a *body*. A shirt, an item of clothing, screwed up and cleverly hidden, would be easy to overlook.

"You roomed among the servants," Sir William said. "If asked to meet someone on the roof – and we must assume it was a guest, with a key – would they? And would they keep their own counsel if requested?"

Thomas considered.

"It would have to be someone they respected or trusted. If...if Sir Perifan asked, for instance, I'm sure it would have been talked about."

Sir Marcus snorted, "I can understand that."

"Or," Thomas felt himself blush, "if Lady Aranda had arranged to meet with someone they'd probably talk about it even though no-one would believe them."

"What about Baldon?" Sir William asked.

Thomas thought. "He was liked; he was trusted. The right person might keep quiet about it."

"And Zachariah?"

"Definitely." A lot of the servants had been in awe of Zachariah, of the stories that surrounded him: killing a man with a single touch, slaying a bull with the Red Death upon it using no more than a rock. It made little difference if these tales were true; Zachariah was one of them – no title, no rich family, a man who came from nowhere and who had the trust of the Prince himself – and it seemed to Thomas that the more outlandish the story about the bodyguard, the more likely it was to be believed.

"But why?" Sir Marcus asked, having sunk to his haunches. "Why kill any of them?"

"Some people just…like to kill," his brother returned. "The crush of life that a summons to this castle would represent – for someone with that itch of insanity upon them, that would be difficult to refuse. Especially after so long spent cowering alone, or among a household who would know when murder was done, or may see the stain upon them if it was unleashed."

So many victims who would never be missed on the top floor, and an explanation for their absence – frustration at their masters' wasteful, selfish behaviour – already provided. It was, Thomas realised with a shiver, the perfect opportunity for the right person.

"You say those bodies are old," Sir Marcus pointed towards the moat, "and there have been nine of us here for…how long? Feels like forever. And Fenwick and his cronies before that. No-one's been murdered for a long time, Will."

Sir William conceded the point. Thomas tried to remember when the last servant had disappeared; the killings must have stopped since then, at least, as there had been no other sudden absences to explain.

"Can such an urge be repressed at will?" the older man

continued. "If those people were killed because of this insanity of which you speak, I say whoever killed them left a long time ago."

"Someone here could still know who was responsible, though."

"But why kill Laurence to hide it?" Sir Marcus asked. "Why would anyone care if it was found out? What harm could knowing do now, with the person responsible gone and the Red Death killing us all anyway?"

"Maybe they killed Laurence for another reason," Thomas said, remembering the red speckling in his friend's eyes.

"Because he had the Red Death upon him, you mean? Then why keep quiet about it?" Sir Marcus insisted. "We'd be furious, but it's understandable. And Laurence would have been dead inside an hour anyway." He picked a small stone from between his feet and threw it into the distance in irritation.

They sat thinking.

"If the bodies were all sunk in the same way," Thomas pressed his fingers to the underside of his ribs to indicate the wounds on Sir Oswin's torso, "how many people would know how to do that?"

"It's an old army trick, you're taught it very early on," Sir William said, and then, to his brother: "How many military men were here?"

A shake of the head. "Fifty?"

In that case it told them nothing.

The creak of hinges and the sound of the hatch in the roof being thrown back brought them up short.

Sir William jumped to his feet, moving towards the corpse. "We must hide this…"

Sir Marcus rose, making a calming gesture with his hands, and walked away from them, towards the hatch, disappearing from view around the chimneys. Thomas and his master waited, and the faint murmur of conversation was brushed towards them on the breeze.

"Will! Thomas!" There was no urgency in Sir Marcus' raised voice, and Sir William raised a finger to keep them in place for a few moments, lest they hurry too eagerly and arouse suspicion.

As they rounded the roof they saw, beside Sir Marcus, Sir Baldon Gregory, his rough beard disarranged as if he was newly woken. His hands shook faintly.

"Percy has news," Sir Marcus said as they approached, and Thomas saw the older man's face darken at Sir Marcus' insistence on using his birth name.

"Ah, Sir William, Thomas, I thought you might be found here." He ignored the mud that caked Sir William. "Some good news at last – the Prince has awoken."

Sir William smiled. "Good news indeed, Baldon, thank-you for letting us know."

"There is—" a twitch of confusion showed on the man's face, and he smiled as if trying to hide it. "This is a little unorthodox, but in the circumstances you will no doubt understand." He looked from Sir William to Sir Marcus and then, much to Thomas' surprise, turned to Thomas himself and smiled a little wider, the confusion on his face only growing as a result. "His Highness wishes to speak to...to you, Thomas."

Thomas blinked. "To me?"

Sir Baldon nodded. "He was most insistent on the matter; he would like to speak with you immediately."

~

His mind was a whirl as Thomas, leaving Sir William and Sir Marcus on the roof with the soaking, broken body of Sir Oswin, followed Sir Baldon down the spiralling stairway to the first floor. These were the very stairs on which Laurence had died – undertaking this very journey, in fact, down from the roof. Which of the men in the castle had he met on his descent? Would Sir Baldon's unsteady hands account for the blade failing to find its mark? Would pushing the man now ahead of him down the stairs, breaking his neck, see justice served?

Thomas shook his head; that was the anger again.

He tried to concentrate on other things. The castle always smelled stale when returning from outside, as if the entire building were somehow rotting beneath them. He breathed deeply as they descended, waiting for the aroma to become familiar again.

They emerged practically outside Sir Baldon's own room and, turning to the right, walked along the front corridor of the castle – past two unused rooms, the now-empty room which had been used by Sir Oswin, and finally the room occupied by Zachariah, all the doors standing open to allow the morning sun to penetrate the gloom – until they reached Prince Prospero's own closed door.

Zachariah stood in the corridor, dried fruit in one hand, the military knife drawn from his belt in the other, his jaws working. He watched them approach, his expression unreadable in the shadows as he sliced the last piece of fruit in two and put both slices into his mouth. Wiping the flat blade on his trousers, he sheathed it on his left hip and raised a hand adorned with flashing stones to indicate that they should stop.

"Master Highstone is with the Prince at present."

"Have you spoken with him?" Sir Baldon asked.

"The Prince? No."

A moment of silence passed.

"W-when did he wake?" Thomas asked.

He thought at first that the bodyguard would refuse to acknowledge him, but then Zachariah spoke: "Master Highstone apparently…accessed the stairway within the room and found the Prince to be awake. He had been too weak to unlock the door—" this said quickly, almost defensively, "and so Master Highstone himself opened it from within and...*requested* that others be told."

Thomas had failed to appreciate that Highstone would be so quick to use the key Sir William had given him. Was this the source of the bodyguard's apparent irritation? He took orders from Prince Prospero alone, so being sent on mere errands by Highstone would probably hurt his pride. Or perhaps he was annoyed with himself for failing to think of the private stairway, unwilling to consider that which tradition dictated only the Prince was to access.

The three of them waited in silence.

"I will, um..." Sir Baldon said, raising a finger as if remembering something. "Yes, please forgive me if I..." he pointed to the nearest stairway and walked quickly away. Thomas watched him descend from view, in little doubt as to where he was headed.

If he had left Thomas alone with a killer – well, the bodyguard *was* a killer, if the stories about him were to be believed – at least somebody had seen him in Zachariah's company. An image of the puckered wounds, weeping water, along the line of Sir Oswin's ribs leapt unbidden to his mind.

"Have you been here all night?" Thomas asked, to distract himself.

"I guard the Prince."

Thomas remembered that there had been no sign of the bodyguard outside the Prince's door when he and Sir Marcus had descended to the dungeons that morning.

"You must...sleep."

Again he got the impression that the bodyguard was reluctant to answer.

"Briefly."

"It must," Thomas heard Isobel's voice in his head, when the abuse from his fellow servants on the top floor became exhausting – 'Be nice to them,' she had said and, amazingly, it had worked – "be a comfort. To the Prince. To know you are always nearby if he needs you."

The bodyguard was only vaguely visible in the shadows, but something in his manner seemed to relax.

"Thank-you."

Caught by surprise at this gratitude, an idea struck Thomas: Zachariah would surely be willing to act in any way that served Prince Prospero's needs. If the Prince were in some way responsible for the bodies found in the moat, Zachariah would no doubt do whatever it took to prevent knowledge of them coming to light.

'I say whoever killed them left a long time ago.'

If Sir William and Sir Marcus were wrong – if those people in the moat died for some reason other than as victims of a mind touched with madness or the lust for blood – then the killer could still be here.

And who would have more to lose than Prince Prospero?

And who would be more willing to protect him than Zachariah?

"You must have been resting when Sir Marcus and I went to the dungeons early this morning."

The bodyguard said nothing.

"Sir Marcus has a lot of respect for you."

That sounded false even to Thomas' hopeful ears, and he felt the bodyguard's eyes run over him sceptically.

"He said," Thomas tried to find firmer ground, "how much he appreciated you coming down to the main hall after we had discovered Sir Oswin's body."

"I will waste no time talking about Marcus Collingwood, boy," the bodyguard's voice became harsher, his accent heavier, at his use of Sir Marcus' name. "He can have his opinions. I have mine."

Remembering what Fergus Highstone had said about

Zachariah being first to arrive at the Prince's rooms following the attack yesterday, and the suspicions the bodyguard had voiced first about Thomas himself and then Sir Marcus, Thomas sought to reassure him.

"I know you think he attacked the Prince, but he was out here with me when we opened the door and saw whoever was dressed as the Red Death. And it was Sir Marcus who chased the attacker down the stairs – I just followed him."

The bodyguard was unimpressed: "I will believe what I see with my own eyes. You may be brave, boy, but Marcus Collingwood has gotten out of tighter jams than this before. He would find a way to make you think you saw what he wanted you to think you saw. If he can outwit justice, he can outwit a mere boy."

Thomas was used to this, to being dismissed because of his youth and position, to the aggressive way he was practically blamed for being the age he was. But being familiar with something was different to accepting it, and so he tried again.

"Whoever was in the robe was shorter than Sir Marcus—"

"I suppose *he* told you that," the bodyguard cut in and Thomas, having learned from Lady Suzann the value of giving up a pointless fight, remained silent.

"A man can," Zachariah continued, crouching slightly, "make himself shorter, after all."

Thomas was pleased that the darkness would mask the heat in his face. He remained silent, concentrating instead on the anger that had stirred within him on the roof. It was better to save his energy for unravelling these mysteries than to waste it arguing with someone convinced of a truth with no substance.

The twitch of the bodyguard's shoulders indicated Zachariah's conviction that he had scored a point, that Thomas' silence was an admission of failure. Let him believe so. It would do him no good if he turned out to be responsible for the murders they had uncovered.

The door to the Prince's room opened inwards, barely reducing the shadows that surrounded Thomas and Zachariah. Fergus Highstone backed into the corridor and pulled the door closed, his long crimson sleeves in the darkness bringing to Thomas' mind an image of Sir Oswin's blood drying on the wooden floor upstairs.

He was to be haunted by images of death, it would seem.

"Ah, Thomas," the medical man sounded pleased to see him. "His Highness is ready to speak with you."

"I will go in with you," said Zachariah, and a little of the pleasure dropped out of Highstone's bearing.

"The Prince said nothing of this, Zachariah."

"Nevertheless," the other man pressed, "I am his bodyguard."

"And you take, or so I understood, orders from Prince Prospero himself. Had he wanted you present, he would have told me."

"But the Prince, unchaperoned…" the bodyguard pressed, and Fergus Highstone laughed.

"Unchaperoned with an 11 year-old boy…"

Thirteen year-old boy.

"…who acted out of bravery and helped save his life yesterday?" The tall man's eyes widened in mockery, "Good heavens, Zachariah, you're right – the risk to his safety is unimaginable."

Thomas had never heard anyone besides Sir Marcus put so much scorn into their words.

Highstone continued, his voice a thorn dripping honey, "You will wait out here, as you did all last night. You were content to be elsewhere when the Prince was attacked yesterday, and you should be grateful to be allowed even this close to him now that he has thankfully recovered. Thomas here," a hand fell on his shoulder, "poses no threat to his safety at all."

The bodyguard was silent.

"Or," Highstone pressed, "I can waste more of the Prince's time by going in there myself and confirming that you were useless to him in his hour of need and *remain* useless now that neither he nor anyone else in this castle has any faith in you."

Thomas almost felt bad for the bodyguard. He was embarrassed for the man, but mostly he wished he had this ability to use words to make other people feel as Zachariah must be feeling at this very moment.

Highstone lifted his hand from Thomas' shoulder, and his voice was pleasant once again:

"Please," he indicated the closed door. "The Prince is waiting."

Relieved to leave these men to their posturing, Thomas pushed open the door and stepped into the room beyond.

ELEVEN

After the dimness of the corridor, even the faint light filtering through the diamonds of cloudy glass in the far wall was momentarily dazzling.

"Lock the door please, Thomas," the Prince's voice said softly, disembodied and unreal.

Having pushed the door shut behind him, Thomas slid the bolt across, a hole drilled into the edge of the panel there to receive it – part of him wondering what effect the sound would have on Zachariah standing outside.

"Was that Fergus and Zachariah arguing again?" the Prince continued as Thomas turned back to face the room. As his eyes adjusted, he found himself looking at the drawn curtains at the base of the bed.

"Yes, Highness," he replied, unsure if he should approach.

There was a sigh from behind the curtains.

"I shall have to calm some ruffled feathers, then." His voice was thinner and rougher than Thomas had heard it before while also more delicate.

Thomas waited, and more of the room revealed itself to his adjusting eyes: the clothes trunk across the bottom of the bed, the fireplace in the wall to his right, the flicker of a candle visible on that side of the bed.

"You may approach, Thomas,"

He walked round the trunk at the bed's base, heading to his right. The curtains on this side had been tied back, and as Thomas rounded the end of the bed Prince Prospero came into view.

He was propped up on pillows at the head of the bed and, even in the flickering light of the candle by his side, it was clear that his skin was waxy and his eyes sunken. With his face turned to the light of the candle, his dark eyebrows and the dark hair which fell to his shoulders contrasted sharply with his

112

hollowed features. He was a handsome man – Isobel had called him 'beautiful' once – but the events of the last day had clearly left their mark on him. Grey smudges beneath his eyes failed to shift and dance like the other shadows cast about the room.

A smile danced on the Prince's lips as he saw Thomas staring. "Yes, forgive my appearance – it has been a trying time."

"No, Highness, it's—"

The Prince raised a hand and Thomas fell silent.

"Thomas, your Prince feels awful, so he trusts that he looks it. And the truth is that we might look even worse but for your fast thinking and bravery."

Thomas still felt that the praise of himself was unearned. "It was really Sir Marcus, Highness, who chased away your attacker."

"Yes," the Prince shifted his weight on the bed, and a strand of his dark hair – Isobel had said that he washed it in a mixture of oil, salt, and honey – slipped out and hung down the side of his face, "Zachariah seems unconvinced of Sir Marcus' innocence, but some people do so struggle to let the past go."

'If he can outwit justice...'

"He was in the corridor with me when you were attacked, Highness. And it *was* Sir Marcus who chased the Red Death down the stairs, and fought with him in the dungeons."

The Prince shifted on the bed, perhaps in pain, and Thomas' eyes, now adjusted to the low light of the curtained space, fell upon the high-necked shirt he wore, the collar rising up to brush the underside of his chin, hiding the bruising that must be on his neck from being throttled. Thomas had always taken Prince Prospero to be somewhere between Sir William and Sir Marcus' ages, slightly less than forty, but the grimace as he moved and the drawn pallor of his face added at least a decade to that estimate now.

"Well," the Prince said, looking away, "many men – mark

me, Thomas, many *men* – would lack the bravery to have acted as you did. Your Prince is grateful, very grateful indeed, for your intervention. You do your father tremendously proud."

In the closeness of the room, Thomas felt a chill of surprise cut through him.

"D…did you know my father, Highness?"

The Prince shifted on the bed again, perhaps to get comfortable.

"I'm sorry, Thomas, your Prince misspoke. You were raised in Sir William's house, I believe."

"Yes, Highness."

"So many young men follow their fathers into the same service, we forgot that you never knew your own. It is, then, Sir William, to whom you do credit, since he is the one who raised you."

"And Sir Marcus, Highness. And Lady Suzann."

"Of course," the Prince acknowledged with a dip of the head.

Thomas tried to examine his own feelings and found that he had none. It would be foolish to miss a father he had never known and a mother who had given him up at the instant of birth. Whether they had been responsible for placing him in the care of Sir William and Lady Suzann he never knew, but a newly-knighted servant of the King with lands to his name would at least have had the means to raise Thomas past infancy. A dusty corner of his mind suspected that he had probably outlived his parents by now – if their own lifestyle had failed to catch up with them, the Red Death would have almost certainly claimed them in the last year.

"I was—" the thought of family had prompted Thomas to speak, and a thorn of fear pierced him at the idea that the Prince might be unaware of what he was about to say, "very sad at the death of Laurence Tolworth, Highness. He was a good friend to Sir William."

And to me.

The Prince turned his eyes to Thomas again, and the sharpness of his features seemed for a moment less the markings of illness than of resolution. Despite the frail edge to his voice, he was once more a man to be obeyed without question: able to demand the sacking of a town with a word, to ruin a family with a voiced suspicion. He was again the heir to an empire on whose speech you hung because of how finally his judgements could determine your own fate, and that of so many men, women, and children.

"So much death, Thomas, and so senseless. This murder of our friend we shall never forget, or forgive. We refuse to let Laurence go unavenged. He...he was a loyal friend to Sir William, and Sir William has had need of friends in recent years."

Disagreement was on the tip of Thomas' tongue before he remembered to whom he was speaking. The one thing Sir William had never seemed to need – in his manor where almost no-one except Laurence visited – was friends. A man more comfortably isolated from those around him, taking joy in the small circle of his wife and household, could be found only in Sir Marcus. But then, Thomas supposed, the Prince had summoned hundreds of powerful men and women here to the castle; he could hardly be expected to know all of them intimately.

"And," Thomas spoke now purely to cover the awkwardness that seemed to have fallen upon them, "you know about the death of Sir Oswin – a-about the oddness of its circumstances."

"I do. Sir Oswin was a staunch supporter of my father. The loss of his life is, of course, one of the most marked tragedies of this whole affair."

Thomas had no reply. So many people had died – the lands were half-depopulated, some said, before the Prince had summoned them here – it felt obscene somehow to care only for those known to you, to elevate personal tragedy above the widespread horror of the Red Death.

He thought, too, of those who had been in service and whose bodies rotted in the moat – waking on the other side after death without gifts, without the knowledge of love and care in the lives they had left – unmourned because they were simply the faceless ones who served, who enabled, who allowed the notable few to live the lives they did. To care only because someone was a friend, and the Prince's speaking of Sir William showed that he knew his 'friends' less well than he might suppose, was perhaps more awful than remaining indifferent to it all and imagining that the world would fix itself while you hid away.

He took a breath; the new anger refused to subside. He clenched his fists behind his back and took a deeper breath, and the threatening flames inside him sank to low-burning embers.

"At our meal this evening," the Prince continued, unaware of the turmoil he had stirred in Thomas' mind, "we shall find the man responsible for these misdeeds. We shall ensure that he is cast out of our presence, and that anyone who may have stood with him is punished alongside."

Thomas was only half-listening. When he made no reply, the Prince turned to look at him and smiled as if embarrassed.

"I am sorry, Thomas; this attack upon my person must be punished. But it is perhaps better for you to be unaware of what is to come."

Thomas waited, thinking better of saying what was on his mind.

"Thank-you for your quick action and bravery – and, yes, I shall be thanking Sir Marcus, too, this evening. You may leave us, and please ask Fergus to come in again."

Remembering Highstone backing out of the room, Thomas retreated from the bed, his foot banging against the unseen edge of the clothes trunk as he reached it. Only when at the entrance to the room, certain he was out of the Prince's view, did he turn. Sliding the bolt out of its housing, he opened the door and stepped through.

Back in the corridor, the darkness that enveloped him was momentarily blinding. He blinked as he pulled the door closed, and the waiting figures of Zachariah and Highstone loomed out of the shadows.

"The Prince would like to see you, Master Highstone," he said and, seeing the scornful smile the medical man flashed at the bodyguard, walked quickly away.

~

Round the stairs he hurried, up and round. Past where Laurence had died, all the way up among the rafters and level with the looming, massive bell. As he approached the hatch to the roof, voices from outside reached him. Slowing his step, he stood inside the hatch and pressed his ear to the crack where it sat partially open.

"...could never have known," he heard Sir Marcus say, the sound deadened by the slates of the roof.

Sir William's bitter laugh sounded dully.

Sir Marcus spoke again. "And what of the other matter?"

"The other matter?"

"Yes. Of Thomas. What do we do about him?"

What was this? He pressed himself closer to the hatch and heard Sir William grunt in agreement.

"He knows too much, that's for sure."

"I agree," Sir Marcus replied. "We'll have to kill him."

Thomas tried to hold his breath, to freeze himself in place.

"We should definitely torture him first, though," Sir William said, far too lightly.

"Oh, of course," Sir Marcus replied. "Really, really badly.

117

With knives. And a cat."

Thomas stood, and pushed the hatch open, his cheeks burning. He was greeted by the sight of Sir Marcus standing over him, grinning from ear to ear.

"It's a good job we never asked you to spy on anyone," he said. "You breathe so loudly you'd scare away horses."

Thomas made no reply.

"Come on," Sir Marcus offered him a hand, "come out here and bring good tidings of our lord and master."

Thomas allowed himself to be pulled out to stand beside one of the chimneys, and turned to see Sir William sat on the pitched roof picking at the drying mud on his trousers, a faint smile pulling at his mouth and eyes.

"I think he fails to see the humour in us, Marcus," his master said when he saw Thomas' face.

"Well," Sir Marcus replied, turning away, "someone's always unhappy."

"How's Prospero?" Sir William asked, closing the matter.

"Exhausted."

"Did he have anything interesting to say?" Sir Marcus asked.

Thomas worked to deny his irritation, "He plans to eat with us this evening. He says he will catch whoever attacked him and killed Sir Oswin and Laurence."

The brothers exchanged a look.

"So he knows?" Sir William asked.

Thomas tried to remember exactly what had been said. "I think so."

'You do your father tremendously proud.'

"Well," Sir Marcus pushed himself off from the ramparts, and stooped to pick up the bow and quiver of arrows at his feet, "if he's joining us to eat this evening I can guarantee Percy's already planning the meal as a glorious return. We'll be lucky if there are fewer than seven courses. I better get down there and ensure we still have some food left for tomorrow."

Thomas stepped aside from the trapdoor, and the big man lowered himself through, tucking the bow and the arrows inside. He exchanged another look with Sir William, smiled at Thomas, and sank from view, slamming the hatch after him.

Thomas took Sir Marcus' place beside the winch, his back against the ramparts, and watched Sir William. His master's eyes were on the horizon when Thomas spoke:

"I'm sorry, I just heard voices and—"

Sir William waved this away, a flake of mud flying from his fingers and vanishing over the ramparts. "Oh, Thomas, please. I'm sorry – it's been a…" he scratched at his head, "…horrible few days. We were just trying to relieve some tension."

Thomas waited, unable to let go of a slight resentment.

"Was anything else said that might help?"

'If he can outwit justice…'

"Did Zachariah and Sir Marcus know each other before coming here?"

Sir William had assured them that Sir Oswin shared no history with anyone in the castle, living as he had in the King's court. But Thomas had failed to consider that others here may have met before. He was curious what the Prince's bodyguard could possibly hold against Sir Marcus. The only person Thomas had met from outside their household who knew the brothers before the war was Laurence. Could Sir Marcus have encountered Zachariah before the war, and done something that meant the bodyguard bore a grudge all these years later?

"Marcus never mentioned it if so," Sir William said.

The mystery only deepened, then.

"What's he been saying?"

Thomas simplified: "He thinks Sir Marcus attacked the Prince."

Sir William sent another flake of mud spinning away. "Hardly a deep thinker, Zachariah."

"I did tell him that we were both outside the room when the Prince was attacked."

If Zachariah was able to convince Prince Prospero otherwise, could anything be done? Thomas knew Sir Marcus was innocent, but how much weight would the word of a servant, and a child at that, carry among these men?

"The Prince is more intelligent than he looks. He knows Marcus is innocent of the attack, there is no cause for concern."

Thomas hoped his master knew the Prince better than the Prince seemed to know his master.

"Where is Sir Oswin's body?"

"Back in the moat," Sir William flicked yet another flake of mud over the edge of the roof. "If we are to hide the discovery of these additional murders, it seemed the most sensible course."

Silence fell.

The warmth of the sun was wonderful.

"What do we do next, Sir William?" he asked after a while, and his master turned to face him and paused in his ablutions.

"Honestly? I have no idea."

Thomas' heart sank; he had seen his master frustrated before, but never defeated.

"There's no sense to any of this. Oswin is murdered in a sealed room, and his body moved and hidden in the moat. Laurence is murdered while trying to find out about it, presumably to hide the discovery of yet more bodies none of us even suspected were here. If the same person killed all of them, why? Why throw dead servants from the roof yet kill Oswin in a manner that makes it look like suicide only to *then* throw him into the moat?" He resumed the removal of the dried mud. "Laurence was a necessity, I can understand that, but how did Laurence even know there was anything in the moat to examine?"

"And how did the Red Death get to him? *And* there's the

attack on the Prince," Thomas added, aware that he was probably making it worse for Sir William but desperate to have an explanation for what he had seen.

"And that."

Thomas waited, and Sir William rose to his feet.

"I just hope," he said, "that it gets no worse from here."

Thomas had nothing to add.

His master turned and opened the hatch, and Thomas pushed from the stone wall to follow him, but Sir William raised a hand. "Stay here as long as you please, Thomas, I need to think," he looked at his mud-caked arms and legs, "and to wash. Just remember to lock the hatch when you come down."

Thomas was so used to going where the Collingwoods went, he had forgotten that he now possessed a key which now effectively granted him almost complete freedom of the castle.

Without delay, almost as if fearing that Thomas would force his company upon him, Sir William climbed down and disappeared from view.

With the opportunity to do so unobserved, and in the glorious rising heat of the day, Thomas walked around the edge of the roof to the castle's back wall. From here, he stepped onto the wall that surrounded the courtyard, and set off to walk the full loop around the castle's perimeter. Following the oppression of recent events, there was joy to be found in this: the sun on his skin, the breeze in his hair, and the knowledge that he was entirely free to be out here without fear of challenge or a demand from someone more important than him that he go and perform some trifling errand they were unwilling to undertake.

As he walked, his mind worked furiously.

TWELVE

Thomas was sitting on the bed on his room perhaps an hour later, once again using the boards in the ceiling above him to practice his counting, when there was a knock at the door. He opened it to find Sir Marcus standing outside.

"Percy wants a new table," the big man said.

The tradition was typically reserved for only the most notable occasions: the crowning of a new monarch, a general's glorious return from battle – the feasting table destroyed and burnt, and the new era or the victory marked by the breaking of bread over a virgin surface. Thomas was unsure if two days spent laying in bed was quite the same achievement, but it was just another example of the unusual behaviour the men in this castle adopted in trying to please Prince Prospero.

They descended to the main hall, empty but for the table and chairs at its centre, the cavernous space above them open all the way to the bell hanging in the roof. Thomas waited beside the table as Sir Marcus exited by the door to the kitchens.

The big man returned a few moments later, carrying the axe used to chop and prepare firewood – a squat affair perhaps the length of a man's forearm. Stopping on the threshold of the hall, he looked from the table to the axe in his hand and then back.

"Hold on."

Putting the axe on the floor, Sir Marcus turned and left the room again.

Most of the light in the room came through windows either side of the castle's main door in the eastern wall, and in through the doorway on that side of the room. In the evening, when they gathered here to eat, candles stood on the table and torches burned in sconces on the walls. The room could be heated on cold nights by the huge fireplace that stood in the wall opposite the door to the kitchens. For now, the room was quiet, cool, and bathed in half-light.

Sir Marcus returned shortly, carrying one of what Thomas had always assumed were decorative axes from the castle's entry hall – a savage-looking instrument standing as tall as the man carrying it, the massive blade, Thomas saw now, finely sharpened.

"Are you going to use that?" he asked with a smile.

"No," the big man said, crossing the room and holding the weapon out in front of him one-handed, "you are."

Thomas assumed this was a joke, but when Sir Marcus simply waited, the axe extended, he reached out and took it in one hand. The unsuspected weight nearly pulled Thomas over, and his feet danced as he tried to rebalance. Eventually he got the weapon under control and stood holding it one-handed, the base of the handle by his feet and the head seemingly pulling away from him with an intent of its own.

"We'll make a fearsome executioner of you yet, lad; you might even kill some people on purpose."

Sir Marcus had taken him to his very first public execution at around the age of five. When the executioner had severed the kneeling man's head, Thomas had watched the corpse with rapt attention, half expecting it to spring to its feet and run into the crowd as did the chickens he had been learning to slaughter at home. And Thomas remembered, too, the tears he had cried some months later when attending his first hanging – the body of the condemned man dropping through the hatch, the neck cleanly broken, and the loose stillness of the suspended form seeming suddenly nightmarish in how quickly the life had simply vanished from it.

Thomas shivered the memory away.

"Go on, then," Sir Marcus indicated the table, then approached it and dragged out his chair, pulling it well clear before sitting in it, facing the centre of the room. "I'll be right here if you have any questions."

He closed his eyes, and feigned sleep.

Laying the axe on the floor, Thomas first moved the remaining chairs clear of the table, reaching around their high backs and lifting them by the arms, carrying each out from its place to describe a larger circle around the edges of the room. He returned, then, to the axe and, lifting the handle with both hands, addressed the table.

"Hold it by the blunt end, remember."

Thomas smiled to himself and, taking the end of the handle in both hands, raised his arms over his head, the blade resting on the floor behind him. Leaning back and taking measure of the weight, he tensed his stomach and heaved with all his might, picturing the blade rising in a curve over his head crashing down into the surface of the circular table, shattering it.

Instead, he toppled sideways and fell over.

Scrambling up, he darted a quick glance at Sir Marcus and thought he saw one of the big man's eyes in the last flicker of snapping shut. Neither of them spoke.

Again Thomas gripped the end of the axe's handle in both hands, his arms stretched back over his head, his feet wider this time. He tensed his stomach, heaved his shoulders, threw his entire strength into the action, and tried to ignore the low, strangled groan that emerged from him as the axe head shifted minutely and then remained still.

"The feast starts at sundown, Thomas."

He dropped the handle and began to laugh helplessly as the tension poured out of him. He understood now, that need for release – the need to crawl out, however briefly, from the press of the horror that had descended upon them all.

As if bemused, Sir Marcus waited while Thomas' laughter filled that empty, towering space.

"We could just tell them that it's a new table," Thomas

suggested, when he had himself under control.

The big man smiled and rose from his chair. "We could, but Percy probably carved a sigil on it somewhere and would be able to tell. I'm in enough trouble as it is."

He approached Thomas and stooped to lift the axe from the floor. Holding the handle horizontal, the base in his left hand and his right hand close to the blade, he turned so that the table was on his left.

He sniffed.

"You might want to stand back."

Thomas retreated.

Sir Marcus tested the weight of the axe for a moment and then rocked his arms out to the right, the blade moving away from him and out from the table. As his arms began to rise, he slid his right hand down the length of the handle until it met the left, and bent his elbows and arched his back as the blade rose, rose, rose over his head behind him. With the smoothness and a power of massive waves breaking against a cliff, he wrenched his arms forwards and, at full stretch, the blade arced through the air above him and swooped with terrifying speed into the top of the table where it stuck fast with a thundering, echoing crash.

Brushing hair out of his eyes, he turned to Thomas and gestured to the table, the axe handle rising from it at a sharp angle. "See? Like that."

He approached the table and took the axe by the handle just below the head, bracing a foot against the table's edge as he pumped the handle up and down, working the blade loose. He then extended the axe to Thomas one-handed again.

"Want to try?"

Thomas smiled, shook his head.

Sir Marcus rolled his eyes, and turned to face the table again.

He took up his two-handed stance a second time and swung

the axe once more into the surface of the table, this time to be met by the loud splintering of wood.

"Right, let's get on with this."

They fell into a comfortable pattern: the axe rising, falling, often accompanied by an echoing yell of exertion, the wood splintering off in all directions, Thomas collecting the fragments and gathering them before the fireplace. Using the kitchen axe, he split the larger pieces of wood into more useful sizes and, with the flat blade of Sir Marcus' knife, feathered the smaller pieces into tinder.

Soon only the very centre of the tabletop, attached to the wooden spindle which held it in place within the collar of the five-footed base, remained.

Sir Marcus, his face covered in a sheen of sweat, his chest heaving, more energised than Thomas has seen him for a long time, sank into his chair and dropped the axe on the floor beside him with a resounding clatter. While he rested, Thomas collected the broom from the kitchen and swept the splinters of wood into a pile, placing these in the fireplace with the other wood already there. It was too warm to light a fire outside the castle this early in the afternoon, but the coolness of the stone walls and the height of the bell above them meant that rendered such considerations unnecessary in the hall.

Thomas worked loose the metal pin through the collar of the base and lifted the wooden spindle free. This he also arranged in the fireplace. The nails which held it together would be collected from the ashes later, in case they were needed.

"Do we destroy the base, too?" Thomas asked, eyeing the five legs splaying out from the circular collar.

"No. Save the wood."

Of course; anything that might be useful later was to be kept.

Casting an eye around the walls of the main hall, he looked

at the other table tops propped there. "Which one do we choose?"

Sir Marcus stood. "Which one has the fewest ghosts?"

Be it the spirit of a late king, or those of brave soldiers who had lost their lives in battle, the presence of ghosts at a feast was said to reflect badly on any house that failed to hasten the departure of the slain to whatever rewards were found on the other side of death. This tradition of replacing tables came from the belief that the dead were unable to recognise they were dead while they remained in this world and so would return to their banqueting halls expecting to be fed. Only if a new table greeted them, and if items known to belong to others were found about their person, did these spirits realise their fate and move on in peace.

Thomas wondered how many of the people who had sat at these tables were now dead. And since they now knew of those in service who had been killed and thrown into the castle's moat, would it be necessary also to replace the table in the kitchens? That should perhaps remain to hide the discovery of those murders, but he had to ask himself whether, in the eyes of Sir Baldon, these lives would warrant such consideration.

Sir Marcus strode to one of the shield-like table tops and eased it away from the wall, rolling it on its side to the base that now stood unadorned in the middle of the hall. Between them, they tipped the circular surface horizontal and lifted the spindle at its centre into the collar of the base. Thomas crawled underneath and pushed the metal pin back through the collar, the hole through the spindle, and out the other side of the collar to keep the top from rotating. Finally, they carried seven of the nine chairs back to the table itself, spacing them out appropriately around the table's edge.

The other two chairs – those of Sir Oswin and Laurence – were carried to the fireplace.

On the mantle of every fireplace in the castle – the six in the revel rooms, the four in the kitchen, the one in the main hall, and in every single guest and servant bedroom – could be found both a flint and a firestriker, the curved strip of hard steel which when gripped in a fist left a bar of metal running close to the knuckles. This bar, when struck against the flint, would cause sparks to dance free that must be caught in a piece of char cloth and fed to tinder to make a flame.

Taking a scrap of char cloth from his pocket and placing it atop the flint, and placing atop the cloth a piece of the finely-feathered wood Thomas had whittled earlier, Sir Marcus took up the firestriker and fed the fingers of his right hand through the curved metal strip. The shape of this metal matched so closely the handle of a military knife precisely because the knife was also intended to fulfil this role when troops found themselves in need of fire in the wilderness. Holding the flint, char cloth, and tinder in his left hand, Sir Marcus struck down rapidly and repeatedly on the edge of the flint with the metal strip, causing sparks to fly outwards which were caught in the cloth. Gently blowing on the thin band of orange that grew on the cloth, Sir Marcus fed the flame to the feathered tinder.

Fire flickered to life in his hands.

Sir Marcus had taught Thomas how to lay a fire on the many inspections they had made of the Collingwoods' lands – journeys of some eight or ten days, at all times of the year, when a quickly-established fire could be the difference between survival and freezing to death. The flame Sir Marcus now held was touched to the wood Thomas had laid, and before long the fire had taken hold. Once the wood of the table had started to burn, they set about Sir Oswin's and Laurence's chairs with kitchen axe and knife, stacking this fuel alongside the wide fireplace, to be fed in later.

Then, with no other demand on their time, they stood back and watched the fire burn.

Thomas started to cry.

He felt the big man's hand press between his shoulders, and knew that Sir Marcus assumed his tears were for Laurence. The truth was, the anger Thomas could feel growing inside him now smothered any grief. When Laurence's killer was found, and when the events of the last two days could be given some shape, there would be plenty of time to grieve his friend.

These tears could have simply been the tension of the last few days, of an unknown terror stalking the corridors, ready to pounce on its next unsuspecting victim, but death had been an ever-present threat for longer now than Thomas cared to remember. These tears could also have been shed at the slowly-poisoning atmosphere in the castle, of men so desperate to stay close to power that they would neglect their own families and subjects to come and pander to the Prince's whims, to play petty games of loyalty and position, uncaring of the threat posed elsewhere because they were mostly safe from its clutches.

In truth, though, Thomas was scared.

Perhaps the Prince's mistake about his father had shaken it loose in his mind, but here, today – especially now – Thomas was aware of how much he owed Marcus Collingwood. They could never be friends, it was Thomas' station in life always to be in service, but he had long believed that this man who had so little time for so many people actually enjoyed his presence: the jokes Sir Marcus would make, the language he would use, the easy way they fell into jobs such as these together. The stories Isobel told of working in Terrington Fenwick's household, and the impressions Thomas had picked up from the other servants who had roomed here on the top floor, had made him realise how uncommon it was to be treated as the Collingwoods treated him.

It was Sir Marcus – more than Cook or Elena, more than Lady Suzann teaching him to use numbers, more than Sir William who, for all his encouragement, remained a distant presence at times – who had spent time with him, given him a sense of what was right and what was wrong, taught him how to joke and when to be serious. Thomas was who he was today because of Marcus Collingwood.

And it scared him to think that Zachariah, with his ignorance, his lies, his prejudice, could take away the person who Thomas cared about more than any other. That Sir Marcus might die at any point, without knowing what he meant to Thomas, seemed unbearable. And knowing that it would have to remain unsaid made it even worse.

"Save your worries, lad," the big man said now, glancing around to see who might be nearby. "Will has some ideas. He and Oswin were involved in something, and Will thinks that's why Oswin was killed. You can trust Will to get to the bottom of this; he seems lost now, but when it all fits up here," he tapped his temple, "he'll know what's going on."

Thomas felt the urge to ask Sir Marcus outright, then, what it was that Zachariah held against him, trusting that the big man would tell him the truth. But what business of a thirteen year-old servant boy was the past of two grown men? To have lived a life without making enemies seemed impossible, as Thomas had seen first-hand in the way he'd been treated by the other servants here simply on account of his youth. He just wished that Sir Marcus' enemy here in the castle was someone other than the Prince's closest, most trusted man.

And so, Thomas decided.

Whatever happened – if others were to insist that Sir Marcus was responsible for the attack on the Prince, for the murder of Sir Oswin, even…he faltered here…even the murder of Laurence – Thomas would do whatever it took to save him. He would defy the Prince himself it if became necessary, so save the life of this man who had raised him.

"Go and get some rest, I can finish here," Sir Marcus patted his shoulder. "There's a big night ahead. Prospero's going to unmask our killer, remember."

Thomas knew it was meant lightly, but the words rang horribly in his ears as he made for the stairs. When Sir William appointed to them the task of finding Laurence's murderer, Thomas knew that his own opinions would count, and that Sir William and Sir Marcus were cautious, intelligent men who wanted to get at the truth. That opportunity was lost to them now.

Now, they were all in the Prince's hands.

THIRTEEN

That evening in the main hall, as they stood behind their chairs awaiting the arrival of Prince Prospero at the feast table, Thomas marvelled at the difference that a few small changes could make.

The men of the castle were always summoned to the table before the Prince, and, at Sir Baldon's request, tonight they had dressed for a celebration: the military men with formal leather jerkins over their shirts, their military belts in place over the jerkin, and Fergus Highstone in a shirt whose baggy crimson sleeves, gathered once at the elbow and against the wrist, spoke of its purely ceremonial function. Thomas, lacking any formal wear, had been presented by Sir William with an assortment of clothes gathered from the abandoned rooms, and was all too aware of the ballooning of the ill-fitting shirt tucked into his trousers, and the unfamiliar scent of someone else's body rising from it.

Sir Baldon had just rung the bell twice more to indicate that all was ready, that the Prince would no longer be kept waiting, and before long Zachariah preceded Prince Prospero into the hall – the latter now sporting a decorative ruff at his neck, whose tightness around the bruises on his throat made Thomas wonder at the discomfort he was in and the show of wellness he was attempting to put on.

"Quite a feast, gentlemen," the Prince said, running his eyes over the food before them, then twisting at the waist to look around the table. "And a new table, your Prince believes. Your work, no doubt, Sir Baldon," he bowed to the man across the table, the white ruff at his throat catching the candle light. "Your Prince is indeed honoured."

Sir Baldon raised his chalice in his right hand, and everybody matched the action.

"Gentlemen, to the King!"

"The King!" they echoed, and drank. Thomas, who found the bitter taste of the wine hard to abide, raised the base of his cup and pinched the metal rim between his lips. The red liquid touched the outside of his mouth for a moment or two before he lowered his arm and, certain no-one was looking, wiped his lips with his left hand.

"Gentlemen," Sir Baldon said again, his voice sounding louder against the cracking of flames in the hearth, "to Prince Prospero!"

"Prince Prospero!"

Thomas pretended to drink once more.

"Thank-you again, Sir Baldon," the Prince bowed stiffly, "your Prince is humbled to see his return treated so joyously. Shall we sit?"

Following his lead, they sat.

No-one was to eat until the Prince ate and, since there had been no-one to serve food for some time now – Thomas would have been unsurprised if told by Sir Baldon that this would be *his* role during the meal – all the food had been prepared in advance and was already placed in front of each diner, a small bowl of salt water for cleansing the hands beside each plate. Looking at the food before him, Thomas wondered at the arguments Sir Marcus and Sir Baldon must have had about how much could be spared for this one meal.

Turning at the waist again, Prince Prospero looked around the table, the twitching of his fingers the only sign of his irritation.

"It saddens your Prince, gentlemen, to know that we must break bread this evening in the absence of our good friends Laurence and Sir Oswin – no, Baldon, there shall be no toast drunk to the memory of dear friends while the man responsible for their murders sits among us."

The bland tone the Prince adopted for this statement made Thomas' heart lurch.

"And of course," he continued, "the matter of the attack against myself will hardly be forgotten. And so, while I am grateful for your efforts, this evening we shall remain here at this table until the fiend who hides among us is unmasked."

In the flickering flames of the candles at the table, and the more distant light of the recently-fed fire, Thomas saw five frozen faces watching the Prince closely. At the edge of Thomas' vision, in contrast to the frustrated twitching and flexing of the Prince's fingers, Sir Baldon's trembling hands rested either side of his meal.

The Prince lifted a piece of cured meat from his plate and placed it in his mouth.

Nobody else ate.

"So," he said around his food, "does anyone wish to say anything?"

Sir Baldon raised his shaking goblet to his lips. Sir Marcus kept his face downturned. Zachariah, his formal leather jerkin shining in the candlelight, glanced around the table with thinly-disguised interest.

Nobody spoke.

Prince Prospero placed more food in his mouth, chewed, brushed a hanging strand of his dark hair away from his face, and asked in the same mild tone: "Does no-one wish to speak? Your Prince assures you, gentlemen, that this is far the easiest way."

Thomas could feel his heart thumping heavily, and a sick feeling building below that. When the scrape of a chair being pushed back from the table sounded, his heightened senses barely recognised the noise for what it was.

Sir William rose to his feet.

"If it pleases Your Highness," he said, raising his eyes to meet those of the Prince, "I believe that I can explain."

~

In the horrible silence that followed, Thomas was unable to tell if the look upon the Prince's face was genuine amusement or simply a trick of the flickering candlelight.

"You may speak, Sir William."

The sickness in Thomas' stomach grew.

"I have been examining the matter of Sir Oswin's death, and I believe, Highness, that only one explanation fits."

"And you wish to accuse someone at this table?"

Sir William hesitated. "If Your Highness will allow me to tell it in my own way…"

The Prince raised a hand to indicate that Sir William should continue.

Thomas dare hardly even glance at the large man to his right. Did Sir Marcus know what his brother was about to say? Had Sir William really found an answer?

"Many of you will be aware that Sir Oswin and I had spent much time in discussion lately. Our foremost concern is, of course," he bowed to the Prince, "your safety and well-being, Highness, but of late Sir Oswin had been most disturbed. It had been my pleasure to serve under him in the war, and I had recognised the change that had begun to steal over him.

"He, at first, denied any unhappiness but, in time, I think he came to appreciate the opportunity to discuss the profound fear and the concerns that had begun to weigh so heavily upon him. He was sent here, of course, under the excellent auspices of your father, Highness, and had your interests at the heart of everything he did, but of late he worried that his own preoccupations were clouding his judgement and his ability to serve and he spoke," he swallowed, "of ending his life."

"He gave no such indication to me," the Prince replied.

Sir William nodded. "He was a proud man, Highness. The thought of his own weakness when your safety should be uppermost in his mind was shameful to him, and it was with the intent of clearing his mind to better focus on your well-being that he and I spent many hours in discussion. To, I fear, no avail."

The Prince's face was unreadable. "You infer that Oswin killed himself."

"I do."

Thomas' mind raced.

"I have examined the privy in which he was found – I have even looked over the castle walls and examined its roof – and there is, simply, no way that someone could have entered it, affected Sir Oswin's death, and then left it sealed as we found it. He was a brave man, Highness, and a loyal servant to you and your father, but we all have our limits."

The Prince sat, eyes hooded.

"I can accept your thinking, Sir William, and I thank you for your efforts in consulting with Sir Oswin to address his unhappiness. But I have difficulty with the part where Sir Oswin, a dead man, made himself disappear."

The light scorn in the Prince's tone was a warning that Thomas hoped Sir William would heed.

Sir William seemed unaffected. "Of course, Highness. Let me put your mind at rest: Laurence moved the body."

"Laurence?!"

It was Sir Baldon who had spoken, and he immediately half-rose to bow his apologies to the Prince, but Thomas could see the surprise of this revelation on the faces of all gathered.

"Please forgive Baldon's interruption, Sir William," the Prince said, the dropping of Sir Baldon's title no doubt stinging that worthy like a whip, "and continue."

"Laurence and I both had the honour of serving under Sir Oswin, and I had shared with Laurence the unhappiness of which our former commander spoke. Laurence, as expected, shared my concerns for his friend. When Sir Oswin failed to present himself yesterday morning following the attack upon your person which still troubles us so…"

Had it really happened only yesterday?

"…I anticipated that Sir Oswin may, as he had spoken of before, have jumped from the battlements to end his suffering. I arranged, therefore, that I should examine the roof and that Laurence should remain in the dungeons and so be saved the burden of discovery. Laurence, I fear, saw through this and, instead of remaining in the dungeons, followed me to the top of the castle and waited out of sight to see what was discovered.

"We found Sir Oswin, instead, in the privy and Laurence, unseen but within earshot, heard our discussion. I doubt he heard the details, he would have wished to be at a safe distance, but he would have heard enough to know we had found Sir Oswin dead and the manner of the discovery made suicide the most likely explanation. After waiting for us to depart, and wishing to save his commander from the ignominy of being known a suicide, he collected Sir Oswin's body and carried it to the roof."

Sir William turned then from the Prince to address the others at the table:

"Those of you present for the meeting will remember that Laurence was among the last to arrive, that I had to send Thomas into the dungeons to find him."

'Terrible news about Sir Oswin.'

Fergus Highstone and Sir Baldon assented.

"I believe that Laurence took Sir Oswin's body out to the roof and, worried his absence might be noted, hid it among the chimneys before hurrying back down the stairs to the dungeons, arriving just before Thomas – and so giving the impression that he had been there the entire time."

Thomas gasped.

Sir William glanced at him and away, "I was—"

"I think, Sir William," the Prince interrupted, "that Thomas may have something to add."

The request could hardly be refused, and so Sir William waited.

Thomas stood, his head feeling too big and his legs too weak. "W-when I went downstairs," he glanced between Sir William and Prince Prospero, unsure which he should be addressing, "it was dark in the revel rooms. None of the braziers were lit, and Laurence carried no lantern or candle." His hand tremored as he tried to find the words, "I just realised that he could hardly have been down there searching for Sir Oswin the whole time in the dark."

The Prince nodded, and Thomas sank back into his chair.

Sir William licked his lips. "It is, then, as I suspected."

The Prince looked from Sir William to Thomas and back again, genuine interest on his face. "Continue."

"We met here, I broke the news of Sir Oswin's death, and then Thomas, Laurence, my brother, and I went to the kitchens—"

"For what purpose?" the Prince enquired, and Thomas felt ashamed at his outburst being recalled to them all.

Sir Baldon half-rose out of his chair before Sir William could reply. "To set up the morning meal, Highness."

The Prince glanced in Thomas' direction; Thomas found himself unable to meet anyone's eye.

Sir William resumed his narration: "Fergus and Baldon ascended, intending to view Sir Oswin's body, and, of course, found it missing."

The Prince looked to Fergus Highstone, who rose to his feet, his crimson sleeves flashing. "That is correct, Highness. We searched the rooms either side of the privy, and then Laurence came up, having followed us, and said that he wanted to investigate the roof."

"Did you go with him?" the prince asked.

"N-no, Highness," Highstone was clearly unsure whether this counted against him. "I thought the others should be told of the disappearance, and so I descended and, finding Sir William here in the hall, informed him of the situation."

Highstone sat, and the Prince turned to Sir Baldon.

"Did you see Laurence, Baldon?"

Sir Baldon rose, "No, Highness, I was searching the rooms, but I heard Fergus and he talking."

Sir Baldon sat and, at an indication from the Prince, Sir William pressed on:

"Laurence, then, headed to the roof, retrieved the body, and I believe that he threw Sir Oswin over the ramparts and into the moat – first puncturing his lungs so that he would sink and be hidden from view."

"How can you be so sure?" the Prince asked.

'It's an old army trick...'

"Simply because I have searched the castle and can find no sign of Sir Oswin anywhere."

The Prince sat back. "All this, just to protect Sir Oswin from being called a suicide?"

Sir William spoke gravely: "For a man like Sir Oswin, who had lived his life in the King's army, with the honour of having served your father as he did, and being as highly regarded by his men as he was, such reputations matter."

Whatever the Prince saw in the faces of the men around the table, men who had served in the King's army, clearly convinced him.

"And so," he pressed, "who killed Laurence?"

"Are you aware, Highness," Sir William asked, "of the title bestowed on Sir Oswin by his men?"

"The Man Who Would Never Die, I believe."

"That is correct. Sir Oswin never came to harm in the war, and when the Red Death descended over a year ago the name took on a new significance because," he paused, to ensure he had their full attention, "Sir Oswin is the only man known to have been touched by the Red Death and survive."

The claim was, at first, too ridiculous to entertain. And then, as a series of confused glances passed among the men present, there was a race to air their disbelief.

"I simply fail to…"

"God's wounds…!"

"Come now…"

Even the Prince's raised hand failed to silence them, and it took Zachariah banging the flat of his hand on the table to bring them to order.

The Prince's voice was low: "No-one survives the Red Death, Sir William."

Thomas' master pressed his palms together, as if gathering his thoughts.

"Highness, you will – we all will – have had occasions when your household has been caught by the fevers that are so common, and yet there is usually someone who remains unaffected. These fevers lay their marks upon us, as the Red Death does; they kill a great many people, as the Red Death does. And yet people survive them, people walk among those touched by these maladies and remain themselves untouched. Why, then, should it be so preposterous for the same to be true of the Red Death?"

No-one spoke.

"I claim no understanding of it, and we fear the Red Death more, as we should, because of its speed and because we are unaware of anyone surviving it, but examples of such survival have surrounded us for generations – blight in crops, illness in cattle. That even a tiny number of men could stand against the Red Death is surely unsurprising."

The Prince regarded Sir William in silence. Thomas glanced across at Fergus Highstone, fearful of any disdain the medical man might show, but, if anything, he looked *interested*.

Perhaps this decided for the Prince:

"Are you guessing, Sir William, or do you know this to be

the case?"

"Oswin told me how one of the things that sustained him in his despair was the feeling that he had been saved for some purpose as yet unknown to him. Once, at home, he said, he was attacked by a bird that clearly had the Red Death upon it. He had felt a great agony as the plague seized him, and then suddenly the feeling passed and he awoke, some hours later, as surprised to be alive as anyone ever has been. He never told the story, fearing he would be thought a liar, and in time he came to regard this good fortune as a curse, being forced to live while so many around him perished. He described it to me in these terms on the evening before he killed himself."

Everybody waited, the silence now as loud as the voices that had previously tried to shout Sir William down.

"How, then, came Laurence to die?"

Sir William took another drink from his wine.

"Laurence would have been most agitated, I'm sure. He had just disposed of the body of a man he cared deeply for, he would have been exhausted and overwrought. He would also have been holding his knife, having punctured Sir Oswin's lungs as I suggest, and that knife would have upon it blood touched by the Red Death.

"Doubtless in his haste to get down from the roof, to cover up his actions, perhaps while wiping the blade upon the leg of his trousers, I believe that Laurence slipped, and cut himself here," he touched a hand to his upper thigh, "and that the Red Death had, then, its chance to claim him."

'There are some scratches upon his hands, and what looks like a fresh cut on his thigh...'

Thomas closed his eyes; he wanted to throw up.

Fergus Highstone half-rose to his feet. "We did find such a wound upon him, Highness."

Prince Prospero nodded, and Highstone sat.

"When he realised what he had done," Sir William

141

continued, "I believe he panicked, and came racing back down the stairs to explain to someone before the Red Death could claim him. By pure chance we happened to be heading up the same staircase and..." he shook his head, looked away from them all. "Who knows? Maybe he suddenly realised the danger he was putting us all in, maybe he felt his control slipping – none of us know the touch of that evil upon us, how it feels as it overpowers the spirit.

"But I knew Laurence, and I am prepared to say that as soon as he heard us climbing the stairs towards him he would have understood the danger he had placed us all in. He would then have done the selfless thing and...stabbed himself in the heart to save us."

Thomas' entire body was wracked with shivers, and he could see how exhausted Sir William looked. Everyone sat in silence, doubtless none of them as confused as Thomas: after insisting that Sir Oswin had been murdered, was this what Sir William now believed? Had they been wrong before?

Had *he* been wrong?

And was it really possible to *survive* the Red Death?

At length, the Prince spoke:

"If this is indeed how Laurence died, he deserves to be remembered for his final acts of loyalty to his commander and bravery in keeping safe those of us who remained." He stood and raised his wine, and everyone did the same. "To Laurence."

"To Laurence," they all echoed, and Thomas forced back a drop of the bitter, blunt wine in memory of his friend.

"And to Oswin," the Prince said. "We honour his bravery and lament his own unhappiness before his end. Let no stain of shame ever mar the memory of a man overwhelmed by life."

"To Oswin," they repeated.

The foul taste filling his mouth, Thomas only pretended to drink.

They waited in silence for Prince Prospero to sit first, and then did likewise.

"Thank-you, Sir William, for your clarity in seeing that which was so obscure to the rest of us. We are forever in your debt."

Sir William ducked his head in acknowledgement. Prince Prospero, turning at the hips again, looked around the table, flexed his fingers once more, and smiled thinly.

"And now, gentlemen, to the attack upon my person. Let us identify the guilty party there, that we may know whom we are to hang at sunrise from the battlements."

FOURTEEN

Clearly pleased with the effect of these words, Prince Prospero sipped delicately at his wine.

"Highness…" Sir Baldon was the first to break the silence, again half-rising to his feet.

"Sit down, Baldon."

The rising man cowered again from the sting of this whip.

"To be quite clear," the Prince continued, his speech clipped in the sudden coldness of the hall, "one of you disguised himself in order to launch a murderous attack upon my person, for reasons we can currently only guess at but shall, here and now, learn fully." He turned to look at Thomas. "I am, of course, grateful for your intervention, Thomas, and," his eyes shifted around the table, "yours, Sir Marcus. Fergus, who is always so concerned for my well-being, kindly examined my injuries a little while ago and assures me that the discomfort I feel will lift in a few days. But for your prompt actions, gentlemen, I may have been far less fortunate. We accept absolutely that neither of you can be to blame."

Thomas almost sagged with relief. Sir Marcus was safe.

"Nevertheless, an attack upon my person is treason, and shall be treated and punished accordingly. Unless, of course, our attacker is hoping that we believe these stories I hear of phantoms vanishing through walls."

Nobody spoke.

"So let us be clear: my father is the credulous old man. Perhaps if the mad old bastard had sired me earlier I would be now of an age to jump at stories of ghosts and witches, but I am thankfully young enough yet to resist such superstitious drivel. I felt hands around my throat, a body clambered over me in my own bed. That was one of you. Sir William tells me that you are all able to account for the presence of at least one other person, and so the answer is simple: two or more of you are lying to protect each other, and so are guilty of treasonous conspiracy against the crown."

Fergus Highstone rose to his feet.

"Highness, please, we beseech you – every man here is loyal to you and your father, even...even if you choose to believe otherwise at present."

Highstone may as well have said nothing, for the effect his words had.

"These are blandishments, Fergus, and they belong to an older age – an age of naïve old men who refuse to believe anyone would dare stain the sanctity of the crown. I built this castle that we might bid defiance to the ridiculous and ignorant fancies of men who have never seen life. I invite my friends here so that they are freed from the constraints of the outside world – here, a man has no need to pretend to be sad that the wife he hated has died; here, he is free to enjoy the company and the attention of other women. Outside, that would be frowned upon. Here, he is free to enjoy the company and attention of other men if he wished, and outside that would *certainly* be frowned upon." He curled his fingers into fists. "So keep your empty words, and stop expecting that I adhere to the ignorant assumptions of the men who have gone before me."

"Of course, Highness, I—"

"Had I *finished*, Fergus?"

Everyone at the table froze, Sir Baldon with his cup to this lips, Highstone with his hands raised in apology.

"I am sorry, Highness. Please continue."

The Prince's face contorted in disgust.

"Do you give me permission to speak at my own table, Fergus? How *very* kind of you."

Highstone, wisely, offered no reply, and simply sat with his eyes downturned.

"If none of you were alone," the Prince continued after a

pause, "the only other option is conspiracy. We shall commence proceedings with the Oath, and then the examination shall begin."

A murmur of unease washed around the table.

"Wh-what is the Oath?" Thomas asked, realising too late that he had forgotten to stand.

Sir Baldon raised a hand as if requesting to speak, and the Prince indicated his consent, and the other man rose to his feet.

"The, uh, the highest judgement in the land is of course that of the crown," Sir Baldon bowed to the Prince, "and all accusations of treason are heard before him. In taking an oath, those who speak before the crown pledge that they shall be bound by the testimony of all who speak. In the event of any differences in testimony, those who insist on the contradictions are held equally guilty and executed."

Thomas thought he must have misunderstood.

"It is often the quickest way," Sir Baldon continued, "even if it is far from pleasant."

"Sir Baldon," the Prince said, "if you would be so kind."

Sir Baldon bowed and lifted his wine, stepping back from the table. He walked to the fire, emptied the wine out into the flames, then approached the Prince and placed the goblet between Prince Prospero and Zachariah. The bodyguard wiped out the inside of the goblet with his sleeve, then took the jug of wine from the table and refilled the cup. Candlelight flickered on the jewelled bands that adorned his fingers.

Everyone stood.

In the candlelight they looked now ghostly, unreal, and their collective fear crept into Thomas' bones. He wondered which of them would leave this room alive.

Zachariah raised the cup with his right hand and, looking around the table, said, "I pledge loyalty to the crown and shall speak the truth."

He drank, and handed the cup to his left, to Sir William,

who also raised it in his right hand.

"I pledge loyalty to the crown and shall speak the truth."

He drank, and passed the cup to Fergus Highstone, who raised it in the same way,

"I pledge loyalty to the crown and shall speak the truth."

Highstone drank, and passed the goblet to Sir Baldon, who took it eagerly with tremoring hands.

"I pledge loyalty to the crown and shall speak the truth," he said, before raising it to his lips and drinking deeply.

Sir Marcus was next.

"I pledge loyalty to the crown and shall speak the truth."

After drinking, he looked at Thomas and then up at the Prince.

"There's no need to include Thomas in this, is there, Highness?"

"Marcus," his brother said, a warning in his voice.

"What, Will?!" Sir Marcus snapped. "You may remember that until recently some of the people at this table were insisting that he should slop out their shit; I can hardly see them conspiring with him to attack the Prince."

"But you might," Zachariah said.

"I beg your fu—"

The Prince raised his hand. "If nobody conspired with Thomas, Thomas has nothing to fear."

"Then we agree."

Sir Marcus reached past Thomas to hand the cup to the Prince.

"But his evidence!" Sir Baldon screeched, his nerves apparently under great strain. "Without taking the Oath, what he says has no value in condemning the guilty."

"You misunderstood me, Sir Marcus," the Prince said, quietly. "Sir Baldon is quite correct; it is my intention that Thomas be included."

Sir Marcus sighed and, muttering under his breath, handed

the cup to Thomas.

Holding it in his right hand as everyone else had done, Thomas looked into the cup, now almost empty, and took a breath: "I pledge loyalty to the crown and shall speak the truth."

Raising the goblet to his mouth, he again pinched the rim of the bowl between his lips and tilted the stem upwards past his nose until the small pool of flat, foul liquid once again only touched against his lips.

He lowered the cup and, with a shaking hand, passed it to his left, to the Prince.

Prince Prospero raised the goblet above his head, and looked around the table, once more with that awkward twist of his waist. "Gentlemen, the crown thanks you for your loyalty. May the light of truth shine forth, and may we visit punishment upon those who oppose justice."

Placing the cup against his lips he tipped back his head and drained its contents.

Thomas prepared to sit down, but no-one moved.

Prince Prospero licked his lips and turned to look at Thomas, a faint smile on his face. "I…" he said, and raised a trembling hand to his face, "I…"

He stumbled sideways, away from his chair, and collapsed to the floor, gasping.

Thomas froze, could feel the bulk of Sir Marcus similarly immobile beside him, and watched as if from a distance as Zachariah dropped to his knees beside the Prince, Sir William and Fergus Highstone both racing to the fallen man.

The crush of bodies around the prostrate form were confused, but Thomas could see Prince Prospero's feet protruding, the heels of his soft-soled shoes kicking and scraping at the floor, as voices clamoured for superiority.

"Breathe, Highness, breathe!" Zachariah could be heard to shout, while Highstone seemed to be trying to force his fingers into the Prince's mouth.

Unable to take his eyes away, Thomas saw, on the edge of his vision, Sir Baldon approaching the body at a funereal pace, terror and fascination mixing on his face.

Still the Prince's heels drummed on the stone floor.

A retching noise could be heard, and the feet rolled over as the Prince was turned onto his side.

His kicking feet skidded less urgently.

"Breathe, Highness!" Zachariah repeated, his voice desperate. A series of flat sounds could be heard, and Thomas saw Sir William pounding the Prince on the back, as if to dislodge something from his throat.

Only one foot kicked now; the other lay still.

"Highness!" Highstone could be heard shouting, "Highness!"

Zachariah howled, Sir Baldon kept walking in his long arc around them, his eyes fixed on the four figures on the floor.

The foot scraped one last time, and was still.

"Highness!" Fergus Highstone shouted into the sudden quiet.

Sir William, kneeling beside the body, turned to face his brother over Thomas' head.

"Is…?" Sir Marcus asked.

Sir William stared at his brother, eyes uncomprehending. "He's dead."

~

The stillness had barely settled before Zachariah spun to face Thomas.

"What did you do?!" he demanded, snarling as he took a step forward.

Thomas stared as the bodyguard approached. It was Sir Marcus, hands outstretched, who stepped forward to stop him.

The two men scuffled, Zachariah's wide eyes on Thomas whenever he appeared around the bulk of the bigger man.

"What did you *do*?"

"He *did* nothing," Sir Marcus said between grunts as he tried to hold the bodyguard still.

"He was the last to drink the wine! He poisoned it!"

"No, bodyguard, you're wrong."

"I saw him!"

"You're wrong!"

"Then it was you!" Zachariah spat, jabbing his finger into Sir Marcus' face. "You poisoned it, then passed it to him—" he jabbed a thumb at Thomas, "and he—"

"Yes?"

The bodyguard's eyes, filled with hate, bored into Thomas: "Give me the antidote!"

"What?" Fergus Highstone exclaimed.

"*You*," Zachariah jabbed a finger at Sir Marcus, "poisoned the wine, *he*—" a finger jabbed in Thomas' direction, "survived drinking it. There is an antidote and I will have it or I will kill you both for murdering the Prince!"

"You're wrong, Zachariah." Sir Marcus sounded exhausted.

"Explain, then, how this *boy* survived—"

"*He never drinks it!*"

The bodyguard stopped struggling. "What?"

Beyond these two men, Thomas saw Sir William's back stiffen. Highstone, still on his knees beside the Prince, also raised his head. Behind them both, Sir Baldon continued his slow, unstoppable progress to whatever destination made most sense in his own mind.

"What did you say, Marcus?" Sir William asked quietly.

Sir Marcus' head dropped. "He never drinks the wine," he said quietly. "He's a thirteen year-old boy, Will; I imagine it tastes bloody foul to him."

Sir William's eyes moved to Thomas. "Is this true?"

Thomas nodded, numb.

"I've sat next to him for however many meals," Sir Marcus replied, "of course it's true. He never touches it."

"Then you *did* poison it!" the bodyguard cried into Sir Marcus' face. "You poisoned the wine and passed it to him knowing he would be safe. All that talk about whether the boy should take the Oath was to distract us while you put your poisons in…"

"And I would draw attention to myself while doing it, would I? And then admit that I knew Thomas would be safe?" He waved a hand scornfully. "No wonder Prospero has died under your protection, with brains like that looking out for him."

Zachariah bellowed with rage and launched himself at the bigger man. They staggered away from the table, snarling and wrestling with each other until Sir William and Highstone, having scrambled to their feet, were able to separate them.

"Enough!" Sir William shouted, gripping his older brother by the shoulders. And then, more quietly, leaning close to the dishevelled mane of shaggy hair, "Marcus."

The fight dropped out of Sir Marcus. His shoulders sagged, and Sir William stepped away. Fergus Highstone had backed Zachariah up several paces, the two men standing with their fronts pressed together, the bodyguard snarling past his captor's shoulder.

Thomas glanced at the body of the Prince, lying once again on its back, shirt pulled open and ruff torn away from its throat in the struggle to save the prince's life.

Sir William raised his hands to his face, and rubbed them back over the top of his head. "What just happened?" he asked no-one in particular.

"Your *bastard* brother poisoned the Prince!"

"With what, Zachariah?" Highstone asked, in the voice of one trying to be reasonable.

"Every morning, these two," he jabbed his chin at Thomas and Sir Marcus, "they go to the cellars and they poison the rats."

Highstone looked over his shoulder at Sir Marcus. "Is this true?"

Sir Marcus nodded.

Highstone seemed confused: "With what?"

"They make the poison – why does it matter?" Zachariah insisted. "If it kills the rats, it kills a man. Do you deny this?"

Sir William and Sir Marcus exchanged a look, and the younger Collingwood deliberately turned his back on the bodyguard.

"Everybody drank," Sir William said.

"Except Thomas," Sir Marcus replied.

"Nobody else died."

"No."

"You were the last one to drink."

"I was."

They both turned to Thomas. He knew this had been coming, it was the only explanation left. He refused to raise his eyes from the dead body, watching instead the firelight flickering on the pale skin of the corpse's exposed chest and neck, the shadows dancing about its eye sockets and nose. Any moment now, surely, Prince Prospero would sit up and reveal this to be one big jest. Any moment now...

"Thomas put nothing in there," Sir William said.

"How are you so sure?" Zachariah demanded, as if about to change his mind over who he wished to accuse.

This is what Thomas dreaded: defending himself when it was only his word against those who might be convinced otherwise – and Zachariah was clearly a man who believed what he wanted to believe.

"Because he's cleverer than that," Sir Marcus said quietly.

Thomas was grateful for their certainty, but he knew it

would take more than that to banish the suspicion he found himself under. With the Prince dead – *dead* – was there anyone who could silence Zachariah's accusations? Would he, Thomas, always be under suspicion now?

How could the Prince be dead?!

"It is good that we can clear Thomas of any involvement," said a voice, and Thomas realised that Sir Baldon had now progressed around the room and was approaching him slowly. "There are other matters we must attend to."

"Baldon," Sir William said, something like warning in his voice.

"But we must ensure…"

"Percy," Sir Marcus' voice was equally cautious, "now is hardly the time."

"The Prince is dead," Sir Baldon said, as if that explained everything. "Now is exactly the time."

"No-one has told him, Percy."

"And I have always been against that."

What is happening?

Sir Baldon stopped in front of Thomas, and smiled sadly. "It is a shame you have to find out this way…"

"Baldon," again the warning tone in Sir William's voice, harder now.

Sir Baldon, ignoring this, sank to one knee and lowered his head. "My liege."

Thomas watched, more confused now that at any time previous in the last few days.

Surely…

"What has no-one told me?" he asked, the answer scratching at the back of his own mind.

Sir Baldon lifted his head, but remained kneeling. "About your father."

'You do your father tremendously proud.'

"My father?" Thomas turned to Sir Marcus, whose eyes

were downcast, and then to Sir William, whose drawn features were perfectly blank.

Sir Baldon continued: "No doubt he would have wanted to tell you himself, but now that he is dead…"

'You do your father tremendously proud.'

"…it is only right that you continue in your father's place. As Prince."

"What?"

The room was suddenly too warm, too small, too cold, too big. Everyone was staring at him, but none would meet his eye.

"The Prince," he glanced again at the stationary form on the floor, "the *Prince* was my father?"

He looked again at Sir Marcus, and the big man met Thomas' eye and then glanced away as if in pain. He turned to Sir William, and found himself unable to read the empty look that had remained fixed on his master's face.

"Is this true?" he asked.

Nobody moved. Beyond Sir Baldon, Thomas could see that Fergus Highstone had turned to face him and Zachariah was standing with his mouth open, both men's faces showing a confusion that was the smallest part of what Thomas felt boiling within himself.

"*Is this true?*"

Eventually, minutely, Sir William nodded.

'You do you father tremendously proud.'

His head swam, his legs buckled; Sir Baldon jerked to his feet as if to catch Thomas were he to fall, and the sudden concern the man showed for his wellbeing – after so long being dismissed, feeling like an impostor – spoke volumes.

Thomas turned, and ran for the stairs.

FIFTEEN

He had picked a third floor bedroom at random, leaving the door open to give no hint of his presence. Sitting behind the vanity screen in the corner, he had cried for over an hour, scared of something he no longer understood. Raised voices had occasionally drifted to him from the hall below, an argument in full force. It must have been the small hours of the morning when they came looking for him.

At the growing light of a flickering candle and the sound of footsteps approaching along the hallway, Thomas made himself as quiet and small as possible.

The footsteps stopped.

"Told you," said Sir Marcus from out in the corridor, "loud enough to scare the horses."

Thomas waited in silence.

He heard footsteps and saw the glow of light enter the room, heard the creak of furniture as Sir Marcus settled his weight against the bed, heard the big man sigh.

"Do you want to talk about it?"

"No."

Silence.

Above the screen, he could see the crazy shadows thrown against the ceiling by the dancing flame. His throat hurt, his chest burned, his mind raced.

"Why did no-one tell me?"

"So you *do* want to talk about it?"

Annoyed, Thomas kicked out at the screen, sending it toppling over with a crash. Sir Marcus, propped against the side of the bed with his feet out in front of him, sat watching. They locked eyes, something like concern on the bearded man's face as he waited.

"Why did no-one tell me?"

Sir Marcus placed the candle holder on the floor and sat

back. "We had our reasons. It was, in part, to protect you."

"Why?"

He rubbed his beard as if tired. "How much do you know about the war?"

Thomas gestured angrily at this man who had lied to him for his entire life. "What does that have to do with anything?"

"You've waited nearly fourteen years to hear this, lad. Let me tell it so it makes sense."

Thomas rested his forehead against his raised knees.

"How much do you know about the war?"

There was no point to this, it would answer none of his questions.

'You do your father tremendously proud.'

"Let's start with an easy one: how long did it last?"

Now it was Thomas who sighed; why were adults like this? "The Thousand Days War? How long did it last?" He could barely be bothered to keep the scorn out of his voice.

Sir Marcus waited.

Thomas shrugged without lifting his head. "A thousand days."

"No."

Thomas sighed again, picked his numbers carefully, checking they made sense before saying them: "Nine-hundred and fifty-eight days, then." Obviously the war was unlikely to have been *exactly* one thousand days.

"No. Worse than that."

Worse? "Two thousand days."

"Nineteen."

Nineteen thous—?

"Nineteen days, from first blood to last."

His irritation momentarily forgotten, Thomas raised his head. He checked the numbers in his head. Surely that was wrong.

"Then why do we call it the Thousand Days War?"

Sir Marcus ignored him. "Here's another one: name one person who stood against the King. I know Will and Suzann refuse to talk about it, and Maude and Elena have both tried to avoid telling you anything about it, but come on – if someone leads an uprising against the King, their name must be well-known. Name one of the men we've come to call the King's enemies: a general, someone humiliated in battle."

Thomas tried to think.

"Come on," Sir Marcus encouraged him, "these people opposed the King. We should spit their names into the mud. Tell me just one name."

Eventually, he had to give up: "I have never heard any of them."

"Hardly your fault. The King's enemies had no leader, no general, no army even."

Thomas' curiosity rose. None of this made sense.

"Now," Sir Marcus looked at him keenly, "what two questions does that information raise?"

"How can a war last only nineteen days?"

"Good. And?"

"How can you have a war without an opposing army?"

The war had always been about sides. What little he could gather had always been about the King's army – lead by men like Sir Oswin Bassingham – versus the King's enemies. Sir Marcus and Sir William had fought in the war, they had been given their titles, their land, their home in recognition of their service to the King. How could that be if there was no opposing army?

"The Thousand Days War was no war, Thomas. Forget the glorious meeting of two armies that comes to your mind when you try to imagine it. It was a massacre – a series of massacres, in fact – and we have been pretending otherwise ever since. Have you ever heard of Rawley?"

Thomas shook his head. "Who's that?"

"It used to be a town, one of the wealthiest in the kingdom. When increased taxes were announced by the King, Rawley sent an emissary to the palace, requesting that, as the ones funding the King's lifestyle, the people as a whole would like a say in how their money was spent, and the control the crown would have over their own lives.

"The landowners were invited to the palace to discuss the matter and, while they were away from the town, one hundred soldiers were sent to Rawley and burned down the houses of those who were absent, killing anyone who resisted."

Fear fluttered in Thomas' chest.

"Now, of course," Sir Marcus was scornful, "much was made of this resistance, of the soldiers fearing for their lives, but how much danger can those who work the land – fruit-growers armed with rakes – pose to a battalion of trained soldiers on Terrington Fenwick's horses? It was a massacre, a show of strength, and people knew it."

"Why?" Thomas could barely croak out the word.

"A king who lets others tell him what to do remains king for only a short time. And our King has always been aware of anything that might be seen as a challenge to his power. Some say he had gotten worse around this time. Stories had circulated that he was hardly himself, could be found at night wandering the corridors and crying, would forget conversations, would repeat himself, would contradict himself and fly into rages when asked to clarify. Last I heard, he was sleeping with four guards in his chamber and four without, and he was so furious when they tried to oppose his wanderings that he bit one man's finger clean off."

Sir Marcus drew in a shuddering breath.

"Some say he saw this request from the landowners – for the right to make decisions on punishments for theft, for instance, without the need to wait for judgement from a representative of the King – as a challenge to his rule, that he was scared to see his power threatened. Some say it had been a while since he last stamped his foot and he was looking for an excuse." He looked away, scratched his nose, "I think that if you make a frightened animal believe it's backed into a corner, it attacks you."

"You said it lasted nineteen days…"

"That was day one. Some of the survivors escaped, fled to the next town, told of what had happened – it could hardly have been kept quiet – and dissent grew. Some went on to spread the word elsewhere, and the less intelligent ones took up what meagre arms they had and went to make their displeasure known."

"Why was it less intelligent to resist?"

"There is no opposing violent men given an outlet for their violence. Raise a man to be a killer, train him and pour into him the glory of battle to protect the life he knows, and then give him the chance to kill, he probably never stops to think. The army has one hundred trained, violent men stationed a half-day's ride in any direction – they began to warn their soldiers, to spread the word themselves, to get to towns ahead of the news from elsewhere and to tell men of an uprising against the King. And when the King's army arrives in your armpit of a town on Terrington Fenwick's horses and tells you of a threat to the King, well, you believe them. They recruited what men they got to first, and then set them against those who were opposing the violent acting out of a madman."

"What happened?"

"Nineteen days," Sir Marcus said slowly. "That's how long it took for the King's army to scare any opposition out of any towns they encountered. The anger of the mob usually vanished in the face of armour, weapons, and training, but every so often the bloodthirsty bastards would get the chance to enjoy themselves, until there was no energy for any more death. It was," he almost spat the words, "a glorious victory for His

Majesty."

He pushed himself off the bed, began to pace. "Afterwards, people started calling it the Thousand Days War. I've heard that someone toadying up to the King said how a victory so complete would normally only be expected after a thousand days of fighting, and I've heard that those on the other side picked the name in mockery of so disgraceful a slaughter, that it should have taken that long for that many to be killed. About the only thing both sides agreed on was that it should never be mentioned again: the King's court because they feared the loss of support from the people, and those they called the King's enemies because they were picking up the pieces of their lives and had no desire to be crushed under the heel of His Majesty's boot once again."

Thomas sat, trying to make sense of this new understanding. *Oh no.*

"You and Sir William…"

"Go on." Sir Marcus' eyes were blank.

"You…took part in this?"

Sir Marcus paused for a few moments. "The army arrived in Will's town looking for recruits. He was 20 years old, full of piss and vinegar, newly married. He and Suzann had…well, he had a wife to support. The glory of protecting the King was poured into his ear and he took the King's shilling, yes. He soured on it pretty quickly when he realised what was happening. Tried to burn outbuildings rather than houses, to scare people away rather than see them perish."

It was too big, too much to take on at once, so Thomas seized the one detail he could comprehend:

"You could have refused."

Sir Marcus smiled humourlessly.

"Two measures of power, lad," he counted them on his fingers: "how little it costs you to give or take whatever you want, and how certain you can be that what you command will be done. The King's army does what the King says firstly because they're paid to and secondly because they know that someone else *will* do it if they refuse. Refusing the King is treason, and treason is punishable by death. Someone keen to prove their loyalty, to get for themselves what might be coming to you, is only too happy to kill you and take your share. Will did far more good alive than he ever could have dead."

Thomas shook his head.

"You disagree? Look at our house, at the land we now command. Prospero gave us all of that – took it from Sir Runciman Jellico when *he* stood against the King – and tomorrow the King might learn his son is dead and decide he wants it back. He could send a hundred soldiers and ruin us like—" he clicked his fingers, "and they would do it because they'd see what had been given to *us* and would realise it might be given to *them*. The King says 'Kill William Collingwood' and a hundred men race to do his bidding – because the King's money puts food in their bellies and companions in their beds, and he might give them a big house and a title if they're nice to him."

Thomas had lived in that house, on that land, his entire life. The idea of it being taken away so easily was terrifying.

"There must be more to it than that."

Sir Marcus smiled sadly, "Must there?"

They sat in silence while Thomas tried and failed to find a flaw.

"I think I understand," he said slowly, "why you hated everyone here so much."

Sir Marcus who had never attended the revels, who had risen early and avoided people for as much of the day as he could.

"I would hardly say I *hated* them," he said, as if giving the matter serious thought. "But when Prospero gathered us here, people flocked partly because they thought he had a plan – you

saw some people, those with principles, walk out in disgust –
but many of them *hoped* he was going to lock them away, keep
them safe, and they were more interested in their own safety,
and in getting close to a man who could give them *anything*.
Some of them woke up and left, some of them…well, some of
them thought it more important to remain."

"You stayed."

"We did."

"Because of me."

"Partly."

"Because of who my father is."

'You do your father tremendously proud.'

"Because of who your father is."

"I had hoped, Sir Marcus," came a voice from the other side
of the door, "that we might have gotten to this sooner."

"If you can do a better job, Percy," Sir Marcus said evenly,
"come and do it. I'm all talked out."

"You have told far more than is needed—"

"Oh, for pity's sake, he needs to know how it came to
pass…"

"—and given quite the wrong impression of what the
King's army faced."

Sir Marcus gestured angrily, and sat down heavily on the
side of the bed. "If you think I'd let him be told the version
you maniacs have made up for yourself—"

"This degrading of the King's name—"

"I'll do more than degrade his precious name…!"

"How is the Prince my father?" Thomas asked quietly,
silencing them both.

Sir Marcus stood glowering at the doorway, and Sir Baldon
entered, pushing the door closed so he could see Thomas seated
on the floor.

"May I, Sir Marcus?"

This big man muttered and swept an arm through the air,

turning away.

"After the war," Sir Baldon said calmly, the flame of the candle lighting him from below, "Sir William and Sir Marcus had titles and land bestowed upon them by the generosity of the late Prince."

"Why?"

Sir Baldon inclined his head. "An agreement was reached. The Prince was at the time, and seems to have been ever since, reluctant to consider settling with a bride of his own, and was also under tremendous pressure from his father to supply an heir."

An heir.

"He gets that from his father," Sir Marcus muttered, and Thomas remembered the Prince's comments earlier about how late in life this own father had waited before having a child.

"It was agreed that Prince Prospero would – hurrum – would lay with Lady Suzann," Sir Baldon glanced awkwardly at Thomas and then away, "and, provided she bore him a boy, that child would be recognised as his heir if no other male child came from any future wedlock he might enter into."

Thomas' throat felt thick. "L-Lady Suzann is m-my *mother*?"

Sir Baldon looked embarrassed. Behind him, Sir Marcus nodded.

Thomas desperately wanted to recall her face, but found it eluded him.

"But I was a servant…"

"Thomas," Sir Marcus said gently, "you are in that house far more as a son than as a servant. You eat at the table, you share in the company of Laurence when he visits, you are taught to count and to think for yourself. You told me about the treatment of that girl in Fenwick's house – what was her name?"

Thomas swallowed, everything coming at him too fast.

"Isobel."

"The treatment of Isobel, and other stories you will have heard in your time here, *that* is being a servant. Carrying plates and cooking food while your masters cavort and screw and deny the end of the world, *that* is being a servant."

Thomas thought Sir Baldon might contradict this, but the other man stood silently.

He started to weep. "So why did no-one tell me?"

"Because," Sir Marcus looked genuinely distraught, "what if Prospero had married, and had a son? You would have been raised your entire life being told you were the Prince's heir only for it to be swept from beneath you. Suzann and Will would hardly sit around like these other over-privileged inbreds simply waiting for what was coming to you – yes, Percy, calm down – only for you to be denied and then be unprepared to cope in the world without that security."

"Was I ever going to be told?"

Sir Marcus and Sir Baldon exchanged a look, and the big man raised his hands in a gesture of uncertainty.

"It was Prospero's decision to make. But you slept one door away from him, you sat on his favoured side at dinner…"

Prince Prospero was to Thomas' left, so he was on the Prince's *right*, the side of the favoured guest. How had he overlooked this?

"…so maybe he was building up to telling you, who knows? Those from the other side of the blanket must wait until the age of seventeen to be designated an heir, but maybe he saw the mistake his father made in leaving it so late in life and was ready to declare you before us all."

Thomas tried to make sense of this, to understand a world in which *he* was heir to the throne.

"Do you have any other questions?" Sir Baldon asked, as if he expected none.

He plucked one from the whirlwind in his mind: "Why

Lady Suzann?"

"I'm sorry?"

"Why did the Prince choose Lady Suzann to provide his heir? He must have lain with plenty of women," Thomas thought of the stairway downstairs, of the close attention paid to the various women – married and otherwise – who had been selected by the Prince and sent up ahead of him to share his bed, "and he could have other heirs by now."

"Yes," Sir Baldon seemed uncertain, and glanced at Sir Marcus. "But there is no obligation for an illegitimate child to be acknowledged."

"He could have thousands of illegitimate children for all tradition cares; he still gets to choose which one takes over," Sir Marcus clarified. "Prospero could give the women he favoured, whether they bore him a son or otherwise, anything – land, titles, security, whatever they wanted, so they could have no complaints if their child is overlooked for the role. Remember, it would cost *him* nothing."

Thomas nodded.

'You do your father tremendously proud.'

"Yes," Sir Baldon interjected, "the Prince was very free in rewarding his favoured partners."

"So why did he lay with Lady Suzann?"

Sir Baldon glanced at Sir Marcus, clearly uncertain. Something passed in the air between them.

"Tell him, Percy."

Still Sir Baldon hesitated.

"Just," Sir Marcus rubbed his face, as if tired to the marrow of his bones, "tell him."

"Sir William," Sir Baldon started slowly, turning to Thomas as he spoke, "had a friend who stood with the King's enemies and was captured and imprisoned. Sir William begged that his friend's life be spared, and so an arrangement was reached. Sir William was required to provide the opportunity for Prince

Prospero's line to continue, freeing the Prince from the encumbrance of a wife while ensuring the child came from…good stock. In return, titles and land were given to Sir William and Sir Marcus to ensure that, should the child be a boy, it could be raised as well as possible in safety."

Thomas' mind was in disarray, but he suddenly remembered the events of the other day – Sir Baldon's words when they had gathered in the hall following the discovery of Sir Oswin's body – and saw now the reason for them:

"This is why," he said to Sir Baldon, "you thought the King's enemies might be behind the attack on the Prince? Because Sir William had a friend who opposed the King in the war?"

Sir Baldon shifted uncomfortably on his feet. "In a way, yes."

"So, were you talking about Sir William?"

"No," Sir Marcus said. "Baldon was speaking of the friend he saved."

"But how could Sir William have gotten someone into the castle unobserved?"

"The man is," Sir Baldon said, sounding nervous, "already inside."

Thomas thought back to the conversation with Sir William in Laurence's room, and realised that his master had broken that off when Thomas had suggested the possibility of someone else hiding in the castle. But, if his master had been hiding something, how did Sir Baldon know about this extra man? Had Sir William now admitted this? Had that been what they were shouting about while Thomas was hiding up here?

Thomas looked back to Sir Baldon and opened his mouth to speak. In the gloom behind him, Sir Marcus pushed away from the wall, his eyes fixed on Thomas the whole time, and what they were trying to tell him suddenly broke through.

'You know, the Prince, he told me about you…'

'Every man here is loyal to you and your father, even…'

'Marcus Collingwood has gotten out of tighter jams than this before…'

Sir Marcus, seeing Thomas' face change, nodded.

"Yes, well done – it was me; I fought against the King in the Thousand Days War."

PART THREE

And the Revel Went Whirlingly On

SIXTEEN

Thomas awoke to a new world.

He now knew who his father was, but the man was dead; he now knew who his mother was, but had abandoned her to watch powerful men vie for position and influence; he was no longer a servant in the house of a titled man, but instead stood on the verge of possessing a power that, for his entire life, had been used to keep people in fear; and the man he cared for most in the world had risked his own life to oppose what Thomas was due to become.

Was this a world he wanted?

The Thousand Days War had been over before Thomas was born, and learning of the conflict, and of Sir Marcus' role in it – his opposition of the King, making him guilty of treason – was to Thomas rather like learning the name of his father: it filled no gaps, replaced nothing that had been missing, and so made little difference. But he had no doubt that it would be *expected* to impact on him because of who he now knew his father to be.

Would Isobel agree to marry him now, he wondered, or would she simply be marrying his title, the security that came with being the wife of someone with such power? The more Thomas considered it, the more he understood why Prince Prospero had done what he had and avoided choosing a wife. Surely you would want to know that you were loved for who you were.

Power complicated everything.

He could tell that the day was older than when he usually woke, Sir Marcus having decided against calling for him this morning. With a heaviness in his chest, Thomas dressed, unbolted his door, and stepped into the corridor to find Zachariah waiting. Unsure how much suspicion should fall on the bodyguard, and equally unsure what he was doing there, Thomas nodded, received a nod in return, and headed for the stairs without a word.

Zachariah followed.

Thomas stopped and turned, "Did…you need me for something?"

Confusion showed on the other man's face. "I was…your father's bodyguard, sire, and now I am yours."

Thomas had no response to this.

Zachariah dropped his head, his long hair falling forwards, hiding his face from view. "I recognise that your father was attacked and killed while I was responsible for his safety, and that I spoke harshly the other day and you…may resent that, but," he raised his head again, "if you will permit me, I would be honoured to continue."

Thomas tried to muster his thoughts. It seemed absurd that a man who had survived the battles and challenges that Zachariah had should be here seeking reassurances from a 13 year-old servant boy.

"D-do you think I *need* a bodyguard?" Thomas had failed to consider the matter.

The question seemed to confuse Zachariah: "The Prince always has a bodyguard, sire

With no idea what to say, Thomas tried to think.

"Right now, I just want to talk to Sir Marcus."

"He was in the kitchens only a little while ago, sire," Zachariah offered, straightening up eagerly. "Shall I fetch him for you?"

Prince Prospero never went to *see* anyone, Thomas remembered; they were *brought* to him. Is this how it would be now? Would everyone be offering to bring him anything or anyone he mentioned?

"No. Thank-you. I'll go and find him."

The bodyguard seemed on the verge of response, but stayed silent.

Thomas turned away.

"Would you...?" Zachariah ventured.

Thomas turned back.

"Should I accompany you, sire?"

With a start, Thomas realised that this was the first time anyone in the castle had sought his permission to do something.

"The Prince," Zachariah continued into his silence, "was always accompanied."

"I just want to talk to Sir Marcus."

"Of course, sire"

Thomas saw that more was required, and ventured onto unfamiliar ground:

"Probably alone."

"Of...course, sire. But...you are also aware that Marcus Collingwood is an enemy of the King."

Thomas again felt that anger stir inside him, this time at how these men saw the world. You were something once, over a decade ago, and so that's who you were forever. He opened his mouth to speak, and then remembered the bodyguard's mocking attitude of the day before – *'A man can make himself shorter, after all'* – and realised the futility of arguing with such a man.

Zachariah clearly saw something in Thomas' face and quickly dropped his head in apology.

"That was wrong of me, sire, I spoke out of turn. Forgive me."

Was *this* power? People who would normally disagree with you now apologised for holding a differing opinion? All this change was too much. He turned away, fighting the urge to run lest the bodyguard follow him anyway.

Zachariah remained behind.

Descending to the main hall, Thomas was unprepared for how normal it looked, with no indication of the drama that had unfolded the previous evening. Prince Prospero's body had been removed, and the room was as familiar and still as it had been on countless mornings before. But for the bodyguard's attitude, all of the events which had shaken them so fully – the Prince's impossible death, the revelation of Thomas' parentage, the things he had learned about the war – may have been his own delirious fancy.

He crossed to the kitchens and found Sir Marcus sitting at the central table there, a bread plate in front of him bearing what looked like the remains of the evening meal. The big man stopped chewing when he saw Thomas enter, and rose slowly to his feet.

They looked at each other in silence.

"Sh-should I bow?" Sir Marcus asked. "This is new to me."

Thomas smiled, hoping to mask the sadness he felt. "To me, too."

The big man grinned awkwardly, remained standing.

Another silence grew.

"I have a bodyguard now," Thomas said, to be saying something

Sir Marcus grunted. "We shall expect you to be dead before the day is out, then."

The ice between them cracked a little. Thomas approached the table, and Sir Marcus turned and collected another plate from the counter along the far wall. Realising how hungry he was, having consumed nothing the night before, Thomas sat in his usual place and the big man placed the plate in front of him before sinking back into his chair and resuming his meal.

"We need to do the frogs."

"Done 'em."

Thomas ate, watching Sir Marcus, his eyes downcast, pick at his own food. The long-stored dried meat and fruit was flavourless at the best of times, but especially so today.

Silence stretched again. Why was it so difficult to talk?

"It makes no difference to me, that you opposed the King."

"You're in the minority there, lad."

"I just – I want to understand."

Sir Marcus sat back from the table, chewing the last of his food while his eyes rested on Thomas. This silence felt different, as if something was coming.

Eventually, the big man asked, "You know why they built this castle?"

After last night's revelations, Thomas felt no impatience at this starting point. Sir Marcus was welcome to tell whatever story he wished in whatever way he chose.

"For the Prince's revels?"

"No, Prospero *took* it for his revels. It was a place of worship before that."

Religion had been outlawed when the King – Prospero's father...and so Thomas' grandfather, he realised with a start – had taken the throne. To acknowledge someone or some*thing* as having more power than the King was branded treason, and so punishable by death. People still observed their beliefs, just in smaller groups, kept secret from authority.

Sir Marcus smiled humourlessly.

"What?"

"I was just thinking, the fact that Percy was able to walk through the doors without being struck down answers any questions about a god, given how many religious heretics he executed on the King's orders."

"Sir Baldon did that? Killed people?"

"Percy did what the King told him to. Always has. You've heard what happened to his family?"

"Some of the stories, yes." The servants liked to gossip just as much as their masters.

"People assume that's what drove him to drink. But, no. He was a drinker before that. Percy went to war for the King in the hope of bathing in enough blood to drown the memories of what he had done before, because the wine was incapable of doing it for him. That's what obeying the King gets you."

Thomas had never seen Sir Baldon in this light. As a murderer he had always seemed so unlikely, but if he really had that much blood on his hands, surely killing for a suitable reason would prove no problem at all.

"Anyway, it would be hard to overstate the time, the lives, the money that went into modifying this place when Prospero decided – about ten years ago, after the war – that he wanted it to hold his revels with all his little friends," Sir Marcus shook his head. "Those rooms downstairs, do you have any idea what all that material cost? And how many people were expected to give it for free because it was for the Prince? Everyone let it happen because the wake of the war was wide and long, and left many too terrified to oppose anything related to the King; but it's the exact kind of waste we had seen before the war, too: taking more and more, purely to please himself."

Could he, Thomas wondered, really be expected to become a part of such a system?

"People starve for lack of food, but the King has spent his life simply holding out his hand so that whatever he wants may be placed into it. And the more he took, the more he wasted, and the more people suffered. And the ones giving it to him – men with titles, with land, with influence given to them *by* the King – hoped he might listen to some reason, and see the request as a hope for just sheer base human decency, but—" he threw his hands up into the air.

"Did the other guests here know you opposed the King?"

Sir Marcus smiled without joy. "It's hardly the sort of thing you can keep quiet."

"But the Prince pardoned you."

"He did."

"How?"

"We were in jail, Will and I, as traitors to the crown. Prospero sent a man with the proposal; Will accepted and we were set free that very day."

"And people had to accept it."

"They did. Though none of them *liked* it."

'Two measures of power, lad…'

"Did they – the guests here – know that you were pardoned because of me?"

"That Suzann bore you as the Prince's heir, you mean? There were rumours – try keeping a secret among that lot. I was unaware that Percy knew, for one. But you forget: if the King decrees it, and the Prince is an extension of the King, then it *happens*. No-one gets to demand justification from the crown. Maybe some of the King's circle heard of it, maybe even the King himself – but I doubt he cared; the war was over by then, he was looking elsewhere for his amusements. Some of the guests here might have heard of you, fathered by Prospero and being raised by Will. But whether they'd have had the guts to ask to see your tattoo in a couple of years is another thing. If they had offended you here, well, they might fear you'd turn and bite them in the years ahead."

Thomas tilted his head:

"My tattoo?" He had no tattoos.

Sir Marcus smiled.

"There are stories – and they may just be stories – of men turning up, claiming to be the true heir to a throne, having been swapped at birth with another baby. It's hardly unexpected – desperate people try desperate things. And so to ensure power passes the right way, either to a newborn son from wedlock or—" he motioned to Thomas, "to an illegitimate son who is of age, a tattoo is etched on the heir to identify him as such. It's said it comes from the days when princes would join their armies in battle, so an important body could be more easily identified among the dead, but…"

"They tattoo *babies*?"

"They do."

"But then someone could tattoo themself and claim to be

the heir."

A smile crept through Sir Marcus' beard, as if he was pleased with this observation.

"They could, but only the father – the King, the Prince – and his closest allies know what the tattoo looks like and where it is. A record is kept in the palace, and two witnesses are sworn to complete secrecy to protect the heir against kidnap or," he gestured vaguely, "influence – allowed to pass on their knowledge only if they know they are to die.

"You," he gestured to Thomas, "are too young. Seventeen was selected as the minimum age of acknowledgement of those from the other side of the blanket, to give the father a chance to ensure his heir had grown into the sort of man who *should* receive such power. If you're raised outside the palace, well, you might encounter—" he gestured to himself wryly, "— corrupting influences."

Thomas thought back to the early days in the castle, when guests and other servants alike had been present. Had his treatment at the hands of the other servants been due to rumours about his parentage? Would they pick on him as a way of attacking the Prince? Or – and this would take some getting used to – would they have been too scared of him? And would any of the Prince's guests even have trusted their servants with such knowledge?

"No-one ever said anything. About my father. No-one here, I mean."

"They may have been ignorant of it; for all his faults, Percy knows how to respect tradition; he'd keep his mouth shut. Someone obviously spoke out of turn – with all due respect to Percy, he'd hardly be in Prospero's confidences – but at best you would have been a rumour. You've never been to the palace, never been in the Prince's presence before now." He gestured and changed the subject, "For all we know, the King himself might be dead, yes?"

"Yes," Thomas felt uneasy even thinking this.

"We may find out in a year, or someone may walk up to the castle today, having come to collect Prospero so that he can take the throne. It takes time for that sort of information to spread, even something as important as the death of the King. No-one apart from the six of us knows that Prospero is dead, after all. So maybe someone had heard of you, maybe someone was convinced they *knew* Prospero was your father, but as to spreading that information around…"

Thomas swallowed.

"Wh-where is he?"

"Prospero? After we were done shouting at each other last night he was put in the food stores to keep cool."

"He's next door?"

Sir Marcus nodded.

"Can I see him?"

The big man sat perfectly still for a moment.

Thomas shifted uneasily under his gaze. "What?"

"You're probably in charge now. If you want to see him, say so and we'll all fall over ourselves to make it happen."

Thomas stood. "Can we?"

"Of course."

Sir Marcus rose and they stepped into the corridor and turned to the right. The food stores were in the western wall of the castle on this level, against the moat where the warm sun never struck and the stone-walled rooms remained cool. Taking his key from around his neck, Sir Marcus put it in the lock of the first door. "He was moved while you and I were speaking last night. To which room, I am unaware."

The first room, windowless and dry, stood maybe a quarter full of casks and boxes, with no sign of the Prince's body. The second, emptier of provisions, was also bare. The third room contained only the body, which in the faint light from the doorway could be dimly made out laying on the floor close to the rear wall.

"Do you want to go in?"

Thomas bristled at the suggestion of his fear.

"Calm down, lad," Sir Marcus said, sensing his rising hackles, "you only said you wanted to *see* him, nothing more."

Thomas felt himself flush. "Sorry. I would, yes. T-to say goodbye."

"I'll get a light."

Sir Marcus headed back to the kitchens, and Thomas stared into the windowless room. As his eyes adjusted, he thought he could make out beneath the body the edge of a wooden vanity screen from the bedrooms, presumably used to carry the dead Prince into the room.

Sir Marcus returned with one of the oil lamps, its flame brighter than that of a candle. Handing it over, he said "I'll wait here," and stepped back from the door.

Thomas drew in a breath, and stepped into the room.

The light of the lamp filled the confined space, tapering out only at the edges, and Thomas could make out the body more clearly now – lying on its back, the head towards the left-hand wall and the feet to the right, arms by its sides. An impression of wrongness struck him briefly, doubtless due to the odd shadows thrown by the lamp. He stepped closer, his eyes moving up from the wooden screen on which the body lay to look at the man he now knew had sired him, and suddenly he saw that the wrongness came, rather than from the dancing of shadows, from the body itself.

He screamed.

Sir Marcus was by his side in an instant, and all Thomas could do was raise his hand and point.

"God's bones!"

On the floor in front of them, the Prince's head leaned oddly to the side because it had been severed at the neck, and then placed back as if still attached to the body. The ragged flesh of the throat leered at them in the lamp's glow. In the shifting light, they could see also that the right hand, nearest to them, had been severed at the shattered wrist and replaced as if resting by the Prince's side. The right foot had similarly been cut at the ankle, above the top of the shoe, and replaced.

Sir Marcus took the lamp from Thomas' petrified fingers and approached the body. He lifted the light as he moved forward, enabling them to see that the left foot had also been cut through at the ankle and placed back as if still attached.

The left hand had also been severed, and was missing.

On the floor by the stump of the left wrist lay the short axe used for chopping wood in the kitchen, its blade stained with blood. Sir Marcus used the lamp to look into the corners of the room. No sign of the missing hand could be found, nor any gap large enough for it to have been taken through.

He turned and inspected the corners of the room behind them, while Thomas stood staring at his father's broken corpse.

When Sir Marcus spoke, his voice was dry and strained: "We need to tell Will."

Thomas, uncomprehending, allowed himself to be ushered out into the corridor. Sir Marcus locked the door, placed the lamp on the floor, and led the way to the stairs.

SEVENTEEN

They ascended the nearest stairs to the first floor and turned to their left; Sir William's room was the second one along.

"Will!" Sir Marcus called, banging on the door with the underside of his fist. "Will, open the door!"

There was no reply.

"Will!" he continued to hammer.

A sudden fear gripped Thomas, a memory of the body of Sir Oswin Bassingham found in a sealed room only two days before. What if...?

He heard bolt slide open. The door drifted slightly ajar.

Thomas and Sir Marcus exchanged a look, relief on the big man's face that no doubt mirrored Thomas' own, and stepped into the room.

"Lock the door, lad, er, sire," Sir Marcus said, and Thomas did, turning back just in time to see his master disappear behind the curtain of his bed, still dressed in the clothes he had been wearing the night before.

"Will," the elder Collingwood's voice was kinder now as he stood by the side of the bed. "Will we need you to—"

"To what?" Sir William's voice snapped from behind the curtain. "What could you possibly *need* me for now, Marcus?" He sounded exhausted, defeated.

Sir Marcus took hold of the edge of the curtain and eased it back. The pale, angry face of his younger brother appeared in the gloom, and Thomas had to suppress a gasp at how drawn and tired his master looked – more so even than the Prince after he had been attacked, the same dark circles under his eyes, dark slashes of his eyebrows standing out on his waxy skin. The death of Laurence had struck him hard, Thomas knew, but these added mysteries were clearly taking their toll.

"Will..."

"It's the Prince's body, Sir William it—" Thomas was

stopped by the bitter, wolfish look that sprang to his master's face.

"What do you think, Marcus?" he turned to his brother, "Am I *Sir* William because I am *his* master or because he is *mine*?"

Thomas swallowed. He had no idea what to say; it occurred to him that Sir William might be drunk, but there was no smell of stale alcohol in the room.

"Will…"

"What, Marcus, *what*?! You need my help? Three men are dead and you need my help? I stood over the Prince while he fought for his last breath and you *need my help*?"

He eyed them furiously.

Sir Marcus' reply was low and calm: "You said yesterday that you had an idea what was going on."

Sir William's laugh was more of a bark: "Ha! Yesterday, yes. Oswin wanted to declare the Prince unfit to rule, to remove his powers – that was what we had spent so long discussing. It takes time, you know, to tear power from the hands of those who cling on so desperately. Someone *killed* Oswin to stop him doing that, to keep Prospero in place."

Thomas stood aghast: they had been going to remove the Prince from power?

"But that hardly works, does it, now someone has also killed Prospero." Sir William pressed the palms of his hands hard against his eyes. "It is unlikely, I think you'd agree, that someone would kill one man to keep a second in power only to then kill that *second* man." He sagged forward on the bed, letting out a exhausted sigh and simply hanging in place without breathing in. Thomas waited, watching, half expecting the man to have died, another impossibility to add to those of recent days.

"So," Thomas ran the previous evening's conversation through his mind, "Sir Oswin *was* murdered?"

Everything was happening too quickly. He felt as if he was sprinting just to keep up.

Sir William turned his head, opened one eye. "He was."

"But you said—"

"Yes, I lied to Prospero; I had told him I would, I thought it would keep us safe. And then somehow he—".

"Was Laurence murdered, too? It is untrue that he was touched by the Red Death while hiding Sir Oswin's corpse?"

"Come on, lad," Sir Marcus said as if it were obvious, "even I knew *that* was a lie."

Thomas tried to think:

Sir Oswin had been murdered.

They had been going to remove the Prince from power.

Laurence had also been murdered.

They had been going to remove the prince from power!

"B-but the cut on Laurence's thigh…"

Sir William smiled genuinely for the first time; only faintly, but enough to give Thomas hope. "I may have done that when Fergus was distracted."

"Why?"

"Because," his master's voice, though weary, was measured and reasonable, "when somebody stabs your closest friend in the chest in the middle of a plague that travels in the blood, it's worth considering how you can put the bastard at ease so you can fit together the explanation that will later wring his neck."

Thomas tried to imagine the cold fury of being able to plan that far ahead while standing over the dead body of your closest friend. Sir William's foresight was either impressive or terrifying, Thomas found it difficult to choose between them.

Still, he had questions:

"So did Sir Oswin survive the Red Death?"

"Nobody survives the Red Death," Sir William said, his eyes closed again. "Nobody."

"But—" this to Sir Marcus, "you called him The Man Who

Would Never Die."

Sir Marcus looked at him oddly. "Do you know what generals do in a war?"

Thomas had no idea.

"They sit at the back and send men like Will forward to do the fighting. Oswin was good, his tactics were the very best even against farmers and women, but he was hardly going to risk himself in the fighting – *especially* against farmers and women."

The Man Who Would Never Die, hiding from the violence he orchestrated.

"So," this to Sir Marcus, "how did you know Sir William was lying? About Sir Oswin having the Red Death?"

His real question: *What did I miss?*

Sir Marcus raised his hand to his chest. "Because Will said—"

"Enough!" Sir William said. "Oswin was murdered, Laurence was murdered, Prospero was murdered, none of it makes sense."

They fell silent.

"There might be more than one killer," Sir Marcus said.

Sir William raised his head with great effort. "What?"

"You say someone killed Oswin to keep Prospero in power. Maybe someone else, knowing of Oswin's plan, killed Prospero because there's now no other way to remove him with Oswin dead. Who else did you discuss it with?"

Sir William shook his head. "No-one here."

Thomas thought he understood: it was probably treason, and so punishable by death. You would guard that closely.

Aware of the difficulties he was reopening, he asked "Could whoever attacked the Prince before have killed him this time?"

Surely nothing was impossible for a man who could vanish into thin air.

Sir William waved a hand, dismissing this. "The man who

attacked the Prince before had no interest in killing him."

"How do you know?"

"Because—" Sir Marcus started to say.

"Because," his brother interrupted, "in a castle filled with people who have killed for many, many years, none of us would attempt to murder Prospero by choking the life out of him. It is," he swallowed, "a horrible, drawn out way to kill a man, and takes so long that you would risk discovery if he fought back. We, any of us, would stab him in the chest, or slit his throat, and be done with it."

Thomas was aware that he should feel some connection to this; they were, after all, discussing the murder of his father. Instead it remained still a series of questions with no answers that made sense.

"Well," Sir Marcus scratched at his hair, "whoever killed him last night, they made sure of it when they cut his head off."

Sir William's head snapped up. "What?"

"That's why we're here – I would have mentioned it sooner, but you were too busy being…" he gestured, "sad."

"What happened?"

"The body downstairs," Thomas suppressed a shudder, "someone has cut off the head and hands and feet."

Sir William, suddenly alert, looked from one to the other. "And taken them?"

"Taken one of them," Sir Marcus said.

"*One* of them?"

The big man nodded.

"You really should see this for yourself, Will. I think we're in serious trouble"

~

Back in the storage room, Thomas stood against the inside of the closed door while Sir William and Sir Marcus examined the

Prince's corpse. As he waited, he thought about how Sir William's explanation for the deaths of Sir Oswin and Laurence had been pure invention. And yet somehow he had missed what Sir Marcus had spotted.

'Because Will said—'

Said what?

He brought his mind back to the present, watched Sir Marcus holding the lamp so that his brother could examine the wounds inflicted upon the body on the floor. Sir William moved carefully; having first examined the body as a whole, he was now engaged in picking up each of the severed extremities and looking closely at them and the stump of the body from which they had been severed. He replaced each carefully before moving on.

That the cutting had been done in here there was little doubt: Thomas could see the scored marks on the vanity screen beneath the corpse where the small axe had bitten into the wood after passing through the flesh. Several blows had been required to cut through the muscles and bone, and the tissue at neck, wrist, and ankle alike was a pulped ruin from which no observations could be drawn.

After examining the stump of the left arm closely for some time, Sir William replaced it beside the corpse and sank to his haunches. Sir Marcus backed against the wall and, Thomas staring at the curve of his master's shoulders, they waited for Sir William to speak.

"Prospero's hand bore no scars or injuries, did it?"

"None that I saw," Sir Marcus said.

"I suppose," Sir William said slowly, "these *are* Prospero's hands and feet. Of the head there is no doubt, but the others…"

"Where would they have come from otherwise?" Sir Marcus asked after a pause.

"Laurence?" his brother suggested. "He was wrapped in a sheet."

Thomas' stomach lurched.

"No," Sir Marcus said quickly. "Before I carried Laurence into the courtyard I gave him back the ring he had given to me. He had his hands, I promise you."

Sir William held his brother's eye for a moment, and nodded slightly.

"So unless someone *else* here is dead and handless…"

A chill went through Thomas as he took Sir William's idea and turned it around. What if…?

"I suppose," Sir Marcus said, "whoever cut the hand off *is* the person who took it."

Sir William backed against the wall opposite his brother and Thomas saw him grin, a face made horrible by the dancing shadows that nevertheless gave the appearance of his old vitality returning.

"You're both so keen to see two plots at work."

"Is that so unthinkable?"

"It would require one man to come in here with that," Sir William pointed to the kitchen axe, which lay at Sir Marcus' feet, "with the express intention of chopping off parts of a dead body only to leave them behind. And then someone *else* comes in, discovers – or maybe suspecting – the butchery and steals the hand as a souvenir?"

Sir Marcus remained quiet, admitting the point.

"If there were twenty men and women this castle, I would happily concede that these parallel plots, these seemingly contradictory plans, might exist. To accept that two of Baldon, Fergus, and Zachariah have separate, rational, and such starkly different intentions is too much."

"They must have stayed for a reason," Thomas said, his horrible idea still churning inside him. "At the castle, I mean, for all these months."

He understood now why he the three of them had stayed – or he thought he did – but could the others have more than the obvious reasons for still being here after all this time?

"They're all loyal to Prospero in their own way," Sir William said. "I see none of them wanting to kill him."

"So it was one of us three?" Sir Marcus said, and his brother smiled grimly.

"Is it really the Prince?" Thomas asked, trying to voice his idea.

Both men turned to look at him.

"You recognise him, yes?" Sir Marcus pointed his free hand towards the butchered head, the face still clear despite the damage to the throat and neck.

How to explain?

"It's his head. But if it might have been someone else's hands and feet, could it be someone else's...body?"

The brothers exchanged a glance.

"So," Sir William said slowly, "someone *else* was killed last night, after we went to bed, and their body put here because we'd *expect* a body to be here – their head was removed so Prospero's head could be put in its place, and the hands and feet cut off so the severed head drew no undue attention..."

"Why would they have to be killed last night?" Thomas asked.

"There are no other fresh bodies – Laurence was cremated, Oswin we threw back into the moat and, anyway, he was too badly injured to pass as Prospero. Someone else would have to die to complete the illusion. Have either of you seen anyone else today?"

"I spoke with Zachariah," Thomas said, and Sir Marcus shook his head.

"But why only take one hand, Will? And what would they do with Prospero's body? That would still have to be hidden somewhere."

"One thing at a time."

Thomas remembered then: "Would he have a tattoo?"

Sir William looked at him.

"Sir Marcus told me they tattoo heirs—" he started to say, but stopped when he saw Sir William's smile.

Without a word, his master turned to the body and began to undo the buttons down the front of the garment the Prince had been wearing when he died. Sir Marcus approached, holding out the lamp to aid his brother's task. When the buttons were opened to the crotch, Sir William eased the shoulders out of the clothes, the severed head rolling grotesquely on the floor as the neck was lifted, and pulled the sleeves down over the stumps of the arms, revealing the close-fitting undergarments around the corpse's legs.

Thomas stepped forward, transfixed.

Sir William turned and took the knife from his brother's belt, and slit the corpse's undergarments from the thigh down, tearing the material aside to expose the Prince's nether regions. Taking the thigh in his hands, he turned the leg outwards until a dark mark was exposed.

Sir William sighed with relief. "It's Prospero. That's his mark."

Thomas had seen few tattoos in his life, and leaned in to look. The shape of what might be a crown, blurred at the edges and with what looked like letters underneath, was drawn on the skin of the Prince's inside leg.

"How do you know?" Thomas asked.

"He showed us once, when drinking."

Thomas tried to picture Sir William and the Prince drinking together.

"Recently?"

"No, a long time ago. Before the war."

"And you remember?"

"Remember the heir to the kingdom getting his dick out?" Sir Marcus asked. "Yes, he probably does."

Thomas could find no argument against that.

"But it could have been done to someone recently. The tattoo. It still might be someone else's body."

"No, lad," Sir Marcus stood back, the light moving with him, "tattoos fade and blur over time. That's an old mark."

Thomas stepped back and Sir William stood, his knees popping.

"So," Sir William said, "it *is* Prospero. We know that someone killed him, and, after his body was placed in here, that someone came back down in the night, took the axe from the kitchen, chopped off his head, his hands, and his feet, and then took the left hand away with them. We know they *took* the hand because there are no gaps anywhere in this room large enough for it to have passed through, even if a rat could get in here. So why? Why take that hand?"

"To hide it somewhere and make someone else look guilty?" Thomas said.

Sir William's face twitched in disagreement.

"But then we would have to accept that someone would carry away, and hide somewhere telling, a hand – a *hand* – that they *know* would see them accused of...something, possibly murder, if discovered."

"Maybe someone cut the hand up into pieces and left it here so that rats could come and take it away," Sir Marcus suggested.

"Then where are they?" Sir William asked. "The taste of blood would bring them out in large numbers. They would hardly take the hand and leave the body...unmolested."

Sir Marcus conceded the point.

The three of them stood in silence, thinking.

"The only person who has ever harmed the Prince," Thomas said, "is whoever attacked him. I know, I know—" seeing Sir William about to object, "but if we could understand that..."

Thomas expected some argument, but instead Sir William simply looked at his brother and the big man put the lamp down at his feet, turned for the door, and stepped into the corridor, closing the door behind him.

Thomas looked at Sir William.

"He'll be back."

Faintly, Thomas heard another door being unlocked.

Sir William stood in silence.

"Were you really going to remove Prince Prospero from power?" Thomas asked, aware of the oddness that had descended with Sir Marcus' sudden exit.

"We were. He was hiding here, abandoning his people, doing nothing. He had the wealth and the influence to help, and he refused. Either he had to be persuaded to leave, or someone else should have been given his means and put them to good use."

"Is that why you stayed? To try to convince him to help?"

"In part."

Thomas now knew the other part.

The door opened, and Sir Marcus entered carrying a wooden box, in which would normally be found the larger candles used around the castle – perhaps a cubit to each side. He closed the door behind him, and looked at his brother.

"It is perhaps time we cleared this up," Sir William said, "as it is getting in the way of your thinking and I need your help. Whoever attacked the Prince before – the man you saw dressed as the Red Death who vanished into thin air – was in no way responsible for the Prince's death, or for this desecration."

Thomas was unconvinced, "How can you *know* that?"

Sir William gestured to his brother, and Sir Marcus raised the box above his head and dashed it against the stone floor, the *crack* of its impact loud in the closed space. Thomas saw a flash of colour as the wood splintered.

A flash of red.

Sir Marcus kicked away the broken slats of the box, and the red peeping out became more pronounced.

And, within, something white.

Something smooth.

"Because it was me," Sir William said.

Sir Marcus' feet moved more broken wood aside. What remained took on a form that sent Thomas' mind reeling: red fabric and a smooth, white, grinning skull from one of Terrington Fenwick's battle horses looked up at him from the floor.

"I was dressed as the Red Death," Sir William continued. "I attacked the Prince."

EIGHTEEN

The problem of the disappearing man had loomed so large in Thomas' mind these last few days, at first he refused to believe that a solution to it would ever be found. For the solution to come from *this* source and in *this* form made it even harder to accept.

"N-no," he said after a few moments, "you...y-you followed Sir Baldon down into the dungeons..."

"And how do you know that?"

"Because yo—" suddenly he saw it. "Because you told me."

Sir William spread his hands. "You and Marcus, you accounted for each other; Fergus, Zachariah, and Laurence were in the Prince's room together, and Fergus sent Baldon away down to the dungeon *after* you had chased the man in the robe down there. No-one ever said they saw me follow Baldon – I told *them* that, and trusted that they would have been too busy at the time to notice or care otherwise."

Understanding tumbled into place in Thomas' mind; he looked to Sir Marcus for confirmation and saw the big man watching him without emotion.

Thomas pressed his hands against his eyes, saw colours spark in the darkness before looking to his master again. "So what happened?"

Sir William almost smiled, "Well, firstly you were supposed to get out of the way so I could flee into the castle, hide the robe, and reappear. When you refused to move I feared that, were I to push past you, you might grab at the robe and reveal me, so I had to come up with a new plan." He motioned to his brother, "Thankfully, Marcus was on hand to help with that.

"Marcus followed me into the dungeons while everybody else gathered upstairs, and we devised a plan on the spot: I would run into the red room, pull the robe off, wrap it around the skull and hide it against the back wall, where the sails of material would mask it – it's the same material, from the same source, so it was easy to overlook. Marcus would collect it later and hide it next door."

"You would have been suspected," Thomas said.

"Yes," Sir Marcus agreed, "it was a bad plan made on the run. Thankfully we heard you coming down the stairs to balls it up for us."

Thomas waited blankly for his master to continue.

"We pretended to fight, so that Marcus would be unable to chase me, and I ran around the *other* way to get far enough ahead of you so that I could take this off," he poked a toe at the material on the floor, "and hide it in the red room as planned. So long as I was the one to search where I had hidden it, its presence need never be known.

"Once the robe was off, I was going hide in the Prince's stairway until you came into view, and then emerge into the dungeons – you may have seen through it, but I was hoping we would have time to explain afterwards. Instead, I heard Marcus shout Baldon's name – in warning to me, I assumed – as he appeared in the dungeons. So I ducked down behind the furniture in the white room, masked by the skirts of a couch, and after Baldon passed I stood up and followed him just as you came around the corner."

Thomas' brain was in a frenzy.

"No."

Sir William looked confused. "No?"

"Laurence and the others in the Prince's room would have seen that you failed to follow Sir Baldon down the stairs."

He shook his head at the way he expressed it, but the confusion on Sir William's face cleared.

"You mean when Baldon came down the staircase from the Prince's chamber – Laurence or Fergus or Zachariah would have noticed that only Baldon entered those stairs, and that I was nowhere to be seen?"

Thomas nodded, but Sir William seemed unconcerned.

"How many times have you used the Prince's private staircase since we have been in the castle?" he asked reasonably. "Aside from that morning, I mean."

Thomas remembered the disapproval in Fergus Highstone's voice when they had spoken about this. "None."

"Correct. None of us *can* use it. It has its own key, it is clearly there for the Prince's private use – and that of anyone he permits, of course, but they're going *up* it rather than down." He moved half a step closer to Thomas. "Now, would someone like Baldon – married to tradition, insisting on a new table for the Prince's return, desperate to secure the succession of the crown even while Prospero lays newly dead at his feet – ever *dream* of using the private staircase of the Prince, even in a moment of crisis? When Fergus said that he sent Baldon immediately down the stairs, I knew that Baldon would have *left* the Prince's room and taken the stairs off the corridor without even *thinking* of setting foot in a stairway reserved for royalty."

Unable to deny this, Thomas turned to Sir Marcus. "You knew."

The big man nodded. "I did."

"The fight was staged."

"It was."

"You were unhurt."

He flashed a disappointed smile. "I'd hardly be cutting up dining tables with a giant axe if I had taken the kicking it appeared, would I?"

In a daze, Thomas remembered the ease with which the heavy axe had flowed through Sir Marcus' hands – and, now he thought of it, the nonchalant way the big man had pulled himself one-handed up the brazier tripods to light the flames there. If attacked as it had appeared, Sir Marcus would surely have had injuries that prevented him from doing these things.

'Still got the bruises to prove it.'

"That is also," Sir Marcus continued, "why the Prince's plan to join us for dinner was a problem. I knew Percy would be in here – well, next door – picking through the supplies. I'd hidden the costume in there. If he had found that, we were probably done for."

How had all of this passed him by?

"You could have told me earlier."

Sir William failed to disagree. "We could, but think of it as a test of your reasoning. I wanted to see if you would notice that *I* was the flaw, the one who was making the problem seem impossible. There was no harm in playing along, since I knew that the disappearance of the Red Death had no bearing on the murders we have since confronted. And, by asking questions about that attack, we have also been able to make progress in our true intention: finding out who killed our friend and—" he indicated the corpse at their feet, "others."

Any growing resentment in Thomas' mind was pushed aside by the body in the room, by what it represented. "W-why would you attack the Prince, though? Was it because...because he...lay with Lady Suzann?"

Sir William sighed, a sound as sad and heavy as Thomas had ever heard his master make. "I have had plenty of years to regret that arrangement. You really think I would wait until now to enact such a petty vengeance?"

"Then...why?"

Sir William turned to look down at the broken body on the floor. "You said, a short while ago, that those of us who have stayed here must have our reasons for doing so. But why did we come in the first place? Oswin was here on the orders of the King, to keep an eye on his heir; Fergus and Zachariah are in the Prince's service, so have an obligation to be wherever he is; Baldon came because of the attraction of power, hoping that the old ways would be restored. But Marcus and I, why do you think we came?"

Thomas knew the answer now: "Because Prince Prospero was my father."

Sir William tilted his head without looking up. "We could have come simply because Prospero requested your presence. But is that enough? Had we refused, he may have sought answers, but Marcus and I have done more for him than many of those who surround him – fear is a motivation we barely feel any more. So why would I abandon the woman I love, leave my home and the people I care about, and drag you and Marcus here, and *stay* here to rot here surrounded by men who want only to preserve their influence?"

That word – 'influence' – recalled to Thomas that which Sir William had said only a short while before: '*He had the wealth and the influence to help, and he refused.*'

"You wanted to change his mind."

Sir William looked almost grateful.

"When the people who have given you everything start to die, and when the avatar of their death is sweeping the kingdom and destroying lives without pause or remorse or pity or reason, surely you owe those people more than just hiding away and deciding that the external world can take care of itself. We came because I hoped that Prospero had a plan, I decided we should stay because he had no interest in forming one."

"How did attacking him change that?"

"If I could stop him feeling safe, if I could get him to look beyond his own comfort, get him to imagine the fear of the people he had turned his back upon..." he shook his head. "When I found the costume, in a room on the top floor, Oswin had already resolved to speak with Prospero to convince him to stand down, to give up his powers. I hoped that, if he was shaken out of his complacency that morning before Oswin spoke to him, he might finally see sense and step aside, let those of us who wanted to do some good have a chance before it was too late."

"You could have reasoned with him."

"What do you think I've been *doing* for the last..." he gestured futilely with his hands, "...how long have we been here?"

Sir Marcus grunted in agreement.

"Every chance I had, I have tried to speak with Prospero, to plead with him." He flung a hand out in Thomas' direction, the fingers splayed "I kept his secret, he had no cause to doubt my loyalty or my intent. But there was no reasoning with the man; he was content to cower here, afraid, like the spoiled child he always was."

Sir William sank to the floor.

"You were angry with him," Thomas said after a pause.

"I was disappointed in him."

"You were angry with him."

Sir William looked up, "Why do you say that?"

"Because you choked him half to death!"

"No." Sir William was resolute.

"What?"

"No. He came to no harm at my hands."

How could Sir William possibly deny this?

"He was recovering his in room for over a day!"

"Will never hurt him, lad," Sir Marcus said, "I can promise you that."

Thomas looked at his feet, and the blank sockets of Terrington Fenwick's long-dead horse gazed up at him from the sea of red on which it sat. Would they really seek to deny what he had seen with his own eyes? He looked at the Prince's body, and saw that the severing of the head had left far too much damage around the throat and neck for the bruises there to prove his point.

Sir William evidently saw where his eyes had gone: "What

did you see, Thomas, when you and Marcus burst into the Prince's room that morning?"

Thomas was suddenly exhausted. He had expected more of them both.

"You were standing behind him, with your hands—" he raised his hands to his own throat, his thumbs pointing backwards.

Sir William agreed with him on this point, at least. "And when summoned to his room the next day, he showed you his throat, the bruises there?"

"No, they were hidden by a high collar."

Sir William tilted his head. "They were hidden by the ruff he wore at dinner, too."

"Yes."

"And when he died, and we were trying to save him, do you remember what you saw?"

Thomas thought back to the Prince's feet scraping at the stone floor of the main hall with less and less urgency as his life ebbed away. He started to nod, then paused, the image fixed in his mind.

...the firelight dancing on the bare skin of the corpse's chest and neck...

"There were," he looked from Sir William to Sir Marcus, and then to the body on the floor, the throat ragged and bloody where the bruises should have been, "there were no marks on his throat."

Sir William was watching him closely.

"You're certain?"

...the firelight dancing on the bare skin of the corpse's chest and neck...

...the bare skin of the corpse's chest and neck...

Thomas thought again. He was. The skin of the Prince's neck and throat had been bare, unmarked, without any indication that he had come to any harm.

200

The madness deepened.

~

It was a few moments before Sir William spoke.

"I promise you, Thomas, that I used no violence on him; I wanted him unsettled, waking to find a masked man in his room and knowing that he was no longer safe. That moment of shock would have been enough – it was all managed so that Marcus could intervene quickly: I tied back the curtains at the base of the bed so it was easy to see what was happening, Marcus was to ask if you had heard a noise so that I would know you were both outside.

"To stop Prospero doing anything foolish, I had planned to kneel over him and hold him down on the bed, but as I approached him after unbolting the door he awoke and jerked upright, cried out at the sight of me and tried to twist away. I grabbed his nightshirt to pull him back and was holding him against the wall one-handed when you entered. He was no fighter – look at how he simply lay down on the bed while you two chased off his attacker, then allowed others to flock around him as if *he* was injured."

"He did love attention," Sir Marcus said, almost admiringly.

"Whoever has done this to his body, I believe now that they are trying to hide the lack of bruises to Prospero's throat. When the ruff was torn away, someone noticed the absence of bruising, and has hidden this because he wants the attack on the Prince by the Red Death – by me – *and* his murder to be seen as part of the same scheme, and blamed on the same person."

Thomas thought hard, trying to make sense of this new design. "Then why take the hand?" he asked, his mind still spinning.

Sir William shrugged. "Perhaps because if we are asking *that* question then we may forget to look at the throat and the destruction of the evidence there. If just the head were severed, it would be clear that the destruction of the throat was the killer's purpose; cutting off the extremities, and removing one of them and probably throwing it into the moat – that seems to be where our killer likes to hide things – throws us into disarray if we allow it to."

They sat in silence. Thomas stared at the blank eyes of the skull on the floor.

"I am sorry to ask, Will," Sir Marcus said, "but are you any closer to understanding how he died?"

"The poisoning of Prospero defies explanation." Sir William sounded defeated again.

"Could someone have thrown some poison into the cup, as I was passing it to the Prince?" Thomas asked.

"They could," Sir Marcus said. "Prospero could even have put the poison in himself. Problem is, he would need some poison to do it."

Thomas was confused. "But, the rats."

"Yes?"

"We...poison the rats."

Sir Marcus shook his head. "We boil frogs, lad."

Sir William exhaled sharply through his nose as if in bitter amusement, and Thomas looked between the brothers waiting for an explanation.

"You put a frog in boiling water," Sir Marcus said, "what does it do?"

"Jump out?"

"Right. It's too hot, the frog knows straight away that something is wrong. You boil a frog slowly: put it in cold water, put a little fire under it, heat it up a little at a time – warmer and warmer, so to frog fails to notice the rising temperature. By the time it notices the water is too hot, it's probably too late."

Thomas waited.

"Rats are the same – canny little bastards. Put food down for rats, and they typically wait for another one to eat it first, wait to see if *that one* dies before they'll eat it themselves. If the poison is instant, only a few of them will have eaten it, and the rest avoid any further poison you put out. So you poison rats like you boil frogs, a little at a time: we put a little in the bread every day – it's hardly strong enough to kill them right away, but every day they eat a bit, then a bit more. It builds up over several days, poisons them slowly, kills them once it's too late for them to stop eating. And, hopefully, the others fail to make the connection and so keep eating and keep dying."

"But it's still poisonous for people."

"It is," Sir Marcus agreed, "but can you imagine swallowing a single apple seed and dying on the spot?"

Thomas had never considered it. He had swallowed plenty of apple seeds in his life. "How much would you have to eat?"

The brothers exchanged a look, Sir William gestured vaguely. "A handful, a cupful – a lot."

"Too much for someone to put in the cup at the last minute without us noticing," Sir Marcus said.

A new idea suggested itself: "Could the *Prince* have been poisoned slowly, like we do with the rats? Someone feeding him a little, day after day?"

"And he just happened to drop dead at the most dramatic moment possible?" Sir Marcus asked flatly. "Will?"

Sir William bobbed his head in thought. "It's possible, but I find it hard to believe. After weeks of slow poisoning, someone just happens – without any of us seeing – to introduce into the cup the exact amount of poison at the exact moment needed to make him drop dead in front of us all? No. If we had found him dead in bed one morning, I could believe someone had been poisoning him for a long time, but dying as he did makes it doubtful. And, anyway, he would surely have shown signs of poisoning long before he died."

"Fergus," Sir Marcus said, and Sir William inclined his head in agreement.

"Master Highstone?"

Sir William turned to him. "He would know if Prospero showed signs of long-term poisoning. And, as he examined the Prince after my attack, he would surely have seen that there was no damage to Prospero's throat."

Sir Marcus exhaled through his nose. "We have to tell them."

"We do."

"They're going to be angry."

Sir William stood and smoothed his hands down his clothes. "They are. But one of them killed our friend."

Sir Marcus nodded, the brothers locked eyes.

"Right," the big man said with false brightness. "Time for a council of war."

NINETEEN

Having rung the bell, Sir Marcus retreated to the kitchens to finish eating, leaving Thomas and Sir William sitting at the table in the main hall. It was still too early to expect anyone to be awake, and so they anticipated a little wait while Sir Baldon and Fergus Highstone roused themselves, dressed, and descended. Thomas expected Zachariah to appear at any moment, however, and wanted to speak with Sir William before the bodyguard appeared:

"Could we fetch Lady Suzann a-and the others and bring them here?"

Sir William's eyes flickered briefly. "Why?"

For a moment, Thomas was unsure how to answer. Surely Sir William would be happier knowing that his wife was safe, and – the selfishness tugged at something inside of him – Thomas wanted to meet his mother face to face now knowing who she was.

"I…"

"You assume we are better off here."

"I just—"

"Do you think," Sir William continued calmly, "I would have left Suzann, left all of them, if I had doubts about their safety?"

"No…"

Sir William's voice became heavy with more than just wistfulness: "I think about her every day, I miss her every day, I have wanted to go to her every single day. But I would hardly have left her if I doubted her ability to look after herself, and the others we care for."

He stopped and Thomas waited, embarrassed.

"We are running out of food – you saw the stores – and we're dying one by one. We're stuck out here at the end of the world with an alcoholic, the world's worst bodyguard and, in the middle of a plague no-one survives, a medical man who is scared of blood. And somehow one of them is killing us. There is nothing here for anyone beyond slow starvation, except that we might get lucky and be murdered first." He sighed. "Honestly, I no longer know why we remain. We will convince Prospero of nothing now that he is dead, and even if we can discover who killed our friend, what kind of justice would they face?"

"S-so you want to leave?"

"I want to see my wife, Thomas; I want to hold her in my arms, I want to smell her hair, I am tired of pretending that I can cope without her. But if we leave, does Laurence go unavenged? And could I live with myself in that case?"

Thomas was saved from replying by the appearance of Fergus Highstone, his coloured sleeves in the gloom telling Thomas who it was before any more of the man was visible.

"Is there news?" he asked, emerging into the hall, his robes perhaps a little more disarranged than usual.

"We will wait for the others, if you agree."

Highstone made a noise of assent, approached his chair and stood behind it. Before sitting, he bowed to Thomas.

"Good morning, sire. I am sorry that you had to learn of your father as you did. It came as a surprise to me, too. We are, however, relieved to know that there is the opportunity for his line to continue."

Thomas dipped his head, with no idea what to say.

Highstone sat, and Thomas heard Sir Marcus enter the hall. "No Percy?"

"I knocked on his door," Highstone said. "He may be some time; it was a…late night for all of us."

Sir William leaned forward, eager.

"Fergus, before Baldon and Zachariah join us, I need to ask you something in confidence."

Interest flickered across Highstone's face. "Of course."

Sir William leaned in further. "We," he included Thomas and Sir Marcus in his glance, "have examined the Prince's body this morning and," Thomas wondered how much Sir William was about to reveal, and how much Highstone might already know, "it seems that there is no bruising around his throat from what we had assumed was the attack upon him."

Highstone's eyebrows rose minutely. "Truthfully?"

Thomas was unable to tell if this surprise was from the revelation of the lack of bruising, or from the ability of Sir William to perceive a lack of bruises on a corpse whose neck – Highstone might already know – had been destroyed under the blade of an axe.

"Truthfully. The Prince trusted you, Fergus, more than any of us – the King would hardly have appointed you to care for him if you were unworthy of trust." Highstone acknowledged the compliment, and Sir William continued, "You examined him after he was attacked, you must have seen that he was unharmed. I am asking you, please, to take us into your confidence that we might finally see some sense in these events."

Highstone sat in silence, as if weighing his responsibilities to the dead Prince.

"The body shows no signs of bruising, you say?"

"Thomas and Marcus," Sir William said after a pause, "both remembered that last night there was no discolouration around the Prince's throat, as might be expected had he been throttled."

This, at least, was closer to a version of the truth.

Highstone's eyes went to Thomas, then to Sir Marcus, and back to Sir William. The presence of other witnesses seemed to convince him to speak:

"Well," he said with a sigh, "it is no confidence now that the Prince is dead, I suppose. You are correct. When I examined the Prince in his room, I saw that there was no marking upon him – he told me that the attacker had held their hands around his throat, but his distress was more really a result of shock than any harm he had come to."

Thomas felt himself relax – he had never doubted Sir William's word, but hearing it confirmed by Highstone meant that the others, and he was thinking specifically of Zachariah, should accept this when told.

"We gathered in the dungeons, obviously concerned for Sir Oswin's whereabouts, and I was able to put the Prince's well-being out of my mind while I searched because I knew that he was unharmed. Upon hearing the bell, I came down past his room and spoke to him briefly in the absence of his bodyguard," a slight sneer in Highstone's voice here, "and suggested that he lock his door against any other attacks. As I came away I heard the bolt being engaged and then…"

Highstone sat back, and dropped his hands into his lap.

"And then?" Sir William prompted.

"Something *happened* to him. We were unable to rouse him. I had assumed at first that he was hiding, or that he was sleeping, and had no intention of disturbing him. It was only the following day that I was able to borrow from you the key to his private stairway and risk an entry. And, honestly, he looked…*awful*. I fear now that I missed something, that my understanding of my craft may be lacking. He had seemed in perfect health and good spirits, and it haunts me, gentlemen, what may have happened to him as a result of my oversight."

Thomas remembered their discussion about poisoning: "Did he eat anything?"

"I am unaware if he did. I took him no food, and the Prince was unlikely to sneak into the kitchens and feed himself. Perhaps Zachariah could tell us if he took anything up."

"You spoke with the Prince before he summoned Thomas," Sir William said.

Highstone regarded him in silence before replying. "I did."

"And before he joined us at the evening meal? Forgive me,

Fergus, I imply nothing by this, but Prospero himself said that you had assured him any discomfort he was in would ease in the coming days."

"Yes."

"And so the decision had been made between you both to give the impression that the Prince's injuries were more serious than they appeared."

"Why do you say that?"

Sir William gestured to his own throat with one hand. "He wore a high collar when Thomas spoke with him, and a ruff at dinner. We all assumed that this was to hide the bruises, but now it would appear it was instead to hide the *absence* of bruises, and to give the impression, added to by his words, that he had in fact been injured."

"Yes," Highstone said slowly, "that would be correct."

"Why?"

It was a simple question, but Thomas felt Highstone's manner chill.

"I thought better than to question the Prince when he made that request, Sir William."

Sir William seemed keen to smooth ruffled feathers. "Of course, of course. I mean no offence. I am simply trying to make sense of these events, as are we all."

Highstone smiled and bowed his head again, and Sir Baldon Gregory entered the hall. Bleary-eyed and unkempt, he made his way to his chair and sat.

"I apologise," he said, his voice thick. Thomas could smell the stale wine no doubt still coursing through his veins.

Sir William smiled. "Relax, Baldon, we are still waiting for Zachariah."

"That bodyguard's never around when you need him," Sir Marcus grumbled. "Should I ring the bell again?"

"I am reluctant to be kept waiting. Especially as there are important matters to discuss."

"Has something happened, Sir William?" Sir Baldon asked, then looked at Thomas as if in apology. It took Thomas a moment to realise that *he* might now be the senior person at this table.

Sir William paused, as if weighing the frustration of further delay, and, with a glance at Thomas, said: "Gentlemen, the Prince's body had been desecrated."

It took a few moments for these words to be appreciated. Sir Baldon drew himself up sharply in his chair and Highstone looked at Sir William more closely.

"When you say 'desecrated', Sir William..." the medical man prompted.

"His head, his hands, and his feet have been severed."

Sir Baldon swallowed thickly, Highstone sat back as if in shock.

"B-but," Sir Baldon stumbled out, "why?"

"I believe to hide the fact that there was no bruising to his neck, since the attack upon the Prince by the figure Thomas and Marcus saw was, in fact, no such thing."

Sir Baldon looked a lot more awake now. "But he was choked, he was unconscious in bed for most of a day..."

"No," Sir William said, "I barely touched him, as Fergus will confirm."

Thomas counted to three in his head before the reactions came:

"*You* attacked the Prince?!" Sir Baldon practically shrieked

"It was no attack," Sir William said calmly.

Highstone recoiled, as if distance between himself and Sir William was necessary to communicate his lack of collaboration. Sir Baldon jerked his head round, eyes wide, to look at Sir Marcus and then at Thomas, the lack of reaction from Sir William's household evidently being enough to convince him.

"Of course," Highstone said slowly, "we had only your

word for your presence. None of us saw you..."

Sir William met his eye unblinkingly.

"You realise, of course, that you have committed treason."

"I do."

"You seem," Highstone said, with the first touch of irritation in his voice, "oddly calm, Sir William, given that your actions set Prince Prospero on a course that may have seen one of us killed."

"How so, Fergus?"

Highstone gestured to the room at large, "When we were here last night, the Prince commanded we take an oath that would have seen us give testimony about this attack—"

"And," Sir William interrupted, "your testimony and the testimony of those with you would have seen you all cleared, since you had done no wrong. I put myself at risk, no-one else."

Highstone subsided as if in thought, and Sir Baldon finally found his voice:

"Doubtless your brother's poisonous views have impressed themselves upon you. It was obviously an error of judgement on His Highness' part when he trusted you with raising his issue—"

"Oh, do be quiet, Percy," Sir Marcus sounded tired. "There is no-one here to impress."

"It goes to show that inventing new titles for those who hardly deserve them—"

Sir Marcus shouted him down: "My brother earned his title trying to save the lives of innocents who were ordered slaughtered by a raving tyrant! And for raising the child of the Prince to ensure the continuation of his line. *You*, Percy, were simply the first life to crawl out of your mother's crack so that when your father died—"

"Marcus!"

"Your brother's title and *his* service are hardly in doubt, *Sir*

Marcus—"

"You think I *wanted* this?" the big man returned. "To be dressed up like the rest of you inbred, unctuous, murderous—"

"*Marcus!*"

"—to have every bastard here laughing behind their hands at my brother for the last thirteen years—"

"*Marcus!*"

Both men fell quiet, glaring hatefully at each other.

Fergus Highstone was the next to speak, his voice quiet: "You have your reasons for confessing to this, I presume, Sir William."

"I have two. Firstly to clear away any suspicion surrounding that attack. The Prince was unharmed – if I had wished him injured or dead, it would have been easy to achieve. Harming Prospero was never my intent, and neither was killing him."

"And the second?" Highstone asked in a frozen voice.

Sir William looked around the table, his voice unruffled, unhurried, infuriatingly calm when compared to the nervous itch Thomas could feel building in his hands and feet.

"The second is that since I bear no responsibility for the death of Prospero, nor Oswin, nor Laurence, you, Fergus, and you, Baldon, may consider yourselves warned."

"Warned?" Sir Baldon's anger at Sir Marcus seemed forgotten.

"Yes. You see, Zachariah should have joined us by now, especially as he is bound by his role to offer his services as a bodyguard to Thomas – and, indeed, would want to keep close to him in light of his recent events."

Thomas realised with a start that he had forgotten about Zachariah.

"So," Sir William continued, "I assume that whatever scheme you are pursuing required his death, and that when we search the castle shortly we shall find him murdered by the same hand that carries responsibility for the other deaths we have seen."

The horror was almost too much to face: Thomas had been speaking with the bodyguard that morning. Surely the man was still alive, and simply watching things from a distance. That one of the men at this table might have murdered him and then calmly joined the rest of them here chilled Thomas deeply.

"It will be difficult to kill us all," Sir William continued, "because we shall be even more watchful now, but let me promise you one thing: if any harm comes to Thomas or to my brother, I will throw both of you from the roof of this castle just to be certain that their killer has been punished."

Both Sir Baldon and Fergus Highstone endeavoured to look indignant. If Zachariah was dead, one of these two men knew it, and was hiding that knowledge behind an affected affront that surely only insanity could provide.

Eventually, Highstone spoke: "I think that is quite clear, Sir William."

Sir Baldon seemed reluctant to let his anger go:

"You seem certain, Sir William, that your brother bears no responsibility for this suspected murder. Are you certain that your fraternal bond is allowing you to see clearly?"

"I saw Zachariah this morning," Thomas said, aware for the first time that he was doing more than simply interrupting, and that the men had all turned to look at him as he spoke. "And I came down to the kitchens immediately afterwards to see Sir Marcus and have been with him ever since."

This was largely true – Sir Marcus had gone to collect the lamp to allow Thomas to view the Prince's body, and had been eating in the kitchen while he and Sir William waited here – but, as he had learned from his father, some claims are above question when the correct person makes them.

"I apologise, sire," Sir Baldon said with a bow of the head. "If Zachariah is indeed dead – and we must hope he is otherwise – then Sir Marcus is, of course, freed from all suspicion by your word."

Perhaps power had its benefits after all.

Sir William looked around the table.

"Any other question?"

There were none.

Sir William stood. "Then let us search, and hope we find nothing."

~

Sir Marcus was asked to provide them all with oil lamps to aid their searching, and haggled his brother down to just two on account of dwindling supplies. While he collected them from the equipment stores, Fergus Highstone rang the bell again in the hope of summoning the bodyguard from wherever he may be.

Zachariah failed to appear.

And so, provisioned with two burning lamps, the five of them began to comb the castle.

First the ground floor – the kitchens and the storerooms, enabling Sir Baldon and Highstone to see the damage wrought upon the Prince's body, one of them for the first time – and then upwards. If they found no sign of Zachariah in the bedrooms, Sir William said, he and Sir Marcus would search the revel rooms below. However, that space being so large and so complex, it made sense to examine the upper rooms first.

Between the floors, Sir Marcus was first to ascend the stairs, Sir Baldon went second, and Fergus Highstone followed. Thomas was next, and Sir William came up last of all. Beyond simple instructions of order and direction, no-one spoke. A quick meeting of eyes – sometimes anxious, sometimes resentful – was all Thomas saw by way of communication.

One of these men surely knew what this searching would

find, and where.

From room to room they went, taking it in turns to enter and look in the clothes trunks, under the bedclothes, atop the canopy of the bed and under its skirts, in the fireplace, while eight eyes watched carefully from the doorway, anticipation building uneasily with each room, each corridor. In the Prince's chamber, Sir William unlocked the stairway door in the corner and descended alone, then Fergus Highstone repeated the search in case he, Sir William, had any reason for lying about what he had seen.

Nothing untoward was found on the first floor. The unused rooms on the second floor were searched in the same methodical, watchful way, and nothing was found there, either.

It was on the south-western corridor of the third floor that they finally found a door standing closed. Sir Baldon pressed upon it, discovering that it was secured, and Sir Marcus put his shoulder to it a few times to confirm this.

The group separated either side of the doorway, and Sir Marcus raised his foot and unleashed a series of almighty kicks at the height of the bolt. These were met with increasingly harsh splintering sounds before the door crashed back on its hinges, disappearing suddenly to reveal the room beyond. Thomas, standing beside Sir William on the far side of the corridor, craned to see around Sir Marcus, and Sir Baldon and Highstone approached from their side of the doorway.

Zachariah's body, hanging from the ceiling, greeted them as they crowded forward.

TWENTY

The body hung from the centre of the room, hands loose by its sides; the chest, the neck, the head were hidden by the wooden panels above the door. To the right-hand side of the body as they looked on, the room's chair lay on its back. Behind the hanging feet, the clothes trunk lay overturned, its curved lid towards the door.

The looseness of those hanging feet stirred in Thomas the same revulsion as always. He tried to swallow the rising bitterness in his stomach, to hold on to the food he had eaten that morning.

Motioning for the others to remain where they were, Sir William patted his brother on the shoulder and they stepped quickly into the room. Without speaking, Sir Marcus went to the body and wrapped his arms around the hanging legs and Sir William approached the bed, which stood in the rear left corner of the room. While his brother lifted the weight of the body in case any life remained, Sir William drew his knife and crouched by the corner of the bed nearest the wall. Thomas could see the rope running from the ceiling down to where Sir William crouched, presumably tied off there. After a few moments' work, Sir William straightened, holding the rope in one hand. He wiped his knife on his hip before sheathing it again, and turned as, with some small effort, Sir Marcus lowered Zachariah's body from the ceiling.

The bodyguard's head, hanging forward so the face was obscured by his long hair, came into view, and Sir Marcus rested the corpse's stomach over his shoulder before gently lowering his burden to the ground. The legs bent and the body folded as it was lowered, assuming a shape that no living man would find tolerable.

Sir William released the rope, and the severed end hung suspended in the air above him. He bent and worked his fingers under the hair across the bodyguard's face, presumably checking for a pulse, before standing back with his eyes on the body.

He looked exhausted once more.

"Surely," he said quietly, "he is the last one."

"But," Thomas heard the disbelieving note in Sir Baldon's voice, "Sir William – the door was bolted, he *must* be a suicide."

"Sir Baldon has a point," Highstone agreed. "There would appear to be no other way in or out; it seems fanciful to lay the blame for this at *our* feet."

Sir William watched them in silence, then glanced at his brother.

"Why should he kill himself, now of all times?" Sir Marcus asked no-one in particular, his eyes on the corpse.

"Well," Highstone said slowly, "the Prince was attacked by your brother *and* killed while in his care. If he felt that this was to be used against him…"

Thomas felt eyes turn to him.

Oh, no.

"Did you see Zachariah this morning, sire?" Sir Baldon asked

Thomas nodded.

"I thought he might find you, yes. Did he offer you his services as bodyguard? It is how these things usually go: from father to son."

Thomas closed his eyes. "Yes."

"A-and what did you say, sire? If I may be so bold."

Thomas tried to think; what *had* he said?

"Did you," Highstone ventured, "take up his services?"

"I…" he tried to remember; it had been so unexpected. "I…"

"Well," Highstone said in the tones of one offering help, "whatever you said, might it have given Zachariah cause to doubt how welcome he would be in your service? Is that fair, sire?"

Were people really going to start paying this much attention to what he said? His eyes grew hot.

"I never—" he could feel tears rising, and hated himself for it.

"There you have it, Sir William," Highstone said. "Perhaps suspecting that his own poor judgement was being held against him – and I feel that Master Thomas was perfectly correct in that, and should feel no responsibility – Zachariah saw that his role here was at an end. Who would, after all, wish to use a bodyguard who had seen the Prince attacked and killed? Faced with staying here in disgrace or venturing out to face the Red Death alone he chose instead to…"

Thomas closed his eyes, and heard Sir Marcus grunt.

"You disagree, Sir Marcus?" Highstone asked.

Sir William replied in reasonable tones, perhaps sensing another argument in the making: "There has been a lot of death here recently, Fergus. Three apparent suicides in as many days."

"'Apparent'?" Sir Baldon asked, "I thought that you had provided the answer to what happened to Sir Oswin and Laurence."

Thomas opened his eyes; of course, only the killer knew the truth. Was Sir Baldon genuinely confused here, or did the tremor in his voice come from the realisation that he was further from safety than he had assumed?

Sir William ignored him: "And then there is the Prince."

"But last night we decided—" Sir Baldon pressed.

"We decided," Sir Marcus' voice was heavy, "that we could reach no agreement. Which means that you still think I poisoned him."

Nobody contradicted him.

"I should," Sir William raised his eyes to look around the

inside of the front screen of the room, "examine this room for any signs of deception. I'm afraid that I am unwilling to risk any one of you coming in here and hiding what indications there might be of murder, and so I request that you all return to your rooms and..."

Sir Marcus stepped away from the body and turned towards the door.

"If I understand you correctly," Fergus Highstone said without rancour, "you are soon to level an accusation of murder at either Sir Baldon or myself. As such, I would be fascinated to see the process by which you come to these conclusions of yours, Sir William. Might I be permitted to stay?"

Sir Baldon fluttered his hands, indicating that he felt the same way.

Sir William sighed. "If you wish these conclusions to be accurate, Fergus, it would be best if you left. Either of you might find a way to...*interfere* with this room."

"We could," Highstone looked at Sir Baldon, "watch from out here."

Sir William watched them in silence, unblinking.

"Of course," he said at length. "But please do remain outside the room."

"I'll make sure they do, Will." Sir Marcus stepped into the corridor.

Sir William extended a hand to Thomas.

"Come on, Thomas, let's—"

"Do you," Sir Baldon interrupted, "really think it fitting that the heir to the throne be involved in such grisly business?"

"I do," Sir William said, and Thomas stepped into the room.

There was no staleness rising from the body as Thomas approached, only the musty aroma of the bodyguard's clothes. He wondered how long ago the man's life had departed. Might a quicker search of the lower floors have got them here in time? Had one of the men now outside this room deliberately slowed the searching to ensure that Zachariah was definitely deceased when inevitably discovered?

Something crackled under Thomas' foot as he approached the body.

"Stop," Sir William raised a palm, fingers splayed. He curled the thumb and three lesser fingers in so he was pointing upwards. "Look."

Tilting his head back to look to the ceiling, Thomas was confused at the sight of the rope hanging down in two apparently unconnected lengths.

"Do you see?"

The confusion cleared, and he saw.

As in all the rooms, the floorboards, as wide as a man's foot is long, ran from side to side, resting on rafters that ran between the castle's inner and outer walls like spokes from a wheel. The floorboards of the room above formed the ceiling of this room. The lengths of rope appeared disconnected because a hole had been drilled in the ceiling at the edge of one board and the rope passed through into the room above. A second hole had then been drilled at the far edge of the next board back, so the rope would cross two floorboards on the floor of the room above before re-entering this room.

Thomas looked at his feet, and saw the sprinkling of wood shavings that had crackled under him as he had approached.

"How did he do it?" Sir William asked.

"He made two holes," Thomas saw it in his mind. "He passed the rope up through one of them, then went into the room above and passed it back down. Then," his eyes dropped to the bed in the far corner, "he tied the end of the rope to the head of the bed to anchor it in place."

"And then?"

Thomas looked around, his eyes falling on the overturned chair. "He stood on the chair and…" he swallowed, unable to continue.

Sir William shook his head. "No. Why is it unlikely that he used the chair?"

Thomas looked at the seat of the chair, and thought of the hanging feet when the door had swung open.

"It is too low."

Standing on the chair, Zachariah's feet would have been closer to the floor than they had been when he was discovered. His weight when he placed his neck in the noose – Thomas shuddered to picture it – would pull his feet lower again than they started, so unless he was willing to jump into the air and hope he got his neck through the noose, Zachariah needed to have been standing on something of greater height.

"How, then?" Sir William asked.

Thomas looked at the overturned trunk, disappointed at how obvious it seemed after only a little more thought. "He stood on the trunk."

"Go on."

The overturned chair made sense now, too. "He stood the trunk on its end and put the chair next to it, then climbed onto the chair and up onto the end of the trunk. He put his head in the noose, kicked the trunk over—" as that fell, it could have hit the chair, knocking that over, too, "and…"

A sudden weightlessness, a sudden drop, and it was over.

Lightness tingled in Thomas' fingers to imagine it. He flapped his hands, trying to chase the feeling away.

"That is how I see it, too."

Horrible as it was to contemplate, Thomas was pleased with this agreement.

"It rather sounds like suicide, then," Sir Baldon said from the corridor.

Sir William smiled grimly. "I wish it was always that simple, Baldon." He turned to Thomas, "How could it have been done if he was already dead, or unconscious?"

"Why dead or unconscious, Sir William?" Highstone asked.

"It is," Sir William replied, "rather difficult to induce a living man to place his head in a noose, would you agree?"

Thomas pointed to the ceiling. With the mystery of the robed Red Death resolved, it was easier to attribute these actions to a living, flesh and blood man. "The rope was already in place. Zachariah could have been," he felt awkward saying it with the people they suspected so nearby, "killed elsewhere, or in here, and his neck put in the noose. He was pulled into the air and the rope tied off on the bed."

"One-handed?" Sir Marcus asked from the door way.

"Marcus is correct," Sir William said. "No man could hold the weight of a dead body with one hand while also tying a knot around a foot of the bed with the other."

"So the body would need to rest on something."

"What?"

Thomas looked around the room. "It could be sat in the chair."

"But the chair is too low."

He had realised his mistake as he had spoken. "What if the trunk was stood on its end—" that still seemed too low, "—and the chair stood on the trunk?"

"That would be better."

"So, the rope is put around the body's neck, the body is hoisted into the air and placed in the chair. Then the rope, no longer holding the weight of the body, was tied to the bed and…"

The trunk kicked away, the chair falling to the ground, the body left hanging in place.

"That would leave this killer in the room with his victim, however," Highstone said from behind Thomas.

Sir William bobbed his head in agreement, his eyes on the floor. "Then there must be a gap."

"A gap?" Sir Baldon asked.

Sir William stepped past Thomas, to the doorway. "A gap,

Baldon, big enough for a man to pass through. Shall we start with the obvious one?"

He reached out and swung the door shut in their faces.

Glancing back over his shoulder, Sir William said, so softly that Thomas knew it was intended only for his ears, "Keep them out of the room above."

There was barely time to indicate his understanding before his master turned back to face the door and started talking again in a louder voice:

"You see, the bolts are hardly foolproof. A gap around the door big enough for a piece of twine to be fed through could be used to pull the bolt across from outside."

As he spoke, he ran his eyes and hands around the edge of the door. "This is the Prince's castle, however, and no shoddy workmanship is allowed. So we can rule that out." Indeed, it was clear that no gap around the edge of the door existed. Sir William crouched down and examined the length of draft-excluding material at the door's base, and Thomas saw beyond his master the T-shaped auger that would have been used to drill the holes, thrown into the corner of the room and so obscured until now behind the open door.

"We know the door was bolted, since two of you tried to open it." Sir William continued, tapping the side of the doorframe where the hole drilled for the bolt to slide into presented itself now as a jagged tear in the wooden panelling. "This was clearly broken in the process. It's also fair to assume that, if murder it was, the murderer would seal the door ahead of time in case of interruptions."

Sir William opened the door.

"Admirably clear, Sir William," Fergus Highstone said. "And so?"

Sir William pointed to the fireplace.

The fireplaces were back-to-back in adjacent bedrooms, sharing a chimney, and Thomas knew from games of hide-and-seek played with Isobel how quickly the openings narrowed too greatly for even someone of his slight stature to fit through. None of these men could hope to climb into a fireplace in one room and over into the next, but Sir William would want to check anyway.

As in every room, the uneven shape of a flint and the metal strip of a firestriker rested on the mantle, and these were quickly dismissed. Some time was then spent looking for loosened bricks or other modifications, and for signs such as disturbed soot in the hearth that might tell of a string run across from the next room that could have been used to pull the bolt from there. Fergus Highstone was invited into the room, under close watch by Sir William, to investigate the narrowing of the flue that was described to him, and to confirm Sir William's observations about the lack of disturbance in the soot of the fireplace itself.

Next, the wooden panels that lined the walls were checked closely, recalling to Thomas the examination of the same in the privy only two days before. Here, as there, the panels had obviously been in place for some time, with the nails showing no sign of loosening or having been struck in recent days. The panels were also checked individually and found to be securely fixed to the frame behind – removing the possibility of an exit hidden by the mere *appearance* of nails holding a panel in place.

Throughout, Sir William kept up a steady rate of chatter about their search and the tricks that could be played, seemingly happy to have an audience. At some point, chairs were collected from the adjacent rooms, and Thomas looked to the doorway to see the three men sat outside paying varying degrees of attention to proceedings.

Standing the clothes trunk on its end and climbing atop it, Sir William pushed at the floorboards of the ceiling, going first down one side of the room and then the other. He examined

224

the rafters and found them unmarked and undamaged. He inspected the glass of the narrow windows – lozenges held in strips of lead, as everywhere – and the stone of the castle's outer wall.

Nothing was out of place.

Indefatigable, Sir William then enlisted Thomas in dragging the furniture of the room around, first placing Zachariah's body in the trunk – checking the floor carefully, looking for loose boards, missing nails, and any gaps through which anything might be passed. Given the purpose to which the castle was put, it was perhaps unsurprising that no gaps could be found: the Prince's guests would want as much privacy in their rooms as could be achieved, and gaps between the floorboards would hardly allow this.

Finally, after what must have been close to a couple of hours, Sir William lowered himself with a groan into a sitting position on the bed and smiled at the men in the corridor. Thomas, his legs and back aching, sat in the room's chair, relieved to be finished at long last.

'Keep them out of the room above.'

"And there you have it, gentlemen," Sir William said, "there is no way out of this room."

"There is only one answer then, Sir William," Highstone said, a twist to this lips. "The killer must be in there still."

Sir William smiled in return, and stood, rubbing a hand across his hair.

"Gentlemen I am sorry. I have put you through a great deal today. The Prince's death grieves me, as it grieves us all, and the desecration of his corpse is an action I struggle to understand or forgive. It now seems possible that Zachariah, mad with grief at his failure, attacked the Prince's corpse for reasons of his own and, realising what he had done, killed himself in remorse. I hope that is the case, I really do."

After a moment of silence, Fergus Highstone stood from his

chair.

"It was a most instructive demonstration, Sir William, and I thank you for the care you have invested here. I hope we can put this behind us and find a sensible solution to these mysteries. Perhaps young Zachariah was responsible after all."

'Keep them out of the room above.'

Sir William sighed. "I need some rest. Thomas, you should do the same. I know Baldon is keen to discuss your herald, and we should be rested to give that due consideration."

The tiredness on Sir Baldon's face cleared briefly at this suggestion.

"My herald?"

Sir William flexed the fingers of one hand, dismissing the matter. "We shall discuss this later."

"And the body?" Highstone asked, nodding towards the closed trunk.

"Yes," Sir William nodded, "Zachariah should be given the funeral he deserves. Later this evening. For now…" he raised a hand, indicating that they should depart.

The men in the corridor stood, leaving their chairs in place, and Sir Marcus began to lead them away. Sir William turned and gave Thomas a meaningful look, then preceded him into the corridor.

Outside the room, Thomas was surprised to see everyone waiting for him as he prepared to head in the opposite direction.

"A-are you coming with us, sire?" Sir Baldon asked.

"I…need some things from the top floor," he said, unable to think of anything better in the moment.

"I could fetch them."

Sir Baldon began to approach, but Thomas raised a hand and, incredibly, the other man stopped in his tracks.

"I know them. I will find them quickly. Thank-you." He turned his back to them and headed for the nearest stairway, hoping no further objections would be raised.

Spiralling up one level, he found the room above that in which Zachariah's corpse now lay. Five single beds were arrayed there, and Thomas understood now why the other servants he had lived with on this floor had accepted these conditions without complaint: this was simply how they lived, in contrast to the opulence of their masters and mistresses. *This* was the life of a servant, a life he had been spared to prepare him for the day he might rule the kingdom they called home.

He hoped that day was a long time coming.

The servants' quarters had no bolts on the doors – in part because servants could be pressed into service at all hours, and so needed to be able to return unimpeded by those who had been fortunate to get to bed earlier in the evening – so Thomas pushed the door closed and dragged one of the narrow beds across in front of it. Unsure of what to do or how long he would be required to wait, he sat on this bed and regarded the two holes drilled at the edges of the floorboards, and the rope running between them.

After a while, he lay down. His eyes drifted closed.

Suddenly aware of a gentle tapping, or maybe of being rocked, he awoke with the impression that the door had just been pushed from outside and, meeting resistance, pushed again, harder.

He held his breath and listened.

The door eased inwards to touch the frame of the bed on which he lay. There was no force behind it, this could be merely a draft, but Thomas, alert and terrified, hoped that he had given no indication of his presence.

The door drifted closed and, after another pause, there might have been quiet footsteps receding.

Newly cautious, Thomas sat on the edge of the bed and waited.

TWENTY-ONE

A short while later, a gentle tap sounded at the door and Sir William whispered, "Thomas."

Thomas stood from the bed and pulled it aside. He opened the door to see his master alone in the corridor, a lit candle in his hand.

"Sorry about before, I was nervous."

"Before?"

"Someone attempted to open the door a little while ago; I thought it might have been you."

Sir William stepped into the room. "No."

"D-does that mean…?"

"It might mean anything," Sir William said lightly. "It might be someone coming to check this room in innocence or because they had a sudden realisation – though I would like to think they would share any ideas with me – or it might be our killer coming to see what signs he left *in case* anyone has a sudden realisation."

He had pushed the door closed, and was stood looking down at the rope as it appeared up through the floor, ran across the width of two floorboards, and then disappeared down again.

"Why do you believe Zachariah was murdered?"

It was tempting to see every death, every act of violence, as part of whatever pattern had started with the murder of Sir Oswin, but that could be wrong. Zachariah seemed an unlikely suicide, but any other interpretation seemed less likely still.

Sir William glanced up at him, and then stepped to one of the beds and sat. He bent and placed the candle holder on the floor by his feet. Thomas sat on another bed, facing his master across the room.

"There are four reasons," Sir William said, his voice low. "Firstly, there are easier ways for a man to commit suicide. He could climb among the rafters around the bell and hang himself there, if he insisted on hanging, or, since climbing to the bell would see him almost on the roof, he could simply throw himself from the walls of the castle."

Thomas was relieved to have the question answered rather than thrown back at him; the weight of any more questions might crush him.

"Instead, we're asked to believe that he finds some rope and an auger in the stores, picks a bedroom – one out of the way, so he will cause no disturbance – and drills two holes in the ceiling. Then he ties the noose and feeds the rope *up* into this room, then comes up here and feeds the rope back down, and then goes back *down* to the room below and ties the rope off. That is too much work for a man suffering under such anguish."

Thomas had failed to think of this; his own fear of hanging making him blind to what must have come before.

"Secondly, if we assume that for his own reasons Zachariah wished to hang himself in this way – perhaps he is scared of heights and unwilling to jump from the walls – he would be much more likely to pass the rope over the rafters that run from the inside wall to the outer," Sir William ran a pointed finger along an invisible line in the air from the door of the room to the windows. "For certainty that the rope would hold, a practical man like Zachariah would bore those holes either side of the strongest support he could find."

This, too, seemed obvious now Sir William pointed it out.

"Zachariah was," has master seemed to search for the correct flavour of word, "*displayed* by being hanged facing the door: someone wanted us to break that door down and be confronted with his dead body – it's a much more striking image, and one designed to inspire disgust and shock and so forestall thought."

Thomas wondered how much death this man had known, that violent scenes such as these made so little impact upon his

229

own ability to reason.

"Like with Sir Oswin?"

"Exactly."

Could the desire to shock out of their reason whoever discovered the bodies be an indication that the same hand was responsible for both murders?

"Thirdly, the rope is too thin."

"Too thin?"

"Yes. Downstairs we have plenty of twine, and a fair quantity of spare rope. Nothing in between. Twine is too thin to support the weight of a body, and rope too thick to fashion a noose. This," he rubbed a toe on the floor in the direction of the strand passing between the two holes, "has been unwound from the thick rope, so that it is thin enough to tie a noose in. That would have taken time. I doubt Zachariah would have set up his noose before coming to speak to you in case he was turned down, and I doubt he would have had time after speaking to you to decide on suicide, find and cut a length of rope and unwind half of it to make the noose, and set up the room as we saw. That is too much to expect from a man who has ending his life suddenly thrust uppermost in his mind."

Pleased to be able to contribute something, Thomas said, "The rest of the rope – the length from which this was unwound – should be somewhere in the castle, then."

"Hidden somewhere that implicates no-one, I'm sure, or simply thrown into the moat."

Thomas agreed, and tried to hide his disappointment.

"Finally," Sir William pointed at the floor, "these two boards over which the rope has been passed. I already had my suspicions as I have said, but when I was examining the ceiling I saw that, of all the planks in the ceiling, these are the only two adjacent floorboards," he now ran his finger in the air from one side of the room to the other, "that both began and ended between the walls of this room."

The floorboards along each side of the castle ran under the frames that had been put in place to make the rooms; all manner of different lengths of board would have been used, with the majority starting in one room and disappearing under the 'wall' into the next. If two adjacent boards began and ended in the same room, however…

"It would be possible to lift them up and…"

"…create a hole in the floor," Sir William finished for him. "Or, indeed, in the ceiling of the room below. And, when removed, two floorboards would make, I think you would agree, a gap wide enough for a man to climb through."

Thomas stared, wide-eyed. That must be how it had been done.

"So he drilled the holes in the ceiling first—"

"The killer first," Sir William interrupted, "finds a room with two adjacent floorboards that can be removed. It would surely be possible, with over seventy rooms to search. Or," he threw his hands out in a shrug, "perhaps it was seeing these boards that gave him the idea in the first place. Someone has clearly given much thought to achieving these effects, and I suspect that this plan has been in someone's mind for a long time in case it was ever needed."

"So, deciding he needs to kill Zachariah, the murderer bores the holes—" Thomas said.

"From where?"

"From below?"

"Perhaps, though drilling them from up *here* would make less work. He could drill the holes, feed the rope down through both of them, and then go to the room below to tie the noose. Otherwise he is running between rooms: drilling the holes from below, running up here to put the rope in place, then back down again. Too much time wasted, too great a risk of discovery. We found the auger in the room below – poorly hidden, you no doubt saw, on purpose so we would fail to connect the killer with *this* room and so examine it for any signs he left."

Thomas tried to picture what came next.

"He prises the floorboards loose—" Thomas prepared to stand and examine the boards, but Sir William raised a hand to stop him.

"Let us discuss it first, to see if it could be done."

Thomas sat, and continued:

"He loosens the floorboards and leaves them in place with the rope over the top of them. He gets Zachariah into the room below, k-kills him, bolts the door, fixes the noose around his neck, and hangs him." He swallowed thickly. The sight of those limp, lifeless limbs would live in his mind for a while yet.

"So how does he leave the room?" Sir William asked.

"The ceiling."

"Go on."

Thomas tried now to picture their killer, ignoring the lifeless horror in the room with him.

"Oh! He takes the chair down—" the body would have been sat it this prior to hanging, Thomas recalled now "—climbs onto it, then onto the end of the upturned trunk, and lifts the planks to one side."

"How does his lift them? The body is hanging from them, remember."

"No," it was clear in his mind now. "The planks stay flat, the body is hanging in the middle of the room." He held his forearm horizontally across his chest and, keeping his elbow in place, swept his hand outwards, describing an arc with his arm like a door opening. "He would have to lift them from beneath and twist them so they went..." he paused, unsure of the word.

"Diagonally."

"Diagonally across the hole. The body remains hanging from the middle and he pulls himself up and through the gap and into this room."

It was a huge risk – the planks might be too awkwardly

placed to lift – but hardly more of a risk than killing a man.

Than killing four men.

"The trunk and chair in the room below," Sir William said, "were kicked over as he lifted himself free to give the impression that Zachariah was the one who set them like that – that *he* kicked the trunk aside when taking his own life."

"The floorboards could then be twisted back into place," one would probably be underneath the other, but this could be achieved with a little effort, "and then the nails hammered in again, and…"

"And our killer has performed another impossible murder."

Since finding Sir Oswin's body in the moat, this was the first solid answer they had provided, and the sense of triumph Thomas felt seemed somehow unsuited to the seriousness of a man's life being taken. Maybe so much death had made him callous, or maybe so many unanswerable questions had made this one piece of clarity too wonderful for anything to spoil.

"So there will be marks on the floorboards, where they were prised up?" Thomas asked.

Sir William blew out his cheeks. "I hope so, because I can think of no other way to explain what we have seen."

They stood, and stacked the beds atop each other in the rear half of the room. A short examination of the boards in question was enough. Light scratches, clearly recent, could be seen in places along the sides of the floorboards where nails had been driven through them into the rafters. In the light of the candle's flame it was possible, too, to see pale ripples on the heads of all the nails, indicating that they had been struck recently.

"You saw Zachariah this morning, correct?"

"Yes." Thomas' elation faded. He had no desire to think too much on that final meeting. Had he mastered his frustration and allowed the bodyguard to accompany him, might Zachariah be alive now?

"Clearly whoever killed him had to act quickly, once the

body was in place. Perhaps by ringing the bell after we examined the Prince's body we hurried their hand and they were unable to finish their work, to cover their traces as fully as they would have liked. Perhaps whoever tried to get in here before me was our killer coming back to examine these marks and see if they could be disguised."

Finally, however, they had an answer as to how one of these killings, these apparently impossible acts, has been achieved. Might the other answers follow now? Might they finally put a face to the terror who stalked this castle, who had taken their friend from them?

Thomas almost hated to ask: "Does knowing how this was done help?"

"It banishes ghostly spectres vanishing through walls, at the very least," there was no mockery in Sir William's voice, but Thomas felt himself redden as he remembered the eagerness with which he had previously grasped at other-worldly explanations. "I am far more interested in why these men have been killed, though. Finding out why will tell us who, and then maybe *they* can tell us how they achieved these effects. Oswin's murder to keep the Prince in power makes no sense in light of the Prince's murder, and if Zachariah knew something why would he keep it to himself? And please—" this as Thomas opened his mouth to speak, "let us dispose with the idea of parallel plots. One scheme behind this madness is hard enough to fathom, but two or three would be…" he threw his hands out.

They sat in silence.

"Well," Sir William said after a few moments. "We have been through every step of this together, you and I. You know all that I know, you have seen everything I have seen. The answer must be in there somewhere."

And, for the first time, Thomas believed him.

~

There was no sense in securing the room any more. If whoever was responsible for Zachariah's death wished to interfere now, the truth was already suspected.

Sir William led the way down the spiral stairs to the first floor in silence, and as they emerged by his and Sir Marcus' rooms a peculiar light-headedness gripped Thomas and he wavered on the spot.

Sir William reached out and gripped his arm. "Are you ill?"

Thomas shook his head. "I feel..."

A kind of sickness gripped him. Somewhere nearby, a door opened.

"Hello?" Fergus Highstone called. "Who's there?"

"Just us, Fergus," Sir William replied, shaking his head. The door closed and the sound of approaching footsteps brought the red sleeves and tall form of Highstone into view.

"Can you smell it too?" he asked, and that made Thomas realise: it was a smell rising to them. The smell of— "Someone's cooking meat."

After so long living on the barrelled provisions in the stores, the sweet, spicy freshness of the aroma had struck them all especially hard. Thomas' mouth had never felt so empty, even after all these days of strict rationing.

"We have no fresh meat," Sir William said, and the pleasure of the smell turned to dread that spread amongst them in a heartbeat.

They turned as one and ran for the stairs.

If it was another body, Thomas suspected that he would finally surrender to the lunacy that was so intent on devouring them.

The sound of their breath echoing in the stairway as they descended seemed loud enough to deafen him. Emerging in the

235

main hall, Sir William at the front, they made hurriedly for the kitchens, the likely source of any cooking – the smell growing stronger, more enticing, more hideous with each step.

Sir William threw open the door on the far side of the corridor, and, Highstone having struggled to keep pace with them, Thomas entered the kitchens to find them empty, the air smoky. They turned to the right, to the fireplace whose cinders were kept continually burning, and ran alongside the empty central table. The final pleasure of the aroma was torn away as Thomas reached the hearth only moments after Sir William and saw the source of what had summoned them.

A disembodied hand lay on the embers, slowly blackening, its fingers curled skywards.

Sir William leaned into the double wide fireplace, stretching his arms out over the rising heat, and, unable to reach or to tolerate the temperature, stood back, looking around.

"Where *is* everything?"

It had struck Thomas, too: the hearth was clear of the pokers and shovels typically used to stir the embers.

Fergus Highstone appeared at Thomas' shoulder and looked into the fireplace, his nose wrinkling at the tang of smoke. "What…?"

"It's the Prince's hand," Thomas said, hoping this was true and that no-one else – where *was* Sir Marcus? – had come to harm.

"Allow me, sire."

Highstone pushed Thomas aside, crouching down and reaching out, using his greater height in the hope of being able to reach, while Sir William tore around the kitchen swearing, clearly looking for any implement long enough to dislodge the hand before more damage was done.

Around the severed wrist, Thomas thought he could make out a length of twine – no, of rope, of *thin* rope – tied and resting on the embers. It was from this that the smoke seemed to be rising.

That hand, Thomas realised, must bear the hint they needed.

In that instant, everything changed: Highstone screamed out in shock and fear as the sleeve of his extended arm burst into flame, and he lost his balance and pitched forward into the fireplace.

His arm outstretched, he landed on the embers in a shower of sparks.

His scream rent the air, rattling Thomas' teeth in their gums.

Without pausing to think, Thomas tried to grab at Highstone's thrashing feet, eventually seizing one and pulling with all his might, straining desperately, hopelessly, to pull Highstone away before the fire consumed him. His eyes streaming, his feet slipping, Thomas dragged Highstone's twisting form backwards a pace and then another, and suddenly Sir William and Sir Marcus were beside him, both pulling and raising the injured man out of the fireplace, the once-promising smell of cooking meat replaced now by the horror of charred flesh and the bitter stench of burning clothes.

Thomas became aware of Sir Marcus patting him down for injuries, face creased in concern, his voice coming from far away. Thomas had eyes only for the still form of Fergus Highstone, black smoke rising from him as he lay on the central kitchen table, Sir William beating at the flames on his body with a thick piece of cloth.

"Water, Marcus, water!" Sir William shouted, and the big man turned from Thomas, looked around the kitchens in haste, then ran for the door to the well.

Thomas retreated to the nearest wall, and sank to the ground, unable to take his eyes from the inert form on the table. Was this murder? Was this the next stage in the killer's plan?

A door opened and Sir Baldon entered, doubtless also drawn by the smell and the noise, a horrified look upon his face.

Everyone was safe.

Thomas' brain threw reason to the winds and simply gave up trying to make sense of these events.

"Marcuuuus!" Sir William shouted, and his brother re-entered then, a bucket in his hands which, striding to the middle of the room, he emptied unceremoniously over the smoking body of Fergus Highstone.

Had he…?

Sir William sagged with relief, and Thomas saw Sir Marcus lean in and whisper in his ear.

Sir Marcus looked over, and saw Thomas sat against the wall.

"Come on, lad, I need your help."

Thomas stared at him, uncomprehending.

"Come on, stand up," Sir Marcus said kindly yet with urgency as he approached, "there's still more to do."

Rising to his feet – confused, overwhelmed, terrified – Thomas allowed himself to be guided to the door. Before stepping into the corridor, he glanced back over his shoulder at Fergus Highstone and, just before his view was blocked, saw his question answered, saw that at least one good thing had come from this tragedy, saw even at this distance that the burned man's fingers were entwined with those of the dead Prince.

TWENTY-TWO

The funerals were held that evening.

Sir Marcus had carried Zachariah's body down to the main hall and, having examined it to determine how the man had died, told them of the bruise discovered in the bodyguard's hairline that implied he had been rendered unconscious and then hanged. Thomas hoped that it had been a quick death: a sudden drop, a swiftly-broken neck. The lung-bursting horror of asphyxiation was too hideous to want to consider. He remembered the way Sir Marcus had lowered the body to the ground, hiding the bodyguard's no-doubt purple and twisted face behind his fell of hair. Perhaps unconsciousness would have been a mercy, and saved the bodyguard from knowing he was being slowly, tormentingly deprived of air.

The Prince's scorched, severed hand was examined before being reunited with its owner, and showed nothing beyond a near-total blistering and blackening of flesh. The rope which had been tied to it – clearly the other half of that with which Zachariah was hanged, and so sweeping aside any last suggestion of suicide from his death – had been charred by the embers but, waxy and difficult to burn as it was, had failed to be destroyed as intended.

Sir Marcus prepared the two corpses with lamp oil and sewed them into sheets, then carried them one at a time into the courtyard. Side-by-side: the bodyguard and the man he had failed to protect.

Everyone then ascended to the roof, where Sir Baldon held an arrow with its head to the flame of the lamp, took aim into the courtyard with the bow, and fired the burning missile into the cobblestones an arm-span to one side of the bodies. It struck the ground with an echoing *clak!* in the stillness of the evening and snapped into two burning pieces. Without a word, Sir Marcus took the bow from Sir Baldon's frozen fingers, touched another arrow to the flame, and fired it into the shapes below.

They stood in vigil as the bodies burned, Thomas aware that he felt no sadness at the death of a father he had never known.

As the flames rose, it was difficult to avoid thoughts of Fergus Highstone, bandaged and blackened in his room three storeys below, the flesh on the underside of his right arm and down that side of his body seared and fused with the melted material of his clothes, his hair partially burned away, reeking bitterly.

When Sir Marcus had taken Thomas from the kitchens, they had headed to Highstone's room and searched out the close-fitting undergarments which kept them warm at night. Those moments of scrabbling through a man's belongings, knowing his life may hang in the balance, were perhaps more terrible than sitting in the kitchens and watching him suffer. Every moment they searched was a moment wasted, a moment they were responsible for Highstone creeping closer to death.

Back in the kitchens, Sir William had torn a sleeve from these vestments and eased this over the burned flesh of Highstone's arm. He fashioned bandages from the rest, securing them around the injured man's torso. Once these were secure, Sir Marcus had carried Highstone up the spiral staircase to his room on the first floor, and left him there to recover.

He would live, of that Sir William was certain. He would also be in agony.

Thomas, Sir William, Sir Marcus, and Sir Baldon stood on the roof watching the bodies burn, the breeze once again carrying the smoke away from them. Overhead, birds of prey circled lazily and, deterred perhaps by the heat, retreated to doubtless return later in the hope of an easy meal.

Behind them, the sun crept lower; the sky darkened.

They descended to the main hall together, perhaps drawing close from the encircling tragedy – caution had provided little protection, so trust could hardly be more dangerous. Sitting at the round table, the smell of burned fabric and destroyed flesh in the air, Thomas stared at the food that had been placed in front of him and wondered if he would ever feel hungry again.

It was Sir Baldon who broke the silence:

"If I might be permitted to speak, sire..."

It was a few moments before Thomas realised that he was the one being addressed.

"Um, of course."

Sir Baldon coughed and looked around the table. "I am sorry to raise this, gentlemen..."

Sir William sat up straight, but Sir Marcus, staring at his hands, rumbled a noise of discontent:

"Are we really going to talk about this now?"

"Baldon's right, we should."

"Talk about what?" Thomas asked.

Sir William looked across at him. "Now that Prospero is dead, his son would be expected to assume his father's position and rule in his stead. However, there are dual difficulties: you are too young, and Prospero never acknowledged you as his heir."

"But *some* people knew I was his son."

Sir William smiled unhappily. "People are welcome to think what they like; unless you are a legitimate son of the Prince, your right to succeed him must be acknowledged by the Prince himself, acknowledged only past the age of seventeen by the mark upon your skin made and recorded in the presence of two trusted witnesses."

Sir Baldon coughed again. "It is a way of ensuring that, should a Prince be *incautious* with his favours, there is still the chance to select the most suitable of his...issue. Without trusted witnesses and the Prince's mark upon you, your claim to the throne, would be open to challenge."

"So," Thomas felt something like relief bloom in his chest,

"I'm unable to follow him, to assume his position?"

Sir William and Sir Baldon exchanged a look.

Sir Baldon wetted his lips, "There is an additional consideration."

"The King has lost his mind," Sir Marcus grumbled.

"Rumours," Sir Baldon said firmly, "of the King's health have circulated – without basis – for some time. Some claim that he has lost his reason, others that he is perfectly lucid at all times and there is no cause for concern."

'...could be found at night wandering the corridors and crying, would forget conversations, would repeat himself, would contradict himself and fly into rages when asked to clarify...'

"If there is any truth in these rumours, he can be deemed unfit to rule and," again Sir Baldon's tongue darted out from between his lips, "his heir would take his place."

Thomas blinked.

"Or," Sir William added, "he may already be dead, and it may be assumed that Prince Prospero is ready to take over from his father."

"But the Prince is dead," Sir Baldon stated needlessly.

Thomas felt sick; he wanted none of this.

"So, if the King is dead or removed from power, and Prince Prospero is dead, and I was never acknowledged as the heir, what happens?" It seemed a problem with no solution.

Sir Baldon's lips moved as he thought.

"I am unaware of the King having acknowledged an illegitimate heir to take up the crown in the absence of his son, so..."

"It would mean war," Sir Marcus said grimly.

Thomas felt like he had been slapped: "War?"

Sir Marcus sat forward. "Power like that, with no-one there to claim it, people will try and take it for themselves. It comes down to who has the most support, and then who can kill the most of their opponents first."

"No."

"Wars are fought over ideas, Thomas," Sir William said gently. "An idea has no power if you kill the people who believe in it."

"But you were going to remove the Prince – you said that you and Sir Oswin were going to remove him from power," Thomas could no longer remember what was supposed to be kept secret, and no longer cared. "That would have had the same result; you were going to start a war…"

Sir Baldon had turned to Sir William, struck amazed beyond mere shock, "T-to *remove* the Prince…?"

"No," Sir William said, answering Thomas. "A general of Oswin's standing would have the loyalty of the King's army, and that would kill any rebellion before it could get started."

Because people are terrified of the King's army.

"Y-you seem very certain, Sir William," Sir Baldon spluttered.

"We had discussed it with Terrington; he had agreed to support us, he would have brought others into line."

This revelation was too much for Sir Baldon, who surged to his feet. "With Terrington Fenwick? So your treasonous action was being discussed openly in the Prince's own castle—"

"Sit down, Percy."

"An action performed in the interest of the people is no treason, Baldon. Treason presumes that a threat to the crown is a threat to the people they represent. Oswin, Terrington, and I shared concerns about Prospero's lack of care for his people – echoing that of his father, of whom we have had no word in far too long. Our intent, far from harming the crown, was to reassure people that the crown was here to support them in this time of suffering, rather than hiding away and holding opulent parties."

"Is this why Terrington left? To prepare the ground for

your...*coup*?"

"Yes; it would be madness to commence such an action without being sure of one's ground. Terrington said that he would need thirty days to check with his trusted friends, and so asked Oswin and I to wait that long before we did anything." He sighed, "Our plans have been...disrupted."

The fight, the indignation, seemed to seep out of Sir Baldon in an instant, and he sank into his chair with a glance between the brothers.

"You realise," he said in a tired voice, "that you would have been denying your ward his birth-right."

A balm pressed itself upon the raging uncertainty in Thomas' heart. "W-what?"

Sir Marcus spoke, his eyes on his brother. "If removed on the grounds of neglect or failure of his people, a royal's offspring are similarly denied the right to rule, for fear that their father's influence over them may force their hand in decisions."

"But," Thomas pointed at Sir Baldon, "you said that Prince Prospero might take *his* father's place—"

Sir Baldon pressed his hands together. "Yes, sire, the Prince could take his father's place if the rumours of the King's poor health proved founded, whereas Sir William was acting due to what he saw as Prince Prospero's..."

"...incompetence," Sir Marcus finished.

They sat in silence.

"Then," Thomas said, "could someone *else* be found to take Sir Oswin's place?"

Sir William stared into the distance. "I have tried to think of someone..."

"Kincaid?" Sir Marcus suggested.

Sir William shook his head. "Dead."

"Evelyn?"

"Dead."

"Gaudan Cross?" Sir Baldon suggested.

Sir Marcus snorted, "The King's army would rather line up behind me."

"There must be *someone*," Thomas pressed.

"Oswin was a special case," Sir William replied. "The overthrow of the crown is hardly something one treats lightly; men who can unite the sides afterwards are rare."

"So what happens if the Prince is dead, and there is no-one to take over?" Thomas hated to ask, but wanted to know.

"The King is too old to sire another child," Sir Baldon said, "so…"

"War," Sir Marcus finished.

Thousands would die. Countless thousands were already dead, of course, but the Red Death had no selfish lust for power at its heart. That men would go to the effort to raise armies at a time like this seemed absurd, but Thomas had no doubt it was true.

Sir William coughed. "We could…lie."

They all turned to look at him.

"No-one but us knows how the Prince died. His body is," he gestured to the front of the castle, "mostly ashes, and what little survives the fire will doubtless be carried or washed away. If we say he fell ill and perished, having transferred his power to Baldon—"

"Why me?" Sir Baldon asked, in alarm.

"You're the most suitable one left, Percy."

Sir William pinched out his thin, humourless smile. "There's no formal deed of transfer, but we were hardly prepared for such action: I have raised the child many people already believe to be the Prince's son and that might carry some weight, and Terrington would doubtless support us."

"And Fergus?" Sir Marcus asked.

"We explain to Fergus, when he's well enough. I am certain that he has no appetite for another war."

They looked to Sir Baldon, who was clearly uncertain.

245

"It is a lot to take on," Sir William said, gently, "and it breaks every tradition there is – but it might save a lot of lives, and it would give us a chance to test the waters for Thomas as Prospero's heir."

Thomas' stomach lurched.

"But you said I was too young…"

Sir William nodded. "You are. No prince can choose his name and accept the mantle of king before his seventeenth year. But in the event of an heir assuming power before that time – a legitimate son whose father dies before he is of age, say – someone is appointed to act for him, and known as the prince's herald."

"Percy could be your herald, if Fenwick and the others he has rallied are willing to support the legitimacy of your claim."

The hope Thomas had been nurturing withered.

Sir William must have noticed something change in his bearing: "There would be no need for your to assume power, Thomas, or it would be a few years distant, anyway. But if people were willing to believe in you, to accept someone other than Prospero without the need for bloodshed, it might keep things stable enough to find an alternative."

Thomas had to cling to this possibility.

"Well, Percy?"

"I…" he swallowed, "I would have been honoured to act as…as your herald, sire, and I suppose this falls under that banner…"

Sir Marcus raised his hands. "It's practically the same thing," he said lightly.

They waited in silence; Sir Baldon stared at something only he could see, and spoke again at length: "As Sir William says, there would be no deed…"

"They would have to call all four of us liars," Sir William reassured him. "And Terrington had no love for Prospero's actions. I am sure he would be willing to mislead people about

246

the dates, to say that he was here when Prospero died and witnessed the transfer, if it would keep things peaceful."

"But then he would have mentioned it when he left—"

"He would have said nothing if we had asked him remain quiet," Sir William said easily. "There was already enough uncertainty to contend with; news of Prospero's death coming out at the wrong time might have seen chaos erupt."

Thomas could see Sir Baldon trying to convince himself. The man held his breath, then sighed. "If it is necessary, then I shall do it."

Sir Marcus stood, leaned across the empty space between them, and extended his arm. Sir Baldon, seeming overawed by the mantle he was adopting, however temporarily, smiled, and took the proffered hand gratefully.

"Gentlemen," Sir William said, smiling, "we may have just prevented a war."

~

Thomas was sitting on his bed later that evening, the churning uncertainty of the day having left him too agitated to sleep, when there was a knock at his door. He opened it to find Sir William outside.

"May I have a word?"

Thomas stepped back, and his master followed him in.

"I wanted to reassure you," he said as he eased the door closed, "that nothing is being taken from you—"

"No," Thomas shook his head, "I know."

"Baldon has his faults, but he is honest. If it comes to it, if there is the support for it, he will stand aside and let you rule."

Thomas barely knew how to express his feelings. He had never expected any of this, and losing his seat on a throne that two days ago had never been his to lose was no loss – particularly when weighed against the loss of Laurence, and the death that seemed to creep ever-closer in recent days. He was, he knew, a long way from being any sort of ruler, especially in this demanding time of the Red Death. Passing power to someone who understood that world, its expectations and traditions, and who had no difficulties with the history Thomas had only just learned about, was a relief he had no words to explain.

He was almost afraid to ask the question uppermost in his mind: "Can they make me rule, if it is undesirable to me?"

Sir William blew out a breath.

"If you are nominated as heir, you typically get to enjoy a life that is beyond the means of most people," he gestured to indicate the castle in which they stood, the people who had been summoned to this place. "To enjoy those benefits and then refuse the mantle is seen as harmful to the crown and, as such, is treason."

Thomas swallowed drily.

"I would be executed?"

Sir William scratched at his short hair. "There are stories of those who chose to duck their responsibilities being burned at the stake, like witches were once—"

It was difficult to think of anything except Fergus Highstone's seared flesh, and his screams as Thomas had struggled desperately to drag him from the flames.

"—but they may just be stories. You may simply be imprisoned, as an example. But in the age of the Red Death, are there even prisons any more? Who knows?"

Thomas felt light-headed, felt heat rise to his eyes, and feared that he would cry. "So I would have to do it, no matter what?"

Even though I hate everything it stands for?

Sir William surprised him by stepping forward and taking Thomas' head in one hand, leaning in so their foreheads touched.

"If you let this fear rule you now, it always will. There are many obstacles to face and many years to go before anything is settled."

They stood with their heads together for a few moments before Sir William seemed to remember himself and stepped back.

"It has been a long day, you should rest."

Thomas stood again, his eyes downcast. Without another word, Sir William turned to the door. On the threshold of the room, he turned to look at Thomas once more, something like sadness in his eyes, before stepping into the corridor.

Thomas bolted the door and climbed into bed. Blowing out the candle, he released the curtains to wrap himself in darkness. For now, at least, he knew Sir Baldon would carry the weight of the Prince's power. Someone so keen to see order observed, to see tradition retained, was surely the best man for such a role...

He sat bolt upright.

The thought came to him in an instant, and took root with a conviction that was difficult to shake. If Sir Oswin had been killed because he was going to remove Prince Prospero's powers, someone clearly wanted the Prince to remain. But what if Sir Oswin had been killed *so that* there was no-one else to take over from him once Prospero's powers had been removed? With the prospect of a war to settle the matter – which someone of Sir Baldon's experience would easily anticipate – and knowing the terror the Thousand Days War had provoked, those who remained would turn to a likely candidate to act as a herald for Thomas: Sir Marcus being unsuitable because of his opposition of the King, Sir William because of his support of his brother, Fergus Highstone doubtless of unsuitable birth and station, and Zachariah as a mere bodyguard left only—

Sir Baldon was drawn to power, was desperate to preserve

the accepted order of things. And had, with no word of objection, now ascended to a position where he could assume the type of power and influence that thousands of men would be willing to kill and die for.

And he had needed to kill only four men to achieve it.

'Baldon has his faults, but he is honest.'

What would the prospect of power just within his grasp do to a man who had spent his whole life worshipping it?

Thomas was tempted, there and then, to run to Sir William and share his thoughts, but two considerations held him back: firstly that Sir William would likely have already considered this, and secondly that, having realised it, the placing of power into Sir Baldon's hands may have been done precisely *because* it made the rest of them safe.

Laying back in the darkness, Thomas considered the possibilities.

PART FOUR

A Multitude of Gaudy and Fantastic Appearances

Thomas awoke early by habit, and was in bed considering his conclusions of the previous evening when the knock sounded on his door. Clad in his sleeping robe, he climbed out of bed to let Sir Marcus know that he would need a few moments to dress.

He drew back the bolt and opened the door to find Sir William waiting.

"Marcus is doing something for me this morning," his master said by way of explanation, "but we still need to check the rats. I'd let you sleep, but I have never checked the dungeons before."

Thomas rubbed his eyes. "Do you want to go now?"

"I do."

Thomas closed the door, dressed quickly, and exited his room to find Sir William leaning against the opposite wall, waiting. He was swinging his key on its loop of twine around his finger and, at Thomas' appearance, gave his hand a final twirl, wrapping the twine around his fist twice before catching the returning key in his open palm. He then pushed off the wall and headed for the stairs.

Thomas stood, watching his back.

As Sir William turned to descend the stairs, he glanced back and saw Thomas frozen in place.

"Are you...joining me?"

Thomas saw him, but his eyes were elsewhere, his mind conjuring images of the privy above them. "I know how it was done."

It came out as a whisper.

"I'm sorry?" Sir William dipped his head.

"I know..." he coughed, "I know how it was done; how Sir Oswin was sealed in the privy."

Sir William watched in silence, his eyes suddenly sharp.

"Then maybe the rats can wait for now."

~

The door to the privy stood slightly ajar, the ragged and splintered hole Sir William had made only three days before to its right-hand side. A stench of uncleanliness hung in the air.

Thomas stepped in first, the candle Sir William had collected from below throwing dancing light over the bloodstains on the floor, and moved to the right; Sir William followed, his own candle and a reel of twine in his hands, and stepped to the other side of the door.

Thomas closed the door, shutting them inside with Sir Oswin's blood.

They stood facing the skeleton of planks that made up the wooden screen, the panels fixed to its far side. The screen was made of four horizontal beams: one at floor level, one halfway up the door – these split half way along by the doorway itself – one at the top of the door, and one at the very top of the screen. These horizontal beams were held in place by vertical ones, starting at the edge of the screen and spaced approximately a cubit apart.

Thomas pointed to the two nails that had been used the seal the door: the first halfway up the door near its edge and the second at the same height in the doorframe, each protruding about half the length of a finger.

"We have to wrap the string around these two nails," Thomas said.

"And then leave."

"No," he realised the mistake now. "Whoever did this—" he must remember to share his suspicions of Sir Baldon, "–left the privy first with Sir Oswin already dead, waiting to be discovered."

Just as with the murder of Zachariah, the sight which was to greet those who discovered Sir Oswin was designed to inspire fear and shock, to prevent thought and force upon them the *conviction* of suicide.

Fear, Thomas had come to realise in recent days, was a powerful weapon.

"So how?"

"The knife." How had he missed this before?

"The knife?"

"Sir Oswin would have been dead or unconscious when his wrists were slit—" just as Zachariah had been unconscious before being hanged, "—so he could be killed in a way that made it appear he was alone in here when it happened."

"So why the knife?" Sir William was patient, interested.

"Because they needed a reason for his knife to be out of its sheath. And more than just out of its sheath: for it to be *on the floor*."

Sir William straightened, understanding in his eyes. "They used the knife to seal the door."

"Yes. If Sir Oswin had been stabbed in the chest, say—" a flash of Laurence, lying dead, which he shook away "—we would expect the knife to remain in the wound. But because we were to think that he slit his wrists…"

"…we would assume he had dropped the knife as he died."

"Or at least give little importance to it being on the floor." Thomas remembered noting how far the knife had been from the body, seeing this as an error on the part of the murderer and then thinking about it no further. He turned and placed his candle holder on the seat behind them. "May I have your knife?"

Sir William placed his own candle on the floor, then unsheathed his knife and handed it across.

"Because the handle is hollow," Thomas ran his finger over the loop through which the fingers could be passed when the knife was used as a firestriker, "twine can be tied around the end." He indicated the reel Sir William was holding, and a length was unspooled from this, cut, and tied around the handle's end. Thomas held the other end of the twine between his fingers so that the knife was suspended vertically, its blade pointing downwards.

"The other end is tied to the nail in the back of the door."

Moving to the door he looped the loose end of the twine over the nail there and adjusted it so that the point of the knife hung just above the floor. Thomas then tied the twine to the nail so that the knife hung in place.

Sir William took a breath as if to say something, and then stopped.

Taking hold of the knife, Thomas raised it as he would a pendulum until the taut string was parallel with the floor and the knife itself level with the horizontal beam halfway up the door.

"The door could be opened slightly and the knife rested here on this beam. Then the killer leaves and pulls the door shut, and so pulls this from its resting place and..."

He let go of the knife.

As he expected, as had the key in Sir William's hand downstairs, the twine stayed taut and the knife swung like a pendulum. It described an arc down to the bottom of the door, the tip of the blade swinging just above the floor, and then began to rise, rise, rise towards the second nail in the doorframe...

...and without rising to the height of the nail, the knife fell back, swinging towards him once more and rising to a lesser height before changing direction and swinging to a lesser height once again, describing a series of decreasing arcs as it swung.

Thomas' hopes sank.

"I thought..."

Interest flickered in Sir William's eye. "It is well

considered, however."

The knife swung gently, mockingly, to a rest.

Thomas seized at the first idea that struck him: "What if it dropped from a greater height?"

Hope bloomed in his chest. He took hold of the knife and raised it, as before, so the taut string was parallel with the ground, and then raised it higher. True, there was nothing here to support the knife before the door was closed, but if they could make it work...

He released the knife.

...it fell straight down...

...the string pulled taut...

...the knife rose, wobbling...

...dropping away, as before, without reaching the height of the second nail to which Thomas had been so sure the string would rise. Indeed, the knife's greatest height had been lower than on the previous try.

He had made it worse.

Burning with embarrassment, he raised the knife one more time, higher still, but when released the knife fell straight down before the string became taut, and the sudden interruption of its descent caused the knife to wobble and bang against the door without the string swinging to anything like the heights it had before.

He watched the knife rattling back and forth at the end of the string, wishing he had kept his mouth shut.

Sir William raised the knife again to the middle of the door, the twine parallel with the ground, and stared at it as if transfixed.

"It's no good," Thomas said, a heaviness in his stomach, "I was wrong."

"It sets a man to thinking, though," Sir William replied. "We have been kept too busy elsewhere to give this any attention."

He let go of the knife.

Thomas, resentful of watching his stupidity play out again, put out his foot to stop the knife swinging past the bottom of the door and then, realising that he had placed his toes in the path of a descending blade, raised his leg so his foot would be struck by the string rather than the knife.

"Thomas…" Sir William said as if in reproach.

The pendulum swung, the string met Thomas' toes, and the knife changed direction sharply, swinging upwards, over the toe of Thomas' boot, wrapping the string around his toes before dropping down the side of his foot from which it had approached.

He yelped in surprise and jumped back, and the knife slipped off his foot and wobbled above the ground at the end of its string.

His eyes rose to those of Sir William; a spark of excitement lit the air between them.

"It's in the wrong place," Sir William said in wonderment. "If we want it to wrap around here," he touched the nails in the middle of the door, "we need to hang it from somewhere higher."

As Sir William stepped forward to untie the twine from the nail, Thomas' eyes travelled upwards, remembering the two nails he had seen at the top of the door when they had first examined the privy.

The nails were gone.

The light coming through the window, even this early in the day, was sufficient for him to see two holes in the wood – one at the edge of the door, one in the frame – to reassure him that they *had* been there before. But someone, presumably the man they sought, responsible for these murders, had returned and removed them in the intervening days.

"They've gone," he whispered, and something between terror and relief flooded him.

"What?"

He pointed, "The two nails here when we found Sir Oswin. Remember? We thought they might have been used before to seal the d—"

He stopped and groaned.

Surely that was what he had been intended to think; just like the knife on the floor being explained by Sir Oswin's slit wrists – one nail in the top of the door would be suspicious, but two in similar positions to the ones below could be dismissed on the grounds Thomas had, once again, been directed towards.

Sir William leaned in, investigating the holes in the wood.

"We need a nail."

They used the knife to prise up a plank in the seat in the window, removing the nail there. This was then pushed into the hole in the back of the door, and hammered in slightly with the knife's handle. The twine on the handle was then removed and a new length, enough twine to reach from the top of the door to the floor, tied in its stead. The other end was drawn over the newly-placed nail, the string hanging straight down from the top of the door so the knife's point was slightly above the floor, and tied off. The nail they had tied the string to previously was now approximately in the middle of this longer string.

Sir William crouched and took hold of the knife, then straightened and raised it to the height of the door, drawing the string taut out to the side, where it could rest on the higher horizontal beam.

He looked at Thomas and smiled.

"Stand back."

Thomas stepped up onto the privy seat, caring little now about the blood, intent only on the solution to this problem.

Sir William released the knife.

It swung cleanly in an arc all the way to the bottom of the door and then, when the string was vertical, the nail halfway down the door arrested the path of the top half of the twine.

The twine below the nail, however, continued to swing. The knife changed direction sharply, and swung upwards.

The string rose, rose, rose...

...and met the second nail in the door's frame, and in a blur the knife passed over the top of the nail and was falling down the other side, then rising again and it wrapped around the nail a second time and fell once more, then rising and falling for a third time, continuing faster and faster, until there was no more twine to wrap around the nails and the knife hung in the middle of the door, the twine tightly wrapped.

The door was sealed.

Eyes wide, Thomas looked from the knife and up into the smiling face of Sir William. He wanted to scream, he wanted to cry.

They had done it!

And then a realisation hit him.

"There's too much string."

Now, a length of twine ran from the nail at the top of the door to the two halfway down where it was tightly wrapped, but when they had found Sir Oswin's body there had only been twine wrapped around the two central nails.

And, Thomas saw, the knife was hanging *from* the string around the nails now, whereas when they had discovered Sir Oswin's body the knife had been on the floor.

Celebration turned to disappointment again, and he swallowed.

Sir William raised a hand. "One problem at a time. First we need to see if this works from the outside."

They unwound the twine from around the nails and extended it out to the side of the door, past the hinges. Sir William rested the knife atop the horizontal beam there and Thomas opened the door wide enough for a man to fit through. Sir William then moved the knife further out along the beam so that the twine remained taut.

They opened the door – it could be opened fully now without dislodging the knife – and stepped outside, and Sir William gently eased it back to its starting position. Thomas stepped up to the broken panel to watch and Sir William called him back.

"We know what happens, I want to keep out of the way in case something goes wrong."

He closed the door.

Perhaps they had left the door open too wide, or perhaps Sir William pulled it too sharply, but as the knife fell it clattered against the inside of the screen and could be heard swinging back and forth within. When the swinging had become less erratic, Sir William stepped into the privy and, leaving the door open just enough to squeeze through, reset everything for a second try.

He stepped out, opening the door fully again and then pulling it closed.

They heard the knife slip loose; Thomas waited, his heart in his mouth.

A few slight scrapes were heard from inside, then silence.

They exchanged a look, and Sir William raised a hand to indicate the broken panel.

"It was your idea."

Thomas approached and leaned in. The string was, as before wrapped around the two nails, holding the door closed.

"Yes!" Thomas shouted in triumph and turned suddenly to Sir William and hugged him, then jumped back in embarrassment. "Sorry."

Sir William grinned. "One is rarely hugged by a king."

A moment of silence fell.

"Shall we try it again? To confirm?" Sir William asked, and Thomas agreed hastily, leaning in to unwrap the string from around the nails.

They tried it five more time to be sure: Thomas setting it up three times and Sir William twice, until they could be certain of the conditions under which this method would succeed: the door must be left open a mere crack when the knife was placed on the horizontal beam, and pulled shut sharply so the string would clear the hinges as it fell.

They had really done it!

Stepping into the privy and sealing the door once more, they addressed the matter of the twine.

"Tell me the problem," Sir William said.

"There is string running from the nail in the top of the door to the ones in the middle."

"Yes."

"And the knife is still tied to the twine and hanging from the middle of the door."

"And you fail to see how the string could be made to vanish?"

Thomas paused. Did this mean Sir William knew?

"What did we find in here, when we broke in?"

"Sir Oswin sitting," Thomas pointed to the seat, "there, his knife on the floor here, twine wrapped around the two nails."

"And what else?"

It took him a moment to remember: "A candle holder containing a burned out candle."

Sir William waited, and Thomas saw the connection he had failed to make:

"The twine was burned."

"That is my suspicion, yes."

Thomas remembered the smell of smoke he had detected in the privy that morning – a smell he had attributed to his fear of the blood.

"You could smell it."

"I could. Some smoke escaped around the edges of the screen, and drifted away overnight, but some definitely remained. I mistakenly attributed it to the candle."

"But the twine is hard to burn."

The twine was waxy, flaxy stuff, which would smoke horribly when you tried to burn it, as had the spare rope from Zachariah's murder, tied to the Prince's severed hand and placed on the embers of the kitchen fire.

"It is. So how do we burn that which fails to burn well?"

Thomas thought of white sheets against the grey cobbles in the courtyard.

"Oil."

"Right. Whoever killed Oswin doubtless met him here intending murder – it might even have been his killer who made the appointment. They must have brought a length of twine up from the stores," he indicated the length hanging from the nail, "so could have also brought one of the oil lamps, too. You agree?"

Thomas did.

Sir William unwrapped the twine from the nails in the door and arranged it as before, the knife resting on the horizontal beam to the right-hand side of the door as they looked on. He pointed to the nail in the top of the door, and then to the knife resting on the horizontal beam.

"We have deliberately cut off the correct amount of string. What if the string were longer? An extra hand's length at each end: overhanging the nail at this end, and beyond the knot on the handle here.

"Some of the twine then has oil from the lamp rubbed onto it: from the extra length overhanging the nail to about halfway along, and from the knot at the handle to the end. Oswin is in place, his wrists slit, the knife and twine set up as here. Our killer simply," he mimed the action, "puts the flame of the candle first to one end of the string and then to the other, and steps outside and pulls the door shut.

"The knife falls and wraps around the nails while the extra

twine at each end burns away. It takes only a few moments for the knife to swing into place, and you saw how it hangs down on one side of the nails when the twine runs out. The flame at the nail," he touched the top of the door and ran his finger downwards, "continues to burn, and when it reaches the part of the twine untreated by oil it simply dies out."

Thomas thought. "And at the other end the knot is also burned off…"

"…and the knife falls to the floor."

Thomas groaned in frustration, his delight overtaken by his blindness. "I should have seen it."

Sir William's forehead creased. "Thomas, you did – we are here because of your insight."

"No," he took from his pocket the twine he had removed from the nails that first morning. "Sir Marcus said that the twine used to secure the door was normally *hung from* one of the nails." He opened his fingers, "When I unwrapped this, it came loose in my hand. There was no knot tying it to a nail."

He remembered, too, how the rough ends of the string had prickled his fingers, the threads hardened from having been burned rather than cut.

"It was easy to overlook," Sir William reassured him. "We had other things occupying our attention at the time."

"We might have saved lives if I had thought of it."

We might have saved Laurence – the swell of emotion felt unworthy, like valuing the lives of the guests in the castle over the unknowns laying murdered in the moat, but the thought crept in all the same.

"And," Sir William was unmoved, "you may have said something to the wrong person and *you* might be dead – Laurence, remember, was killed because of something he knew, or something he saw."

It was difficult to deny this; nevertheless…

"Do you know who it is?" Thomas asked, rubbing at his

eyes.

"I thought I did – Marcus and I were discussing it last night – but with enough certainty, to charge a man before the King and convince others of his guilt? No."

"Does," Thomas tried to keep the desperation from his voice, "does *any* of it make sense?"

"Most of it, yes."

The conviction in his master's tone brought Thomas up short. "Really?!"

Sir William nodded.

"I know why Oswin was thrown in the moat, I know how the Prince died, I know how Laurence knew of Oswin's death before being told along with everyone else, but the murder of Zachariah, the Prince's hand being burned – that makes no sense. Until then..." he gestured frustratedly.

"W-will you tell me?"

Sir William smiled without any happiness. "No. I would be in a significantly worse place without your help, Thomas, but the man must go unsuspected, and the safest way to ensure that is to keep my thoughts to myself."

Thomas tried to swallow any resentment. "Sir Marcus knows."

"Yes, and that is why he is helping me with something else at this moment. Which," he seized upon the change in subject eagerly, "reminds me that we must check those dungeons. Catching our killer means nothing if the Red Death is allowed to take dominion over us."

He took down the knife, untied the twine, and stepped out into the corridor. Thomas picked up the candles and the spool of string and followed.

"You will find out before too long, Thomas, I promise." Sir William said, turning to face him as he stepped out of the privy. "I have a feeling that we may be near the end of this thing now. And, in all honesty, I am relieved."

Thomas tried again to reason with his resentment, to trust this man who could see much farther and much clearer than he, and followed his master to the stairs.

TWENTY-FOUR

In the darkness of the spiralling stairway, Thomas considered Sir William's words. He, Thomas, had been present at practically every stage of these examinations, so how had Sir William come to conclusions that were still so far out of Thomas' reach?

He tried to think as they descended.

They emerged into the main hall and headed to kitchens, the sharp odour of burned fabric and ruined flesh still clinging to the corners of the room. Placing the spool of twine on the table, Sir William picked up the bag Sir Marcus had prepared the previous evening and turned to Thomas.

"Is this it?"

"Yes. The gauntlets and clubs are downstairs."

They turned for the stairs to the dungeons.

As Thomas followed, his eyes stole to the fireplace into which Fergus Highstone had fallen the previous day, and he stopped, staring. Sir William was unlocking the door before he looked up and realised.

"Thomas?"

"The poker, the shovel." These were now back in their place on the hearth.

Sir William took a couple of steps towards him. "Yesterday, whoever placed the hand in the fireplace had thrown them into the well. That was why Marcus was so long getting water, because the poker had jammed in the shaft of the well and he struggled to pull the bucket up."

"So someone really meant for the hand to burn?"

"It seems so," Sir William sighed. "What makes no sense is *burning* the hand. The smell was sure to attract our attention. It could have been thrown into the moat, or hidden in an unused room. It might have been discovered eventually, but it would have taken some time."

It seemed to Thomas that, far from just being thrown into the moat, something as small as a hand could have been thrown *beyond* the water, to the land on the other side, where it would likely be scavenged by some animal and never found again. He rubbed at his tired eyes, and Sir William, clearly reading his frustration, unlocked and opened the door to the stairway.

The shadows from their candles crept close as they descended. Emerging again at the boundary of the blue and red rooms, Sir William locked the door and Thomas went ahead, drawing out Laurence's key to let them into the brazier corridor. Cool morning air fell through the grates above them, and Thomas shivered as he locked the door after Sir William had stepped through.

"Which brazier do we light this morning?"

Thomas tried to remember. The morning of the attack on the Prince, they had lit the blue brazier, and then the following day the red. Yesterday, when Thomas had slept late, Sir Marcus would have come down alone and lit the next brazier around, by the white window, and so...

"It...it should be the green window, but..."

Sir William waited, and when no more was forthcoming, asked, "But?"

"On the morning that the Prince was attacked, Sir Marcus lit the blue brazier, but when I got to the other side he had also lit the green one. It should be green today, but since Sir Marcus lit that a few days ago, I suppose we should do purp—"

The look of shock on Sir William's face stopped him.

"Say that again."

Uncomprehending, Thomas repeated himself:

"On the morning that the Prince was attacked, Sir Marcus lit the blue brazier—"

"Three days ago? The morning I staged my attack on Prospero?"

"Yes."

"You're sure?"

"Yes."

"And another brazier was also lit that morning?"

"Yes. When I got round to the green window, Sir Marcus had also lit the flame there."

"Which way did you go?"

Thomas pointed into the corridor behind the blue room, towards the moat.

"And Marcus?"

Confused, Thomas pointed in the other direction, to the corridor behind the white room and the wood store beyond.

Sir William pointed to the blue brazier, "You would normally meet here, yes? You kill rats, you collect the rats, you burn them here?"

Thomas nodded.

"But on that morning two braziers were lit, and you burned your rats in the one on the opposite side, by the green window, because Marcus had lit it for you."

"Yes."

"Have you ever lit two braziers at the same time before?"

"No."

Sir Marcus had rationed everything carefully: food, oil, candles. Anything that could be consumed had to be used sparingly, lest they run out too soon.

"How long was it after Laurence and I left you in the kitchen that you came down here?"

Thomas struggled to think in the face of his master's sudden intensity.

"Almost immediately?" Sir William pressed.

"Almost."

"And it was definitely that morning that the two braziers were lit?"

"It was."

"Did you ask Marcus *why* he had lit a second when you saw

him?"

He shook his head. "We were working in different parts of the corridor."

"And afterwards? Did you ask him later?"

"No. You came down to tell us—" Sir Oswin's body had vanished, to be found the next day in the moat. And then Laurence had...

Sir William pressed the palms of his hands to his eyes. After several moments, he took a deep breath and dropped his hands to his sides.

"Baldon," he said with conviction.

"What?" Thomas jerked round in surprise.

"Baldon, we need to speak with Baldon."

"Now?"

"Now. I know who is responsible for these murders, and I know why they thought them necessary."

CHALLENGE TO THE READER

It is traditional at this stage to reassure the reader that all the information required to solve the mysteries contained in the narrative has been presented, and to encourage them to spend a few moments thinking over what they have read to see if they can beat the author to the answers.

The reader may consider themselves to have solved the mystery if they have a sequence of events that accounts for and explains all of the foregoing occurrences. The following questions, when answered individually, may help elucidate the solution:

1) Why was Oswin Bassingham killed?
2) Why was his body subsequently thrown into the moat?
3) How did Laurence Tolworth know of Sir Oswin's death?
4) How was Prince Prospero killed?
5) Why was his body desecrated and the left hand burned?
6) Who is responsible for the murders?

In answering all six questions correctly, you will have solved the puzzle of The Red Death Murders.

I wish you good luck, and hope you enjoy the explanation to come.

TWENTY-FIVE

It took some time for Sir William to return from rousing Sir Baldon, and the waiting was beginning to frustrate Thomas when the men eventually appeared in the stairway door. Sat in his accustomed place at the table in the main hall, trying to keep his mind from churning through the possibilities, he did his best to remain seated when all he wanted was to jump to his feet at the sight of them and start demanding answers.

As he had the other morning, Sir Baldon seemed slightly confused at being awake this early, his eyes struggling to focus and his growth of greying beard unkempt.

"Should we ring the bell for the others?" he asked distractedly, as Sir William preceded him into the hall, and Sir William shook his head as he sat.

Spotting Thomas, Sir Baldon stood behind his chair and bowed his head. "Sire."

"Good morning," Thomas said, unaware of what was expected.

"I have no desire to disturb Fergus," Sir William replied, "and Marcus is busy at the moment. Please, Baldon, sit."

Sir Baldon sat, and rubbed his hands over his chin to tame his facial hair. He then laid his hands face down on the table and blinked in an exaggerated manner to wake himself.

"Thank-you for rising so early, Baldon. The key information that explains these bizarre events has just now come into my possession, and I wanted to talk to you for two reasons."

The other man looked surprised. "You have an answer for what we have endured of late?"

"I have."

"I am very pleased to hear this, Sir William. It is true that we have feared your methods over these last few days to be rather aggressive, but if they have guided you to a solution to these problems, I am sure they can be justified."

Sir William raised his hands briefly in apology. "The murder of my friend, the murder of our Prince – these events should face no opposition in being brought to light."

Sir Baldon tilted his head placatingly. "Quite so."

Thomas' palms itched.

"The first reason we needed to talk immediately was that, as agreed last night, you are to stand as Thomas' herald, and so all information should be laid before you, Baldon, as it would have been our late, lamented Prospero."

Sir Baldon smiled faintly, looking pleased. "Thank-you, Sir William, I am indeed humbled. And the second reason?"

Sir William locked eyes with Thomas across the table, and exhaled a heavy breath. He then turned his attention to the other man and said evenly:

"The second reason, Baldon, is that you are responsible for at least two of the deaths, and I want to give you the opportunity to explain."

~

Thomas got the impression that, had the accusation been less serious, Sir Baldon would have laughed. To sit in this empty hall in this empty castle and be accused of the madness that had pursued them for four days was surely the ultimate joke.

Sir Baldon's lips barely moved as, frozen in place, he said, "I'm sorry?"

The itch in Thomas' palms spread to his arms and his elbows. He saw Sir Baldon's hand, still flat on the table, tremble, and wondered at the cause.

"Last night," Sir William said in the same even tone, "we sat at this table and bestowed upon you the power of a prince and, for all we know, possibly that of a king. None of us have an appetite for war, and Terrington's support all but ensures that anyone who steps into the Prince's role would do so unopposed—"

"I have," Sir Baldon's frozen appearance was now easing into wobbling indignation, "been a loyal follower and supporter of the King for more years than—"

"Yes," Sir William was still calm, still measured, "of the *King*. Of the old ways. A new table for the Prince's return, the need to immediately recognise Prospero's successor upon his death. All the pomp, all the formality. Everything Prospero himself rejected.

"Had Oswin and I removed Prospero from power, that stain, that corruption of your desires, would be cut from the royal line. Oswin stepping into the role was much more preferable to you – a man who has spent his later years as one of the King's closest confidants is bound to have adopted the habits, traditions, and ideas that Prospero scorned, ideas close to your own heart."

It started to make sense, but...

"So why would I *kill* him?"

"Because," Sir William looked at Sir Baldon with something close to pity, "you realised that you *could*. You have spent so long so close to so much power, this was your one chance to have some of it for yourself. It's only human, that temptation. Killing Oswin *after* Prospero was removed would have been too obvious, but before anyone else knew what was happening...well."

"Sir William," a begging note had entered Sir Baldon's voice now, "I assure you—"

"You knew that, with Prospero killed, the son you also knew about," here a gesture towards Thomas, "would assume his responsibilities and, since he has yet to achieve the necessary years, he would need a herald. Marcus was never going to do it with his history of opposing the King, and I, even as the man chosen to raise the Prince's issue, was too close to my brother to be considered. But you, Baldon, you could use your service of the King as proof of your suitability."

'You're the most suitable one left, Percy.'

Thomas felt no joy at being right. It seemed so petty when put into words. To kill four men just so you might have control of the lives of others – what kind of person did that?

"But," Sir Baldon's eyes seemed to dance in his head, his hands trembling, "Sir Oswin's body – if I killed him, I could hardly move his body. I w-was the first person here in this hall and," he seemed pleased with the idea that suddenly struck him, "your own brother will tell you as much." As he grew in confidence, his words came faster: "I was here when he rang the bell, and remained at this table between it being rung and the moment Fergus and I ascended together to view the body, which had disappeared by the time we got there."

Sir William and Thomas had been looking upon the corpse at the time the bell had summoned everyone back to this room. Sir Baldon was correct, he lacked the opportunity to have moved it.

And yet…Sir William was unmoved.

"I am aware of that difficulty, and Marcus has, on a number of occasions, assured me that you were indeed here in the hall the whole time."

"And still," Sir Baldon chuffed, perhaps a bit too mockingly, "you accuse me of responsibility for these acts?"

"I do."

Some of the confidence fell away from the other man. "I-I should like to know why."

Sir William glanced at Thomas, and the itch in his arms grew to consume his chest.

"Because Marcus moved the body," Sir William replied. "Because the two of you were working together."

~

"No!" Thomas was on his feet before he knew it, the word exploding out of him.

"Thomas," Sir William raised a palm in his direction.

"No!"

"*Thomas!*"

The room tilted, his head seemed to be growing and shrinking at the same time. "You're wrong. He would never..." he swallowed. He became aware of the two men looking at him, and realised he was behaving like a child – always bursting into tears and running from the room when he heard something he found displeasing. He remembered the quiet way Sir Baldon had accepted Sir William's accusation only a short time earlier, and was, for the first time, struck by the man's composure.

He fought to get this breathing under control, to lessen the thundering in his chest and the screaming in his mind.

"You're wrong," he said, more quietly, his voice shaking.

Something like regret crept into Sir William's face for the first time.

"Thomas, I told you that Marcus was doing something for me this morning. That was a lie. The truth is, we sat up late last night discussing the matter, and this morning I found he had disappeared—"

Fear stabbed through Thomas, and Sir William was quick to reassure him:

"He has come to no harm. I checked all the rooms except Fergus', and Marcus is no longer in the castle. His clothes were missing, the door to the roof was unlocked, a rope leads over the battlements."

Thomas wanted to remind him of the bodies found in the moat under similar conditions – assumed deserters who had come to a worse fate – but something in his master's manner told him there was more to this.

"We had talked last night, running over the possibilities until late. Marcus surely realised that I had exhausted every avenue, and that only my blindness provoked by love of my brother was keeping him free from suspicion. He knew that, before too long, I would *have* to examine his own movements, and that when I did I would realise how it had been done."

"How?" Thomas' throat was dry as he asked. Knowing what Sir William thought was the only way to convince him otherwise.

"Oswin was killed first—" Sir William began.

"Sir Oswin was *killed?*" Sir Baldon said, and Thomas was unable to tell if he was pretending ignorance. "But you said he was a suicide."

"I did. At that stage I had no idea how his murder had been achieved, but I wanted his killer – and it makes no difference to me if it was you or Marcus – to feel safe."

Sir Baldon looked shocked.

"Then you *lied* to Prince Prospero?"

Sir William watched him in silence for a few moments, and Sir Baldon indicated that he should continue.

"Oswin was killed and sealed in the privy – Thomas and I have established this morning how it could have been done. Right now, it is irrelevant. The method provides no clues to the man who enacted it."

Sir Baldon waited.

"Marcus knew I was to stage my false attack on Prospero in the morning, and doubtless arranged the timing of Oswin's murder so that the additional confusion of the next day might complicate things."

Thomas recalled Sir Marcus' insistence on suicide when the privy had been broken into, when the signs of murder were there for all to see. Was he trying, even at that early stage, to spread confusion?

"After Oswin was found, we all gathered down here, and

then Laurence, Marcus, Thomas, and I went to the kitchens. Laurence and I left shortly thereafter and Marcus and Thomas went to the dungeons to check on the rats."

So far, he could find no flaw, no argument to convince Sir William of the wrongness of his conclusions. But he would. He would.

"Marcus, I have just learned," another glance at Thomas, "lit two braziers downstairs for the burning of the vermin. Two braziers on opposite sides of the dungeons."

Thomas' heart plummeted. He sank back in his chair, horrified.

Oh, no.

"This meant that his absence would pass unnoticed."

"His absence?" Sir Baldon asked.

"Marcus was in the dungeon only long enough to light the braziers, knowing Thomas would be kept busy, hoping that the second brazier would keep him on that side of the castle. And then, this done," Sir William swallowed, "he ran up the stairs to dispose of Oswin's body.

"Marcus was," this to Sir Baldon, "more mobile than yourself or Fergus – indeed, we know how long it could take Fergus to climb the stairs, and I am sure the two of you would have ascended together. You are of a similar age and, after all, it would provide you with a witness who could swear that you had no chance to get to Oswin's body before it vanished."

Sir Baldon raised a finger. "And if I tell you that Fergus and I made very good time up those stairs? That your brother would have been unable to ascend before us?"

"Well, you would say that, of course. And you forget that Thomas, Marcus, and I followed Fergus up the stairs later that morning, and can attest to his lack of sprightly movement."

Sir Baldon made no reply.

"Marcus could get to the top floor ahead of you, remove Oswin's body – that would prove no problem to a man of his size and strength – carry it out to the roof, stab the lungs, and throw it into the moat."

"Why?" Thomas croaked out the word.

Sir William smiled unhappily. "That was my fault. I had been foolish enough to insist on Oswin having been murdered, when Marcus would have been hoping it go unsuspected for at least a little while longer. Hiding the body might delay any certainty, until Marcus and Baldon here could find a way to convince me otherwise."

"You seem very certain, Sir William, that the body was indeed hidden that way."

"Well," Sir William replied blandly, "I did find the body in the moat and view it for myself."

Sir Baldon looked at him in frank surprise.

"In the moat? But the drawbridge has been raised this whole time."

"I climbed down a rope over the walls," irritation clipped Sir William's words. "Does it really matter?"

The other man dipped his head in apology, something like despair on his face.

"Marcus was probably still coming down the stairs when Laurence arrived up there and saw whatever he saw." Sir William's voice was grim, "Which means that you killed Laurence, Baldon."

Thomas watched Sir Baldon closely, the itch in his chest now shrinking to a point of hardness.

"Maybe you heard him tell Fergus he was going onto the roof – you were reluctant to admit it when first asked, I seem to remember – or maybe you waited for him to go out and come back. Either way, Fergus came downstairs to tell us about the missing body and you..." his voice faltered, "you stabbed Laurence in the chest, to protect yourself."

Thomas curled his fingers into fists, and placed them on his thighs.

"Do you really think I," Baldon raised a shaking hand, self-loathing on his face, "could beat Laurence Tolworth to his own knife?"

"No, but there was no need to stab Laurence with *his* knife. You stabbed him with yours."

The military knife, given to everyone who served in the King's army.

The military knife, worn by most of the men in this castle.

"You simply needed to surprise him, which I'm sure was no difficulty – none of us would suspect you capable of such an act. But you have been away from violence for too long, Baldon, and your attempt missed. You left him on the ground thinking he was dead, took his knife and put it in your own belt, and returned to your search. We would probably be suspicious of you, but you had denial on your side; so long as you were away from the corpse when he was discovered...well, we could never *know*.

"And you *were* away from his body when we found him, but through no design of your own. Because you had left him alive, Laurence was able to—" he swallowed as his voice faltered, "to stumble down the stairs in search of help before the effort killed him."

Sir William glanced over at Thomas with something like a warning in his eyes and Thomas did his best to act other than a child might, to hold onto the rage and the hatred, the horror and the disgust, surging inside of him.

"And the signs of the Red Death upon Laurence's body?" Sir Baldon asked. "You are simply ignoring that?"

"You and I have killed enough men to know that a sharp blow to the head, the neck, can cause blood to rupture in the eyes; doubtless as Laurence fell he struck his head on the steps with enough force for this to occur. I never believed that he had the Red Death upon him. Zachariah's eyes were red when I cut him down, and I hid his face so that no-one would spot it and realise the lie I had allowed to grow. Again, I was making you feel safe, Baldon, so I could finally confront you now."

There was less confidence in the older man now, Thomas saw.

"The murder of Prince Prospero," Sir William continued evenly, "was accomplished exactly as suspected: you drank enough of the wine to ensure that only a little remained, Marcus having assured you in advance that neither he nor Thomas would drink any. Drawing attention to himself was simply to cover the fact that Marcus *did* sneak poison into the cup – probably before he even pretended to drink, when no-one was looking that closely at him."

"But," Thomas seized at the last hanging thread of a chance to clear Sir Marcus' name, "the poison we use for the rats hardly affects people, you said."

Sir William scratched at his head. "This is something I would need Marcus to explain. He assured me that the poison was fatal only in large quantities, but I see now that it suited his needs for me to believe that. Clearly there was some way to strengthen the poison, to intensify its effects. And until he is found, we may never know how that was done."

"And why," Sir Baldon asked, with an air of shock in his tone again, "did we desecrate the corpse? That detail can hardly be excluded."

Sir William looked unconcerned. "Precisely for the reason that Marcus feared I was getting too close and so should be given an additional problem to worry about. He knew that if I came to suspect him, my inability to see the sense in the removal and burning of the Prince's hand, to make that part of the events elsewhere which *had* to be connected, would stop me from accusing him. My weakness," he said with a sour smile, "is that I like everything to fit."

"So was Zachariah killed for the same reason?" Thomas asked.

Sir Baldon looked confused. "But Zachariah killed *himself.* W-we watched you...examine the room; there was no way out."

Sir William was silent for a few moments, staring at Sir Baldon.

"I'll confess, I see no purpose behind the murder of Zachariah. I was hoping that you might see sense, recognise that your scheme has been exposed and my brother has fled and abandoned you to carry responsibility, and that you might therefore tell *me* why the bodyguard had to die."

"You insist it was murder, then?"

"I do."

"Well, since I carry no responsibility for his death," Sir Baldon's confidence was growing, now that Sir William's explanation was before him in full, "I am unable to aid you."

A thought struck Thomas then, the last chance to save Sir Marcus: "But, Sir Marcus and Sir Baldon, they..." there was no nice way to say it, "they *hate* each other."

Sir Baldon was almost eager in his agreement, but Sir William was yet again unconcerned.

"They appear to, yes, but such behaviour was necessary to divert suspicion. Come, now, even after hearing what I have to say, do you really believe that these two would conspire to commit these acts?"

Thomas gave that some thought. "No."

"And yet they must have – look at the mistakes they made."

"Mistakes?" Sir Baldon asked, with a sharp note of alarm.

"The biggest one was asking Marcus to replace this very table – unless you knew he was uninjured from his fight with the figure dressed as the Red Death, with me, the day before, you would never have asked for that, because he should have been too bruised, too sore. And he forgot to refuse because he knew both sides of the lie – the fight with me was staged, and you and he were only pretending to be at each other's throats.

He forgot that *you* should be in ignorance of the staged fight, and so he agreed and gave you away."

"And if I tell you that I was unaware of Sir Marcus having fought with anyone? All that was spoken of was, er, His Highness chasing the figure, er, you, before you disappeared."

Sir William looked at him sadly. "What else would I expect you to say?"

Sir Baldon steadied his hands on the surface of the table, and looked from Sir William to Thomas and back again.

"I maintain this is all the purest invention, Sir William, and I had hoped you would be more careful than simply to jump at the first and easiest explanation you could find. I wonder if you might answer one more question for me."

"Of course."

"You say I did this to seize power, which I deny. Why, then would your brother aid me? His history is now," a gesture towards Thomas, "understood by everyone here, and any involvement he sought in the running of the kingdom would hardly go unopposed by those of us who remember his treachery. He despises the very system you claim I have murdered to uphold, so why would he help me achieve this aim?"

Sir William scratched roughly as his head again, as if forcing back tiredness.

"For all his flaws, Marcus believes in the rights of the people. The two of you were bound together in this, and he would have used the knowledge he had of your ambition to ensure that, once the chaos of the Red Death is laid to rest, a fairer, a kinder, and a better system emerged. Marcus will never have power, because people possess long memories, but he can stand beside it and steer it occasionally in a better direction."

Sir Baldon eyes dropped to the table and then up again at his accuser. "That is perhaps the first thing you have said with which I agree completely. And now I have only one more question."

They waited.

"What do you intend to do with me? I maintain my innocence, but I see that you are unlikely to be swayed in your conclusions. And so the matter of my treatment from here should be addressed."

Before Sir William could speak, a rhythmic slapping sound echoed out into the room. As if a spell had been broken, all three of them turned their heads in search of the source of the noise, and Thomas saw Fergus Highstone emerge from a doorway.

He was clapping.

He appeared to be smiling.

The skin on the right side of his face was pink and blistered, and livid red scarring could be seen on his neck above the collar of his nightshirt. He shuffled awkwardly into the hall, bearing his weight on his left side, determination in every line of his body as he approached the table.

"An excellent story, Sir William," he said, dropping his hands, approaching Sir Baldon from behind, "you are to be commended. A quite marvellous use of the glare and glitter and piquancy and phantasm that has engulfed us in these recent days."

He reached Sir Baldon's chair, patted the man's shoulder in a reassuring manner and, inclining his head towards Thomas, sank into Sir Marcus' seat.

"How are you, Fergus?" Sir William asked, his eyes hooded.

"Oh, you know," came the cold reply, "in agony. But I am saddened to be excluded from the crescendo of our little drama."

"I thought you should rest."

"I imagine you did."

Thomas looked from one man to the other. What was happening?

"Poor Baldon here, accused and friendless, was exactly what you wanted, that you might better ply him with your false accusations and bully Master Thomas into accepting them."

False accusations?

"Is that so?" Sir William's face was blank, unreadable.

Highstone nodded. "And I think this farce has played out long enough."

Sir William dipped his head. "I agree."

"Farce?" Thomas blurted out, unable to follow the meaning both men seemed to have packed into their words.

"Yes," Highstone said casually, his eyes never leaving Sir William. "Your master – your ex-master, I suppose, sire – tells a good story, but I think it is perhaps time for the truth."

"The truth?" Sir Baldon said, as if hardly daring to believe.

"Indeed," Highstone replied. He reached out and placed a reassuring hand on the other man's arm. "We know that no blame lies at your door, that you committed no murders, that you – most laughable of all, Sir William – were in no pact with Marcus Collingwood."

"You do?"

"We do, Sir William and I. Am I right?"

Sir William offered no response.

Thomas realised suddenly that the three of them sat together, facing his master across the table, almost as if...

"Because you killed them, Sir William," Highstone said. "No blame lies at Baldon's feet, it lies at yours."

TWENTY-SIX

Thomas expected his master to laugh, or at the very least to pinch out that thin smile of his, and for Fergus Highstone to grin in reply with a resumption of his usual manner, this whole proceeding revealed as a jest. Instead, the two men watched each other across the table, their eyes locked, their faces unmoving, their breathing slow and level and controlled despite the high emotion in the air.

A sharp sweetness rose from Highstone's burned flesh, and Thomas was unable to tell if it was this or the gravity of their manner that made him feel so uneasy.

"You see, Sir William," the burned man said, "as I lay upstairs recovering, it struck me that you had been very clever in assuming the mantle of examining these problems for yourself. With time to reflect, I see now the pattern behind it all, the pattern you have sought to hide from the rest of us by pretending to look for explanations in murders and actions that you have yourself committed."

"It was *him*?" Sir Baldon screeched.

Highstone's eyes stayed fixed on Sir William. "It was."

Thomas, quelling again that childish urge to spring to his feet and shout otherwise, sat, waiting, his fists bunched ever-tighter in his lap.

Sir William held Highstone's gaze. "I should be interested to hear your explanations, Fergus."

"Very well," Highstone replied, and grimaced in pain. "You say you have deduced the method by which Sir Oswin came to be sealed in the privy, and I see no need to press you on the details. Since Master Thomas was with you, I am sure he has either seen a working method or, as you so skilfully managed elsewhere, has been misled away from it. I think, though, that whatever method you have shown him is genuine, your discovery of it *together* no doubt used to assure him of your innocence."

Sir William remained relaxed but alert, and Thomas wished for just one reassuring glance in his direction; just one, before the world burned down around him.

"Under the guise of sympathy for Sir Oswin's desire to remove Prince Prospero from power, you met him in the privy – all the better to keep it secret – killed him, and sealed him in. You had planned your own attack on the Prince for the following day, trusting, as you attributed elsewhere, that the additional confusion would unnerve people further and make them look in entirely the wrong places.

"Better yet, since you know Sir Oswin is already dead, you arrange for us to search each floor – it was, after all, you who deployed us around the castle to look for him – making sure that someone who would have little suspicion of you discovers the body and would most likely seek your advice before all others."

Thomas tried to deny the sense of this. He *was* the perfect choice to discover Sir Oswin, because he could be expected to call Sir William and Sir Marcus to the privy ahead of anyone else.

Had he been manipulated this whole time?

Fergus Highstone continued:

"You realised the flaws in your presentation, or wanted to further divert suspicion, and so insisted that Sir Oswin had been murdered – no murderer would set up a suicide to then immediately point out it was murder, after all – and you no doubt invited your brother and servant into your confidences by asking them to keep this suspicion to themselves."

'For the time being, say nothing about murder.'

Thomas' uneasiness grew.

"You summoned us here and told us of your discovery, after which Master Thomas, Laurence, Sir Marcus, and yourself headed into the kitchens, and Baldon and I headed upstairs to view the body."

"Which had, by this point, moved," Sir William said reasonably.

"Which had moved." Highstone agreed.

"Then how...?" Sir Baldon asked, echoing Thomas' thoughts. They had left the corpse in place at the ringing of the bell, and Sir William was never alone between then and the body's disappearance.

"Because Zachariah was helping me," Sir William said, and Thomas' stomach lurched at the admission before his master continued: "Is that correct?"

Highstone dipped his head once.

Sir William's voice remained reasonable, "As the only person who was unobserved at that time, he is only one who *could* have moved the body."

"Exactly. Sir Marcus spoke to him on the way down, and we know Zachariah refused to leave his station. However, as soon as your brother was out of sight, Zachariah raced upstairs, getting there probably just as you had started to descend, and carried the body – as you had agreed – out to the roof and threw it into the moat. It was, Baldon told me when we spoke of this before, yourself who sent your brother up to summon Zachariah to our meeting after a suitable time had passed. The bodyguard agreed to join us that second time only because he had fulfilled the task assigned to him: disposing of the body."

'It's an old army trick.'

Zachariah, who had served in the armies of many lands.

"And did Zachariah also kill Laurence?" Sir William asked.

"I am unwilling to be rushed, Sir William," Highstone replied, his voice stern, and Sir William raised a hand in apology.

Thomas rubbed his sweating palms on the rough material of his trousers. Listening to a description of Laurence's murder for a second time that day was again something he wished to flee, but he forced himself to sit still, to listen.

"After leaving Master Thomas and your brother in the kitchens, you followed Laurence upstairs – you knew his intelligence, and feared that he, of all of us, might spot something Zachariah or yourself had overlooked. Keeping out of sight, you heard his conversation with me and, fearing he perceived some truth and unwilling to risk whatever he might notice out on the roof, you waited until I began to descend and, I imagine, confronted and attacked him there and then."

Thomas drew in deep breaths. No-one looked in his direction.

"However, again as you have attributed elsewhere," Highstone indicated Sir Baldon, "you are also a long way from violence, and in your haste – and, to be fair, in distress at having to kill your friend – your own blow was wide of the mark and Laurence was, as you said, clinging to life when you left him."

"But you found me here, in this very room," Sir William objected. "If you had a head-start on me descending the stairs – and I would have waited for you to be some distance away before killing anyone, I think we can agree – I would have been out of breath from racing down a different stairway. If I had even managed to make it down here at all. You do admit that?"

"I do."

Sir William nodded, satisfied.

"Yes," Highstone continued, "that was the one part I could see no answer to, until you enlightened me when trying to hang your misdeeds on Baldon here."

And he pointed upwards, to the bell.

"You told Baldon, and I noticed you make brief work of doing so, that you found Oswin's body in the moat, and climbed down a rope to do so. Well, if you can climb down a rope on the outside the castle, you can climb down one *inside*."

"Oh!" the word slipped out before Thomas could stop it,

and Sir William glanced over at him, looking nervous for the first time.

"Are you able to clarify something for us, sire?" Highstone asked, turning to him.

"You," Thomas felt awful saying it, but there was no malice in the look Sir William turned upon him, no warning; "you slid down the rope outside so quickly." He thought of the bell rope, descending from the roof through the middle of the open space above them.

Five storeys.

Straight down.

"Surely the bell would ring?" Sir Baldon asked.

Thomas shook his head, unable to take his eyes from his master. He could see it so clearly, so perfectly. "The rope could be disconnected from the clapper and tied to the rafters easily enough, then reconnected later." Provided no-one wanted to ring the bell, everything could be put back without any suspicions being aroused. Sir William could have easily snuck up to the roof without being seen before the burning of Laurence's body...

No emotion showed on Sir William's face. "That is very clever."

Highstone jumped in before Thomas had time to feel horrified at what sounded like an admission: "You admit that this is indeed what happened?"

"I admit the cleverness of the insight; nothing more."

Highstone's eyes glittered in the rising morning light.

"The murder of the Prince and the desecration of his body are, then, simply parts of the same problem. You do yourself no favours, Sir William, with this talk of unknown poisons that may be made stronger by a process beyond the ken of any of us. The answer, as you well know, is far simpler."

"Prince Prospero *was* poisoned, then?" Sir Baldon asked.

"He was."

"So how did the rest of us survive?"

A little of the urgency went out of Highstone's bearing, as if these interruptions wearied him, "Because there was no poison in the cup."

"Then how...?"

"Think. What happened? Zachariah filled the cup and drank, and we all in turn drank. After Sir Marcus' little drama – far from the distraction Sir William claims, but simply an expression of the disdain he holds for our traditions – the cup came round to the Prince who, like the rest of us, took it in his right hand, drank, and fell down dead."

Took it in his right hand.

"Supposing, at the moment he drinks, someone were to seize his *left* hand and – with, say, a ring designed for such a purpose – pierce the Prince's skin so as to place poison directly into his blood."

Thomas remembered the whispered stories surrounding Zachariah, stories they had all heard: that he had once killed seven men with a single swipe of his sword, that he had killed one man simply by touching him.

Simply by touching him!

Zachariah, who had been sat to the Prince's left.

Thomas bunched his fists again, feeling his nails digging into the skin of his palms.

"There are poisons which if swallowed leave a man unharmed, but if placed in his blood kill him in a matter of moments. Whatever you are using to kill these rats is, I wager, one of these." His voice became grim, "And I intend to prove it later."

How, in the middle of a plague spread through the blood of its victims, had Thomas failed to consider poison placed into the Prince's own blood? He tried to deny the sense that Highstone was making and yet...

"Zachariah again," Sir William said.

"Indeed."

"And so the desecration of the Prince's corpse—"

"Yes," Highstone said, "was to hide the wound on his hand. You were unable to predict how soon the desecration might be discovered, and had only the *left* hand been severed we might have guessed the significance. With our attentions then directed to Zachariah, he may have been persuaded to talk before you could silence him forever. By perpetrating those additional horrors of severing the Prince's feet and head you sought to hide the importance of that one missing appendage, which could be burned at a later time. And, of course, only the site of the wound need be destroyed, so the discovery of the hand and," Highstone gestured to himself, "what happened afterwards was of no consequence."

Sir William raised one more objection: "And the fact that I was nowhere near the kitchens when the hand must have been placed in the fire…"

Highstone was unworried.

"The hand was, I seem to recall, tied to a length of rope?"

Sir Baldon nodded.

"Then it would be a simple matter of fixing this inside the chimney with some wax, and waiting for the heat of the embers to melt it. Or perhaps you placed the hand on the embers atop a thin piece of wood, which would have burned away only once you were able to provide a witness to affirm that you were elsewhere. Really, Sir William, it is no defence at all."

Where *had* Sir William gone after the discovery of Zachariah's body? How long had Thomas dozed in that room on the top floor before his master joined him?

Sir William placed his hands flat on the table. "At least now we know why Zachariah was killed."

Highstone continued joylessly. "You said a little while ago that your brother would use Baldon's complicity to manipulate him at a later time. You had already anticipated this from

Zachariah, so you killed him to prevent it – and used the examination of his death as proof, once again, of your innocence, as you have done throughout this affair. Why else would a killer seek the answers behind a murder *he* had committed?"

"The fact that I was with Thomas and Marcus when Zachariah was killed?" he asked, infuriatingly calm.

"Proves nothing," Highstone replied. "Zachariah's body was found two floors above your own room. I heard your brother knocking on your door – we probably all did – and I remember it took you rather a long time to answer. You could have been racing back from having committed that murder, and could have entered your own room using the same method by which you had exited the room with Zachariah's body in."

If there were loose planks in the ceiling of that room, surely there could also be some in the *floor* of another. Again, Thomas was furious with himself for failing to think of this: always distracted by his own immature concerns – fear of hanging, blind trust of a man who…

"Are you finished?" Sir William asked.

Highstone looked to Sir Baldon on his right and then Thomas on his left, as if judging the impact of his words. Thomas found himself unable to meet Highstone's eye, reluctant to admit the sense of what he had heard and yet unable to find a flaw. He felt completely lost. Had he really been deceived so easily?

"I am."

Sir William sat up straight in his chair. "Good, because you have forgotten a few things."

"I have?"

"You have; how, for instance, did Laurence know that Oswin was dead when he joined us here at the table that morning?"

'Terrible news about Sir Oswin…'

"Well, it hardly seems important—"

"But can you explain it?" Sir William asked. "My weakness, you see, is that I like everything to fit."

Highstone sighed. "Laurence Tolworth was a man to whom life and death were equally jests; he was probably making a joke that he hoped would be tasteless enough to earn him some reaction."

Sir William dismissed this with a wave of a hand. "And the fact that two braziers were alight downstairs the morning we found Oswin's body?"

Highstone's sigh was heavier this time. "It does you no justice, Sir William, to seek solace in such distractions. You are exposed; admit it and face what is coming to you."

Sir William shook his head. "But my brother's parsimony in all things is well-known. Why, when he had fought tooth and nail to make our provisions last, would he break the habit on that morning in particular?"

"Well," Highstone's face took on a pleased look, "we could ask him."

"Ask him?" Sir Baldon blurted out. "But he has left the castle."

"No, Baldon, you forget," Highstone said, "Sir William told us that as part of his attempt to shift the blame for his actions onto you. Sir Marcus is, I am sure, within the castle still."

"Then let us ring the bell and summon him to us," Sir Baldon said confidently.

Nobody moved.

"Wh-?" Sir Baldon looked from Highstone to Sir William. "What is the delay?"

Highstone inclined his head. "No, it is a good idea, Baldon. Unless—"

"Unless?" Thomas had to ask, fear gripping him.

Highstone turned to him. "I am sorry, sire, we could all see how fond you were of Sir Marcus. But when we have gathered here of late, what reason does anyone have for being absent?"

Thomas found that he was unable to raise his eyes to Sir William's face, for fear of what he might see there.

"Am I right, Sir William?" an edge of nastiness crept into Highstone's voice. "Did Sir Marcus see through your plans and also need to be pushed aside? We could, if you prefer, waste time as before searching the castle, or you could tell us now in which room we shall find his body.

"Or," he smiled thinly, and raised a hand to indicate the bell above them, "you could put an end to these speculations and summon him to us."

There was a tremor in Sir William's hands and voice both when he spoke. "Why?"

"Why?" Highstone was taken aback. "Well, because it would prove me at least partly wrong, and no doubt set the mind of Master Thomas at ease."

Sir William shook his head, "No, I mean why did I do all this? I claimed Baldon was motivated by power, but I have achieved no power, no position, as a result. So why would I kill all these men?"

Highstone seemed pleased at the question.

"You say you have no power, no position, but come – that is hardly true."

"How so?"

"You raised the Prince's son who, because you prevented Sir Oswin from removing the Prince's powers while he lived, can now ascend to his father's place and may, in time, become King. Baldon may be accepted as herald, but as the man who raised the Prince's heir, who taught him so much, you would have his ear – an entirely natural result of the trust he has in you. That, Sir William, is true power."

"And that is how I convinced Zachariah to assist me?"

"It is."

"Because he had been so close to power that he, like I

claimed of Baldon, was desperate to taste it for himself."

"Indeed."

Thomas had no interest in this bickering over power, in these games that were being played for the purposes of influencing him in the years ahead. He felt stupid for being misled, and angry at himself for failing to question more, for failing to see what had been right in front of him.

But all he cared about in this instant was whether Sir Marcus still lived.

"Thank-you, Fergus," Sir William said, his back straight once more, his voice level and even and...

...kind?

Highstone, clearly confused, remained silent.

"I am particularly grateful to you for filling in the few remaining gaps in my own reasoning, and showing me that which I had overlooked."

"Th-then," Sir Baldon started to say, "y-you still maintain that I...?"

"Oh, no, Baldon," Sir William said with a gesture, "I owe you an apology, but it was necessary at the time to give the impression that I believed you were guilty."

"Then you know that I—"

"Carry no responsibility for these deaths? Of course."

Sir William glanced at the man opposite him, and Thomas drew a breath against the deepening lunacy he could feel rushing down upon them.

"Because you killed them, Fergus. No blame lies at our feet, it lies at yours."

TWENTY-SEVEN

Finally, someone laughed.

"Come, Sir William," Highstone scoffed, "you are a dog urinating on trees. First you accuse Baldon and then, when I provide proof of your own complicity, you turn your focus on me. Really, this is beneath you."

Sir William smiled his thin smile, and spoke in the same calm tone as before:

"Let me ask you a question, then; one that thus far no-one has asked or answered."

Highstone waited, giving the impression of tolerating the whims of a desperate man.

"Why did Laurence go up to the roof?"

Highstone looked at Sir Baldon, and then back across at the man opposite. "Well, because he suspected Sir Oswin's body had been carried up there. As it had. By Zachariah. Helping you."

"But why the *roof*? You said yourself that you and Baldon started searching the rooms, and Laurence, without speaking to either of you—" he looked between the men and waited for them to confirm this, "decided to skip searching the rooms and go straight to the *roof*. The rooms were the obvious first place to search, so why overlook them?"

Highstone made an elaborate, confident gesture. "Tell us then, Sir William. Why?"

Sir William looked from Sir Baldon to Thomas, as if waiting for them to figure it out. Thomas' mind was in such turmoil, he no longer knew what to believe; trying to piece together coherent thoughts was beyond him in this maelstrom of accusation and counter-accusation.

"Laurence would have gone to the privy first, because that is where we assumed the body was at that time. The only reason he would then go to the *roof*," Sir William said, "would be if something fell past the window – something big enough shape to catch his eye, and send him running."

"So what did he see?" Thomas asked.

"A dead body," Sir William replied. "Oswin's body fell past the window when Laurence was in the privy."

Thomas' blood froze; Sir William turned to face Fergus Highstone.

"Because you, Fergus, sent Baldon to search the rooms and, with him out of the way, headed up to the roof and threw Oswin over the side."

~

"I was correct before," Sir William continued into the silence, "I just chose to lay it at the feet of the wrong person: when we split up to search the castle for Oswin, Laurence remained down here and you, Fergus, instead of searching the floor I assigned to you, crept up to the top floor to await the discovery of the body you had killed and placed there the night before.

"I, foolishly, discussed the possibility of murder, and had Thomas confirm my suspicions. You, having overheard, simply waited for us to leave, knowing that the first stage of your plans had been ruined and that we were now looking for a murderer. So, as soon as Thomas and I left, you carried the body out to the roof for safe keeping and then – it must have taken a little time, wrestling a dead body through that hatch – descended to meet us here, and blamed your lateness on having called in on the Prince."

Thomas remembered: Highstone had been the last to arrive that morning.

'Bugger, sorry…'

"From this meeting, you went upstairs with Baldon," Sir William gestured to his left, "discovered the body missing, and instituted a search. Sending Baldon around in one direction, you ran for the roof, punctured the lungs of the corpse, and threw it over the side of the castle just as Laurence reached the privy."

Highstone raised a finger, "You will forgive me, Sir William, but as the only remaining man in this castle to have been spared military service, I am," he gestured to where his belt would have been, "unarmed at all times. So how could I possibly have stabbed the body as you claim?"

Sir William almost smiled, and looked at Thomas.

"I said it was an army trick, hiding the body like that, but a medical man would know about air trapped in the lungs. A medical man would know much that was useful for effects we have witnessed." He turned his attention back to Fergus Highstone, "As to what to puncture them with, well, that's where you fell down. You had no doubt intended to use Oswin's knife, but I had taken it with me after we found him, which you would have noticed when moving him. And so, if you're heading to the roof and in urgent need of a pointed weapon, you would have to take—"

"The arrows," Thomas breathed, and the first chink of light appeared.

"Why the arrows, Thomas?"

"The wounds on the body," he could slap himself for missing it, "were round, puckered, like an arrow had been driven into the lungs from below – oh!"

An image of Sir Marcus touching his chest came to him: *'Because Will said—'*

"Go on," Sir William prompted.

Thomas swallowed, remembering the sight of his friend lying dead. "The knife in Laurence's chest," he tapped his ribs, "was here. A knife blade would slide between the ribs, so the lungs could be punctured that way, but an arrow would be too wide to force between the ribs by hand and so needed to be stabbed into the lungs from underneath."

His delight at seeing this connection was suddenly swamped by the realisation that the man they were accusing sat next to him. Highstone's eyes flicked coldly up and down Thomas before he turned back to Sir William.

"Any one of us could have used the arrows, Sir William."

"This is true. But you took the bow out with you as well."

"Did I?"

"You did."

"And how do you explain that?"

"Because you sat here knowing you were going back up to the roof at the first opportunity to stab a corpse, and you would therefore have a bloody arrow on your hands, one you would be keen to get rid of as quickly as possible. And we all know how you feel about blood in the days of the Red Death, Fergus."

"You burn it," Sir Baldon said, almost innocently.

"There is a flame on the roof at all times, kept there at my insistence over my brother's protestations. When you went back upstairs, you collected the arrows, stabbed Oswin in the lungs – and then you set fire to that arrow and disposed of it."

Thomas risked a glance at Highstone's face; he was looking much less pleased now.

"It would be a risk to simply wait for it to burn up – someone might emerge onto the roof at any moment – but where to fire it? Into the moat and it might float and attract attention; into the surrounding land and, after this hot weather, you may start a forest fire. But," Sir William raised a finger, "from the roof you can see the courtyard, and at the base of the castle walls are the grates above the braziers – hardly a difficult shot for a man who would fire a flaming arrow into Laurence's body at a similar distance later that same day. So, with time was running short, and still needing to tip the body into the moat, you leaned over the wall and fired the arrow down through the grate, knowing it would burn up in the brazier and destroy itself."

Highstone's eyebrows rose and fell as if unimpressed.

"But the body could have been stabbed with an arrow to make it look like it was done by anyone *but* a military man. Indeed, you have had such foresight this whole time, you may have directed Zachariah to do this precisely so *that* I could be accused."

Sir William looked at the third man sitting at the table.

"What does a military man do with an unclean weapon, Baldon?"

"He wipes it clean."

Thomas thought back to Sir William wiping the knife he had used to cut the rope which ended Zachariah' life, and of Zachariah slicing fruit outside the Prince's room, wiping his blade before sheathing it.

"A military man *could* have stabbed Oswin's body with the arrow, but then would have wiped it clean and placed it back in the quiver – you respect what you might later need. And, I believe, the only smear of blood to be found on Oswin's clothes…"

"…Sir Marcus made when we found him," Thomas breathed, beginning to hope.

He saw Highstone's jaw flex.

"And I suppose I would do this – fire a flaming arrow into the dungeons – knowing that your brother and Master Thomas were due to descend there that morning? That they might even be down there at that very moment? An extra flame was bound to catch their attention."

"No, Fergus," Sir William's voice was still calm, "you had no idea that Thomas and Marcus would be down there."

"Is that so?"

"It is. When Prospero was killed in this very room, Zachariah accused Marcus of poisoning him on account of Marcus and Thomas taking care of the rats in the dungeons. And you were surprised. You had no idea they were down there every morning."

Thomas remembered, from the confused impressions of that night:

'Every morning, these two, they go to the cellars and they poison the rats.'

'Is this true?'

"Even so," Highstone argued, "when Sir Marcus guided Master Thomas from the hall that morning he said—"

"He said they would go and boil frogs – it's Marcus' little joke, and would, if anything, have made you assume they were headed to the kitchens, rather than the dungeons." A little of the light left Sir William's eyes, "I hate to think what you might have done if you'd thought they posed any sort of risk when it came to discovering that flame."

"But they *did* discover it."

"And misunderstood its presence – each, I think, believing the other to have lit it – which is why they failed to mention it to me."

'Just one flame this morning, save the fuel.'

Thomas groaned; it had been a rebuke for what Sir Marcus saw as his wastefulness the day before.

"After Marcus, Thomas, Laurence, and I left, you and Baldon headed upstairs – you're doubtless faster on these stairs than you wanted us to believe, Fergus, as Baldon attested earlier – and Laurence followed a little while after, getting to the top floor while you were on the roof, probably just as you fired your arrow down into the brazier. You tipped Oswin's body over the edge, leaving a smear of blood on the stone, and Laurence, in the privy, saw it and immediately headed for the roof – meeting you on your way back down."

"And then," the sneer in Highstone's voice surprised even Thomas with its strength, "I wrestled a knife away from a trained soldier 25 years younger than me and managed to stab him in the chest. Please, Sir William, stop wasting our time."

"No, I agree, that is ridiculous. Laurence would have been on his guard, you would never have beaten him to his knife, nor in a fight. But you had no intention of killing him by stabbing him in the chest. You left him dead, or so you believed, without needing to take his knife from him at all."

Thomas sat up at that. "But we—"

"We heard Laurence stumble down the stairs, yes, and he was clearly injured. But Fergus thought Laurence was already dead and, realising his failure, raced up the stairs and at *that* point took Laurence's knife from his scabbard and..." he stopped and pressed his hands into the surface of the table, drawing in a deep breath.

"So," Sir Baldon asked, "he stabbed Laurence twice? Was that why there was a cut on his leg?"

Sir William closed his eyes, bunched his fists, and Thomas watched the tension work its way out of him. His eyes opened, and he looked at Sir Baldon.

"The cut on Laurence's leg was made by me, to allow for the false explanation I gave to Prospero before he died. No, Laurence was killed in another way entirely."

"Then, how?"

Sir William inhaled deeply, and became still again.

"The thing I could see no sense in was Oswin's killer moving the body. And then Thomas made me realise, just a short while ago, that we had never thought about *how* Oswin died. The knife on the floor of the privy had been used to seal the door rather than to kill him, but we only realised that today. Oswin was already dead when his wrists were slit, so his body was moved – and thrown into the moat – to disguise how he had actually been killed."

"How?" Thomas asked.

"Well, what did dropping Oswin onto water from such a height do?"

Thomas swallowed, remembering the contorted limbs of the

corpse they had dragged over the battlements. "It broke his bones."

"Exactly," the firmness in Sir William's voice gave Thomas more hope. "It shattered practically every bone in his body, hiding the ones that had been broken *before* he was dropped into the water. Oswin died of a broken neck. And, with murder suspected, the one thing Fergus was keen to avoid was any talk of broken necks." He looked at Highstone. "I think Laurence confronted you – that was the conversation Baldon overheard while searching the rooms – and demanded to know what you had been doing on the roof, and you tripped him and pushed him down onto the stairs and broke *his* neck, just as you had broken Oswin's – just as you would go on to break Zachariah's – hoping to give the impression that he had slipped on the stairs and died in your absence."

"And how did Laurence manage to walk down the stairs with a broken neck?" Highstone's disdain was clearly masking something deeper.

"There are broken necks and broken necks. If you snap a chicken's neck, it retains enough life to run around a paddock for a while; a bad or malicious hangman can break his prisoner's neck just enough to leave them to asphyxiate in the noose. I am willing to bet that it is possible to break a man's neck and leave him alive – that, panicking as you were, you caught Laurence a glancing blow and broke the bone but, like a bad hangman, left enough connection," he rubbed his own neck with a finger, "for Laurence to remain conscious, struggling to breathe but aware of what was happening, with just enough control of his body to get to his feet and fight his way down the stairs to warn us. Only for you to be the first person coming back up the stairs to meet him."

Highstone sat, silent.

"We examined the body, looking for signs of the Red Death – I'll admit, I was too upset to think of much at the time, but I at least wanted an opportunity to come up with some false answers to make his killer feel safe. And then, under the guise of your fear of blood and the Red Death, we burned him and destroyed any chance of showing how he really died."

Sir William paused for a moment, to gather himself.

"Killing Oswin was, I suspect, practice for killing Prospero; no-one could have devised that method of sealing the privy door on the spot, it must have been planned for later use. Oswin simply...hastened your hand, Fergus. I think that, if Oswin's murder had gone unsuspected, we would also have found Prospero sealed in that privy with slit wrists at some point – however long it took between deaths to convince people the two were suicides. Of course, we discovered the murder straight away and that made Fergus change his plans."

"So how was the Prince poisoned?" Thomas asked.

Sir William's eyes were far away before he replied. "I think Laurence walking down those stairs gave Fergus another idea, and examining the corpse before the funeral helped clarify how it might be done. If Prospero could be seen alive, walking and talking, and then die in our presence without Fergus going near him, it would be a perfect way to kill him without attracting suspicion. I think Fergus has an excellent medical mind, and has broken a lot of necks while in this castle – there are some bodies in the moat we need to discuss – and I think he trusted himself to damage Prospero's neck just enough to keep him alive, but so that a sudden movement, a sneeze or a throwing back of the head to drain the contents of a cup, would put enough strain on the broken neck bone to make it finally separate and for the spine to break and suffocate him. Did you see Prospero's hands during the meal?"

Thomas nodded, and Sir Baldon shook his head.

"He kept flexing his fingers, and clenching them into fists. I put this down to his anger at the time, but I now think it was because Fergus had shattered one of his vertebrae when examining him before the meal. And Prospero, like Laurence before him, was losing sensation in his hands and arms on account of the damage."

"And why would the Prince let me *break* his *neck*?" Again, the scorn in Highstone's voice was rich and heavy.

Sir William cast his eyes downwards. "I believe that was my fault. Prospero's throat would have been bruised if, when dressed as the Red Death, I had actually throttled him. When Prospero spoke to Thomas in his chamber, he was wearing a high-collared shirt – Thomas assumed to hide the bruising, but we now know it was to hide the *absence* of bruising.

"I think he wanted a bruise, in case anyone asked to see it, or maybe he was hoping to flaunt it at the meal to mock whoever had attacked and failed to kill him. You told us, Fergus, that Prospero had admitted coming to no harm at the hands of his attacker; doubtless he told you what had happened and you convinced him that a bruise to the back of the neck was appropriate and so you should be allowed to strike him there – harmlessly, of course, though he should expect a little pain – to provide one. You put that ridiculous ruff and tight collar on for the grand reveal, or so you told him, and then struck him in such a way that would end his life at any moment. That collar keeping his neck stiff was probably what kept him alive for as long as it did."

"And Zachariah?" Thomas asked.

"Doubtless Zachariah was gulled into trusting Fergus with stories of my own guilt, and then killed to throw suspicion on me. Prospero's body was desecrated as an excuse to cut off the head to again hide a broken neck. But removing the left hand – there would be less blood to bother you, Fergus, the body having had time to cool – and burning it in the fire also enabled that lovely fiction of Zachariah's involvement to divert suspicion onto me, as did your heroics in rescuing the hand after enough had been burned to disguise that there was no puncture wound."

He turned to Sir Baldon.

"I owe you an apology, Baldon. I have been trying to make the killer feel unsuspected and secure this while time, and once I realised the truth it seemed that only in accusing you could I reinforce Fergus' innocence enough to make him show his hand to clear up some of the finer points. If that second brazier had evaded my notice, I would never have thought of an arrow being set aflame and fired from the roof. And since I knew an arrow had been used to puncture Oswin's lungs and hide his body, and since the arrow would therefore be bloody, there seemed only one reason for someone to burn it…"

He sat back, satisfied.

Highstone waited, breathing heavily. There were no more denials, Thomas noticed. Could they finally be at the end?

Eventually, the accused man spoke: "You tell us that you like everything to fit, Sir William."

"I do."

"So how do *you* explain Laurence's knowledge of Sir Oswin's death that morning?"

"Oh," Sir William waved a dismissive hand, "I've always known that. Marcus told him."

"What?!" Thomas nearly sprang out of his chair.

"Here's something no-one considered: as the Prince was unharmed by me when I staged my attack, why did he look so terrible when he spoke to Thomas? He had spent a day locked in his room, after all."

"How do you know he was locked in his room?" Sir Baldon asked.

"Because Zachariah was outside the door most of the time, and Prospero would have been unable to leave by his private stairway as I had taken his key the day before."

"What?!"

Sir William looked confused, "H-how else do you think I

got into his chamber? I had to unbolt the door to the corridor so that Marcus and Thomas could enter at the correct moment, and the only other way in was by that stairway."

"That's why you were able to give the key to Laurence in the dungeons," Thomas realised. "You had it on you the whole time."

"No," Sir William said, as if this explained everything. "I gave no key to Laurence.".

"But I saw you."

"You saw Laurence with *two keys*. When Fergus asked for the key I had taken from Laurence's body, I wanted to hide from him that I possessed *both* copies of the key to Prospero's private stairway, because, well, at that point I was uncertain who to trust."

"So Laurence had his own key to...to the Prince's stairway?" Thomas said slowly.

Sir William nodded.

"Think; between the morning of my attack, when the Prince was unharmed, and the next day when you saw him looking terrible, what happened?"

So much had happened, but only one event seemed relevant: "Laurence was murdered."

"Right. And how was Prospero at dinner? He was upset at having been attacked, of course, but how would you have described him?"

"He was," Sir Baldon said, thinking, "pale, he was exhausted, he was angry, he was..."

"...grieving," Sir William finished.

"Grieving?" Highstone asked, in spite of himself.

Sir William turned to look at him. "Prospero and Laurence have been in love for over fifteen years, and have hidden their relationship that entire time. I sent everyone around the castle that first morning because I knew where Laurence wanted to be: by the side of the man he loved. He would be able to access

309

Prospero's room from the dungeons, so I left him down there and sent everyone else away. After the discovery of Oswin's body, Marcus, on his way down here, told Zachariah that Oswin had been found dead – Zachariah, who was at his post outside Prospero's door—"

"And Laurence, in the room, heard him," Thomas finished.

"Exactly. Knowing that everyone would be summoned back from their searching – that's why Marcus would have told Zachariah so clearly, as a warning to our friend – Laurence descended to the dungeons and was down there when Thomas went to collect him. He may, indeed, have only just got there ahead of Thomas."

"Which is why you knew where to send me to collect him that morning..."

'I'd try,' – he remembered his master pointing to the staircase to the right-hand side of the fireplace – *'that one.'*

"...and why he was down there in the dark. Because he had actually been with the Prince."

"Do you see it now?" his master asked. "After hearing of Laurence's death – again, because of Marcus telling Zachariah, again doubtless because he wanted to warn Prospero what was coming – Prospero took a day to grieve and then emerged determined to get justice."

"Come now," Highstone said angrily, "the Prince had that stairway so he could bestow the key on whichever young woman he wanted to enjoy on a given evening. Everyone stared at it, night after night, waiting to see which lady he would send up—"

"Never watching," Sir William interrupted, "the insignificant man in the background who would leave by the normal stairs and take the lady's place in the Prince's bed. It was quite clever, I think you'll agree."

"But the women would talk!" Highstone insisted, "A prince who prefers to share his bed with men! Pah! He would be a laughing stock!"

"He was *very* generous," Sir Baldon said, as if suddenly realising.

Sir William inclined his head in agreement. "A title, a house, an income – many others besides Marcus and myself have benefitted from Prospero's generosity, several of them women. It buys a lot of loyalty. And it's an easy secret to keep if only a handful of people need know."

That this revelation was new to both men at the table was clear in the ensuing silence.

"And you expect me to believe that you, brother to a traitor to the throne, would be trusted with this knowledge?" Highstone said after a few moments.

Sir William looked at Highstone seriously. "Laurence was my closest and dearest friend; I raised the Prince's son, I spread rumours about his illegitimate heir and pretended a life of subjugation at the Prince's demand to help protect their secret. You are welcome to believe what you like, Fergus. You killed them both, for reasons of your own, and I intend to see you pay for it."

Silence fell again.

"You tell an interesting story, Sir William—" Highstone said, quietly.

"It's a bit more than interesting, Fergus," Sir Baldon interrupted.

"—but you have yet to tell us *why* we should believe anything you have said. What possible reason could I have for killing these men as you claim? I gain no power, I gain no influence; unlike yourself, I get nothing from this carnage you lay at my feet."

"I agree," Sir William said. "You get nothing."

Highstone seemed confused. "Then…then you admit that I have no reason for doing what you claim?"

Sir William's eyebrows collided. "Oh, no."

"I'm sorry?"

"No, you get no power, but that's why you did it. Because you wish to avoid power at all costs. The Red Death has destroyed this land, and doubtless others as well, killed untold numbers, sent our leaders running in fear – hiding in their castles, ignoring the plight of those around them. Whoever ascends to that power, when the King either dies or goes mad and is removed, would have far too much to do, far too much anger and chaos to repel. It would destroy the life of anyone who was in line for such a position.

"What was the word you used when we met here before searching for Zachariah's body? I believe you told Thomas that you were *relieved* to learn that Prospero's line could continue. And you were, Fergus. You were *very* relieved that the Prince had an heir.

"You see, the burning of Prospero's left hand had another purpose, beyond simply appearing to destroy evidence so you could blame me for these deeds. You placed that hand in the fire, and moved the tools with which it might be removed, because you needed witnesses to swear that your injuries had been come by in a natural way."

"His injuries?" Sir Baldon asked.

"The King left it late to have a son, Prospero often rallied against this. He was terrified of women attaching themselves to him only for his power, and so he delayed and delayed until pressure to provide an heir made him choose a queen, marry her, and, after she had given birth, kill her."

Thomas remembered his own fears that Isobel might now agree to marry him purely because of the power it was anticipated he would inherit. He tried to imagine living with that suspicion behind every friendship, every relationship he struck up from now until his dying day. Maybe this was what drove powerful men mad, never knowing who to trust. Or maybe the knowledge of power in the first place was enough to do that on its own.

"But I will wager that the King had many women in his bed over the years," Sir William continued, "especially as a young man, and that he might, before marriage, before the birth of Prospero, have acknowledged an illegitimate heir only to throw him over when his own son was born in wedlock some years later. And who would know about this illegitimate heir, were he to exist?"

"Only his most trusted men," Sir Baldon answered.

"One of whom was Oswin Bassingham."

The light broke through, and Thomas saw everything.

"So when Oswin and I made plans to remove Prospero from power, Oswin *knew* there was an heir – an acknowledged heir, about whom he was sworn to secrecy – ready to take on the mantle. And when Oswin told you the night before that he was preparing Terrington Fenwick's support so that you could adopt your father's responsibilities, Fergus, you killed him to stop your own position coming to light. And I knew Prospero, I have spent much time with him and Laurence over the years, and I can believe that the death of the man he loved would have ruined him, would have made him talk about giving up his powers, and you – his half-brother, whom it would amuse the King to appoint as his son's personal physician, as no-one could be more motivated to assure Prospero's well-being – you would have been *very* unwilling for that to come to pass."

Highstone said nothing, and Thomas could see Sir Baldon looking at him with wide eyes.

"And so, Fergus, I am prepared to wager that somewhere on that ruined flesh – painful, no doubt, but people have recovered from worse – we would have found upon your skin the mark of the King, and that you would need a good reason for such an identifying mark to be burned off, to be able to deny your birthright, preferably with witnesses who could swear to your genuine intentions when you were injured. I'm even willing to bet that Oswin came here suspecting that he might need to remove Prospero from power. And so he would have brought with him the deed he had signed that bears your name and the description of your tattoo should any of us need convincing when he stood up in front of us and declared you the King's son. Doubtless you destroyed this early on, and then concocted your plan to avoid your responsibilities. What do you say?"

A few moments passed, in which Highstone tried to smile.

"It is only too bad that you have no proof, Sir William, for this fancy."

Once more, Sir William's humourless smile cut his features.

"Which is why my brother climbed down a rope over the battlements at dawn. He will find a horse, ride to the palace, break the news of Prospero's death, and – if he can, if the man lives – find the second of the King's witnesses, and the copy of the deed securing your obligations. And then he will return here with a battalion of the King's army and, if they are lucky, I will have been prevented from killing you by the time they arrive."

This finally broke Highstone's defences. He slumped forward in his chair and groaned, all arrogance and scorn dropping from him. On the other side of him, Thomas could see Sir Baldon watching with suspicion and disgust on his face.

"Well, you are a clever one," Highstone murmured without looking up. "How long do I have?"

Sir William shrugged. "Four, maybe five, days."

"And you will lock me away until then?"

Sir William's eyes darkened. "Yes. To keep you safe."

"Oh, well," Highstone sighed, and struck like a snake.

His left arm shot out and he seized Thomas by the hair, pulling him to his feet. Thomas yelled as he was dragged to the side, and something cold was pressed against his neck as Highstone wrapped his free arm over Thomas' shoulder and around his chest to hold him.

"It's unpredictable but easy enough to do," Highstone's voice was sharp. "You can kill a lot of men if they're stupid enough to sit still and let you."

The coldness at Thomas' neck was removed, and he saw out the corner of his eye Highstone's right hand, clenched into a fist, with the metal band of a firestriker across his fingers.

A new coldness went through him.

On the other side of the table, Sir William was out of his chair. Highstone backed away, dragging Thomas with him, his chair scraping across the ground behind them as he walked.

"Those bodies in the moat? Servants who dared don that Red Death costume and cavort among us as if they belonged. I learned so much from their deaths, and from Laurence's, it is true. How about this one, Sir William?" Highstone's voice was friendly now. "Will he die, will he live? Where should I stri–"

Explosively, an arrow sang down from above and, passing just to the right of Thomas, struck Highstone's shoulder. He screamed and Thomas slipped out of his grip and fell to the ground. A second arrow speared down and caught Highstone in the throat as he was looking upwards, and the tall man stopped walking and dropped backwards into his chair.

From his position on the floor, Thomas saw another arrow whizz down, slamming into Highstone's chest, and then almost immediately a fourth hit him less than a hand's breadth away from the third.

Highstone sagged, lifeless.

Thomas, too exhausted to be surprised, simply watched as a fifth arrow broke the stillness, crashing into Highstone's corpse between the last two shots.

"He's *dead*, Marcus!" Sir William shouted.

"Just making sure," came his brother's echoing reply from far above.

Thomas scrambled to his feet to see Sir William, ashen-faced, leaning heavily against the table. At the sight of

Thomas, he dropped back into his chair, spent.

The three of them waited in the eerie silence, Thomas' heart pounding so hard in his chest that he thought he would throw up.

"It is over?" Sir Baldon, on his feet, asked.

Sir William sagged forward, and placed his head in his hands.

"It's over."

PART FIVE

An Uneasy Cessation of All Things as Before

For three days they had debated what to do. At first, there were the practical considerations. Sir Marcus had dragged Fergus Highstone's corpse, chair and all, into the middle of the courtyard, spat on it, doused it in oil, and set it aflame. Supplies had been counted, then recounted. There was wood enough in the furnishings and floorboards to keep them in fire for months, but with food running low this merely meant that they would be warm while they starved. Outside was perhaps a looming war when people learned that the King's son and his selected heir were both dead, that there was no-one else to lead.

Outside also was the Red Death.

Early on the morning of their departure, Thomas climbed through the hatch to the roof and joined Sir William and Sir Marcus in watching the sun rise. As he stood with them, the sky lightening over the hills beyond the raised drawbridge, he was unable to tell if his nervousness grew out of excitement or fear.

At length, Sir William turned from where he stood by the battlements. "Is everything ready?"

Thomas nodded.

Sir William turned once more to look out over the courtyard and view beyond, and drew in a deep breath, savouring one last time that which he would soon leave forever.

His eyes went to his brother.

"Time to go?" the big man said.

"Time to go."

The two of them turned for the roof.

Thomas remained where he stood, blocking the way. Sir William watched him for a few moments, confused, and said, "You first."

Thomas remained in place, his nervousness growing. It was now or never:

"Are you my father?"

The question sent across Sir William's face a flicker that Thomas was unable to read.

"Because Prospero loved Laurence, you mean, and so he could never have lain with Suzann? There are men, and women, who will happily lay with both. And, to secure an heir, Prospero would have been more than willing to perform with my wife if it helped hide his feelings for Laurence."

Thomas shook his head.

"No."

"No?"

"Laurence was your best friend; he would do anything for you, and you for him." He looked to Sir Marcus, "Lady Suzann would have lain with Prince Prospero to save your life, but it would need to result in an heir – in a boy. Had she given birth to a girl, the offer would have been worthless, you would have been imprisoned again or...or killed. Laurence loved you all, he would never put you through that doubt, the months of wondering."

"Will," Sir Marcus said, and Sir William raised a hand to quieten him.

"So what do you think happened?" Sir William's voice was hoarse.

"I think Lady Suzann had already borne you a boy, before the soldiers recruited you, and when you were imprisoned Laurence came to you with a suggestion: if you were both freed, and given lands and a title, people would be bound to ask why and the rumours would take care of themselves."

Sir William watched him silently.

"And you would do that, for your brother, for your friend. Pretend I had been born later, pretend you were merely used for the Prince's benefit." He turned to Sir Marcus. "So would you – happily be thought a traitor to both sides, for Laurence."

"It was a bloody good idea."

"Marcus!"

"What, Will? What?! He's worked it out; there's no need to lie any more, no need for me to see you distrait every time you think he's going to be taken away."

Thomas had been fighting against this conclusion ever since learning of the feelings Laurence and Prince Prospero shared. To convince himself it was true and to then be told otherwise would have broken his heart.

"You're my father," his voice was strangled. His feet wanted desperately to flee, but he was beyond that now.

"If we had told you—" Sir William replied, his eyes downcast. "People needed to believe it was true; if you had…said anything to anyone…"

Thomas' eyes were wet. "I know."

The truth was, he had hardly missed out. Sir William may have been brusque at times, perhaps hardening his heart against the moment Prince Prospero would acknowledge his heir and see Thomas taken away, but never anything close to cruel or unkind. And Lady Suzann loved him, of that Thomas was certain, as did Sir Marcus, his uncle. Many were raised in the certainty of knowing their parents and experienced far worse.

"I have no right to be King."

Sir William's eyes snapped up. "We need that choice…"

"I know, I know. I can pretend, I am happy to say what's needed. But once it is known Prince Prospero is dead, if war is avoided, can we find a way?"

"Prospero may have never acknowledged you publicly," Sir Marcus said, "but he took plenty of credit in private. Even then, rumour and supposition count for little – you would need to be acknowledged as his choice, and that never happened. Tradition goes a long way with these bastards." He turned to his brother, "What say you?"

Sir William, looking at Thomas closely, nodded.

Thomas smiled, "Thank-you."

Sir William averted his eyes.

"Let's get a move on," Sir Marcus said, with forced brusqueness. "Plenty of time to discuss this on the way."

Thomas turned, and they headed back inside.

~

They collected their supplies from the hall and left by the castle's main door, crossing the courtyard to the raised drawbridge. They had dressed cautiously: long sleeves, leather gauntlets, formal leather jerkins over their clothes, a knife within easy reach at their waist. Sir Marcus carried the castle's only sword, in case stronger persuasion was needed. Food, rope, and sleeping materials were divided among them, worn on their backs. They would travel by day to better see any living thing – afflicted with the Red Death or otherwise – that may attack them, and would sleep at night in the safest locations they could find.

Sir Baldon had decided to remain behind, his age and physical condition making him unsuited to the ten days of heavy walking required to reach the palace. He had, he said, no desire to slow them down – the news of Prospero's death should be spread quickly, and he could be collected from here in due course. There was, Thomas knew, ample food remaining for one man. And, perhaps more importantly, ample wine.

Lowering or raising the drawbridge required two men, however, one at either side, and so Sir Baldon crossed the courtyard with them. He went to one of the winches beside the raised door and Sir Marcus to the other, leaving Sir William and Thomas alone.

Sir William kept finding ways to avoid Thomas' eye – checking his equipment, adjusting the straps over his shoulders, wiping at imaginary stains on his boots or his clothes – but at the first sound of clanking chains he paused. His eyes turned towards the great wooden door, and they watched in silence as it crept downwards away from them, the splinter of sunlight at the top widening to show a seemingly endless stretch of clear blue sky, then the distant hills, then trees growing ever-closer.

Behind them, the castle stood empty and still. All lamps extinguished, all doors closed and, where possible, locked; bedrooms strewn with the abandoned possessions of the land's richest and most powerful families, the revel rooms in that magnificent dungeon waiting in darkness. In the cavernous space of the main hall, the single circular table stood bare, seven chairs waiting beneath the dome of the silent bell.

The drawbridge crashed thunderously to the ground on the other side of the moat. A cool wind swept through the opening, carrying the smell of dried earth to them, so unfamiliar after all this time surrounded by stone, all these months spent watching the wider world at a safe distance, scared of allowing it in.

Thomas Collingwood reached out and gripped his father's offered hand, and they stepped forward together.

ACKNOWLEDGEMENTS

You get one debut novel, and you feel like a charlatan most of the time you work on it. As such, everyone who offered support and encouragement requires some thanks.

A typewriter from Jonny Berliner got me started, and, upon completion of the first draft, a conversation with Ali Shaw about climbing the mountain for a second time helped me see a way through. When I outlined the first draft to Brian Skupin, he made an observation in jest which bore wonderful fruit in my rewriting, and his enthusiastic and clear-sighted suggestions after reading the third draft came at exactly the right time.

If Ryan O'Neill offers to provide feedback on your manuscript, accept. His forensic attention to detail made me realise how many tics, anachronisms, and irrelevances I had included ("You've answered a question here that no reader would think to ask," he told me at one point, and I reduced four pages to two lines), and gave me fresh eyes with which to comb through and make the necessary changes.

Nigel Moss provided a thorough and insightful critique of this manuscript in its late stages, helping clarify several key points and improving the book overall. And I know he won't mind that I ignored at least half of what he suggested!

Dr. Sacha Burgess listened to a rambling explanation of my plans and provided some vitally important medical rabbit holes for me to disappear down, and Richard Taylor deserves huge credit for allowing me to risk my life in the name of research. Felix Tindall, cover designer extraordinaire, was a joy to collaborate with from first to last.

And before, throughout, and beyond all of this there is Megs – celebrating every step, every chapter, every milestone, every eureka moment. Without Megs there is no breath in my lungs; anything I have achieved here is because of her.

ABOUT THE AUTHOR

Jim Noy first encountered classic detective fiction when he read
The Murder of Roger Ackroyd by Agatha Christie in 1999.
From that point on, he developed something of a fascination
with the genre's 'Golden Age', and became a huge fan of
Christie, Christianna Brand, John Dickson Carr,
Freeman Wills Crofts, and their peers, with a particular affinity
for impossible crimes and locked room mysteries.

Since August 2015, he has pursued this interest through his
blog The Invisible Event (https://TheInvisibleEvent.com).

He can also be found on Twitter: @invisible_event

The Red Death Murders is his first novel.

'The Masque of the Red Death'
by
Edgar Allan Poe

It would be impossible to overstate the debt that The Red Death Murders owes to Edgar Allan Poe's 'The Masque of the Red Death' (1842). The notion of a group of people hiding from a plague struck me as a perfect closed circle setup when I first read the story in 2010, and the more I played with the idea the more Poe's story came to feature heavily in my planning and many of the details of the setting.

In writing 'The Murders in the Rue Morgue' (1841) Poe became acknowledged as the grandfather of the detective story, a genre I have taken a great deal of pleasure from over the last 20-odd years. In writing 'The Masque of the Red Death' he became, much more directly, the grandfather of The Red Death Murders, and I wanted to acknowledge the huge influence Poe and his writings have had on both this novel and my reading life in general.

So, as a sort of 'bonus bits'– and by way of thanks for your support in buying this book – I thought it might be interesting to include Poe's text and highlight a few places where I took particular inspiration.

There are no spoilers for The Red Death Murders herein, so you could read this first and then read the novel to see how the details bled through, or, having read the novel, you might find it interesting to spot Easter Eggs in this story.

In whichever order you read them, I hope you enjoy them both.

Jim Noy
February 2022

The 'Red Death' had long devastated the country. No pestilence had ever been so fatal, or so hideous. Blood was its Avatar and its seal — the redness and the horror of blood[1]. There were sharp pains, and sudden dizziness, and then profuse bleedings at the pores, with dissolution. The scarlet stains upon the body and especially upon the face of the victim, were the pest-ban which shut him out from the aid and from the sympathy of his fellow-men. And the whole seizure, progress and termination of the disease were the incidents of half an hour[2].

---

[1] Blood is the avatar of Poe's plague, so I wanted it to be the avatar of mine; thus, to clarify the rules of this universe, I needed a medical man to observe and allow some narrative discussion about how the Red Death *is* transmitted. Sure, this might violate some laws of nature and medicine, but this is why we write fiction, right?

[2] The physical manifestation of the Red Death is important, and I tried to keep as many of Poe's symptoms as I could. Half an hour of life seemed insufficient for the disease to spread as I needed, however, so I lengthened that. Expect this elaboration of mine to become important in later books (he says optimistically...).

But the Prince Prospero[3] was happy and dauntless, and sagacious. When his dominions were half depopulated, he summoned to his presence a thousand hale and light-hearted friends from among the knights and dames of his court, and with these retired to the deep seclusion of one of his castellated abbeys. This was an extensive and magnificent structure, the creation of the prince's own eccentric yet august taste. A strong and lofty wall girdled it in. This wall had gates of iron. The courtiers, having entered, brought furnaces and massy hammers and welded the bolts. They resolved to leave means neither of ingress or egress to the sudden impulses of despair from without or of frenzy from within[4]. The abbey was amply provisioned. With such precautions the courtiers might bid defiance to contagion. The external world could take care of itself[5]. In the meantime it was folly to grieve[6], or to think[7]. The

---

[3] I didn't like the name Prospero, but started using it intending to change it later. After six months of thinking and writing about him, however, I came to realise how little picking the 'right' name really matters; you get to know your characters so intimately by the time you're done, their name couldn't be less important.

[4] A classic closed-circle mystery setup right here; I'm amazed (and grateful) that no-one else wrote this before me.

[5] The abandonment of responsibility is the core thread that I had to carry over to The Red Death Murders, in order to do justice to more than just Poe's setting. It took a long time to emerge as a central theme, but once I was able to bolt key ideas onto it, things came together with a surprising swiftness.

[6] These three words sum up an important part of the puzzle-based mystery for me: in real life people would grieve, of course, but in fiction we want a complex investigation that gets more baffling and

prince had provided all the appliances of pleasure. There were buffoons, there were improvisatori, there were ballêt-dancers, there were musicians, there were cards, there was Beauty, there was wine. All these and security were within. Without was the 'Red Death'.

It was towards the close of the fifth or sixth month of his seclusion[8], and while the pestilence raged most furiously abroad, that the Prince Prospero entertained his thousand friends at a masked ball of the most unusual magnificence. It was a voluptuous scene that masquerade.

But first let me tell of the rooms in which it was held. There were seven[9] — an imperial suite. In many palaces, however, such suites form a long and straight vista, while the folding doors slide back nearly to the walls on either hand, so that the view of the whole extent is scarcely impeded. Here the case was very different; as might have been expected from the

---

more intriguing as it goes. Grief is folly, because it wastes time; grief comes after retribution.

[7] These three words, however, are about an antithetical to the puzzle-based mystery as you can get...!

[8] I always interpreted this as meaning that they waited five or six months before having a masquerade, and that never seemed right to me. I got around this by having a tranche of Prospero's guests — perhaps the ones who knew him best — suspect his real intentions and so arrive prepared, for the revels to be the *reason* they came in the first place and agreed to stay.

[9] I have six coloured revel rooms in The Red Death Murders because a hexagonal castle seemed easier to build, and Poe's are end-to-end in weird orientations whereas mine are in a loop to enable...certain effects.

duke's love of the *bizarre*. The apartments were so irregularly
disposed that the vision embraced but little more than one at a
time. There was a sharp turn at every twenty or thirty yards,
and at each turn a novel effect. To the right and left, in the
middle of each wall, a tall and narrow Gothic window looked
out upon a closed corridor which pursued the windings of the
suite. These windows were of stained glass whose color varied
in accordance with the prevailing hue of the decorations of the
chamber into which it opened[10]. That at the eastern extremity
was hung, for example, in blue — and vividly blue were its
windows. The second chamber was purple in its ornaments and
tapestries, and here the panes were purple. The third was green
throughout, and so were the casements. The fourth was
furnished and lighted with orange — the fifth with white — the
sixth with violet. The seventh apartment was closely shrouded
in black velvet tapestries that hung all over the ceiling and
down the walls, falling in heavy folds upon a carpet of the same
material and hue. But, in this chamber only, the color of the
windows failed to correspond with the decorations. The panes
here were scarlet — a deep blood color. Now in no one of the
seven apartments was there any lamp or candelabrum, amid the
profusion of golden ornaments that lay scattered to and fro or
depended from the roof. There was no light of any kind
emanating from lamp or candle within the suite of chambers.
But in the corridors that followed the suite, there stood,
opposite to each window, a heavy tripod, bearing a brazier of
fire that projected its rays through the tinted glass and so

---

[10] This is such a beautifully gaudy visual, and another of the ideas
herein that I simply had to include in order to emphasise the debt I
owe this story.

glaringly illumined the room[11]. And thus were produced a multitude of gaudy and fantastic appearances. But in the western or black chamber the effect of the fire-light that streamed upon the dark hangings through the blood-tinted panes, was ghastly in the extreme, and produced so wild a look upon the countenances of those who entered, that there were few of the company bold enough to set foot within its precincts at all.

It was in this apartment, also, that there stood against the western wall, a gigantic clock of ebony. Its pendulum swung to and fro with a dull, heavy, monotonous clang; and when its minute-hand made the circuit of the face, and the hour was to be stricken, there came forth from the brazen lungs of the clock a sound which was clear and loud and deep and exceedingly musical[12], but of so peculiar a note and emphasis that, at each lapse of an hour, the musicians in the orchestra were constrained to pause, momentarily, in their performance, to harken to the sound; and thus the waltzers perforce ceased their evolutions; and there was a brief disconcert of the whole gay company; and, while the chimes of the clock yet rang, it was observed that the giddiest grew pale, and that the more aged and sedate passed their hands over their brows as if in confused reverie or meditation. But when the echoes had fully ceased, a light laughter at once pervaded the assembly; the musicians

---

[11] I changed the interior lighting by having a fireplace in each section of my revel rooms, but the braziers by the windows are again a superb idea with so much potential.

[12] This description of the ringing bell is what inspired me to use direct quotes from the story in the novel. Goddamn, it's so perfect, and describes the sound I was after far more elegantly than I had managed after about a week of trying.

looked at each other and smiled as if at their own nervousness and folly, and made whispering vows, each to the other, that the next chiming of the clock should produce in them no similar emotion; and then, after the lapse of sixty minutes, (which embrace three thousand and six hundred seconds of the Time that flies) there came yet another chiming of the clock, and then were the same disconcert and tremulousness and meditation as before[13].

But, in spite of these things, it was a gay and magnificent revel. The tastes of the duke were peculiar. He had a fine eye for colors and effects. He disregarded the *decora* of mere fashion. His plans were bold and fiery, and his conceptions glowed with barbaric lustre. There are some who would have thought him mad. His followers felt that he was not. It was necessary to hear and see and touch him to be *sure* that he was not[14].

He had directed, in great part, the moveable embellishments of the seven chambers, upon occasion of this great *fête*, and it was his own guiding taste which had given character to the costumes of the masqueraders. Be sure they were grotesque. There were much glare and glitter and piquancy and phantasm

---

[13] This caused me a crisis about how advanced the technology of my universe was going to be: had they mastered clockwork? It's partly on that account that I've gone for a pan-Medieval feel, to keep the technology simple. Also, it seems to me that if you were going to party away the end of the world the last thing you'd want is a gigantic bell reminding you of every passing hour.

[14] In a way, this is the most horrible part of the story for me: Prospero's abandonment of the outside world not because he is mad – or fleeing it in fear or grief – but because he is perfectly sane and simply sees giving up as the only sensible course.

— much of what has been since seen in 'Hernani'. There were arabesque figures with unsuited limbs and appointments. There were delirious fancies such as the madman fashions. There was much of the beautiful, much of the wanton, much of the *bizarre*, something of the terrible, and not a little of that which might have excited disgust[15]. To and fro in the seven chambers there stalked, in fact, a multitude of dreams. And these, the dreams — writhed in and about, taking hue from the rooms, and causing the wild music of the orchestra to seem as the echo of their steps. And, anon, there strikes the ebony clock which stands in the hall of the velvet. And then, momentarily, all is still, and all is silent save the voice of the clock. The dreams are stiff-frozen as they stand. But the echoes of the chime die away — they have endured but an instant — and a light, half-subdued laughter floats after them as they depart. And now again the music swells, and the dreams live, and writhe to and fro more merrily than ever, taking hue from the many-tinted windows through which stream the rays from the tripods[16]. But to the chamber which lies most westwardly of the seven there are now none of the maskers who venture; for the night is waning away; and there flows a ruddier light through the blood-colored panes; and the blackness of the sable drapery appals; and to him whose foot falls upon the sable carpet, there comes from the near clock of ebony a muffled peal more

---

[15] I love this description, and was very keen to use it in my text so that some sense of the revels can be communicated to the reader; the emptiness of the castle is arguably the point of the narrative I wrote, so I opted not to include flashbacks of any revels, but Thomas' reflection on them using this line is a favourite part for me.

[16] And, honestly, had I ever wanted to write some description of the revels, it could never have lived up to this.

solemnly emphatic than any which reaches *their* ears who indulge in the more remote gaieties of the other apartments.

But these other apartments were densely crowded, and in them beat feverishly the heart of life. And the revel went whirlingly on, until at length was sounded the twelfth hour upon the clock. And then the music ceased, as I have told; and the evolutions of the waltzers were quieted; and there was an uneasy cessation of all things as before. But now there were twelve strokes to be sounded by the bell of the clock; and thus it happened, perhaps, that more of thought crept, with more of time, into the meditations of the thoughtful among those who revelled. And thus, again, it happened, perhaps, that before the last echoes of the last chime had utterly sunk into silence, there were many individuals in the crowd who had found leisure to become aware of the presence of a masked figure which had arrested the attention of no single individual before. And the rumor of this new presence having spread itself whisperingly around, there arose at length from the whole company a buzz, or murmur, expressive at first of disapprobation and surprise — then, finally, of terror, of horror, and of disgust.

In an assembly of phantasms such as I have painted, it may well be supposed that no ordinary appearance could have excited such sensation. In truth the masquerade license of the night was nearly unlimited; but the figure in question had out-Heroded Herod, and gone beyond the bounds of even the prince's indefinite decorum. There are chords in the hearts of the most reckless which cannot be touched without emotion. Even with the utterly lost, to whom life and death are equally jests, there are matters of which no jest can be made[17]. The whole company, indeed, seemed now deeply to feel that in the costume and bearing of the stranger neither wit nor propriety

---

[17] Read those two sentences again. Perfection.

existed. The figure was tall and gaunt, and shrouded from head to foot in the habiliments of the grave. The mask which concealed the visage was made so nearly to resemble the countenance of a stiffened corpse that the closest scrutiny must have had difficulty in detecting the cheat[18]. And yet all this might have been endured, if not approved, by the mad revellers around. But the mummer had gone so far as to assume the type of the Red Death. His vesture was dabbled in *blood* — and his broad brow, with all the features of the face, was besprinkled with the scarlet horror[19].

When the eyes of the Prince Prospero fell upon this spectral image (which with a slow and solemn movement, as if more fully to sustain its *rôle*, stalked to and fro among the waltzers) he was seen to be convulsed, in the first moment, with a strong shudder either of terror or distaste; but, in the next, his brow reddened with rage.

"Who dares?" he demanded hoarsely of the group that stood around him, "who dares thus to make mockery of our woes? Uncase the varlet that we may know whom we have to hang at sunrise from the battlements.[20] Will no one stir at my bidding? — stop him and strip him, I say, of those reddened vestures of sacrilege!"

---

[18] Occluding the face of whoever wears the costume of the Red Death was important, but – technology again – I didn't think there would exist the means to produce something so close to the appearance of death. Hence Terrington Fenwick uses what he has plenty of access to: dead horses. Horse skulls are terrifying, man.

[19] Again the fear of blood, which I wanted to utilise to a narrative end. Hence the burning of the bodies in my story. Expect this elaboration of mine to become important in later books (he says optimistically...).

[20] As the only direct dialogue in the piece, I wanted to use as much of this as I could.

It was in the eastern or blue chamber in which stood the Prince Prospero as he uttered these words. They rang throughout the seven rooms loudly and clearly — for the prince was a bold and robust man, and the music had become hushed at the waving of his hand.

It was in the blue room where stood the prince, with a group of pale courtiers by his side. At first, as he spoke, there was a slight rushing movement of this group in the direction of the intruder, who at the moment was also near at hand, and now, with deliberate and stately step, made closer approach to the speaker. But from a certain nameless awe with which the mad assumptions of the mummer had inspired the whole party, there were found none who put forth hand to seize him; so that, unimpeded, he passed within a yard of the prince's person; and, while the vast assembly, as if with one impulse, shrank from the centres of the rooms to the walls, he made his way uninterruptedly, but with the same solemn and measured step which had distinguished him from the first, through the blue chamber to the purple — through the purple to the green — through the green to the orange — through this again to the white — and even thence to the violet, ere a decided movement had been made to arrest him. It was then, however, that the Prince Prospero, maddening with rage and the shame of his own momentary cowardice, rushed hurriedly through the six chambers — while none followed him on account of a deadly terror that had seized upon all. He bore aloft a drawn dagger, and had approached, in rapid impetuosity, to within three or four feet of the retreating figure, when the latter, having attained the extremity of the velvet apartment, turned suddenly round and confronted his pursuer. There was a sharp cry — and the dagger dropped gleaming upon the sable carpet, upon which, instantly afterwards, fell prostrate in death the Prince

Prospero[21]. Then, summoning the wild courage of despair, a throng of the revellers at once threw themselves into the black apartment, and, seizing the mummer, whose tall figure stood erect and motionless within the shadow of the ebony clock, gasped in unutterable horror at finding the grave-cerements and corpse-like mask which they handled with so violent a rudeness, untenanted by any tangible form[22].

And now was acknowledged the presence of the Red Death. He had come like a thief in the night. And one by one dropped the revellers in the blood-bedewed halls of their revel, and died each in the despairing posture of his fall. And the life of the ebony clock went out with that of the last of the gay. And the flames of the tripods expired. And Darkness and Decay and the Red Death held illimitable dominion over all

---

[21] I had a solution to this apparently impossible death worked out, but could find no way to include it in the novel – my Prospero exits via a different door.

[22] This impossible vanishing, too. Maybe next time (he says optimistically...).

Printed in Great Britain
by Amazon